PEREGRINE'S CALL

ALSO BY ELIZABETH COLE

Honor & Roses

Choose the Sky

Raven's Rise

A Heartless Design

A Reckless Soul

A Shameless Angel

The Lady Dauntless

Beneath Sleepless Stars

A Mad and Mindless Night

Regency Rhapsody:

The Complete Collection

SKYSPARK BOOKS

PEREGRINE'S CALL

ELIZABETH COLE

PHILADELPHIA, PENNSYLVANIA

SkySpark Books
Philadelphia, Pennsylvania
skysparkbooks.com
inquiry@skysparkbooks.com

Publisher's Note: This is a work of fiction. Names, characters, places, and incidents are a product of the author's imagination. Locales and public names are sometimes used for atmospheric purposes. Any resemblance to actual people, living or dead, or to businesses, companies, events, institutions, or locales is completely coincidental.

Ordering Information:
Quantity sales. Special discounts are available on quantity purchases by corporations, associations, and others. For details, contact the "Special Sales Department" at the address above.

PEREGRINE'S CALL / Cole, Elizabeth. – 1st ed.
ISBN-13: 978-1-942316-30-5

Chapter 1

TAKE HEART AND BE STRONG, Robin thought to herself. She straightened her back and took a deep breath. Through the window, she looked out over the gold-touched autumn landscape. Beyond the walls of the manor of Cleobury, the remaining leaves had turned amber and red, but most of the trees displayed bare branches. Winter would creep into the forest soon, and Cleobury would provide shelter not just to the de Vere family, but a whole host of servants and residents who called the place home.

Robin was one of those people. Rainald de Vere had taken her in years ago when she was a homeless orphan and he was a homeless lord in exile. So when de Vere was able to return to his estate of Cleobury, Robin accompanied him, and became his ward.

His daughter, Cecily, along with her husband, Alric, raised Robin...or at least they tried.

Robin feared she wasn't ever meant to be a lady.

She'd been born too poor, and lived too hard and wild a life as a child, to ever be a retiring and gentle creature who was happy to sew by the fireplace. But that was the role of a lady, and the de Veres wanted Robin to become a lady. So she did her best to fulfill the wishes of the people she loved.

Now she's shaking with nerves, wondering if she could look like a lady even when she didn't feel like one.

You can endure this. You can endure anything.

She raised her chin, picked up the hem of her gown, and descended the massive stone staircase to the hall below, where her judges awaited.

There they stood, silent and watchful, like the carved statues of saints in the church. But these were flesh and blood women.

Agnes, a longtime servant and occasional tyrant, spoke first. "Faster, girl, or do you think you'll trip on that gown? If you didn't run about dressed as a lad for so many years, you'd know how to walk in a lady's clothing."

"Oh, hush, Agnes. She's doing her best," said Pavia, who stood nearby. Pavia was well-born, and the maid fell silent at the command. "Keep on, my dear. We need to see you in the light."

Robin hurried the rest of the way, stopping when she reached the long, angled patch of sunlight coming in through the narrow windows. "My ladies," she said, curtseying as she'd been taught.

The third woman's eyes lit up, and she clapped her hands together once. "Lady Robin!" Cecily proclaimed. "What a picture you make!"

"Are you certain?" Robin let out a breath. The dress she wore was the result of many painful hours of measuring, cutting, and stitching...and much assistance from the other three women. The green silk was the finest fabric Robin had ever worn, and she'd chosen it because the color reminded her of the forest in summer. But oh, the challenge of making a bolt of fabric into a gown! Robin nearly despaired. But at last it was done. And perhaps, to judge by the women's delighted faces, it was worth it.

The women circled her, their hands out to inspect the lines of the gown, Robin's silk headdress and the unbound hair cascading below it, and even the tips of her new leather shoes.

Pavia, an older woman who nevertheless radiated youthful vigor, reached out to straighten the pendant at Robin's throat. It was a tiny cross of gold with a single, round-topped crystal in the center. Robin treasured it above all her other possessions.

"Now you look every inch the lady," Pavia said. "I am so proud of your efforts, Robin."

"Praise all the saints for such a miracle," said Agnes, and in a lower tone, "To think that such a tatterdemalion could ever bloom into a rose."

"She's not a flower," Cecily interjected, "she's a bird. And she just needed a bit of a boost to spread her wings."

The blonde woman took Robin's hands in her own. Cecily's smile was as warm as the summer sun. "Alas that tonight can't be a feast—a gown like this deserves to be seen by all."

"Seen by men," Pavia translated. "And in specific, by Geoffrey Ballard."

The son of a neighboring baron, Geoffrey Ballard was good-looking, tall, and well built with thick, sandy hair that usually caught women's eyes. When he was in a good humor, which was often, he had a ready smile and a jesting, teasing way about him that Robin did enjoy. If his mouth was a little thin, and tended to press into a line when something displeased him…well, why should everything about him make Robin swoon?

To be honest, nothing about Ballard made her *swoon*. She liked him well enough. He shared some interests with her—hunting and hawking, and to a lesser extent, the countryside they both knew well. But she was terribly conscious of the need to please him, to pretend to be a lady, and to forgo any actions that might make her seem too willful to be a good bride.

Robin said, "Geoffrey has seen me before. A new gown won't change his opinion of me."

"Oh, it may," said Pavia. "Nineteen is an age to secure a husband, and if another man sees you before Lord Geoffrey makes his formal declaration, he may be too late. Has he asked you to join him for his next hunt?"

"He has." Robin bit her lip, not entirely pleased at the reminder. She loved hunting. Lord Geoffrey owned superb hounds and hawks, and Robin had enjoyed going on hunts organized by him previously. But she shook her head. "I'm not sure it means anything. A hunt is not a marriage proposal. An orphan girl with no name and no dowry is not a prize."

Though Geoffrey certainly expressed interest in her, Robin couldn't imagine a noble family approving of her for a bride. A part of her was always aware of her lacks.

"He's all but spoken the words," Cecily told her. "If Geoffrey's mother had not been so ill, the marriage would have taken place already."

Robin frowned. She was not looking forward to a wedding.

"What's wrong?" Cecily asked.

"Not a thing, my lady," Robin said, trying to believe it herself. "I pray my learning to sew will not be in vain, and that I'll be able to take my skills to the Ballard estates."

"How well said." Cecily smiled.

Robin grinned back. She did have some skills. She was an excellent rider, and she could hunt with a falcon or with hounds. She'd learned proper modes of address for nobility, and she also knew how to read and write quite ably in French—the most necessary language for a lady.

Just then, the door to the courtyard swung open, pushed by a guard. He saw Cecily and huffed out a greeting.

"My lady. Ladies," the guard said, somewhat out of breath. "We just got word that Sir Octavian is approaching the manor. He'll be here within the hour. Perhaps sooner."

At the mention of the name, Robin's breath caught in her throat. "Octavian is coming here? At this moment?" she gasped. Oh, Lord, if he saw her in such a gown, he'd laugh. Little, scruffy Robin dressed as a lady!

"I had no notion of this," Cecily said. "Was there more to the message?" she asked the guard.

The man shook his head. "Nay, my lady."

"I'll see that everything is prepared for a guest," Cecily said, already turning to the task at hand. "No, wait. I must finish brewing the remedy for the tenants who are sick. Robin, you shall see that a chamber is made ready, and that Octavian has what he needs for his stay."

"I should change," Robin protested. "This gown is ridiculous. I must get my own outfit back on…."

"Nonsense," Cecily said firmly. "If we wish to know what effect it will have, how better to test it than by displaying it? Tav is always honest." Cecily used Octavian's nickname with easy affection.

Robin herself never dared to be so familiar with the knight, who was five years older than she was, and a close companion to Sir Alric. To her, Octavian had always seemed a paragon.

The first time she'd ever met him, she was only fourteen and certain she knew everything about how the world worked. Then she saw him.

Octavian wasn't anything like other knights she'd encountered. First, most fighters, even knights, tended to be rough men who relied on their strength and swords rather than words to make their way in the world. He was built as a fighter, of course—tall, with strong shoulders and chest after years of training. And more so than many knights, Octavian was excellently educated because he'd been raised in a strict, religious environment by monks who seemed to know everything, and then passed it on to Octavian. His familiarity with many languages helped him travel from the Holy Land, where he'd been born, through Europe and finally to England.

In England, he was unusual. The son of black Africans living in Aleppo, his skin was many shades darker than Robin had ever seen. And though his parents died when he was just a baby—hence his childhood in a monastery—Robin assumed they must have been beautiful to have given their child such a face. Octavian had warm brown eyes and a mouth that eased into a smile whenever he greeted her. Unlike a lot of the men she'd grown up around, Octavian shaved routinely and kept his hair cropped so short his scalp was visible, which just made his high cheekbones stand out. She thought he looked more like a prince than a soldier.

He'd always been kind to her, and treated her with none of the condescension so many other men did—which made her admire him all the more. But admiring was one thing. Speaking to him as an equal was quite another, and she certainly couldn't imagine saying *Tav* in such a comfortable manner.

It hadn't always been that way. When she was young, she spoke to Octavian—and indeed everyone—with the boldness of a child who feared nothing. But that was before she learned proper behavior, and how to speak to her betters with respect. Over the past few years, she found herself more and more...flustered...around Octavian, despite how much she looked forward to his infrequent visits.

The women separated, and Robin moved toward the guest room, determined that all should be perfect. That was the task of a lady, and wasn't that what Robin wanted to be?

Chapter 2

SIR OCTAVIAN DE LEVANT WAS used to traveling at a moment's notice. He was a knight in the service of Lord Denis of Courci, who in turn swore allegiance to King Stephen. Because Tav spoke many languages and had the full confidence of his lord, he was frequently asked to carry letters from one person to another among the king's vassals—and unwritten messages that were far more covert. He enjoyed such tasks. Tav was an inveterate traveler, and he loved seeing new places, however humble or grand they might be.

But this particular trip would be more challenging than most. It might even get him killed. Tav hoped to increase his chances of surviving by gleaning vital information from old allies. Hence the journey to Cleobury.

Octavian rode on through the familiar countryside. Sheep grazed here and there, since the land was too hilly for good farming. He continued, keeping his horse's pace steady, even though he wanted to hurry.

Cleobury had always been a haven for him. Alric was one of his closest friends, along with the knights Sir Luc and Sir Rafe. Together, they'd fought in numerous battles, and Octavian would trust any of them with his life. Despite being born far away in the Levant, from parents who were commoners, Tav felt he'd found a home in this far corner of the world.

When he reached the manor of Cleobury, the gates stood open. Alric insisted on the open gates as a matter of policy. He wanted the residents to know they were free to come and go.

"Sir Octavian!" a voice called. One of the guards atop the gatehouse waved. "We got your message. Ride in to the courtyard!"

Octavian rode under the gatehouse, noting the thick walls of the manor. If war ever did threaten Cleobury, Alric would have the place sealed tight within moments. Tav dismounted, but before he'd even managed to hand the reins over to one of the stable boys, he was hailed by a new voice.

"Tav!" The name practically boomed out, and the man who called out strode across the wide courtyard to crush Octavian in a fond embrace. "What brings you here? We heard nothing of your coming till an hour ago!"

"That's because I didn't have much warning, but even so, I would not have been able to tell you beforehand."

Alric pulled back to consider this, his expression indicating that he read Tav's true message—he was on business more urgent than the usual tasks his own lord Denis sent him on. Alric asked, "How much of a hurry are you in?"

"I can stay no more than two nights, though one would be better. It depends on how much Lord Rainald can tell me this evening."

Alric shook his head. "Alas, Rainald is not here."

Octavian's hopes fell. "I came this way specifically to

speak to him."

"A private matter required him to travel to Wallingford. He'll be gone at least another fortnight."

"That's unfortunate."

Alric chuckled. "Unfortunate? Why do I have the sense that any other man would have a string of curses on his lips?" It was something of a joke among the knights that Octavian never swore, despite being in many situations calling for a curse or two.

"The brothers always knew how to train a boy out of swearing," Tav noted, remembering the punishments meted out at the monastery where he'd been raised after being orphaned. "I'll explain what's happening after supper."

Alric nodded once. "Indeed. And however short the visit, it's good to see you." He kissed Tav and said, more cheerfully, "Cecily will want to know how you are. I'm surprised she hasn't swept down upon you already." He turned to a passing servant, asking, "Where is my wife?"

"The gardens, my lord," the girl replied.

Of course Cecily was in the gardens, Tav thought. The woman was constantly kneeling in soil, no matter the season. She took her role as lady of the manor seriously, and there was no finer herbalist in the shire.

When the men found her, she was in her garden workshop, carefully blending a concoction as it heated over a low flame. The smell of honey permeated the air.

"Just a moment," she said, eyes on her work. "One of the tenants is ill, and this remedy must not boil or it will lose its effectiveness."

"We'll wait," Alric assured her.

Octavian looked around at the various drying herbs and the many bottles and clay jars on the shelves. Cecily's workshop always had an air of mystery.

After a little while, she removed the pot from the

flame to cool. A smile lit her face as she focused on them at last. "Octavian! How wonderful!" She stepped away from the work table and kissed him once firmly on the mouth. "We just heard you were on the road. Has Alric kept your visit for a surprise?"

"It was a surprise to me as well," Alric said. "And we don't have him for long."

Cecily gave a little pout, but linked her arm in Alric's, leaning against him. Then she held out her other hand to Tav. The three began to walk back toward the manor. She said, "If the visit must be short, let us make the best of it. Octavian, we have fresh venison for supper. I wish my father were here!"

Cecily asked a slew of questions as they walked, everything from the news of London to the latest rumors of the war's progress to the health of his liege lord Denis. Tav answered them as fast as he could, all the while noticing how Cecily and Alric communicated in gestures and glances as much as words. Tav caught the way Alric leaned against Cecily for a moment, and without understanding how he knew, Tav was certain Cecily was with child again.

He didn't say anything, because it wasn't his place, but he smiled, warmed to see the couple so happy.

But underneath that was a layer of cold, drawing the warmth down to drown in it. He'd felt it before, but chose to ignore it. He had work to do, and soldiers never complained about being lonely.

Tav instead answered Cecily's next question, though she interrupted when the manor house itself came into view. "Ah! Look who's come to greet us." Cecily pointed to the doorway.

Octavian looked over to see a young lady in an elegant green gown standing there. He'd never met the woman before, because he surely would have remembered. Petite in stature, but obviously confident in herself, to judge by her posture and the cool, calm smile on her face. Thick brown hair tumbled down her back, contained only by the simple green and gold headdress. He approved, because that let him see her rich blue eyes. Those eyes met his almost defiantly, reminding him of…

"Robin." He said the name aloud without even realizing it.

"Who else?" Cecily returned cheerfully. "You seem surprised, Tav."

Surprised? He was stunned. He couldn't rip his gaze from the woman in green.

This woman was Robin? The Robin he knew was barely more than a child, maddening and charming and mischievous all at once. She dressed in boy's clothes and ran in the woods and in general acted as if she were part squirrel and part imp. She wore mussed-up braids and had dirt on her skin. Tav had always liked her—it was impossible not to like Robin. But he was also very glad she wasn't his responsibility, since she was a whirlwind.

The Robin standing in front of him now was a full-grown woman, and looked it. The green gown skimmed her figure, hiding nothing of what she had become, which was a slight but absolutely lovely lady. He did wish that the neckline wasn't quite so low, because no man should be able to see just how she'd…matured. Tav was uncomfortably aware of being caught up in her presence. She'd become a whirlwind of a different kind.

Then Robin smiled at him, saying, "Sir Octavian! What a surprise to see you."

"Lady Robin."

"It's only Robin," she said, wrinkling her nose in reaction to the title. The gesture was adorable.

Tav leaned forward to kiss her, as he had nearly every time he'd seen her before. But then, once again tripping on the sheer difference of Robin now from Robin a year ago, he hesitated.

Robin blinked, her eyelashes fluttering.

He had to think quickly, so he reverted to humor. He stepped back and bowed, just as he would to a woman on first meeting her. "Not Lady Robin, but only Robin? You're looking well, whatever you wish to be called today. The gown suits you." *Far better than the boy's clothing you used to wear*, he added silently.

Robin's eyes narrowed a fraction, and he wanted to laugh. She heard him whether he spoke it out loud or not. Like that, their previous camaraderie was restored.

"I made it," she said, "thanks to much instruction from Cecily."

"I see you haven't got a bit taller," he said.

"I have too," Robin said hotly. "Quite a bit."

He grinned. Robin had always been little. At least he could tease her about that…and there was something gratifying about watching her gentian-blue eyes flash as she tried to think of a response.

"Well," Cecily said, "you both can spar over supper. Robin, show Octavian to his chamber."

"I know where it is," he said.

"But part of Robin's education is learning how to act as hostess," Cecily countered.

Robin stepped aside to let him enter. "This way," she said, smiling as she led him to the stairs and up to a chamber he'd stayed in a dozen times before.

Tav trailed after her. The silk of the gown rustled softly with each step, and the folds of the skirt rippled past her hips, drawing his attention to the curves he should most definitely not be so enchanted by.

"When did I see you last?" he asked, mostly to say something.

"Wasn't it Easter of last year?" Robin looked over her shoulder at him, her face partly hidden by a few loose waves of hair. The move was unexpectedly, unknowingly alluring.

Tav swallowed. "A long time."

"I missed you," she said, in the blunt, honest tone he remembered. "You said you'd tell me about your visit to Cairo. And don't think you may slip free of the obligation! I've been waiting *ages* for that story."

They reached the guest room, and Robin stepped in with him, looking around with sharp, appraising eyes. "Fresh water. Fuel for the fire. Three candles, just in case. Did I forget anything? The mattress was just restuffed," she added, ticking off items on her fingers. "We had great luck earlier this autumn, hunting geese. I shot more than any other year, I think. We plucked so many, I was picking down out of my hair for a fortnight!"

Her report of shooting so many birds was no surprise. She'd always been a fine archer. But Tav was caught by the idea of running his hands through her glossy, unbound hair, and felt an accompanying jolt of desire that he quickly tamped down. No. This was *Robin*.

"I have everything I need," he said. "You should go."

She looked surprised by his too-brusque tone, but gave him a curtsey. "You must be tired," she said politely, sounding just like Cecily. "I'll see you at supper."

Robin turned to the door, but then paused. "You never kissed me. Alric and Cecily rate a kiss of friendship, but I do not?"

"An oversight. I was distracted."

"Well, you may correct the oversight now."

Before he could respond, Robin stood on her tiptoes

and leaned forward to give him a kiss, the same friendly kiss of greeting she'd give to Alric or any of the knights when they arrived at Cleobury after a long absence.

He bent his head obligingly. But the moment her lips touched his, he slipped a hand around her waist, feeling the heat of her body beneath the sheen of the silk. The resulting rush of desire in his veins had nothing to do with friendship, and he raised his head once more, out of her reach.

"On second thought, it wasn't an oversight." It had been an instinct, warning him to stay away from her.

Robin stepped back, nearly losing her footing, except that Octavian took her by the shoulders to steady her. To judge by her expression, she was more than a little hurt.

"Robin," he said, her name now sounding utterly unfamiliar on his tongue. He had to apologize.

But she'd already begun to blush, obviously embarrassed at how a routine greeting had gotten so complicated.

"Never mind. I have to get back," she said breathlessly. "I'll see you at supper."

She turned and left, closing the door behind her. Tav let out a breath. What had he just done? He'd managed to turn an innocent kiss of friendship into something else entirely.

He'd never thought of Robin as dangerous before—at least, not due to her being a woman. When she chose to launch a volley of arrows, then she was as dangerous as any archer he'd confronted. But she was still the same sweet and innocent girl he knew. He saw her expression after the lightning-quick kiss. The confusion on her face. She must be wondering if he'd lost his mind.

A short rest restored Octavian's sense of equilibrium. He changed from his dirt-stained traveling outfit to a clean tunic and hose.

He'd been gone a long time, and that accounted for his reaction to Robin. When he saw her next, he'd be prepared for her appearance. Children grew up, after all. Robin wasn't going to remain a girl forever. She'd become a young woman, and that had nothing at all to do with Tav. Alric was practically a brother, which made Robin almost a little sister, or a niece.

Supper was served in the great hall. The family all seated themselves at the high table near the massive fireplace while the servants and residents of the manor gathered at the long tables on the lower part of the floor.

As a guest, Octavian was seated by Lady Cecily while Robin sat on the other side, next to Alric. Tav was glad for the slight separation because as it turned out, he *still* wasn't used to seeing Robin in her new guise.

Stop it.

"She's grown up," he said in French.

Cecily nodded. "At last! I think she's finally accepted her role as a lady. She's learned so much. Granted, hawking and riding are her best accomplishments, and I fear I could never present her at court, but she's no longer the wild creature she was when my father took her in."

"She looks like a lady tonight," Octavian said, choosing his words carefully now. "And she could ask for no better guardians than you and your father."

"Thank you, Tav," Cecily said, clearly pleased. "I do hope we've done the best for her, giving her the upbringing she deserved, despite her childhood. And we look forward to her marriage."

He paused just as he was about to drink his wine. "Her what?"

"It's not official yet, but we expect that she'll marry Geoffrey Ballard soon. The match would be a good alliance for our families, but Robin seems to look favorably on him too. He's got several falcons and will use any excuse to go for a hunt."

And Robin loved a hunt. Well, if she found someone she wanted to marry, Tav was happy for her. Except that he didn't quite like the idea of her marrying at all. "Isn't she a little young?"

"You just said how much she's grown," Cecily replied. "And my father won't be at ease until we know there is someone who will care for her and see that she's happy. One can't thrive alone."

Then she put a hand to her mouth, her eyes rounding. "Oh, forgive me. I've been preaching about family and home to you of all people. And here in England you have neither."

He said reasonably, "I chose my life. I chose to follow my lord from the Holy Land to France, and then here. I knew what the life of a soldier in a lord's service would mean."

"Do you miss the Levant?"

"In winter," he said with a wry grin, "I miss it very much, and wonder what madness led me here to the freezing north."

She laughed. "And yet, winter after winter, you stay. Why is that?"

"I serve my liege lord and his liege lord," he said simply. "And the war is not over yet."

Cecily's good humor faded. The war between Stephen and Maud seemed interminable. Though the past two years had been relatively quiet compared to the preceding five, there was no guarantee that violence would not flare up again. The empress's faction held a part of southwest England while Stephen held much of the east. The region where Cleobury sat had been in Stephen's control for some time, and Alric would hold the manor for Stephen if he had to. Or, more likely, he'd march to wherever the next battle threatened.

"Will they never cease fighting?" Cecily said. "Cousins should not be enemies."

"Not in an ideal world. But this world is not ideal."

After supper, Alric nodded to Octavian, wordlessly inviting him to follow him to a smaller room where Alric often conducted the business of the manor.

A high-backed bench stood near the fireplace. Octavian sat on the cushion while Alric ordered one of the servants who'd trailed behind to bring them mulled wine. The boy nodded and dashed off.

Octavian stretched his hand toward the flames. Alric chuckled.

"It's only autumn, friend. What will you do when winter comes?" he asked.

"Move closer to the fire," Tav muttered. "And stay there till spring."

The boy reappeared with the wine, and Tav took his gratefully. "This will help too."

"There's plenty more," Alric assured him. "But you haven't come to Cleobury for the wine. What business are you on? Your lord's?"

"His lord's," Tav responded. "King Stephen has ordered me to carry out a very particular task."

"What task?"

"Several weeks ago," Tav explained, "a northern man sent word to the king that he had valuable information regarding the military plans of multiple rebel lords, including Ranulf of Chester."

Alric's eyebrows rose. Ranulf of Chester had been a thorn in the side of the king for years, first taking up the cause of the empress, then switching to Stephen, and then back again. But despite who he claimed to serve, Ranulf mostly seemed interested in taking as much power for himself as possible. He said, "The king would love to have that man in chains again."

Tav nodded. "He's interested in learning more of what this man promised in terms of information. But, naturally, it's not so simple as inviting him to court."

"Who's the man?"

"His name is Govannon." Tav paused, then said, "And a difficulty arises because he is in the service of Lord Pierce of Malvern."

Alric inhaled, and his expression went dark. Alric had good cause to hate Lord Pierce. The man had once been betrothed to Cecily, and she narrowly avoided the fate of marrying him...largely due to divine providence, and the quick actions of Alric to rescue her. Octavian had been there, and he knew how dangerous and unpredictable Pierce could be.

"So you'll need to sneak past Pierce to find this man? Good luck getting into Malvern Castle."

"That's another difficulty. Pierce no longer holds Malvern Castle."

"Since when? I hadn't heard."

"Apparently, his alliance with the Welsh soured. A force of mercenaries who gained access to the castle seized it from within—on orders of Cadwallader himself. They were supposed to imprison Pierce, but he managed to escape into the Ardenwood with a very small retinue, which includes this man Govannon."

"I still don't see what your role is," Alric said.

"Govannon specifically requested me as the courier of the king's reply."

"You! He could only have met you once, and that was years ago. Do you remember such a man?"

Tav shrugged. "No, but I don't remember all those I met at Malvern. Anyway, I have to find Govannon, and convince him to share what he knows."

"He could be dead by now, murdered by the Welsh. Or by Pierce himself," Alric added.

"If Govannon is dead, I'll carry that news back to the king," Tav said. "Either way, I am to go alone and rely on absolutely no one I may meet. But I wanted to speak to Lord Rainald first." Rainald had lived in the Ardenwood for years, so Octavian had hoped to learn what he could of the forest, and in particular where Pierce might be.

Alric considered it. "You know, while living in exile, Rainald often relied on his men to range farther and bring back news. A few of them came with him here to Cleobury—you can speak with them. And..." Alric stopped as he wrestled with something. Then he said, reluctantly, "Robin knew the Ardenwood very well. Rainald often said she was his eyes and ears."

Tav shook his head. "I would rather leave Robin well out of this." For so many reasons.

"I too," Alric said. "Indeed, I wish she forgot her old life entirely. She makes light of it, but there are few good memories there."

"However," a new voice broke in, "it would do no harm to learn from her."

Both men looked to the door, where Cecily stood. She walked in and over to the fire, saying, "Robin had an unusual life while she was my father's ward in the forest."

"The sooner she forgets that life, the better off she'll be," Alric said firmly. "Cecily, you mean well, but on this matter, I must insist you not interfere."

"Is it interference to help Octavian?" She turned appealing eyes to him. "Tav, if Robin knows even one scrap of knowledge that allows you to succeed—"

"Cecily, leave it." Her husband's tone was still calm, but he wanted to end the conversation. "Robin is a young woman. She can't be involved. This is the king's business, and it may affect the very course of the war."

Cecily's eyes narrowed for a moment, and Tav thought she was about to unleash an uncharacteristic fury toward Alric. But then she looked to the floor, and said, "Yes, I understand. Women have no place in such matters."

Alric looked relieved—and puzzled—to hear Cecily so meek.

"Perhaps you should share your wisdom with the empress," Cecily added, now with a tartness to her voice. "She'd end her fight for the throne the moment you tell her women can't be involved in war." She then turned and stormed out.

"There's my true wife," Alric muttered. "For a moment I was worried." He put his face in his hands for a moment, but then laughed. "I thought marriage would be less dangerous than battle. I was wrong."

"You're happy to be married, though."

"Every day." Alric smiled. "You should consider it."

"I'm not in a position to marry," Octavian said. It was true. While Alric had chosen Cecily for love, he also possessed some lands and could have provided for her even if she lost her own holdings. Octavian had no land in England or France or anywhere else. "I can't even be certain of where I will be from one month to the next. Lord Denis could order me to Paris, or Rouen. Or Acre."

"And you don't mind?"

Octavian shrugged. "Not at all. I was born to wander. I'll wander all my life, and after I die, I hope to wander heaven."

"A true peregrinus," Alric said. Then he stood up. "I'd best go soothe Cecily's ruffled feathers. Tomorrow we'll find those men and hear what they know of the Arden-wood."

"Good night," Tav said.

Tav recalled Alric's words later that night as he got ready for sleep. Peregrinus, the name for the far-ranging falcon, but also the name for pilgrims, those who trudged along countless roads to reach holy places, hoping to find some connection to the divine. That was Octavian. He always felt the need to move on, to see new places, to know the world God had created. As such, he'd mastered a spare, ascetic way of living. He had no possessions he couldn't carry with him. He had no property and no financial interests. He didn't particularly care about worldly matters. True, he fought on the side of King Stephen, but only because he served Lord Denis, who backed Stephen out of loyalty to an oath sworn many years ago. Octavian kept apprised of politics because it was prudent to know what was happening. But the many shifts in power, or the news of a lord changing sides, meant little to him personally.

But the other side of that coin was a sense of isolation, a lack of connection to a larger group. Octavian was truly a man without a country, and in a world were allegiance mattered greatly, that set him apart. He valued the freedom he had—he could always move on. But that was a drawback too—he could always move on.

So he was extremely grateful for the small group of friends he'd made while in Britain. He'd met Alric, Luc, and Rafe while all of them were fighting a battle on the side of the king. Separated from his own company, Octavian had stumbled into their group by chance...or by divine guidance, considering that he probably would have been killed in that battle if not for those knights. He'd repaid the favor in future battles, and now he counted the three among his true friends.

He wished one of them could join him on this sortie north. But he seemed doomed to face the challenge alone.

Chapter 3

THE NEXT MORNING, ROBIN ROSE early, hoping to find Octavian while he was unoccupied by whatever matters he'd been discussing with Alric the night before. Usually, Robin was permitted to listen to such things. In the war between these royal cousins, ordinary people's lives hinged on seemingly distant matters.

However, in this case, no one told Robin anything. Octavian didn't mention a word beyond his first revelation that he was on the king's business. And then Alric spirited him away to the small chamber to talk. Their reticence worried Robin the more she thought about it. What was Octavian doing, and why could he not give a hint of it to Robin? She was nobody! She was the safest person in the world to tell, because who would she share the secret with?

But no one told her. Octavian and Alric were off somewhere around the manor, and when Cecily found her at breakfast, she announced that the morning would be devoted to sewing, causing Robin to heave a sigh of despair.

Sewing took place in the bright room known as the solar for its generous number of windows. Despite the light, Robin still hated the work.

"So fussy," she muttered, stabbing the needle into the wool in her lap. "This shouldn't be so difficult."

"Watch the seam, dear. If your stitch wanders, the garment will bunch up in that spot, and it may chafe at the skin. Not to mention look sloppy."

Robin sighed, tugging the fabric flat and pulling out her last few stitches. She understood what Cecily was saying perfectly well. It was just that Robin could hardly stand to mend a tear, let alone sew a whole gown on her own—even the simplest pattern for the most basic style. She glanced at Cecily's quick-moving hand as she ruched the elbows of the sleeves of her own gown.

"I can't concentrate," she confessed. "What were they talking about all last night?"

"Discussing Octavian's mission, which is urgent," Cecily said absently, her eyes still intent on her work. "I do wish he could stay longer, but his orders are clear, and he must reach the Ardenwood as soon as he can."

Robin nearly pricked her finger with the needle. "The Ardenwood! What takes him there?"

Having inadvertently revealed one key detail, Cecily must have decided that it mattered not to tell the rest. She explained how Octavian had intended to learn more of the forest from the absent Rainald.

Robin blinked in confusion. "I know far more of the Ardenwood than Rainald. Why not ask me?"

"The men fear that Octavian's questions would raise unpleasant memories. You are a lady now, Robin, and ladies must always be treated with care."

"Do they honestly think me too delicate to remember my past?" Robin had never felt so annoyed by the restrictions of womanhood.

Cecily gave a little shrug. "In any case, it's unlikely that you could tell Octavian what he needs to know in a day, or at all. Your knowledge of the forest is inseparable from your own feet and hands and eyes and nose. You couldn't tell him of the secret paths you used to travel, because you knew them through a hundred tiny signs that you couldn't possibly explain to another. You knew where to ford a creek, or which tree was the turning point on the path to reach Rainald's camp. That can't be taught in words."

"True enough," Robin said. She could use her knowledge, but she couldn't translate it.

Cecily went on, "What Octavian truly requires is a guide. But he's been ordered to go alone. The king fears he can't trust any stranger he might hire. A guide could be in the pay of an enemy." Cecily sighed. "I will pray for his success and his safe return. What else can we do?"

Prayer had its place, but Robin could think of several other things she could do to help Octavian...none of which Cecily would want to hear.

What Octavian truly requires is a guide.

The idea was eminently logical, and Robin couldn't let it go. When Agnes came in to the solar to tell Cecily her child was awake from a morning nap, Cecily rose.

"I must attend my little one," she said, smiling. "Robin, that is enough sewing for now. Have you other tasks?"

"Yes, my lady," Robin said quickly. "I can occupy myself till this evening."

Once free of the watchful gaze of Cecily or Agnes, Robin hurried to make herself ready for her new plan. Certain supplies were needed. Food was to be filched from the kitchens. A horse had to be selected and fed well for its unexpected journey. And Robin had to pack all the essentials.

She rolled a set of men's clothing up in a tight bundle,

along with a simple shift and her old brown dress. She pulled out sturdy, heavy-soled shoes, and folded up a fur-lined cloak, which should keep her warm in most conditions.

Thinking of other possible dangers, she also snuck into Cecily's garden work shed, and took several small items. "I'll ask forgiveness later," she whispered, praying that the things she took wouldn't be needed for any patients at Cleobury.

Finally, she packed her knife and laid her bow and quiver in an out-of-the-way spot in the stables.

All was prepared.

She encountered Octavian in the late afternoon, when the weak sun was just sinking below the trees. "When are you leaving?" she asked bluntly.

"Tomorrow at dawn," he replied. "I am sorry I cannot stay, but I—"

"You have your orders," Robin finished. "I understand that, Octavian. I'm not a child, you know."

"I noticed," he muttered.

She went on, "This mission sounds perilous, from what Cecily said." Far too perilous for one person, no matter how brave he was.

"I'm a soldier," Octavian said. "I don't get to choose which dangers to face."

"You *will* be careful," she said, suddenly aware of the sheer audacity of her plan and the high chance of something—anything—going wrong.

"I'm always careful," he told her, reaching a hand to take hers. "I like this life too much to rush out of it."

Robin looked at the large dark-skinned hand encasing her own slender fingers. She wished Octavian didn't have to face any dangers.

She woke well before dawn the next day, sneaking out

of the warm bed she shared with Pavia and Agnes. If either woman noticed her going, Robin would have said she was bidding Octavian goodbye, but as it happened, neither of them stirred.

Robin bundled herself up in warm wool clothing. She slipped down the stairs of the manor house and through the courtyard to the stables. No one was about—even the lowliest servants would linger in the warmth of their beds until the last possible moment.

She saddled her chosen horse and led it outside, keeping to the packed dirt so that no one would hear hooves clattering on the stones of the courtyard. She walked the horse to a side gate just large enough to let a horse without a rider through. The main gate was far too risky, and Robin needed time to get away from Cleobury if her plan was to work.

When she could no longer see the manor walls, she mounted her horse and rode toward the village of Bournham, which all travelers passed through if they wanted to go north. She kept to the trees, in case anyone was awake.

Dawn was just coloring the eastern sky lavender when she halted on a small rise past Bournham. She had a good view of the road, and she'd see anyone passing by. Her breath puffed little clouds into the air. Her horse puffed larger ones.

She patted the creature. "Just a little while, and then we'll be off!" she murmured.

The woods were calm, but not quiet. Birds began to twitter and chirp their morning song. An owl not yet gone to sleep gave a last mournful hoot above the highest branches. Robin pulled the fur-lined cloak closer about her body.

She could turn back to Cleobury this moment. Even if she were seen, she could claim she went on an early ride.

Cecily might shake her head, but Robin could continue on just as before.

While Octavian continued on his task with no help at all.

Robin exhaled, knowing that she couldn't turn back. The cost of her choice might be very high, but she was the only person who could help Octavian, even if he was too proud to ask.

The sound of hooves interrupted her brooding. Robin leaned forward to get a better view of the road. The clear ring of iron meant a well-shod horse, and the particular volume and frequency of the ringing suggested a heavy animal, moving at good pace, followed by another animal. And the sound was coming from Cleobury.

Then she saw him. Octavian, riding his favorite traveling horse, leading another pack animal behind him on a long rope. Her breath caught. It was now or never. Return to Cleobury and safety? Or follow Octavian north toward the Ardenwood, where untold dangers waited?

She glanced back, thinking of the warmth and comfort of the manor she'd left. A lady would return there.

Robin waited until Octavian passed beyond her view, and then turned her own horse north, following him.

Chapter 4

FOR THREE LONG, COLD DAYS Octavian rode northward. The first part of the way was through the Long Forest, which he knew well because he'd traveled this part of the country many times in service to Lord Denis, or to help his fellow knights for one reason or another. He stayed the first night at the home of a local nobleman who asked after the de Vere family and then about the news from London. Octavian ended up staying awake far too late talking with his host, but hospitality and comfort would be hard to come by later on, and he learned to value such gifts when they were offered.

He rode out later than he should have the next day and urged his horse faster to make up for lost time. The land became hilly, the path sometimes narrowing to a thin wedge between much taller ridges. Tav stayed alert, thinking how perfect such places were for an ambush. However, no attack came. Indeed, Tav felt almost alone. Occasionally, a shepherd would hail him from a distant slope, or he'd pass a wagon or rider hurrying from a farm to a nearby village. But this late in the year, few people traveled unless they had no choice.

I have a choice, Tav told himself. He chose to serve Lord Denis. And if he didn't want to travel, he certainly could tell Denis he wanted a different assignment. Denis didn't send Tav out into the cold November to punish him. Yet, as a cold wind rose through the half-barren trees, it felt a bit like a punishment.

He nudged his horse slightly, urging him to a different pace. As he did so, he listened carefully. There it was! Some faint echo of hoofbeats—but not an echo, because the rhythm was wrong.

Someone was following him.

Tav was almost certain of it for a moment, but then doubt crept in again. These hills were deceptive, and sounds could tumble from one hillside to another, or be carried down a stream for miles. Perhaps the sound was just the echoes of his own horses' hooves, distorted by the landscape.

He turned his head very slightly, hoping to catch sight of someone, anyone, who might prove his suspicions correct. Nothing. The browns and greys of the late autumn hid little, and yet he saw nothing. No other rider, no scout or spy.

Tav patted his horse's neck. The creature was getting nervous, picking up on Tav's own tension. "Calm down," he murmured in French.

The horse nickered softly, and resumed its normal pace. Tav kept an ear open for strange noises, but he heard nothing else for the rest of the day.

As dusk approached, he started to look for a place to make camp, there being not a hint of a village or farm in this part of the Long Forest. He rode off the trail to find a suitable spot. He wanted some shelter from inclement weather, and access to water, and some privacy from the road in case unfriendly people came by. He found a place with both water and privacy, though little protection from the elements. He'd simply have to pray that no rain or snow fell tonight.

After gathering what firewood he could find, he set up his meager camp. The fire smoked horribly due to the sodden state of the logs and branches he'd found, but it was better than nothing. His horses grazed on the few grasses that still grew during the cold autumn. The creatures seemed indifferent to the weather, so Tav suffered alone.

It would be a cold, lonely night for him. He ate and then unrolled his blanket as close to the fire as he dared. He was tired from a long day of riding, but sleep was difficult. He imagined footsteps and whispered words, as if a group of thieves planned to attack him and steal the horses. Whenever he woke, he threw another log on the fire, so at least he got a bit of warmth from his restlessness.

The morning came with no sunshine, just a grey layer of clouds. It seemed a little warmer than yesterday. As he proceeded north along the main road, he met a few other travelers, and spent another cold night in the woods.

The next day, he crossed into the Ardenwood proper, though no signs marked the border. The Ardenwood was a vast tract of land, not all forest, despite the name. Tav had ridden through it on this road before, and he remembered open meadows as well as ridges of low mountains as one looked west toward Wales. But no matter what the actual landscape, the Ardenwood was essentially wild, and therefore dangerous.

"Bad things happen there, sir knight," one man told him as they crossed paths. He was a merchant taking a last shipment of leather hides southward. "Thieves live in the woods there, and stranger things too. Monsters, some say. What takes you north? I'll pay you well to escort my wagons to Hereford."

"I am on my lord's business," Octavian said. "So north I must go."

"Good luck to you, then. Keep your sword ready."

The merchant was the last person he saw on the road that day, though he kept hearing the teasing, troubling sounds of other hoofbeats in the distance. Never for long, and never clearly enough to be sure. It was just enough to set him on edge.

He pressed on, through rougher country where the trees grew ever closer to the road, almost erasing the path in places. Tav grumbled to himself, as the road wound around steep cliffs.

Perhaps it was time to return home. To Aleppo, where he'd been born, or Jerusalem, where he'd spent his adolescence. "At least it will be warm there," he muttered as he reached the end of the detour.

Suddenly, he caught the rustle of dried leaves to his right, giving him a moment of warning as several figures sprang out from the underbrush.

"Get him!" one yelled. "Knock him down, and don't harm the horse he rides!"

Bandits. Tav pulled his sword free from its scabbard. They must be desperate, to attack an armed and mounted knight.

He angled his horse to better confront the two bandits coming directly for him. One held a long spear with a sharpened metal tip, which made him the prime threat to Tav. He focused on the spearman, parrying the thrusts of the spear with his longsword. The spearman was fairly skilled—perhaps he'd once served in an army—but Tav was able to deflect the most dangerous attacks.

Seizing an opportunity, Tav swung his sword to hit the shaft of the spear in a way that brought it closer to him.

Dropping the reins for a precious moment, he grabbed the spear in his free hand and snatched it upward, out the other man's grasp. Then he spun it around and hurled it directly at the man, catching him in the shoulder.

The man howled in pain and stumbled backward, cursing. But as soon as he left the fray, another fighter stepped in.

"Come down and fight like a man!" the blue-shirted attacker jeered.

Worried about harm to his horse, Tav leapt down and blocked the attacker's path toward the animal. He parried the first clumsy blow from the blueshirt, but soon found himself flanked on two sides as the others closed in. The horse was the only thing saving him from a knife in the back…so far.

Two of the bandits were actually good swordfighters, reinforcing the idea that this group probably left an army to find an easier life in the wild, preying on mostly unarmed travelers.

He'd make them regret attacking a knight.

For the first few moments, Tav felt that the odds were fair enough. He'd dispatched the spearman, and the two swordsmen were within his ability to defeat, even both at once.

Then a pain burst at his chest. He glanced down to see a fist-sized rock bouncing to the ground. Someone was playing dirty.

The second of distraction made him drop his sword, and one the swordsmen lunged forward, striking Tav. A dull ache spread outward from his bicep. He didn't look at it, but redoubled his attack.

His opponent fell back, unprepared for the speed of Octavian's strikes. Another rock whistled by, missing Tav by inches.

He saw an opening and struck the other man with a quick jab. The sword sliced the man's side, and he yelled out in pain. Tav hit again, and the man collapsed.

But just then, another heavy rock smacked into the side of Tav's head, the chain mail he wore doing little to weaken the blow.

Tav staggered sideways a few steps, trying to regain his balance. But he was now in a worse position, no longer with his back protected by the bulk of his riding horse.

He kept attacking and defending, but the attacks became fewer, and the defense became more and more necessary as the attacking group closed in.

One bandit in a rust-red tunic seized the long lead for the pack horse and started sawing at it with his knife. Tav winced. Losing the pack horse and its supplies would be a problem. The rustshirt shouted in triumph and then ran toward the woods with his prize. The normally placid horse whinnied in distress, but walked as he was led.

Angry, Tav shifted his grip on his sword and hit the nearest bandit with the flat of the blade. The force of the blow stunned the man, who fell to his knees as he clutched his head and moaned.

A whistling sound made Tav freeze in place.

The bandit in blue shrieked as an arrow struck his leg. Did the archer hit one of his own gang?

Make that two, Tav corrected as a second arrow sang through the trees, striking another man in the chest. He looked astonished, and sank to the ground without a word.

Either the archer had terrible aim, or he was not on the bandits' side—which didn't mean he was Tav's ally.

"Halt!" a voice called out from the safety of the woods. It was bright and clear without a trace of nervousness. But also...young? There was something familiar about it.

"All weapons to the ground!" the voice ordered. "Now!"

The three remaining bandits looked at each other in consternation, and lowered their arms, but didn't drop the weapons.

The archer was having none of it. "Are you stupid? I said weapons to the ground. Last man to drop his will get an arrow through his eye."

Hearing that, the bandits all dropped their swords and daggers with a clatter.

Tav slid his own sword into its scabbard, choosing to risk the archer's ire. A knight didn't throw away his sword.

"He's still got *his* weapon," one of the bandits complained to the unseen archer, pointing at Tav.

An arrow struck the ground by the man's feet—a clear warning to shut up.

"What now?" Tav asked the hidden archer, keeping his tone calm.

"Sir knight, kindly restrain these men. Or kill them. Doesn't matter to me."

The familiarity of the voice nagged at him, but he followed the instructions, quickly tying the three men to a broad trunk of a tree with the rope they themselves had carried.

"Well done, Sir Octavian," he heard from behind him.

Chapter 5

SHE WORE THE HOOD OF her capuchin up, so it wasn't immediately obvious that she was a girl. But Tav recognized her form all too well.

"What in God's name are you doing here?" he asked in French, on the off chance the others wouldn't understand.

She responded in kind. "Just at this moment? Saving your life, which I do from time to time, if you'll remember." Robin smiled. "The day we retook Cleobury, that time when Angelet got kidnapped…"

"Enough," Tav snapped. Seeing Robin so calm and self-assured annoyed him to no end. What was she *doing*, dressed as a boy and armed for a battle? The last time he'd seen her, she'd been the model of a proper lady. "We'll address your presence later."

"The fight is over," she said, gesturing to the restrained bandits.

"Not yet. I need to track the others. One stole my pack horse."

Robin raised her hand to stop him. "I stole it back. It's tied up safely with my own horse. Shall we retrieve them and ride on?"

He grabbed her by the arm and led her out of earshot of the tied-up men. When they were far enough from the captured men, he stopped and turned to her.

"Ride on where?" he asked in a low voice.

"To wherever you're going," she said, sounding quite reasonable despite it being a completely unreasonable proposal.

"You will return to Cleobury immediately. I'll take you there myself and see that Alric locks you in a room for your own safety."

"You won't," she said bluntly. "It would mean the loss of many more days. You can't spare the time. Besides," she added, "it's not as if this is the first time we've traveled together alone."

In a flash, Octavian remembered the other time, over four years ago. By complete accident, he'd encountered Robin not far from Cleobury. She'd been less than a year into her new life, and she wasn't adapting well. In fact, she'd decided to run away.

She cursed him the moment she saw him in the town where she was riding through—and Robin knew how to curse very well, thanks to a rough upbringing among some rather dubious people. But Octavian, still a young knight with more ideals than sense, refused to let her continue with her mad plan to run away to London.

Instead, he'd argued, then ordered, then begged her to return to Cleobury with him to escort her there. Robin was barely fifteen then, and though she'd been dressed as a boy—naturally—she didn't look like one. But Tav was not going to let her roam the countryside of England completely undefended.

Over two days and nights, they journeyed back to Cleobury. It was nerve-jangling for Tav to be in the company of Robin because he was constantly worried that someone would see them, realize Robin was a girl, and accuse him of mistreating her. Not that any man mistreated Robin—she always made men who tried regret it very quickly.

Tav strained every inch of his being to making sure nothing he did over those few days could be misinterpreted. He never touched her, and he certainly never took advantage of her. Anyway, Robin was a scruffy little kitten at that point. There was nothing alluring in her appearance, other than her sparking blue eyes, and her laugh, and the way she took nothing seriously—a counterpoint to Tav, who took everything seriously.

All he wanted was to get her home safely, and in secret. They managed it, somehow. Robin returned to Cleobury with a story that worked. She swore she'd never tell anyone of Tav's involvement, and she even apologized at the end, promising she'd behave in the future. And he thought she kept that promise. Until now.

"I don't want to ever think of that incident again," he warned her. "And you can ride back to Cleobury on your own this time."

Even as he said it, he knew that he also couldn't let her do that. Robin got this far unscathed, but the chance that she would return to Cleobury without coming to harm in some way was too slim. Tav couldn't concentrate on his own task if he wasn't certain she was safe. "You waited till so long to reveal yourself for just this reason, didn't you?" he asked.

Robin shook her head. "I revealed myself now because there was no guarantee that you'd win that fight without getting injured."

"I needed no help," he retorted.

"You did," Robin shot back. "You could at least be

gracious about the fact that I prevented that man in the blue tunic from stabbing you while you were attending to the red one."

Tav thought back to the skirmish and realized that Robin was correct on that count. "It wouldn't have been a fatal blow," he hedged.

Robin huffed out, "Oh, men really are intolerable."

He took a breath. "All right. Thank you."

She paused, considering him with those big blue eyes. "You're welcome. You see? You'll be better off now that I've joined you."

Tav sighed. "You can*not* join me. We'll find some other solution."

"No other solution is needed," Robin said, "because I'm most useful with you. You need to go through the Ardenwood, and you need to know what to expect there. Cecily didn't know much, but it was enough to make me think that you needed someone you can trust in the north."

"And you followed me all the way from Cleobury?"

"I actually left the manor before you did," she corrected, her tone defensive. "I didn't technically start following you till after you rode through Bournham."

"Alric will never forgive me."

"Leaving was *my* choice," Robin insisted. "And whether Alric will forgive *me* is the question. You're in the clear."

Tav doubted that. Whether or not the idea was Robin's own, the moment Octavian realized she was here meant he was responsible for her.

But he had no choice in the moment. Retrieving their horses, and a few supplies from the bandits' own stock— Robin proclaimed they were ill-gotten gains and therefore the bandits had no better claim to them—they rode on.

As they went, Tav realized that Robin must have been concealing herself from everyone while she traveled. He asked, "You spent these past nights sleeping alone in the forest?"

Robin gave a shrug of her shoulder. "Obviously."

"You could have been killed!"

"Only if someone had found me," she said in far too calm a manner. "And I know where to camp so that no one will find me."

"The fire…"

"Just attracts attention. I can survive without one."

Tav shivered at the mere idea of a long, cold night without any heat source at all. "It's been far too cold these past few nights. And it will get colder when—"

He turned to look over his right shoulder, but winced as a sudden pain coursed through his arm, and he unconsciously let out a hiss.

* * * *

Robin flinched the moment she heard Octavian. She looked back, expecting some archer behind them, but saw nothing.

"What is it?" she asked. Robin's gaze went to his arm, catching the sheen of blood on his right sleeve.

He put his left hand over the spot, shaking his head. "Nothing."

"You were struck during the fight!" Robin said, aghast. "Why didn't you say anything?"

"It's a minor wound."

"Which will become a major wound if it's not tended to. We need to dress it." Goodness, she sounded *exactly* like Cecily now. "Follow me."

She edged in front of him on the path and started forward, watching for any sign of water. Fortunately, this part of the forest was filled with little streams, and it wouldn't be long before she found a suitable place with fresh water to clean the wound.

At Robin's direction, they rode a little way off the trail. She dismounted and tethered her horse, and he did the same, favoring his right arm.

Octavian was talking to himself in French, and Robin only heard a little of what he said. He was cursing his own inattention to the fight, as if it hadn't been one man against many.

A few moments later, Robin had gathered several items from her own pack. She pointed Octavian to a place near the stream. "Sit. I'll get some fresh water."

She filled an empty leather skin with icy cold, clear water. When she looked back, she found that Octavian had already taken off his surcoat and the chain mail, and was in the act of pulling the linen shirt over his head.

Well, then. Robin blinked. Had the air been cold before? Now it felt like a furnace. She'd seen men half-naked before. Whether it was the men-at-arms training at Cleobury in summer, or the servant boys who ran straight to the pond for a swim, stripping off clothes as they went —despite censure from Agnes.

She knew what men looked like. And they didn't look as perfect as Octavian, with a chest that broad, or shoulders developed from years of training. Why had she not thought of how awkward it would be to travel with him?

Nonsense. He was just a person, in need of her help. She knelt down near him, wet cloth in hand. The water was cold, giving him goosebumps as soon as the cloth touched his skin. Robin chuckled in spite of everything. "The gash didn't upset you but a little cold water does?"

"Everyone has a weakness," he said.

Such as an ideal, incredibly gorgeous knight.

"The cut isn't very deep," she said as she opened a jar of Cecily's ointment.

He looked skeptically at the substance. "You're certain you took the correct jar?"

She glared at him. "I worked with Cecily many times when people around the manor needed help. This is what we use for any wound that breaks the skin."

"Very well." He shifted a little, holding his arm up so she could anoint the wound.

Robin put one hand on his arm to steady it, fearing she'd accidentally jostle the already painful spot. She carefully applied the sticky, strongly scented ointment to the wound, trying not to notice anything else. But it was impossible not to notice Octavian when he was only inches away without anything on above the waist.

His dark skin looked smooth to the touch, and she did indeed want to touch him. Beneath the skin, sleek muscles rippled, drawing her eye to his shoulders and the bulk of his arms. He was so strong, she thought. What was she doing staring at him?

"I...need...a bandage," she said, feeling as if she'd drunk far too much rich wine.

"Please," Tav said, his voice even. "Before I get any colder."

"Right." She grabbed the long strips of cloth bandage and quickly wrapped it around his arm, aware that her cheeks were on fire now. She tied the ends with shaky fingers, but thankfully, she knew what she was doing, and the bandage would hold until it was time to change it.

"There you are," she said at last, not daring to look at him. "We'll need to change the dressing tomorrow, or sooner if it bleeds too much."

He leaned over to examine the bandage. "This was

very well done."

"I told you I had practice." Robin felt the need to defend herself despite the compliment. "You needn't sound so…" She trailed off when she realized that her face was only inches away from his own. *If he wanted to, he could kiss me*, she thought.

For a moment, she thought he would. His eyes roamed her face, and lingered on her mouth, a small sign of interest that made her breath catch in her throat. His right hand drifted up toward her, and she wanted so badly to feel his fingers on her face and her neck.

She always thought Octavian was resistant to such impulses. He never flirted with any women in Robin's memory, and his piety seemed to suggest that his mind rarely wandered to baser things.

Before, when he'd found Robin while she was running away, he'd been furious with her for acting so rashly, and he treated her with an icy reserve that made her feel like the lowest, most common creature. He barely looked at her that whole time he was escorting her back. Robin had been so embarrassed that she'd annoyed the one person she idolized that it was difficult to even speak with him along the way, at least for the first part of the journey. She spent hours wishing he'd relent, and show her a little mercy. And he did, at the very end, which only made her more mortified because she realized how much worry she had caused him.

But back then, he never hinted that he had any interest in her. Now, she could read a few signs, and her heart leapt in her chest at the thought that he might…that the strange almost-kiss he gave her at Cleobury meant something after all, or that the look in his eyes right now signaled a new feeling.

Then he pulled back. "We need to keep riding north,"

he said, reaching for his clothing. "I can't lose any time. With luck, I'll find a safe place to leave you."

Robin hated the way he suggested leaving her behind, and felt stung by his dismissal. As they rode onward, she pled her case.

"You should understand, of all people," she said. "You know what it's like to see the world. You've seen Jerusalem and Rome and the sea and how many mountains, so don't try to speak to me of being content in one spot. What would you know of how that feels?"

"I wouldn't. I grant you that."

Robin seized on his words. "If you grant me that, then you must also grant me the chance to go somewhere because it's my choice."

"This isn't a friendly visit, Robin. This is going to be dangerous."

"I can *help* you, though."

"How? It's been years since you were in the Ardenwood."

"How quickly can the paths change?" she retorted. "Even if things are different, I know more than you. And I'm less noticeable than you." She reached over and tapped the back of his hand meaningfully.

He just shook his head. "You're more noticeable than you think, Robin. You can't get away with what you did years ago."

"I could."

"No, you couldn't. Then you could—barely—pass for a boy. You were young enough, and you had short hair."

"I can cut my hair again. I've no great vanity about it. It will grow back."

"Even if you cut your hair, you can't hide your face."

"My face is the same."

"It is not. You're older. And…"

"And what?"

"You're quite pretty," he said, not looking at her.

"Oh." He thought her pretty?

"And that makes it imperative for you to be somewhere safe. Not out here."

"What sort of arrogance leads someone to ignore help when it's offered? If women were in charge of armies, the wars would be far shorter." She nudged her horse and rode on ahead several lengths, too annoyed to argue further.

A short while later, Octavian caught up with her, and reached out to take the reins of her horse, signaling both horses to halt. "We need to discuss this."

"I thought you had already decided my fate."

He looked frustrated. "You're correct about the situation. I'm at a disadvantage, considering that I don't know enough about the area, and I can't hire anyone I don't know. I know you, and you've already learned about the mission, so it's not exactly violating the king's instructions to tell you more."

She took a deeper breath, relaxing as she felt the glow of victory. She'd convinced Octavian that she was worth having. "Then we can stop fighting."

"I wasn't fighting with you, I was trying to protect you," he said, glaring at her. "And that's still a matter to address because you absolutely can't travel alone with me looking as you do."

His implication was clear. Robin would be vilified for traveling alone with a man who she wasn't related to in some way. And while she knew that Octavian wasn't a threat to her, by the mere fact that they had been together without anyone else to keep watch Robin would be assumed to be ruined, her virginity lost along with her soul. She could almost hear the condemnation from the church

—how she had transgressed, and how she was like all women, wicked and lustful and inspiring otherwise good men to sin.

"I'll be a boy," she said. "I'll get dirt on my face, and cut my hair short." She looked to his own close-cropped hair. "You've got a razor, don't you?"

Octavian's eyes flashed. "Don't touch your hair. How would you explain the damage once you return to Cleobury?"

"I'll…I'll say the lice got so bad that I had to shear all my hair off. That happens!"

Despite the situation, he laughed. "Not to you. So kindly leave your hair alone."

"If I keep my hood up," she said, "I think I'll be safe enough. At least till I think of something more clever."

He sighed. "Spare me your clever ideas, Robin. They're going to get me killed."

Chapter 6

THEY RODE ONWARD, ROBIN RIDING ahead, and Octavian looking behind them frequently in case the bandits decided to chase after them once more. Robin thought it unlikely. Such men wanted easy pickings. Discovering that Octavian was a well-trained knight, and that he was now accompanied by an archer, would discourage any repeat attack.

She sought out a secluded spot to camp that night. The area here was especially wild, and she wanted them to remain well hidden. Setting up the little camp took almost no time at all. Gathering firewood was the most consuming task, but it was now cold enough that she thought they should risk it.

Octavian, though he still looked dubious about her presence, did appreciate the fire. While they ate supper, he looked at the sack of things Robin had liberated from the thieves. "What's in there?"

"More food, mostly," she said. "They owed us something after trying to kill you and steal your horses." She rifled through the sack, pulling items out. "Looks like some smoked pork, a few skins of wine. Ooh, a wheel of cheese! And a blanket." The last item she pulled out was a folded brown cloth. But it turned out not to be a blanket. It was a monk's robe, clean and patched in many places.

Robin made a face. "Ugh. I hope they didn't rob a monk to get some food. Though they seemed evil enough to do it."

Tav frowned at the robe. "If the thieves sunk that low, I should have punished them far more harshly than just leaving them in the woods."

"Too late now." Robin shook the robe out and held it up, trying it on for size. "Perhaps they used it to trick travelers. Monks aren't intimidating."

Octavian tilted his head slightly, regarding her with a more speculative air.

"Put the robe on," he ordered suddenly.

The robe was voluminous, obscuring Robin's figure. She pulled the hood over her head and then tugged it to cover nearly all of her face. When she bent her head, she could barely see more than a few steps ahead of her…but she would be hidden from all eyes.

"Will this work?" she asked Octavian. She tied the simple rope belt loosely around her waist.

"Keep your hands folded in your sleeves," he advised. "And keep the hood up. But yes, as a disguise it should work much better than a boy's outfit. People will see nothing more than a devout traveler, and that should allow us considerable freedom."

"There is a famous holy well dedicated to Saint Winifred in Treffynnon, in Wales. If we say I'm headed there, folk will believe us. It's a well-known place for pilgrims." She pulled the hood away from her face, irritated at the limited vision.

"Pilgrims…" he echoed. A moment later, he put something into her outstretched hands—a collection of small pilgrim medals, souvenirs gathered by people who'd traveled to each holy place as a symbol of their often long, difficult journey. "Pin these to the front of the robe. Then you'll truly look like a pilgrim."

Robin peered at the medals. One was a stamped brass sun with waving rays. One was silver in the shape of a crucifix. One was a brightly painted fish carved from bone. Her mouth fell open. "Octavian! I can't wear your medals! Did you go to all these places?"

"I grew up in the Levant," he pointed out, "so many of those places took no more than a week to reach. As pilgrimages, none were terribly harsh. Don't lose the quatrefoil cross, though, please. I got that in Jerusalem, at the Holy Sepulchre."

"Oh," she said, awed. There was something unreal about holding an object that she knew had come from the city of Jerusalem itself. "I promise I'll take care of it. All of them!"

"Good. Now pin them on, and no one will question your status."

"But what if someone asks me about the Holy Land? I don't know what to say."

"You'll say nothing," Tav warned her. "You, Brother Robin, are under a vow of complete silence, and I'll speak for both of us."

"But—"

"Not even one word," he interrupted. "That violates your oath." He smiled at her. "It's the only way, Robin. You couldn't maintain the disguise if you had to talk."

"But I may need to tell you something!"

"Then you can signal me," he said. "And when we're out of earshot of others, you can speak."

"Are you certain this is necessary? Or do you just want to shut me up?"

"Why would you think that?" Octavian asked, too

innocently. "You wanted to come along. Your silence is the price. Or you can turn around and ride back to Cleobury."

"You know I won't do that."

"Then promise me you'll do *exactly* what I say, when I say it." His expression grew serious. "No arguments, no protests, no going off on your own. Promise me."

"I promise," she ground out.

"Promise what?" he prompted.

"Ugh! I promise to follow your orders, and obey you in all things," she said. "Is that good enough?"

"It is," he said, satisfied. "Now pay attention."

He made a gesture with his right hand, drawing two fingers across his mouth and then pulling his hand down in front of his chest. "Mimic that."

She did so, and again until Tav nodded in approval.

"That gesture communicates that you're under a vow of silence. Make that to any priest or monk and they'll know. Most others will guess, or I'll tell them."

"How do you know that?" she asked, just before re-membering that Tav had grown up in a monastery after he'd been orphaned. He learned many aspects of the reli-gious life, even those that didn't apply to a young boy taken in as a student.

"Never mind. Any other signs I should know?" she asked.

"Let's keep things simple for now. The last thing the world needs is a little Robin running around in the perfect disguise of a monk."

She stuck her tongue out at him, then acknowledged that the move proved his point of her being immature.

She'd just have to show him otherwise.

The night grew colder. Even in front of the fire, Robin shivered. "My front half is roasting and my back half is freezing. Why did this stupid Lord Pierce decide to change sides at this time of year? He ought to have done it in summer."

"Inconsiderate," Octavian agreed.

"I remember when Cecily and Alric fled from him," she said. Robin remembered nearly every detail, for the fateful arrival of Cecily in Rainald's camp was the great turning point in Robin's life. If she hadn't spotted Cecily and Alric in the woods that day, if she hadn't taken them to Rainald…everything would be different. She might still be living in the forest. He never would have come to Cleobury. She never would have met Octavian.

"Robin?"

"What?" She'd grown distracted, lost in the reverie. "What did you say?"

"I said that if we do find Lord Pierce, you need to be wary of him. Treat him the way you'd treat a poisonous snake."

"Don't worry. From what Cecily said, he's no one I wish to befriend." Indeed, the few times Cecily mentioned Pierce, there was a loathing in the other woman's voice that no one else inspired. And when Alric heard the name, his hand always tightened on the hilt of his sword.

Robin was confident that she'd hate Lord Pierce on sight. She shivered again, both from the idea of the man and from the gust of wind that was strong enough to make the fire hiss and spark.

"Come here." Octavian raised his arm, and Robin dove into the sheltering warmth under his cloak. She huddled up against him, her monk's robes gathering around her as she made herself as small as possible.

"That's much better," she said after several moments. "I can feel my fingers and toes again."

"Good. Curse this cold," he muttered. "They say Hell

is fire, but I think it's ice."

"You didn't have such cold in the Levant?"

"Not like this. And never so damp."

She nodded. The damp cold was the worst, seeming to creep right into a person and settle in the bones. "Tell me about Aleppo. I need to hear something warm."

He laughed a little. "It's definitely warm. In summer, the sun burns through the whole city and the land around it. During the day, we'd find any excuse to go into the hills, where the olive trees grew. The shade made it tolerable."

"Who's we?"

"The boys from St. Thomas. Especially Septimus. He was close in age to me, and had been taken in by the monks just the month prior to my arrival. We were raised as brothers."

"Septimus and Octavian."

"He was the seventh orphan that year. I was the eighth. The monks liked order in all things."

"Hold a moment! The *monks* named you Octavian?"

"Of course. You knew that."

"I did not!" Perhaps he'd told others, but Robin never heard anything about his name being changed to suit the brothers of the monastery. "What was your name before? What did your mother call you?"

There was a long pause. "I was too young to remember."

That was unbearably sad to her.

"Don't you want to learn?"

"Yes," he said, after a long pause. "I do. But I never knew how to go about it. I had only a few hints, based on what the brothers had been told when I arrived. My mother was Nubian, come to Aleppo with her family. And my father was a soldier for hire in the city. Protecting caravans, guarding outlying villages during times of strife, that sort of thing. They met and married, and probably thought they'd have a lifetime together. Instead, he died in some skirmish, and she died not long after. So what is there left for me to find?"

"Maybe someone remembers something else. What if they did, and it led you to your mother's home? Or your father's? You could find out so much more. You were really just a boy when Denis asked you to go with him. You probably couldn't have traveled to Africa on your own, but you could now. You can go anywhere!"

"It's a long way to go to answer a question," he said, sounding as if he were trying to convince himself of the argument.

"Yes, but it's a very important question," she countered, even while she wanted to bite her tongue to stop her words. Why was she offering Octavian reasons to leave? She didn't want him to leave. "It's who you are."

"I know who I am," he said, and from his tone she guessed more prodding wouldn't be welcome.

"You know who you are, but I barely do," she told him. "Even if it's been years since we first met, I can measure the total length of time we've been in the same place in mere days. A month at most. To be honest, we're strangers." And yet she was huddled right up against him —very familiar behavior for a stranger. She looked up, hoping to read his thoughts in his face.

He was staring into the fire, not at her, so she could watch him without shame. The truth was that Robin had never seen a more beautiful person in her whole life. Granted, she had lived in some seclusion for years, but she was not completely ignorant of the world. Most people were ordinary, like her. Octavian was astonishing.

And she was alone with him. Risking his life along

with her own.

"Octavian?" she asked.

"What?"

"I can still go back to Cleobury. I'll be safe, I promise. You don't have to get in trouble on my account."

He looked at her, his brow furrowed. "I can't let you go alone," he said slowly. "While I trust your ability to ride and scout and sneak about the whole country like a weasel"—he smiled to let her know it was a compliment—"I cannot risk sending you off again on your own."

She nodded, acknowledging the tricky situation she'd put him in, all out of a desire to help.

"Besides," he added, speaking slowly, "two people are better than one. You aided me in the fight, and you patched me up better than I could myself."

"You're saying I'm useful?"

He nodded. "The night I stayed at Cleobury, I prayed for assistance. Who am I to refuse it when it appears?"

She smiled, though she certainly couldn't claim divine inspiration in her deeds.

"However," he added, more sternly, "you have to listen to me in all things, understand? You know the woods, but I know the minds of the men involved here. And that's the most dangerous part."

"I'll listen," she promised. "You won't regret it."

"Let's hope not."

Chapter 7

AFTER ONLY A DAY, OCTAVIAN had to admit that traveling with Robin was better than traveling alone. He spent half his life on the road, but Robin knew this part of the world far better than he did. She remembered useful spots, such as the clear-running creek in a little valley hidden from the main road, and the sheltered place to camp that allowed them to build a fire with wood that was somehow not sodden with moisture.

"How do you manage to find dry wood?" he'd asked. "I feel as though it rained every other day this autumn."

She laughed. "The first thing is to look in the right places. People like to camp near water, which almost always means they're camping in a flatter, wetter part of the forest. I always search for wood near uplands or hills, if they're around. The water runs down the slope and any fallen wood tends to dry out faster. It means more walking to and from the camp, but a better fire is worth it."

It sounded so obvious when she explained it.

"I need to go on foot for a while," she said at one point, glancing around at the surrounding hills. "It's easier to see where I'm going…" She trailed off without finishing her thought. It was a habit of hers, he noticed. She did it whenever she was focused on what she was doing more than what she was saying. Which was often.

She'd done it when she'd bandaged him up, her words dropping away as she noticed him staring at her like a dolt, half-dressed and dazed by her proximity. Robin had looked fetching when she was dressed as a lady within the walls of Cleobury. But she looked ten times prettier in the middle of the woods, her face streaked with dirt and her cheeks pink from the cold. He thought she'd never looked so vibrant.

The urge to tell her that was strong, or just to show her that with a kiss. But at the last moment, Tav restrained himself. Robin was virtually alone, except for him. The last thing she needed was her protector turning into yet another man to fend off.

Not that she looked in need of protection at the moment. He watched her as she blazed a path through the trees, her steps slow and sure on the forest floor. She barely made a sound when she walked while he seemed to hit every twig and crackle every dry leaf in the vicinity. The horses were quieter than he was, he thought in disgust.

"Ah!" Robin said at last. She looked back and smiled. She indicated a spot in the woods that looked just like every other part of the woods "This trail will lead us to a manor. We won't get there tonight, but by tomorrow evening we'll be inside the walls. Assuming the family is still friendly to travelers."

Tav nodded.

That night they camped once again, after Robin found a good spot, sheltered from the wind. They ate, combining their supplies for a better meal. Robin loved cheese and packed far more of it than cold meat. Tav had done the opposite. Combined with the bread he'd got from his last host, the supper was definitely enough to satisfy any camper.

Robin cleaned up afterward, her movements quick and efficient. He was reminded again that she'd spent the better part of her young life living very rough.

"You never forgot how to live in the woods," he said when she came back from the stream.

"Never will," she said cheerfully. "Cecily says I'm still feral." As soon as she mentioned Cecily, though, her eyes clouded and she sat down on her bedroll. "She's going to be worrying about me. I should have left a message."

"You didn't tell anyone?"

She shook her head. "I didn't want to be stopped."

"You could have left a written note."

"I thought about it, but...I didn't." She looked ashamed. "Everyone will be so angry at me."

"They'll save some rage for me," Tav guessed.

"No. When we get back to Cleobury, I'll take all the blame. Don't worry. You'll be safe from Alric," she said.

Don't worry. It was rather sweet how she was offering to defend him. As if anything would deflect Alric's wrath once he found out what happened.

She yawned then, covering her mouth with the back of her hand.

"You should get some sleep. I'll stay awake."

"I think we're safe enough," she said. "A person would have to be mad to be out in these woods when they could be somewhere safe inside walls."

That describes you perfectly, Robin, he thought but didn't say out loud.

Robin curled up in her bedroll, pulling the blanket up over her head so she was just a little mound next to the fire. Her hip rose highest, but she was a small woman, and surprisingly delicate in form, almost like a bird. It was her personality that made her seem so dominant.

She was much easier to deal with when she was sleeping. Tav shook his head at the thought because it immediately made him think of less innocent reasons for him to see her sleeping.

He really had to stop thinking of her in that way. He deliberately turned himself so his back was to the fire and the sleeping woman. He stared out at the woods. The fire's glow illuminated the nearest trees, but beyond that, the world was dark. A few dry leaves rattled in high branches whenever the wind picked up. Owls hooted to each other. Then a low, dark shape of some creature emerged as it passed into the firelight for a moment. Tav saw large yellow eyes staring back at him.

Then the creature dashed off. He heard the sound of a splash an instant later as the creature dived into the stream to be safe from the interlopers in its domain.

As Tav watched the woods, he thought of how he ended up here. It all started with meeting Lord Denis.

Octavian encountered Lord Denis in Jerusalem. The Frankish lord had gone on a pilgrimage to the Holy Land, bringing along his wife—a somewhat unusual decision, but Lady Muriel was a devout woman who had endured some painful personal tragedies in her life. The couple hoped that a penitential visit to the holiest of places in Christendom might absolve them of whatever sins cost them the lives of their four children.

Denis and his wife stayed at the very monastery where Tav was living when they arrived in Jerusalem, and that was how Octavian first met the man he'd eventually serve as a knight.

Octavian spoke Aramaic, Latin, a little Greek and Arabic, and some French. Languages were like games to him—he could pick up the rudiments within days. He'd also trained with Brother Benuic, who'd been a soldier before he took the cowl. Octavian had a natural athleticism that fit well with Benuic's instructions in knife and sword fighting. The result was that his education prepared him very well to live on his own no matter where in the Levant he chose to go.

He could have remained at the monastery. A part of him was drawn to the order of religious life. But at seventeen, he was far too restless to make that choice. The bald brother Marcus had given him the best advice—the church was eternal, and would always be there to welcome Octavian. But the world was wide, and God would not be displeased if Octavian wished to see it for himself.

On the monks' recommendation, he'd been hired to escort the lord Denis and his lady safely around the city for the few months they planned to stay. During that time, he'd gotten to know both of them quite well. As it turned out, he was the same age as their youngest son would have been if he'd lived, even sharing the same birth month. Lady Muriel took that as a sign and treated Octavian much more like a relation than a hired hand.

One evening, Octavian defended Denis from thieves while the pair returned from a late mass. The small gang thought they'd cornered a rich, lazy tourist and his paid guide—who they assumed would abandon his employer as soon as a blade was drawn. Octavian had instead drawn his own knife and rushed the attackers, shocking them with his ferocity. They'd fought back because a gang's reputation would suffer if they ran at the first hint of resistance. But Octavian fended them off long enough to get Denis to a safer location, even though he was wounded in the fight. He still bore the scar—a slash along his upper right arm. The wound, thank God, had not gone deep. It bled copiously, but the infirmary monk had cleaned and bound it well.

Denis was impressed by Octavian's quick action and character. The bond between them deepened the longer Denis and his wife stayed in the city. Tav took them not just to the well-known holy places, but also to shrines and other places of interest throughout the area. Their collection of pilgrim medals grew accordingly, and in Bethlehem, Lady Muriel said she prayed to Mary and heard the Mother of God tell her that her children were awaiting her in heaven. The lady had collapsed with joy, and had to rest for hours before she was ready to leave the shrine.

When Denis decided that it was time to return to his own land, he extended an offer to Tav. Tav's gift for languages, along with his ability to fight, would make him a valuable addition to Denis's retinue. Out of gratitude for Tav saving his life, he promised that he'd not just employ Tav as a man-at-arms, but see that he was trained as a knight with all due speed. Some men didn't become knights until they were well over thirty, but Tav was knighted in Paris at the age of nineteen—all due to Denis's insistence.

He struggled with the honor, feeling unworthy of it. He nearly died in an early battle, except for the timely intervention of a slightly older knight who stepped in to defend Octavian's weak side during the fight. It didn't matter that Tav didn't know the other man's name or his lord. They finished the day after fighting back to back against an assault by one of Maud's forces.

Afterward, the man introduced himself as Alric of Hawksmere, said that it was clear Octavian needed a bit of watching over, and then brought him into a circle of friends—a tight-knit group of soldiers—that Octavian remained with ever since. When he might have met death on the battlefield, he instead found a new life.

And now, he was riding north with the ward of his oldest friend in England. The irritatingly astute ward, who asked the same sort of questions he'd been asking more and more. Why didn't he go back? Why didn't he search for more clues to his past?

He wanted to. Tav always wanted to know more about his parents and where they came from, and why they chose to leave their own homes. Perhaps he came from a whole lineage of wanderers. Perhaps there were aunts and uncles and cousins who'd welcome his stories.

Despite his yearning, the prospect of tracing that path —with only a few tiny clues to go on—seemed too daunting. Maybe that was why he accepted Denis's offer, because it was a clear path forward. Perhaps he wasn't smart enough or strong enough to follow the other path, the one leading back.

You can go anywhere. Robin had spoken with sublime confidence. And she was correct about one thing. He was older now, and much more capable. Perhaps a task that was impossible for him as a boy would be possible as a man.

The thought stirred him. He could go anywhere, and perhaps even find out where he truly came from.

In her sleep, Robin turned from one side to the other. He glanced down, remembering his more immediate problems. Before he could consider leaving for home, he had to finish what he started, and that meant focusing on the task at hand, and the complicating presence of Robin.

No matter what else happened, he swore silently, he'd keep Robin safe.

Chapter 8

ROBIN AWOKE WITH A RIME of frost on her blanket, but she felt much better than the day before. They broke camp and got riding as soon as possible. The sooner she got her blood running through her veins again, the warmer she'd be.

The afternoon of the next day, they reached the gate-house of the manor she had hoped to find.

"Hood low," Octavian muttered as they rode closer. "Keep your head down and your hands hidden if someone gets too close. This is our first test."

Robin did as he said, bowing her head as if in prayer.

"Halt there!" the guards near the gate called. "State your names and your business if you wish to enter."

"God keep you," Octavian said pleasantly. "I am Sir Octavian de Levant. This is my companion, Brother Robin, who I have sworn to protect while we travel. We aim for the holy well of Saint Winifred in Wales, but we hope to stay the night here."

"The brother does not speak for himself?"

"He has taken a vow of silence," Octavian explained easily. "Yet another penance to chasten his soul while on pilgrimage. He did the same while we traveled to Bethlehem, and spoke not a word until we were in the presence of the relic of the True Cross in the cathedral there."

The guards murmured to each other in a quick conference, and then the one said, "Do you both swear as Christians to uphold the laws of our lord who holds these lands?"

"We do," Octavian said.

"Then you both may enter." The guard still sounded dubious, but he had no grounds to turn them away.

Robin breathed a sigh of relief.

The lord was not in residence, so the guards escorted them both to the seneschal, who governed the manor in the lord's absence. He was a white-haired man, as thin as a rail, but tough-looking as a gnarled oak tree. He looked them over, and at Octavian with special doubt.

"The monk's alliance is clear, though you are a puzzle. You are Christian?" the old man asked, staring hard at Octavian.

He merely gestured to the cross on his shield. "All my life, sir. I was baptized in the Church of Saint Thomas in Aleppo."

"You know the Lord's Prayer, then. Recite it."

No reaction showed on his face, but Robin saw his shoulders tense up, a response similar to her own body whenever she knew she'd have to fight. So this was another sort of fight he had to deal with regularly. He said, "Would you care to hear it in Latin, Greek, French, or Aramaic?"

"Latin is the church's chosen language," the man declared.

Octavian recited the prayer in clear Latin.

"Our priest could not say it better," the man declared, a bit unwillingly. "And everyone knows that devils cannot say the words. Very well. You both may stay the night."

Octavian looked to Robin. "You'll want to spend some time in the chapel, brother," Tav said, his expression making it a clear command. "Go there, and I'll come find you when your meditations are complete. I have a few questions about the road ahead that only the seneschal can answer."

Stay out of trouble, Robin interpreted. She bent her head and shuffled off to the church.

The church was small and dark and cold, with only the candles on the altar providing light. At Vespers and Compline, more lights would be lit, but for now the place was empty except for her.

Robin sat on a bench toward the front, trying to remain calm and think holy thoughts.

She was terrible at holy thoughts. She kept wondering about Octavian, and thinking about Cecily and Alric being either frantic or furious with her, and angry that the seneschal thought Octavian might not be trustworthy simply because he looked different.

The first time Robin had seen Octavian, she'd been surprised. She hadn't seen that many people in her short life, and so it had been a revelation to learn that someone could have skin as dark as Octavian's. But she'd been equally struck by how very much he'd seemed an ideal knight. Beginning that day, Robin admired Octavian the way she admired heroes in tales.

Whereas the seneschal looked at Octavian and made him prove he wasn't a devil.

Idiot.

She looked up at the church altar and tried to look suitably prayerful. There were tales of saints who prayed alone in the wilderness for years. She could hardly make it through an hour before she wanted to take the church walls apart stone by stone. When would he come to fetch her?

She heard the soft squeak of the door, and then footfalls down the center aisle. She shifted slightly, assuming what she hoped looked like an attitude of prayerful calm. She couldn't peek to see who had come in, and anyone who lived here had a reason to enter the church.

Someone slid onto the bench behind her.

"Robin," Octavian said softly, leaning forward to be heard. "Are you hungry?"

"Starving, and you know it!" She plucked her hood back a little and looked to him. "Why exile me to the church?"

"I wanted you in a safe place, with the fewest eyes possible." He handed her a few items, all bundled up in a linen cloth. "Bread, sausages, and cheese. I've got some ale in a jug here as well. Eat, and then we'll go to the dormitorium. It's not private, but I claimed the two pallets in the corner. It should be safe enough."

Robin nodded absently. She was already too engaged in eating to care about sleeping arrangements. The seasoned sausages disappeared first, and then she tore into the bread. It was a hearty, dark, grainy loaf, and she relished each bite.

"Drink." Tav lifted the small jug toward her.

Robin took a sip of the ale to wash down the food, then started to devour the cheese.

"You were hungry," he said. "If I'd known, I could have brought more."

"If you'd let me talk, I could have told you," she whispered.

"Your vow of silence is what keeps this masquerade together. But I will bring more food next time. I'm sorry I thought this was enough, but you're so little."

She finished the last bites of cheese. "Riding all day makes anyone hungry, no matter how big or small."

"So I see. You'll be all right?" he asked then. "Sleeping in the dormitorium?"

"Naturally. I've slept with men many times."

Tav's raised eyebrow made her blush. "*Among* men, I mean. Growing up in Rainald's camp, I was just another boy—till the past couple years, I suppose. Then they insisted I stay with Sara in the women's cottage."

"Good." From his tone, it sounded as though Octavian thought she ought to be locked in a tower.

"You had a whole story ready for the guards and the host," she noted. "I never would have guessed you'd be a good liar."

He smiled a little. "I've learned that it's not always prudent to tell the truth. I'll ask forgiveness for all my deceptions—after this business is concluded."

"Do you have to do that often?" she asked. "Prove yourself?"

Tav hesitated before saying, "More than I'd like. Especially in the countryside. In London, or the port cities, it's not so common."

"It must be annoying."

"Yes."

He didn't have to add the obvious point that if he returned home, he wouldn't have to deal with the ignorance. Robin bit her lip, thinking that it was only a matter of time until he did leave. Why would he want to stay in a backwater when he could easily travel home to the center of the world?

* * * *

After leaving the following morning, they continued

on the road north.

"No hint of Lord Pierce from the seneschal or the guards," Tav said. "Nothing more than we already knew. He's fled from Malvern and no one knows where he's gone." The frustration made his voice tight.

"We'll keep asking," Robin said, trying to reassure him. "All this means is that the manor doesn't have many visitors who might share news. Or that Pierce went another direction. We'll find him, and we'll find this Govannon."

"Even if we do, it might be too late."

"So it might," Robin said. "But not for lack of *you* trying. This whole situation is ridiculous, really. Sending one knight into the middle of nowhere based on a single message from a man who may or may not have secret information to help the king? You're lucky you got this far without incident."

"You don't consider yourself an incident?" he asked with a wry smile.

"I'm an ally. Be grateful," she returned.

"Is that a chicken?" Tav asked suddenly, pointing to the right side of the path.

Robin looked. It was indeed a chicken.

The bird pecked at the ground with determination, and then looked up at them, as if wondering whether they might have feed for it.

"That bird should be on a farm," Robin said. "Nothing that stupid can survive in the woods for more than a few hours."

She dismounted and approached the bird. It squawked, but she grabbed it expertly, keeping her hold on it. "Do we have an empty sack?" she asked.

"Thinking of supper?"

She shot him a look. "I'm going to find out if it belongs to anyone near here."

"Like that goat?" Octavian pointed again, past Robin and into the woods.

Robin turned, expecting some jest. But there was a goat standing just at the edge of her line of sight, chewing on something near the trunk of a tree.

"What is going on?" she muttered. Louder, she said, "Let's go reclaim that animal and retrace the path. There must be a farm nearby."

"A very poorly run farm," Octavian noted. He rode up to Robin and dropped a wad of cloth that proved to be a silk bag.

"Far too fine a transport for you," Robin told the chicken, tossing it in. It protested for a moment, but then quieted.

She remounted while Octavian rode ahead to get the goat. It was a placid animal, and hardly stopped eating while he slipped a rope around its neck.

"Where to now?" he asked.

Robin wasn't a seasoned tracker by any means, but then, the goat wasn't good at hiding its tracks. She followed the intermittent hoofprints through the forest until she smelled smoke in the air.

She raised a hand to signal Octavian to stop. The chicken squawked from its bag. "Hush," she warned it, "or you'll be dinner."

Another squawk—but not from the bag. Robin tipped her head, listening. "That way," she said at last, gesturing to the north. "The farm has to be just ahead. Unless the smoke is all that remains?" She could picture a scene of destruction if a farm was attacked and set on fire. That happened when bands of outlaws struck homesteads. They stole whatever they could carry and then killed the inhabitants, setting everything afire to cover their tracks.

But Octavian said, "It smells like hearth smoke—nothing worse."

She sniffed again and nodded, reassured. "Very well. Let's go and see why these animals got loose."

"Your hood," he warned.

Robin pulled her monk's hood up to cover her head. Around the last curve of the path, she saw the roof of a building, then another.

A modest farmstead lay before them. The few buildings were in good repair, but the fence surrounding the farmyard was destroyed in three spots. Robin saw no one about. A few geese strutted aimlessly about the yard.

"Hello?" Octavian called out. "We've found a goat that belongs here." His words were mild, but Robin noticed how his hand rested on the hilt of his sword.

He dismounted and led his horse to a railing of the fence to secure it. "Hello? Anyone?" he called again, walking toward the house.

Robin noticed a little rustling movement in a stack of hay in the farmyard, and then the flash of a hand, quickly hidden again.

A girl is hiding in there. How Robin knew, she wasn't sure. But she was absolutely certain that someone was at home, and that that someone was a wise little girl who knew better than to trust what appeared to be two strange men—a dark-skinned soldier and a faceless monk.

She dismounted. Then she stepped into the fenced area and put the silk bag near the ground, carefully releasing the chicken.

The hay rustled once more.

She pulled her hood down, earning an annoyed grunt from Octavian, who stood behind her.

"You can come out," she told the hay pile. "We won't hurt you."

The hay didn't move.

"My name is Robin," she said, shaking her long hair loose. "And this knight is Sir Octavian. We were passing by, and thought you might need help."

"If you're a girl," the haystack said suspiciously, "why are you dressed as a holy monk?"

"A disguise for the road," Robin replied. "Just as you disguised yourself as a haystack. We women can never be too careful. Your mother must have taught you that lesson."

"My mother is dead." The haystack shivered and a little straw-covered girl emerged.

"We're sorry to hear it," Octavian said quietly.

"Can you help me bury her?" the girl asked him, her initial wariness now gone. "The ground is hard with frost, and I broke the handle on the shovel."

"Your mother just died?" Robin asked, alarmed.

"Last week. I put her in the barn to be safe from wild animals." The girl looked at the closed barn and then promptly broke down in tears.

Robin rushed to her, kneeling to pull the straw from her hair and then enfolded her in an embrace. "We will help you," she promised. "What's your name?"

"Ada." The girl sniffed. "I don't know what to do!"

Octavian strode up, his form towering above them. "Robin, take her inside the house and clean her up. Find out what happened. I'll take care of…whatever is in the barn." He then walked to the barn, but didn't open the large door. From his expression, Robin sensed that he had some suspicions about the girl's story. He wanted them out of the way before he went inside.

Robin nodded and took Ada by the hand. "Octavian will know what to do," she said reassuringly. "Show me your house."

Ada led her to the house, which was barely warm from the tiny fire in the hearth.

"You need to keep that going," Robin advised.

Ada said, "I need more wood. I was too busy trying to catch the animals. A wild boar ran through here two days ago and ruined the fence. The animals escaped. I didn't know what to do. So I tried to catch them, but I can't repair the fence…"

"Hush," Robin said. "We'll help you. Now, point me to the wood pile."

Not long afterward, Robin had a much larger fire going in the hearth, having refilled the wood supply in the home. She sent Ada for water, and they began to heat it over the fire. Robin heard the sound of digging from somewhere behind the house, and so she distracted Ada by asking her many questions.

She learned that the family had started this farm when Ada was just a baby. She had two older sisters, who'd married and moved to their husbands' farms, and a half brother, who was apprenticed to a carpenter in the nearest town. Ada's father died a year ago, and her mother was hurt badly a few weeks ago when she struck her foot with an axe, and the wound festered, leading to a fever. Ada tried to tend to her, but was afraid to leave the farm to get help. Then her mother died, and Ada was immediately beset by the new problem of losing the animals when the fence was destroyed.

Robin washed Ada's face and hands with the warm water, and then looked at the meager food supply. No bread, a small amount of grain and some vegetables from the harvest, and not any meat to be found. "When did you eat last?"

"I had porridge this morning."

"We'll have to make something more filling." In fact,

Robin decided that one of the chickens would have to sacrifice its life to feed them tonight.

Just then, Octavian opened the door. He looked at Ada. "Come. It's time to put your mother to rest."

Robin and Ada wrapped themselves in cloaks and followed Octavian. On the edge of the property, a little spot had been cleared. A body wrapped in cloth lay at the bottom of a new pit.

"Can you speak Latin?" Ada asked Robin.

"I was dressed as a monk, but I don't know Latin," she confessed. "Octavian does."

Octavian drew his sword and knelt. He held the sword so that the point touched the earth and the hilt formed a cross. He spoke a prayer in Latin, then a few more simple lines in English, committing the body to rest and commending her soul to Heaven. Ada was crying, but silently. She clasped her hands together and kept her eyes on the grave.

Robin put her hand on the girl's shoulder. "We'll let you say goodbye to your mother alone. Come back to the house when you're ready. We'll take care of the grave afterward."

Octavian stood up again and sheathed the sword. Robin had never seen him look more like a perfect knight. She followed him from the gravesite to the house. At that moment, she would have followed him to hell.

When they were all back in the cozy house, Ada looked more at ease. The burial ended her more acute sufferings, and now she looked at both Robin and Octavian with curiosity.

"Why is your skin so dark?" Ada asked.

"Because I was born in a place very far from here where many people have dark skin. My mother and father both did."

Ada nodded at his explanation. "What's the name of your home?"

"The city is called Aleppo, and it's in the Holy Land."

Her eyes rounded. "Really? How far is it from here?"

"Very far. A thousand miles or more, and across the Middle Sea."

She surveyed him with a bit of incredulity. "Why did you come *here*?"

He laughed. "Because here is where my path took me. For now."

"I'm glad." She took his hand. "I prayed every night for help, and now I have help. From a real knight, and a false monk. I suppose God thinks that will be what I need." She smiled at Robin. "It's all right to pretend things if it's for a good cause."

Robin smiled back. "I couldn't put it better myself."

Chapter 9

ADA HAD FALLEN ASLEEP WHILE eating her supper. Robin prevented her from going face-first into her meal, and Octavian picked her up and walked her to the bed in the corner of the cottage. The girl looked tiny and fragile in his arms.

"She'll sleep till noon tomorrow," he predicted when he rejoined Robin.

"She was exhausted," Robin agreed. "Trying to save a farm, while mourning her mother, and just being a little girl…it's impossible."

"She can't stay here."

"No. We'll have to take her somewhere she can be cared for. The village church, or a nearby manor house. They can send a message to her brother or sisters, and one of them will know what to do. Anyway, she shouldn't come back here. It's too isolated."

"You sound very certain."

"I grew up on a homestead like this," she confided. "My parents worked hard to carve an assart out of the wilderness. They farmed it, and raised livestock, and managed the surrounding forest so we had firewood and lumber. I helped my father more than my mother because

I loved being outside, and I had no brothers. Just two younger sisters. So I did whatever Papa needed—I helped fix things, I set traps for rabbits. I was happy."

The last part she hadn't meant to say, and it felt like too intimate a confession. What did it matter if she was happy or not?

Octavian was listening closely. "What made your parents live so far from others?"

"Because they wanted to live on their own terms without some reeve telling them what to plant or which animals to slaughter for a lord's table."

"But without a lord's protection," he pointed out.

Robin nodded sadly. "So they learned too late. One day in spring, a band of men came to the door. They claimed to be foresters for the king—but they were just bandits. My father tried to send them away, but he was only one man, and there were six of them. Two men rushed my father. He yelled at me to run. They didn't even capture him. They just stabbed him with a dagger. I ran. They killed my father and I just ran away."

"That's what he told you to do," Octavian said.

"I should have gone to my mother and sisters in the house. I could have been with them."

"And died as well. Robin, you were a child. You couldn't have changed anything about that."

"If I'd had my bow, I could have shot one of them at least."

"But you didn't. And you probably weren't as skilled then as you became later."

"That's true enough. I swore no one would ever get close to me while I had a weapon. I practiced my archery endlessly afterward."

"It shows," he said. "But all the same, a child can't win against a band of armed men. You were right to run."

"It never felt right."

"Did you return there?"

"Later that night, yes." She paused, remembering the scene. None of the horror of seeing her murdered family had faded, no matter how many years had passed.

Octavian put one arm around her hunched-up shoulders. The gesture nearly brought Robin to tears.

"You don't have to tell me," he said quietly.

"It would help to say it out loud. Does that make sense?"

He nodded, keeping his arm around her.

"I crept back there," she said finally. "My mother and sisters were dead in the house…throats slit." She suspected far worse had been done to her mother before she died. "I dragged my father's body inside as well, and set the house on fire when I left."

"Rough tasks for a child," he said very quietly.

She nodded. "Before that, I took some clothing and gear. I dressed in my father's clothes so I'd look like a boy. I didn't dare stay there, in case anyone came back, so I lived in the woods on my own all through that spring and summer. I hunted and walked and slept and then did it all again. It felt as though I traversed the whole Arden-wood, but looking back, I can't have covered that much ground.

"In early fall, I heard a commotion and went toward it. Some bandits had stopped a very fancy carriage on the road north. But they didn't kill their victims. They just made them hand over what money and jewels they had, along with some supplies, and sent them on their way. So instead of shooting the thieves, I followed them. It was long way to their camp, but it was a *large* camp. I spied on them for weeks, watching to see what they did. They would stop some travelers, but only the well-off ones, never the poor. And they never killed anyone except the armed guards who refused to go peacefully. That intrigued me.

"And then one day, I was careless and crept too close to the camp. One of the guards captured me and brought me to the camp's leader, an older man who wasn't like any person I'd seen before in my whole life—Rainald. And you know the rest."

"Did Rainald and the others know that you were a girl?"

"Not initially. I didn't trust them enough to tell, and the name Robin works just as well for a boy, so no one questioned it. I'd cut my hair short that summer. It was nearly a year before someone figured it out. Then Rainald was fairly angry because he thought I'd put myself in danger. But I knew what I was doing!"

Octavian said, a bit drily, "Of course you did. No one questions your confidence."

Robin sighed, lowering her head to rest on her drawn-up knees. "I do. Sometimes I feel like I've got no more sense of direction than a deer, just bounding through the trees with no idea where I'm headed."

"That does not sound like the Robin I know," he said. "You're tired, that's all. In the morning, you'll feel like yourself again."

"Will I?" Yawning, she leaned into him, enjoying the warmth of his arm around her shoulders.

"Robin," he said in a low voice. "This is not a good idea."

Telling her story had relieved her of a burden she didn't know she'd been carrying, and she was equal parts sleepy and giddy. She teased, "Are you afraid that with me so close, you won't be able to resist the urge to kiss me?"

"Yes."

She waited for him to laugh, but he didn't. Robin turned her head to look at him, and was instantly ensnared by his gaze. His deep brown eyes were serious, watching her with an intensity that made it difficult to breathe.

"You do want to kiss me?" she asked, suddenly breathless.

He reached out with one hand and touched her cheek. "Yes. I shouldn't, but if I'm honest, then I have to admit that I do. More than once since I saw you again."

"Oh." Robin knew she ought to say more. Something intelligent, something inviting. But all she could think was *yes, I want that too.*

"But I won't do anything," he said with what Robin assumed to be reassurance.

"Wait," she countered. "I want you to."

Octavian's fingers grazed her cheek. "Not a good idea."

"I want to know what it feels like, though," she confessed.

"You've been kissed before."

"Not...not the way I think you mean," she said. Mortifying. Admitting that she was almost completely ignorant of such things.

"Never?"

There'd been stolen kisses from time to time, usually from young men who thought Robin was just being coy when she refused their advances. She always shoved them away the moment they thought they'd won her over.

She didn't want to shove Octavian away. She wanted to pull him closer. "There was never anyone who I quite..." She trailed off, uncertain how to convince him. "I just want to know how it feels. Please."

He said something in a language she didn't know, a

quiet phrase that could have been anything from a warning to a promise.

Then Robin felt a jolt when his mouth covered hers. Any thought of being tired fled, chased by the surge of heat in her belly. His lips brushed against her own, then lingered there, and she actually felt faint. Was she falling?

No. Somehow, she'd ended up in his arms, cradled against him as the kiss continued to melt her. She rested her hands on his shoulders, feeling the strength of the muscles underneath. She'd always laughed at the other girls who went moon-eyed over the strongest men at Cleobury. But now she was doing the same thing every time she saw or felt Octavian.

All this tumult from a simple kiss. Robin felt as if she were ice melting into water, warmed just by his mouth on hers. She sighed, and then let out a little unexpected whimper as Tav tightened his arms around her.

A log snapped in the fireplace, and an ember flew out onto the hearth. Robin and Octavian broke apart. She sat up again, her hands shaking from the intensity of the kiss.

Robin reached out and brushed the ember back toward the fireplace, lest it spark a more disastrous flame. As if there could be any flame more disastrous than what just occurred between her and Tav. Then she looked back at him. "Tav…may I call you Tav?"

Unexpectedly, he smiled, making her heart pound uncontrollably. "Yes."

"We…we should not do this again."

"We'd both regret it."

"I don't regret it," she said. "But you're correct about it making life more difficult."

"You're the one who decided to follow me."

"Not for this!" She never planned on throwing herself at him.

"I know that, Robin." Despite everything they'd just discussed, Tav leaned closer. His breath merged with hers as they both hesitated to confess their desires.

Then Robin reached out to curl her hand around his shoulder, bringing him closer. "One more kiss. Please?" she asked.

"We shouldn't." He ran his thumb along her lower lip, and something about the sensation made Robin weak in her *toes*. How could a simple touch do that?

She opened her mouth, and after a second's hesitation, she licked the pad of his thumb.

Tav inhaled in surprise, and then bent his head to kiss her. This kiss was deeper, far more dangerous than the first. She gasped when his tongue touched hers and felt the heat of the kiss tumble down into her belly.

More. More of this wondrous, warm feeling, of having Octavian so very close to her, skin to skin.

I would do anything for you, she thought dreamily. She'd let him keep kissing her. She'd let him touch her, strip her clothing off, lay her down. She'd happily obey every little command, just to be so close to him and feel this swirl of joy in her heart.

Dear Lord, what's wrong with me? Robin's mind recoiled from the unfamiliar thoughts. She'd never granted any man such power over her. Why was she losing her sanity just because Tav kissed her?

Granted, no one had ever kissed her like this before, and she loved every moment of it, but that was no excuse to behave like an animal in rutting season.

"Stop," she gasped out.

He froze and pulled back, watching her with concern.

This kind of behavior, wonderful as it felt, would quickly lead to something less innocent. Robin pulled away, inhaling nervously. "This was a mistake. I didn't know what I was asking. I'm sorry."

Tav also looked as though he needed to catch his breath. "It's not your fault, it's mine," he said, very gently extracting himself from her arms. "I'm responsible for you. You're the ward of my friends and a young girl I've…"

"I'm nineteen," she pointed out, running her hands along her sleeves and the body of the tunic, as if straightening out some rumpled fabric was all she needed to do. "I'm not a child anymore, Tav. Many women are married by this age. I am a woman."

"I noticed," he said. "Believe me."

He took a breath and then stood up, holding his hand out to help her up as well. "You need to go to bed. You need sleep as much as Ada does."

Standing right in front of him didn't help her forget the kiss. It only highlighted how much bigger he was, how strong compared to her own slight frame. "You need sleep too."

He indicated the spot in front of the hearth. "I'll be comfortable right here. And I'll wake up if I hear anything."

And tomorrow, they'd both behave as if this encounter never happened. Robin knew it was the best choice, the only choice. Octavian had a mission to carry out, and she had to help him accomplish it. Any entanglement would hamper that goal.

"Good night," she whispered. She went to the bed, where the sleeping girl was hardly a bump under the blanket. Robin slid in beside her, thinking that a week ago, she never could have guessed she'd be in a stranger's home with Octavian and a little girl who was the shadow of her younger self.

What would tomorrow bring?

Chapter 10

TAV SAW ROBIN CLIMB INTO the bed next to Ada, then put out his own blanket near the hearth. Though only coals remained, it was almost too warm, considering the state he was in.

It had been a few months since he had slept with anyone. The last had been a woman named Colette, who lived on Lord Denis's main estate. He first met Colette on the journey from Jerusalem to France, for she'd been in Denis's retinue as a lady in waiting to his wife. She took a liking to Tav and somewhere along the way, they'd fallen into an easy intimacy that often included sex. Tav never thought himself in love with her, and she admitted that the loneliness of widowhood was too much to bear—she'd lost her husband after only a few years of marriage. Colette was several years older than Tav, and he learned quite a lot from her in terms of how to please a woman. His earlier experiences in Aleppo and Jerusalem, as it turned out, hardly distinguished him from any other lustful young man. Over the years of their intermittent affair, Tav improved.

She wasn't the only woman he had slept with, and he

knew Colette had taken other lovers while he was away. It didn't matter to him. He had no claim on Colette, and no reason to be jealous. He'd always assumed he wasn't susceptible to lust as a sin.

But ever since he saw Robin this time, every day—and night—he remained near her grew more challenging. Robin should not be so alluring to him. She was inexperienced, naive, and the ward of his comrade. She was also unlike any other woman he had known. Robin's disregard for rules was maddening, but he had to admire the fact that when she wanted something, she simply charged through all opposition to attain it. Though this time, her boldness was going to get her killed or shunned. And Tav still didn't have a good idea for how he could save her.

He stared at the coals until he fell asleep.

In the morning, Tav woke first. He added logs to the fire before he went outside to see to the animals in the barn. The air was crystalline, hinting of snow to come. The heavens stretched above the trees, a luminous, steely blue in the predawn. He took a deep breath, filling his lungs with winter. The cold hit him like an arrow. *Why am I still here?* he thought. The weather alone should have driven him back the first year. Cold and sleet and freezing rain.

"Rain shouldn't freeze," he muttered as he slid the barn door open. It was an affront to the natural order of things. Rain was meant to fall in its own season, as it did in his homeland. In England, rain fell whenever it pleased, and half the time turned to ice. Not right at all.

And yet you're here, you fool.

Tav heard his own thought in the voice of his old friend Septimus. Where was he now? Septimus and Octavian had been inseparable growing up. They sat next to each other for lessons with Brother Petrus, they ran through the streets together from the market to the city gate, getting into trouble every chance they found.

Once Tav began to train with Brother Benuic though, Septimus grew more independent and distant, running off on his own mischief. And a year or so later, Tav ended up working for Lord Denis, which led him to leaving the Holy Land entirely. He sent word to Septimus before he left, but he never heard back. The thought of that broken thread nagged at him more and more. He owed Septimus an account.

He shrugged off the memories. He had to think of the present moment. He gathered supplies to mend the broken fences. He was no carpenter, but soldiers often had to learn bits of other trades. Tav had built and repaired shelters while on campaign, and the fence was simpler than that.

Tav chopped down a few saplings, then cut them and tied them to the posts where the former rails had been destroyed. The whole task took perhaps two hours, and Tav sang under his breath as he worked.

When he was done, he stepped back to survey his work. The fence appeared sturdy enough now. It would keep in Ada's animals, at any rate.

The sound of footsteps made him turn to the house. Robin approached. Her hair gleamed with red undertones in the morning light, and her gaze was steady. She wore the boy's clothes she preferred—the monk's robe put away until she needed to hide her identity once more.

"Did you break your fast yet?" she asked.

"No. I wanted to get the fence repaired so the animals could use the yard again."

She surveyed the fence with a critical eye, then took hold of the railings and tried to shake them. Without warning, she jumped up onto the highest railing, testing its strength. "It should do," she said, balancing atop it. "Though it may be for naught. We'll have to take the girl somewhere else, and who knows if she'll ever return?"

"If she doesn't, someone else can use the farm," Tav said, his gaze locked on Robin's feet as she cavalierly walked along the railing. "And please come down from there."

Robin only laughed. "It's not even that high! And I have excellent balance." She swung around on one foot, then flailed her arms as she seemed about to topple over. Tav rushed forward, but she bounced back from his grasp quite nimbly. "Just kidding!"

"Don't *do* that," he muttered.

"What? I'm not going to fall." She bent her knees to bring herself to his eye level. "There's nothing to worry about."

"That's what people say just before something goes wrong," he told her.

She hopped off the fence and landed lightly on the ground. She really did have excellent balance. "Go eat, Octavian. I'll deal with the animals. And then we need to plan where to go next."

There was no hint in her manner of what had happened the night before. *For the best*, he told himself, even as he remembered how sweet she'd tasted.

* * * *

After breakfast, Robin spoke with Ada, learning that the nearest town actually was west, not north along the road they'd been traveling. Ada called the town Sutton, a name that Robin remembered.

She told Octavian, "From Ada's description, it should be large enough to have someone in authority who can care for her while a message is sent to her family."

"You're certain she knows the way? A little girl as a guide might get us lost."

"I'm the guide," Robin said. "She knows where the trail starts from the farm—that's all I need. I can keep us on the right path once we find it."

Octavian looked around the yard and at the buildings. "We leave at first light tomorrow."

"And…we have to bring the animals."

"What?" He swiveled back to her. "I'm not hauling along a menagerie."

"It could be weeks until someone returns to this place, and the animals may make the difference between poverty and wealth for Ada. Who knows if her other family members can provide for another mouth? A cow or a goat might save the girl's life. And the chickens will at least provide some meals."

"All right, you've made your case. God willing, even traveling at a cow's pace, we'll make it to the town eventually. Just make sure there are no other surprises. We've been delayed enough already."

Robin took his warning seriously and prepared everything for the journey that evening, staying up rather later than she ought to while she rechecked the supplies and the now winter-ready farm buildings.

Finally, Octavian stood in front of the door when she announced that she would go out once more. "Go to bed, Robin. We're ready to go in the morning. You're no good as a guide if you're sleeping in your saddle."

"Just one more thing," she wheedled.

Tav put one hand on the door frame, his body blocking the space. "No."

Moving past the knight would be a physical impossibility. Robin sighed, tiredness suddenly washing over her.

"Then will you check that the well is covered? I can't remember if I did so last time."

"I will undertake this sacred mission," he replied, the sarcasm tempered with sympathy, "provided you *go to sleep*. Now."

She turned and walked to the bed, where Ada was already curled up. She glanced back toward Octavian before she began to undress, but he'd already politely turned away. Since the kiss the previous night, he'd maintained his distance, seemingly determined to forget it ever happened.

She stripped down to the loose-fitting shirt that doubled as her nightshift. The men's shirt was shorter than a woman's shift, but the hem fell to her thighs, so it protected her modesty.

Not that it would matter, she thought as she climbed into the bed. She was still an unmarried woman keeping company with a man for days on end. At some point, her indiscretion would be punished. Even if they'd done nothing more than kiss once. Or twice.

Robin pulled the blanket over her head, as if that could conceal the wickedness of her thoughts. The one time she and Tav gave in to that temptation, they'd both agreed that they shouldn't ever do it again. Or let it go further. And yet, that was exactly what she wanted to do.

She heard the door open and close softly. Octavian going out to check on the well, just as she'd asked. The knight always did as she asked—ever since they first met, Robin couldn't recall a time when he let her down. She flipped onto her side, her back to the door. Pursuing any silly romantic notion with Tav would hurt him as much as her. If Robin cared about him at all, she ought to respect that.

"Mary, Queen of Heaven," she prayed in a whisper.

"Help me. Send me the strength to be good. I am full of sinful thought—*very* sinful thought—and I never knew I was so weak. Please help me to do what's right."

Ada shifted in her sleep, murmuring for her mother.

Robin stroked the girl's hair to soothe her, and then closed her eyes. Nothing happened by chance. Ada lost her family at a young age, just as Robin did. It was Robin's duty to see her to safety, just as it was Octavian's duty to fulfill the mission given to him by the king. She would follow through on her own task, and then assist Tav with his. And she would endure any temptation in silence. She wouldn't drag him down due to her own folly.

Eased by that thought, she fell asleep, not even hearing the door open again, or the murmur of Octavian's voice as he went through his own, more lengthy, nightly prayer.

Chapter 11

BEFORE FIRST LIGHT, ROBIN WAS awoken by Tav's hand on her shoulder. "Time to get up," he told her.

Robin dressed hurriedly in the chill air of the morning since there was no point in stoking the fire before they left. She woke Ada and told her to gather the last few items she wanted for the journey.

Ada nodded seriously and then scrambled under the bed, emerging a moment later with a little bundle of cloth. "I'm ready," she announced.

"What's that?"

"Everything of value we owned." She unknotted the bundle to reveal an intricately carved wooden cross, a few brightly colored stone beads that looked like they might be worth a little money, and, surprisingly, two silver coins.

"Wrap that back up and keep it close to you," Robin advised. "You may need it before long."

"I'll keep it close, but I know I don't need to worry because you and Sir Octavian will be with me," she said, with a trusting look on her face that nearly broke Robin's heart. They'd known the girl for two days, and she put her life in their hands.

At Octavian's insistence, Robin put on the monk's robe. He cautioned Ada to only refer to Robin as Brother Robin, and the girl nodded. "Of course. I know how to keep a secret!"

Tav smiled. "I'm sure you do."

They now had, in Octavian's words, a troublesome menagerie. The three horses Tav and Robin came with were now followed by a cow, a goat, two sheep, and a small cart bearing a large wooden cage containing the chickens.

Goats were not known for their obedience, and Ada's goat showed little inclination to follow the line of creatures on the trail. It pulled at its line and wandered to nearby shrubs and in general made Octavian look ready to slaughter it just to be able to move faster.

The fifth time the goat caused them all to stop, Octavian muttered something under his breath and dismounted, striding toward the beast. Robin scrambled down from her horse to follow him. "What are you doing?" she demanded.

"This animal is going to be the death of us. How long will it take to get to a town at this pace? Will we have to sleep outside in the cold two nights? Three? Four?" He reached down to grab the rope line.

"You can't kill it," Robin said.

"I'm letting it go. The forest can kill it—I don't want to waste the time."

Robin knew the pace was torturing him. He was already worried about the delays in finding out where this man Govannon was. Any more obstacles would cause the normally even-tempered knight to snap.

"She likes apples," Ada offered from where she sat in

the saddle. "We could throw some down in the path to make her chase them."

"That will work till we run out of apples," Tav muttered.

Robin had an idea. She grabbed one apple from the sack on the cart—the biggest, juiciest one she could find. She saw a sapling growing near the path and severed a long, thin branch, then speared the apple on the end. Taking the goat's leading rope, she walked back to Ada. Handing her the branch, she said, "Your job is to keep the apple within the goat's sight and out of its mouth. Understand?"

Ada's eyes lit up. "Yes!"

Robin remounted and waited until Octavian did the same. "Let's move on."

The method of teasing the goat with the apple worked well. Ada found the game highly diverting, and Tav's mood went from grumpy back to his usual calm manner.

By late afternoon, they could smell smoke in the air, the first sign that the town was near. When they began to hear some distant sounds of shouting and a dog barking, Octavian rode ahead. "I'll lead from here," he said. "Brother Robin, keep your hood up and keep quiet. Ada, remember the secret."

The girl nodded, her expression serious.

They rode into the town, which boasted a high street with an inn at one end of it, and a mossy stone church at the other. The streets were actually quite busy, with a number of folks going into and out of buildings.

People looked at them, and in particular at Octavian. The expressions on people's faces spanned everything from curious to disbelieving. One older man called out something in a language Robin didn't recognize. Then he added another string of incomprehensible words. At last,

Octavian smiled and responded.

The man grinned and switched to English, though his own accent was Welsh. "Ah, so it's Greek that works! That's all I remember from my seafaring days. *Greetings* and *which way to the drinks*. Knew how to say them in ten tongues. Enough to get by." He gestured to their odd collection. "What brings you here, sir? And with such odds and ends?"

Just then, one of the townsfolk recognized the young girl. "You're Beatrix's girl. What happened to bring you here with two strangers?"

On hearing the short version, the man immediately sent his son running to the carpenter's, where Ada's half brother was an apprentice, and then led Ada and her two escorts to the inn.

A crowd quickly gathered, since any break from the ordinary was welcome. A stable boy took the horses from Octavian and Robin, and the innkeeper offered refreshment, wishing to keep the interesting newcomers at his own establishment.

Ada's half brother arrived soon after. His eyes went wide on hearing of Beatrix's death, and he promised to do what he could to save the family farm, saying, "Oh, I am sorry you had to endure that all alone, Ada."

"I wasn't alone in the end!" She then related the whole story, from the death of her mother to the rampaging boar, the lonely days and dark nights, to the unexpected but prayed for arrival of help in the form of Sir Octavian and Brother Robin.

"Praise Mary, for looking after little children," one spectator said, crossing herself.

Ada told her story well, never hinting that the silent, hooded monk was anything other than what "he" appeared to be. The listeners, from the innkeeper to the village priest, were sympathetic, and a plan was hatched to send word to Ada's older sister and to keep the girl safely housed until then. A woman who lived in town and worked as a seamstress said she had a spare bed, since her own daughter went away, and could take Ada.

"She's a little thing, but she can help me by running errands. I'll keep her out of trouble till her family sends for her!" The matronly woman had round cheeks and bright blue eyes that almost disappeared when she laughed. Robin watched the crowd carefully. Everyone was at ease when the woman talked. She'd be a good guardian for Ada.

Ada said she could pay for her board, but Octavian gave the seamstress a few coins from his own supply. "This should cover her food and other needs for a month."

"Her needs and mine! You're generous, sir knight." She put the coins away in a leather purse at her waist. "She'll not starve, for certain. And I'll see that her clothing is all repaired and patched."

Robin guessed that Ada would end up with an entirely new gown, from the way that the seamstress was smiling at her.

At that moment, the sound of hoofbeats drew everyone to the front doors of the inn. The building lay at one end of the town's main street, and from the south, a group of riders emerged from the woods.

Instead of slowing down on reaching civilization, however, they shouted to clear the street and kept coming at a furious pace. The crowd all turned to watch the horsemen thunder by, and a moment later, only a cloud of dust floated in the air to mark their passing.

A low murmur broke out among the people. Another attack. The sheriff. Who? Who was it this time?

Robin desperately wanted to ask what was going on,

but she couldn't without breaking her character as the holy monk. She elbowed Tav rather sharply in the side to get his attention.

"Ow," he muttered. In a louder voice, he said, "What's happening?"

"There's been a group of men raiding farms and homesteads in the area," a resident said. "That was some of the sheriff's men who just rode by. They'll track the men, but it's dangerous work. Even if they find a trail to follow, who knows how long it's been? It can take a day or even a week to hear of an attack, so it's usually too late."

"Not to mention that if they find the thieves, they'll have to fight them," Octavian said.

"Aye, sir knight. No one wants to attack if they don't know how many men the enemy has got. Meanwhile, these thieves continue to steal from good, honest people and go back to their den to gloat and indulge in who knows what sort of evil."

"Have they taken any people?" Tav asked.

"No. Killed more than a few, but they don't kidnap. They only want the livestock and the chattel, and any wealth or weapons they can get their filthy hands on."

Robin glanced to Octavian, who looked thoughtful.

She coughed, gesturing for Tav to lean toward her, which he did in the guise of asking if she needed water.

"Ask if there's any lord to the west who might send aid," Robin whispered as softly as she could.

He asked, and the answer came back swiftly. "No lords or barons at all until you reach Wales, and *they* won't help us—they want all the English to suffer."

"It's a wide stretch of land to be without any sort of oversight," Tav said.

An older man said, "Oh, kings have tried to tame the

Ardenwood before. The Conqueror sent armies to build castle after castle, anywhere they found a hill or a bend of river to defend. But they didn't last. Last one to fall was Willesden. Kept the roads safe when I was a boy, but it hasn't been used since the old lord died during the Battle of the Standard against King David. Castles are worth nothing if they're empty."

"Where is it?" Tav asked the man.

"Northwest of here. Wise folk steer clear of the whole region. It's a godforsaken place, far out of reach of the king's justice or any other help."

Robin tugged at Tav's sleeve and stepped away from the crowd, around the corner of the building to an alleyway. The smell of the stables grew stronger here, a smell of animal droppings and straw. The indistinct sound of voices filtered in from both sides of the alley, with the stable boys at one end and the yammering crowd at the other.

Octavian leaned closer to her. "What are you thinking?"

"That place he mentioned—Willesden. I saw it once when I was just a child. If I were a lord driven from his home, and I knew Willesden existed, I'd consider regrouping there."

"You think Pierce is there? The man called it empty," Tav said.

"News takes time to travel, and doubly so through a place like the Ardenwood. Lord Pierce *could* have taken over Willesden…"

"And sent his men out to raid to get supplies to make the place livable."

"They kill the folk who get in their way, but they don't kidnap anyone because they don't want ordinary folk to know where they are, at least not until the place is fully defensible."

"Could you find it?" Tav asked, excited.

"It's just a guess," she warned. "We could get there and find nothing at all."

"I've asked people at every point along this journey about Lord Pierce, and no one has offered anything else useful. He hasn't made a name for himself in any other part of the country, as far as we know. So maybe he is at Willesden, which means Govannon is too. It's worth the risk. I'll take care of supplies. You can walk with Ada to her new home. Meet me where we stabled the horses in an hour."

After Ada bid Robin goodbye, with a tight embrace and a whispered promise to keep her secret always, Robin left her in the care of the seamstress and returned to the horses.

The weather turned warmer as they went west over the next few days, a lucky turn of events considering how rough the country was becoming. A few times they had to go around steeply rising hills or avoid a washed-out path. Robin led the way, her sharp eyes watching for any danger from the woods. Octavian rode behind her, almost silent. The few times she looked back at him, he was completely alert, focused on the surroundings. His sword hand was always loose at his side, ready for an attack.

The farther they traveled, the more familiar the land became to Robin. She was close to her childhood home, where she'd first grown up among the rocky hills and the narrow trails of the forest. Farms were barely more than clearings in this area. Some folk herded sheep in the parts of the Ardenwood that were clear of trees, and the hillsides lay covered in tough, dark green grasses.

"Are we getting close?" Octavian asked more and more frequently.

"I'm sure we're near Willesden," she replied, "though I can't guarantee that this is where Lord Pierce chose to flee to."

"If we find nothing, at least we can eliminate it."

"He might have gone directly into Wales," Robin said. "Wasn't he working with the Welsh when he tried to marry Cecily?"

"He was," Octavian confirmed. "But that was five years ago, and alliances don't last. Word is that the Welsh betrayed him. Not to mention that Pierce is an unpredictable sort of man. I wouldn't trust him to saddle a horse, let alone fight a battle with me."

They came upon a group of coppiced trees with chopped wood stacked neatly under a few pines, ready to be used for fuel. She smiled. Here was the best evidence yet that they were near a large estate. Only a lord, or a larger institution like an abbey, had the resources to send foresters out to prepare wood. This must mean that they were now on land controlled by that estate, which she hoped was Willesden.

Then she heard the jingle of horses' reins.

"Wait." Robin put her hand out to stop Octavian from moving forward. "Someone's coming from the other side."

* * * *

A moment later, a group of men emerged from the trees. Tav counted quickly. Ten of them, too many to take on alone. Six of the men were dressed in common clothes while the other four wore armor. All of them carried weapons, though.

The men had carts with them, and it was evident that the group came here to retrieve the stacked wood. The four soldiers fanned out to watch the surrounding forest, and the rest went to work, carrying armfuls of wood from the stacks to the carts.

Robin whispered, "They'll go straight home from here."

Tav understood her point. They could follow the group and perhaps be led directly to Willesden. Who else but a lord could have a retinue of ten men, carts, and horses just to fetch firewood?

"Stay down," he warned her. "No need to risk being seen. We'll be able to track this group easily."

She nodded, then settled down to a crouch, a position she seemed able to maintain for hours. Tav didn't know how her legs didn't cramp up, especially in this cold. But Robin never complained and never appeared uncomfortable. In fact, the longer she stayed in the Ardenwood, the more at home she seemed. *This is where she belongs*, Tav realized. Robin truly was happiest in these cold, wild woods.

At Cleobury, she had an air of awkwardness, of someone trying to fit in and failing. Tav always assumed it was due to her age—the uncertain time between childhood and adulthood. But now he understood that Robin would never be at home in a place like Cleobury. She was too wild.

When the sounds of the departing group faded into the woods, she stood up. "Let's follow!"

"Put the robe back on first," he ordered.

"I can move more easily without it."

"But you'll be safer in disguise. We don't know who these men are, but no matter who they work for, they probably won't kill a monk on sight."

She mouthed something rude at him, but retrieved the brown robe from her pack. She tied the rope belt around her waist, the bulk of the cloth once again concealing her natural form. One hand touched each of the pilgrim medals pinned to her chest, verifying they were still attached.

"Good," Tav said. "And remember you're under a vow of silence."

"Is that for my safety or your convenience?" she retorted. "I can't remember."

He grinned at her. "God in his wisdom can make a single thing serve multiple purposes."

Robin rolled her eyes but pulled the hood over her hair. "Lead on."

Tav went first, guiding his horse between the ruts in the path. Robin rode behind, and held the lead for the pack horse. They'd been riding for half an hour when the trees suddenly opened ahead, revealing a glimpse of a built structure.

Tav rode forward, but the woods around him rustled.

"Halt!" a voice called.

And then the four guards who'd been escorting the wood-filled carts appeared around them. Three stood with bows up and arrows nocked. Two of the guards aimed at Tav, and the other at the less-threatening Robin. The fourth guard stepped onto the path, his chest puffing up as he looked over his new prisoners. He raised his sword and pointed it at Tav. "Who are you to be sneaking about my master's property? Thieves or spies! No one else has reason!" His attitude was boasting and belligerent, like so many men when they gained a small amount of authority.

"We weren't sneaking," Octavian explained in his most reasonable tone. "We were simply following the best trail we found going west. If I'd known that the master here shunned all visitors, we would have taken another way. But I didn't know, because we're strangers to this part of the world."

"That last is clear enough," the guard said, narrowing his eyes as he looked at Octavian. "You don't look like you belong here at all."

It would take more than that to get a rise out of Tav, who heard worse many, many times. He just stared the man down, not blinking.

The guard glared back for a moment, but then seemed to realize that since he was the person who ostensibly had Octavian and Robin in custody, he'd have to make the next move. The three other guards were looking at him expectantly, then glancing to Octavian to see if he was a threat.

As the silence extended, Octavian could practically feel Robin struggling not to offer a sharp comment. Doubtless she had half a dozen to throw at these men. They were luckier than they dreamed that Robin was keeping her vow of silence. For now.

"Go on," the head guard barked at last. "Escort these two spies to the master. He'll want to interrogate them."

"What if they're not spies?" a young guard asked, watching the hooded Robin with an expression of extreme doubt. He was obviously having trouble thinking of any-one in religious garb as a spy. At least some of Pierce's soldiers were sensible.

"That's for the lord to decide, Kevan, not you!" the head guard snapped. "Shut up and take these two into the manor. Lord Pierce should be in the great hall now."

Chapter 12

LORD PIERCE.

The mention of the name felt like victory, even though Tav and Robin were under guard and in no position to fight back.

The contingent of guards fell in around them. The youngest, the one called Kevan, led the way, and the others kept to the right and left, with the head guard at the back. They all kept their hands close to their swords, to be ready in case Tav or Robin tried any sudden moves.

But Tav had no desire to escape. These men were leading him exactly where he wished to go—into the protected home of Lord Pierce, the man who would know where to find Govannon.

They walked past the outer walls, then through the ramshackle courtyard to the large keep where Pierce would be. Willesden was a solidly build place, though with years of neglect to be repaired. The outer wall was partly earthworks—a raised berm created when the place was built. Atop that was a stone wall, crumbled in places. Tav thought it was perhaps ten feet tall. But since it was set on top of the earthworks, the effect was formidable.

Two crews of men worked on the wall in different places.

They reached the keep. The massive oak doors opened a crack to allow them all to enter.

"Come on," the guard said, pushing Robin hard in the back to propel her forward. "Lord Pierce will decide your fate, brother. If you're lucky, he'll let you go and only kill the soldier."

Tav didn't react to that threat. He'd learned long ago that ignoring such jibes was the best way to deal with them. Also, he wasn't going to worry about what a low-level soldier predicted—as he said, Lord Pierce would decide their fate.

He'd only met the man once, years ago when he joined Alric on the journey to take Cecily north to her expected wedding. Pierce had been perfectly civilized... up to the moment he imprisoned Lady Cecily and re-vealed himself as a traitor to King Stephen.

However, Pierce hadn't counted on Sir Alric. Alric led Octavian and the others in the retinue on a rescue, saving Cecily and making an enemy of Pierce. How would the man react to seeing Octavian again?

The guards continued to lead them down a corridor and then into a large room. While the other parts of the building were dark and cold, this room blazed with light from the fire and the dull winter daylight from two tall, narrow windows.

Lord Pierce sat in an ornately carved, high-backed chair near the fireplace. A pure white cat sat on his lap, purring loudly as Pierce petted it. The blond man seemed wholly absorbed by the cat, not even looking up when the guard announced the prisoners.

"Caught these two oddities skulking around the outer walls, my lord. We took them and disarmed the soldier. He claims to be a Sir Octavian. And he says this monk is

Brother Robin. Probably spies. Shall I take them out and have them killed?"

"Not yet," Pierce said mildly, stroking the cat under its white chin. "They may know something of value."

Tav glanced to Robin, who still had her hood on. He wished he could tell what she was thinking, and yet he was relieved that her disguise remained intact. There was a chance he could get her safely out of this situation.

Pierce turned to Tav. "You call yourself Sir Octavian, do you? If you're a knight, who do you serve?" There was no hint of recognition in the man's eyes. Was it possible Pierce didn't remember him?

If so, he certainly wasn't going to remind him. "I am Octavian de Levant, and I serve Lord Denis of Courci. My most recent duty is to see my companion to the holy well in Treffynnon."

"Unusual duty for a knight," Pierce said.

"I do as my lord instructs," Tav replied.

"How pleased your lord must be to have such a reliable lackey." Pierce turned to the hooded Robin. "And who are you to warrant such an escort?"

"This is Brother Robin," Tav said.

"Let him speak for himself," said Pierce, staring hard at the hooded Robin.

"My companion is under a vow of silence," Tav explained hastily, "so you can only interrogate me."

Pierce smiled at last, and Tav wished he hadn't, because the expression revealed him to be as cold as winter. He said, "I'll interrogate whoever I wish, sir knight, and my methods can make even a holy monk forsake a vow of silence in exchange for his life."

"Robin can't tell you anything."

"Then there's no reason to keep the good monk alive," Pierce said, eyeing Tav for his reaction. "Best take care of this intruder immediately. That will allow me more time to find out what *you* know, Sir Octavian." Pierce looked to the head guard, who stood near the door. "Estmar, take Brother Robin outside and slit his throat. Dig a grave, but don't fill it in until this knight is dead too. No sense making more work than needed," he finished cheerfully.

The head guard stepped forward to grab Robin's arm. "As you command, my lord."

Just as the guard reached Robin, she raised her hand, the slight movement nevertheless catching everyone's attention.

Oh, please don't do that, Tav thought, a moment too late.

Robin yanked her hood off, revealing a mass of dark, wavy hair and an all-too-feminine face. The guard saw the transformation from monk to lady, and actually stepped back in confusion, as if he'd been dazzled by a miracle.

"How *dare* you," she raged at Pierce. "My name is Robin, and I am a lady, and I will not be hauled off like some animal to be slaughtered just because you, Lord Pierce, think that every passing traveler is out to attack you. Though why you think you're important, here in your hovel in the hinterlands of the Ardenwood, I can't begin to guess."

As she spoke, Robin straightened up and held her head high, tossing her hair behind her shoulder. Tav watched as Pierce's entire demeanor changed from careless to intense. When Robin accused him of having no honor, the man's hand tightened on the arm of the chair. But he waited until the end of Robin's little speech before standing up, placing the cat on the chair as he did so.

"My lady," he said, his voice calm. "You must understand that your appearance is…unexpected. I saw the unusual pair of an armed soldier and a nameless, robed figure, and I was told only that they were skulking past my own isolated property."

"I do not *skulk*," she replied frostily. "Your men get overly excited at the prospect of strangers."

"I beg your forgiveness, my lady. Robin, you said? Robin of…"

Robin froze for an instant, and Tav knew why. She had no family name of her own, nor would she claim to be a de Vere, despite being taken in by Rainald. In any case, telling Pierce that she was connected to the de Vere family, or that she lived at Cleobury, would hardly help matters.

Just as Tav was about to make some claim about why Robin's name had to be kept secret, she recovered herself.

"I do not see why my name is a concern," she said loftily. "Any woman, whether known or unknown, should be treated in the same manner."

"I do have manners. You two will be my guests here at Willesden," he said then, sweeping a hand out in welcome. "Lady Robin, you will find hospitality worthy of you. And a new gown as well," he added, looking with amusement at her monk's robe. "In return, over supper you can explain your disguise."

Robin nodded cautiously. "I will join you for supper, along with Sir Octavian."

"Naturally. I wish to speak to you both at greater length." He took a few steps toward Robin, blocking Tav's view of her. "I trust you'll forgive the initial reception. A lady should be treated with every consideration."

But then Pierce looked back at Tav and said in a low voice, "Though if the lady misbehaves in any way, someone will have to pay for it." The threat was clear. If she tried to escape on her own, Octavian would be killed for it.

"We'll follow your guard to our rooms. What was the name again? Govannon?" Tav said casually, hoping to learn where the man he'd come to talk to actually was.

"No, that's Estmar, the head guard of Willesden," Pierce said. "Govannon, however, is right here. Trust my faithful Govannon to find the warmest place to sit."

And he pointed to the white cat.

Chapter 13

"THE *CAT'S* NAME IS GOVANNON?" Robin asked, too surprised to stop herself.

"Yes, dear lady, and if you desire to make his acquaintance later, I'll be pleased to chaperone. But now you must be made comfortable. Estmar, after you show our guests to their rooms, tell one of the maids that we have a lady as a guest who will require an attendant."

Robin didn't like the way Pierce looked her over as he spoke, but she just nodded in the most ladylike way she could. *How would Cecily act?* she asked herself. If only she had embraced more of those lessons on proper behavior. She would apologize endlessly to Cecily…if she ever saw her again.

Octavian edged closer to her as they made their way through the dark halls of the manor. Just before they reached a winding staircase, he murmured, "*Tombe.*"

Fall. Robin deliberately misplaced her foot on the second stair, and let her body tumble down, splaying her hands out to avoid hurting herself.

But Octavian was right beside her and swiftly stepped in, reaching for her waist.

His lips at her ear, he whispered, "No one can know

who you are or where you live. No matter what, let me tell the story."

She nodded, even as she straightened up again.

"You're certain you're all right, Lady Robin?" Octavian asked in a louder tone.

"Yes, just tired," she replied, a bit haughtily since she was acting like a lady now.

Octavian moved away before the guards could order him to do so.

Robin was shown her room first, so she didn't know where Octavian would be sleeping. She hoped it wouldn't be far away. Everything about this place set her teeth on edge. The air in the halls was cold and clammy, the shadows flickered in the torchlight, and absolutely everyone was watching her.

The room she was led to was quite large for a bedchamber, and she learned that three women—and now Robin as well—shared it. A massive bed dominated one end, with heavy brocade curtains hanging from the posts to retain the heat of the sleepers.

Moments later, a woman about her own age arrived. She curtseyed. "Lady Robin, my lord bids me to welcome you to Willesden. I am Irene, and I'm to attend you during your visit. I was told you lost your clothing on the road?"

Robin resisted the urge to tell Irene she wasn't a lady. As if it weren't obvious, considering Robin's scruffy appearance, strange outfit, and arrival in the company of just one man.

But Irene acted as if all was normal, and soon produced a gown suited not just for a lady, but a princess. Robin ran her hands over it, awed by the sheer extravagance. The patterned fabric was alternately smooth and velvety to the touch. The deep burgundy color was sensuous, though too bold for Robin's taste. And then there was the trimming.

The neck and sleeves were trimmed in light brown rabbit fur, the softness of it caressing Robin's skin.

"This gown is too fine for me," she said.

"Lord Pierce would not tolerate you being given a lesser quality item, my lady. And we must not make him angry."

There it was. Though Irene sounded calm, Robin noticed the knitted brow and nervous, jumpy fingers when Irene spoke. She was frightened of Pierce.

She didn't want to get Irene in trouble, so Robin just nodded. "I'll wear this one, of course." Supper would be a trial for her. She'd likely spill gravy on her lap or do something similarly horrible.

Irene helped her into the gown and laced it up tightly on both sides, so that the fabric hugged her body and made her small chest far more prominent than Robin liked. Worse, the rabbit fur trim kept tickling the tops of her breasts exposed by the neckline. She touched the small gold cross she wore around her neck and swallowed nervously.

"I must tend to your hair," Irene went on. "It's dry enough now."

Robin expected her to braid it, as it had been before. Irene instead brushed it and used carved wooden combs to pull back the sides, letting the rest fall freely down her back. The lightest silk cloth, also secured with a comb, served as a headdress.

"There," Irene said, surveying her work. "You must feel so relieved to be dressed properly again."

In fact, Robin wanted to grab her boy's clothing and run back into the woods. Her tongue stuck to the roof of her mouth. She'd have to go to supper like this, and everyone would see her in this outfit, and they'd know instantly that she had no business wearing such finery.

When supper time arrived, she stepped into the great hall, now set up with several long tables so everyone could eat the evening meal. The large chair Pierce had sat in before now occupied the center place at the high table, right in front of the fireplace.

Pierce watched her enter, and gestured for her to come forward. Octavian stood nearby, watching her with an unreadable expression.

However, it was clear that Pierce enjoyed the picture she made. His eyes raked over her with approval, lingering on her chest. Robin bit her lip. She couldn't be rude to this man. Not now.

We just have to endure this for a little while, she told herself. Once Octavian discovers what this Govannon business is all about, we can leave.

When she reached the high table, Pierce gestured to the seat next to his. Robin sat on the wooden chair, arranging her skirts to avoid being trampled on by feet or spilled on by wine.

Octavian had the seat on the other side of Pierce, which meant that they couldn't exchange a word or glance without Pierce knowing exactly what was going on.

She ought to be polite and boring. That was the best way to deflect attention. "I thank you for your hospitality, my lord," she said to Pierce, keeping her gaze modestly downcast. "Your servants are very capable, and the loan of the gown was beyond expectation."

"Anything for a lady," he replied, with no hint that he was anything other than a gracious host. It was almost as if he'd invited them there for a hunting party and this was the supper the evening before.

But nothing about this place was normal, she reminded herself. She asked, "Where did it come from? Such a gown seems like an unnecessary expense for a man in your position, here at a keep that holds no ladies of rank."

He shrugged. "Just a lucky chance. I was negotiating with a merchant not long ago, and he had some fine clothing I was willing to accept as part of the exchange. I'm pleased some it can be put to use...and what better use can there be than to adorn such a beautiful creature as yourself?"

She rolled her eyes at the transparent flattery, yet a little part of her enjoyed hearing it. She glanced sideways toward Tav, but he was watching the rest of the hall, as a few servants began to bring out the first dishes.

During the meal, Pierce tried to tease out who Robin was. Warned against doing so by Tav, she took refuge in a lady's prerogative to be mysterious.

"I am afraid that I cannot tell you my full name, or where I call home," she said in answer to Pierce's first and most mild query. "It is a matter of honor, and I have promised to keep silent until I am done with my journey." Inside, she felt that being mysterious might actually be rather fun.

"Did you not even tell your rescuer?" Pierce asked, pointing to Octavian.

"Just her Christian name," Tav interjected. "And the fact that she required protection after the incident that stranded her alone on the road."

"Oh?" Pierce raised an eyebrow and looked to Robin. "That sounds intriguing."

"*Intriguing* is not the word I'd use," Robin said, glancing toward Tav. In a flash of inspiration, she added, "Sir Octavian is better placed to tell you what happened. I scarcely remember the details because I was so upset."

Tav nodded, with a flicker in his eyes to let Robin know he got the hint.

He then spun a story of riding along the forest road and coming upon Robin, alone amid the wreckage of a carriage and the remnants of a skirmish. The Robin in his story sounded frail and fragile, but if she weren't, why would she need protection? Octavian provided enough detail to make the story very convincing. He told about recovering her horse, somehow abandoned in the woods nearby, and even of having a monk's robe handy to help conceal the lady from prying eyes.

Pierce seemed to accept it all, but then asked, "And how did you end up so far from the main road?"

"That was my fault," Octavian said easily. "After finding Lady Robin, and knowing there was a group of outlaws near, I decided we ought to leave the road for a little while. But the Ardenwood is hard to navigate, and I managed to lose my way. It was only pure chance that we happened upon your men, who brought us here."

"Well, these are dangerous times," Pierce replied. "I must protect what is mine."

"Is Willesden yours by right?"

"By right of conquest," Pierce said. "We marched in and took it...not that it was much of a battle. There was no lord here, just a few rough folk living here as squatters."

"Did you kill them?" Robin asked.

"Certainly not. I put them to work in the grounds and in the surrounding lands. They're happy to have a lord. The common folk crave direction. I tell them what to do, and in return I protect them from the threats of the outside world."

Robin looked down. Her own parents had avoided the life Pierce talked about. They'd deliberately lived independently.

And they'd died.

She took a sip of wine, confused and out of sorts. Life had been simpler a day ago, when she'd been alone with Octavian in the Ardenwood. *We can't stay here long*, she thought. However polite Pierce was acting now, he had some ulterior motive for luring a king's knight here with that strange message.

Just then, the white cat leapt up onto the table and sashayed toward Pierce. Rather than shooing the creature away, he offered it a piece of meat from the plate near his chair. The cat accepted the offering and then crawled onto the man's lap, purring the moment Pierce began to stroke its back.

"I know you're curious about Govannon," Pierce said, looking toward Octavian.

"Then tell me more," Tav returned, his voice even.

Chapter 14

TAV GAVE HIS FULL ATTENTION to Pierce, hoping the man would finally explain why and how a message came to the king promising help from someone who turned out to be a cat.

"I don't suppose Govannon is named for a man you know," he said.

"There's only one Govannon," Pierce said. "I named him after a story my nurse used to tell me when I was a boy. She was Welsh, and told me tales at night about a clever spy. Govannon was a hero of the people, fighting against the Danes who came to conquer. I always liked those stories, even though I think she made them all up. Govannon was always getting into one adventure or another, always meeting kings and getting treasure and tricking his enemies," he said. "Anyway, this cat was here when we came, so I named him Govannon. I think he was somewhat annoyed to be usurped as sole lord of the manor, but a little meat and some adulation is enough to win him over."

"A singular creature," Tav agreed. "Where I'm from, cats are considered keepers of secrets."

"I can imagine," Pierce said. "They stalk the night, and who knows what they overhear?"

Robin was listening silently, with an air of utter confusion. She was no doubt wondering if Pierce was completely mad for talking about a cat this way, and if Octavian was mad for asking.

But Tav recognized the meaning beneath Pierce's words. He still didn't understand *why* Pierce had to veil his meaning in a story like this, but he could tell that something made the man too worried to simply share his thoughts out loud.

"How do you get a cat to tell a secret?" Pierce asked.

"Earn its trust, I suppose," said Tav. "Though I think cats know who can be trusted right away."

Pierce gave the cat another chunk of meat. "We'll see if Govannon decides to grace you with his trust. Perhaps in the next day or two?"

Robin kept her eyes on the table as she asked, "How long are we being kept here, my lord?"

"You injure me, Lady Robin, speaking as though you're some sort of prisoner. I hope you'll see my home as a refuge. Tomorrow, I'll show you more of the castle and the area. You'll love it here."

The look Robin shot Tav was flustered and alarmed, so he said, "You mentioned you like to pray before bed, Lady Robin. There's a chapel in the courtyard, on the eastern side of the keep."

She gave a tiny nod to indicate that she understood that he wanted to talk to her there, and then excused herself shortly after the meal. The men at the high table stood up when she did, and Tav did not like the way Pierce looked at the departing Robin, who was far too decorative in her borrowed gown.

When Octavian managed to leave the dining hall a while later, he went immediately to the chapel. Robin sat on a bench directly in front of the altar. The place felt more like a cave than a house of worship.

"It's freezing in here," he said, sitting down beside her. "If I'd known, I'd have asked you to wait somewhere else."

"I don't think this chapel gets much use under the rule of Lord Pierce." Robin sounded lively enough, but her face was pinched and her lips nearly blue.

Tav removed his cloak and wrapped it around her shoulders.

Robin almost disappeared within the voluminous fabric, but she said, "That's much better."

He was glad she was covered, because it was difficult for Tav to avoid staring at her before. It seemed that every time Robin was dressed like a lady, he was bound to gape. The gown did exactly what it was meant to—it displayed all of Robin's most feminine features in a way no man could avoid seeing. The shape of the fabric over her hips made it very easy to imagine reaching out to run his hands over her curves. And the furred neckline was just cruel. His first impulse on seeing her in it was to want to drag the neckline just a little lower and use the fur lining to tease her until she begged him to take the whole gown off.

At that point, Tav gave up trying to deny that he was wildly attracted to the singular woman he was supposed to be protecting. All he could do was hide his increasing desire until Robin was safely home again. Then she'd be truly protected, and she could resume her life. Probably by marrying that young lord Alric mentioned.

Yes, you should remember that she's essentially engaged to someone else. Octavian thought a lot of the obsession surrounding a woman's purity was nonsense. If purity were so important, why was a woman like Mary Magdalen so close to Christ in all the stories, a loyal and beloved follower? But so many people, in the church and in the world, held it up as the sole measure of a woman's worth before the day of her marriage. The de Veres hoped a good marriage would pull Robin up from her common birth to a place where she would be respected and safe. And for that to happen, she would need to remain a virgin.

Which meant he'd need to keep her safe from himself as well as Pierce and every other man.

I can do that, he thought. Then he looked at the altar. *That is, if I ask for a miracle and get it.*

Robin interrupted his thoughts. "What was all the talk about the cat?"

He explained, "Pierce confirmed he's the person with the information the king needs, and he'll talk, but only when it's safe to do so. You should ask him to allow you to go riding tomorrow."

"Why?"

"Because he wants to get one or both of us in a place where he can speak freely, and speaking to a lady will probably be easier for him to do." He didn't want Robin to be alone with Pierce in the middle of the woods, but he also knew that Robin was very capable of defending herself.

"If you think that's best. But I still don't trust him. Or anyone in this place." She looked over and smiled. "Except for you, of course."

Tav wished her words and her smile didn't affect him so much. He was beginning to need Robin close to him, in the same way that he needed food to eat and air to breathe.

"What is it?" she asked, looking at him curiously.

"Nothing. Just be careful tomorrow."

"I will. And what will you be doing?"

"Just lazing around Willesden," he said. In truth, he intended to investigate every possible avenue of escape, from the castle walls to the front gate to the well. He didn't like being hemmed in, and he definitely didn't like being held against his will, no matter how generous the meals were.

"You've never lazed around anywhere," she retorted. "But I won't ask more questions. You carry out your mission, and I'll carry out mine. Shall we meet here again tomorrow after supper, in case we can't speak earlier?"

"I was just about to suggest that."

She grinned. "I'm learning how you think."

He hoped not, because if Robin knew how he thought about her, he'd have no defenses left.

Chapter 15

THE NEXT MORNING, ROBIN BROKE her fast in a sunny ground floor room close to the kitchens. The bread was still warm, and the butter was rich and yellow. There was even honey, which she drizzled on her bread with pure pleasure and a little too much generosity. She sucked the extra off her fingers happily, up till the moment she caught one of the guards staring at her as if she were something he'd like to eat.

"What? Have you nothing better to do than look at me?" she asked.

He grinned. "I can think of better things to do than look, my lady."

"Stop wasting time and go about your duties," Robin said sharply, just as Cecily would have commanded a servant to do. She ignored the innuendo entirely—to admit she noticed would be giving in.

She glared at him until he sidled out of the room, but the simple joy of the morning meal was spoiled for her. Robin hated being watched, especially by churls who thought she existed for their entertainment.

Afterward, Robin found Pierce. This time though, he

wasn't seated in the high-backed chair by the fire. He was leaning over a table, frowning at a map, his arms braced on the edge.

Pierce looked up as she stepped closer and covered the map with another document on the table. "Good morning, my lady," he said. "I trust the accommodations were up to your standards."

"I slept well," said Robin. "Though I've no idea how to spend my day." At Cleobury, she had a number of tasks related to learning how to run a household, or just aiding Cecily and the other women with whatever they needed. She might help gather herbs in the gardens one morning, or go fishing on a summer afternoon, or—ugh—mend and sew clothing as needed. Here at Willesden, all the castle's activities were focused on military matters. Men were hard at work rebuilding the curtain wall, or deepening the ditch outside the gates. Servants bustled about the bakehouse and the kitchens, of course, but Robin had no business among them since she was ostensibly a noble guest. There were no tasks for ladies. Except…

"My horse will need to be exercised," she said. "And there's not enough room within the walls." Even the largest space—the north ward between the keep and the walls—was long and narrow, and hardly offered enough room to turn a beast around at the ends of the ward. "I should like to ride him for a brief time."

Before Pierce could respond, the guard named Estmar shook his head. "Far too dangerous. The lady cannot possibly be allowed out alone."

The look Pierce gave his guard was deadly, but his next words were deceptively mild. "I am the lord here, Estmar. If the lady wishes to go riding, I say she shall. I'll ride with her, and armed grooms can follow to preserve the lady's peace of mind. We wouldn't want her to worry."

The guard stared back at the lord, and then dropped his eyes. "Yes, my lord." He then ordered one of the footmen standing by the door to go to the stables and tell the boys to prepare the horses.

Robin tried to understand what just happened. A guard should never speak so impudently. Was Estmar really going to insist that his own lord couldn't do as he wished?

"Is it so dangerous around here that your guards are afraid of the woods just outside the gates?" she asked.

"Estmar is overprotective," Pierce said smoothly, clapping a hand to his guard's back, a gesture that seemed more violent than friendly. "He knows his job is to keep me alive! But a morning ride will be safe enough, my lady. You have my word."

Not long afterward, Robin was mounted on her own horse, accompanied by Pierce on a spirited rouncey, with mounted and armed grooms riding behind them. Despite the reminders that she was still under guard, Robin felt wonderful. Being in the woods again, out of the castle walls, was a glorious freedom. She couldn't help but smile, and Pierce was actually a charming companion. He rode near her—but not too near—and spoke about his own experiences riding in the area, some stories obviously embellished to entertain her. He talked about the state of the country in only the most general terms, and more or less seemed perfectly content. Robin was puzzled. The Pierce she was seeing now bore little resemblance to the stories she'd heard of him. Maybe he'd changed? In any case, he didn't look like a man on the run, which was what the message to the king suggested.

They rode out of a wooded area to the edge of a wide plain rolling off to the west. Hunched mountains stood blue in the distance, but closer was a tall, solitary hill with the ruins of some ancient stones on the top.

"How beautiful!" Robin said, taking the scene in. "What is that place called?"

"The name has been lost, my lady, but the locals say the fairies guard it, and anyone foolish enough to climb to the top will face their wrath."

Looking at the formidable ascent, she could believe it.

"A proposal, my lady. We'll race to the base of that hill. No fairies will threaten us there."

She nodded. Without warning, she signaled her horse, and let out a laugh as the wind pushed her hair off her face. The horse responded to Robin's nudges and sped up into a smooth canter. Robin felt as if she were flying.

Soon, the hill loomed in front of her, and she reluctantly pulled up so that the horse came to a halt only a few yards from the face of streaky, glittering rock. Robin turned to watch Pierce catch up.

"I've won!" she proclaimed once he was in earshot.

He slowed a moment later, glancing behind him at the grooms, who were struggling to make the same pace as the nobles' horses. When Pierce reached her, he rode close enough to grab the reins of her horse. "Congratulations, that was perfect. We have only a moment of privacy, my lady. You must listen closely."

"What?" Robin asked.

"If this morning hasn't already made it obvious, I'm not free to come and go from my own castle. Your companion is the one man here who can help me. Will you ask him if he's willing to get me out of here?"

"You want Octavian to help you escape your own castle?"

He glanced toward the grooms now thundering up behind them. Then he looked back at her, his gaze intense. *"Will you ask him?"*

"Yes!" The agreement burst out of Robin before she even quite understood what she was promising.

Pierce heaved a sigh. "If he agrees, signal me by saying the word *mouse* when you see me next."

"And then what?"

"I'll arrange a meeting to discuss it. Now hush. We must pretend we're discussing matters of no import at all. And smile, my lady."

When the grooms reached them, Pierce was telling her that if he'd known her horse was so swift, he'd never have proposed a race, and asked for the horse's lineage, which Robin of course didn't know.

"My lord," she retorted. "You should credit the rider. I would have won that race no matter what horse I rode."

He laughed. "That sounds like a challenge, Lady Robin. Would you—"

"My lord, you should not do that again!" the first groom interrupted, his eyes narrow.

"Oh, leave off," Pierce said dismissively. "It was perfectly safe. It's open ground the whole way, and you had us in sight from the beginning."

"We have our orders, my lord," the other man said, more apologetically.

"I'm sure you do." Pierce's voice was dry, and he threw the tiniest glance toward Robin. "Well, that's enough freedom for one day. Lady Robin, you feel your horse had been put through her paces?"

"And then some, my lord," she murmured.

They rode back in a group, the grooms keeping quite close now. She couldn't wait until that evening to discuss what had happened with Tav. She saw him on the east battlements, and climbed up to join him.

He nodded to her once she reached him. "Good ride?"

"For the most part."

"What does that mean?" Tav still looked quite casual, but he'd tensed up.

"Nothing bad happened," she assured him. Since they were in little danger of being overheard up on the walk, she quickly explained Pierce's request.

"In truth," she concluded, "I'm not sure he's entirely sane. He seems to see enemies everywhere."

"He's made a lot of enemies with all his plots," Octavian said.

"But to think his own guards are restricting his movements? To say that he's a prisoner in his own castle and that you—practically a stranger—are the one man he trusts to get him out? I don't understand."

"I don't, either, but my own mission was to get the information that the mythical Govannon claimed to have. Now I know that Pierce is the true holder of that information."

"So I'll tell him you'll help?" she asked dubiously.

"Yes, give your signal. And then we'll have to see what he does next."

After speaking with Tav, Robin retreated to her bedchamber, finding that it was occupied. Govannon stalked the perimeter, his paws silent on the stone floor, his gaze locked on the shadowy spaces under the bed and in the corners.

Robin sank to the edge of the bed, watching the predator's progress through the room. Her mind tumbled over the strangeness of this place. Pierce was supposed to be a terrible person, according to all the stories she heard, and yet he'd been very attentive and kind to her this morning.

The white cat jumped onto the bed and stared at her with unblinking, amber eyes. Govannon was a gorgeous creature, big and sleekly muscled under the pure white coat. He flexed his paws, revealing claws as sharp as dagger points.

"You're a killer," she told the cat.

He meowed in response, then approached her, bumping his head against her leg until she began to pet him. That made him purr, a rumble of contentment that was surprisingly soothing.

"I have no food for you," she said, though the cat didn't seem to want food, only affection.

She was petting the cat when the maid Irene came in with folded clothes over her arms.

"Ah, my lady. I didn't know you were in here."

"Carry on whatever you need to do," Robin said, still petting Govannon, who had gone still at Irene's entrance.

"Gone riding with the lord, did you?" the maid asked.

"Yes, all the way to that hill the fairies guard."

"Your soldier didn't join you."

"He had his own business," Robin said. "Though I'm sure he would have joined us if I asked."

"You seem to know him very well, considering that you only encountered him a short while ago."

Robin said, "Some people inspire trust. Sir Octavian is one of them, at least in my opinion. He saved my life, and I don't want to hear any nonsense about who I choose to travel with."

"My lady, I meant no offense." But the maid had a sly look in her eyes, and Robin feared she'd said too much. But how could she keep silent?

"No matter," said Robin. "I think I'll rest this afternoon. Would you wake me before supper, if I fall asleep?"

That evening, Irene dressed Robin in a different gown, this one a deep blue silk that was blessedly free of the fur trim, but still with a neckline that dipped lower than Robin would like, and with a bodice that was laced up tighter than she thought necessary.

"Can't you loosen it?" she asked Irene.

"Why would you want that?' the maid asked blankly. "Men want a pretty figure to look at."

Robin sighed and gave up trying to explain that she wanted to breathe more than she wanted admiration. She walked into the great hall with her head held high, repeating to herself that she could get through this.

"My lord," Robin said once she sat down at the table. "I found a dead mouse on my pillow today. Is that your cat's handiwork?"

Pierce's eyes gleamed in satisfaction, but he sounded very apologetic when he said, "Govannon is barely civilized, my lady. I'm sure he meant it as a gift, but I'll speak to him later about such activities and how unwelcome they are to ladies."

"I would appreciate that, sir," she said primly. Having delivered the signal that Octavian would help, Robin turned to her supper.

The soup served was rich, smelling of beefstock and onions. After a sennight or so of rough living in the woods, such simple things felt like luxuries. After the soup came a course of mutton. Then a small plate of honeyed cooked apples was placed before her. Her wineglass was refilled by the servant who kept watch behind her seat. Robin barely took a sip before the glass was topped up.

Toward the end of dinner, Estmar, who sat at the end of the high table, spoke up.

"You're a soldier," Estmar said to Octavian. "I assume you have experience in battle and know something of tactics and strategy?"

"Some," Octavian hedged. "I've seen my share of fighting. What is the question that's troubling you?"

"There's an outpost to the west—the farthest point that

might be said to be protected by Willesden, in the sense that we could keep a small garrison there to watch for any unrest. The problem is that I'm not sure the previous owners built the outpost in the right place."

Pierce put down his wine and looked over at his head guard. "What are you up to, Estmar?"

"My lord, we ought to take advantage of having an outsider's opinion. I propose riding out tomorrow so Sir Octavian can look at the tower and tell me if he sees any problem with it, or how we might strengthen it. I know how seriously you take your role as protector, my lord."

Pierce stared hard at Estmar for a long moment, but then said, "An excellent suggestion, Estmar."

The guard was plainly surprised at Pierce's acquiescence, and so was Robin. Why would Pierce want to send Octavian away for a day when he so badly wanted to talk with him?

But Pierce went on, "If Sir Octavian agrees, of course. But I would be interested to hear what you think, sir knight. Consider it a gesture of trust."

Tav's eyes flickered to Robin for a moment, and she held her breath. But then he said, "Certainly, my lord."

"Well, that's settled. Tomorrow you and Estmar ride to the outpost. I shall endeavor to keep Lady Robin entertained here."

Chapter 16

HAD TAV REALIZED THAT THE outpost Estmar wanted him to look at meant he'd be gone from Willesden for more than a day, he'd have objected. Not that it would have made much difference. Tav remembered Pierce hinting that going along with Estmar would serve as a test of trustworthiness.

The sun was fully above the trees when Octavian and Estmar rode out of the gates and headed west. He was confident that he'd hold his own if the man tried to attack him. He only wished that he'd been told of the plan to camp overnight at the tower before they left.

In the late afternoon, Estmar pointed to a tower. The structure was perhaps four or five rods tall. On reaching it, Tav saw it was squared off with each wall facing a cardinal direction. Narrow windows that served as arrow slits were the only disruptions in the stone walls. A single door provided an entrance to the tower.

At the door, Tav turned around. About a hundred paces away, he saw a small stone building. The roof had caved in some time ago, and the stone walls were in disrepair.

"Is that the old barracks?" he asked. The tower didn't

have room to provide living quarters to the guards who would have been on duty here.

"It must have been." Estmar looked at the building with little curiosity. "It's been a long time since anyone kept guard around here. These are difficult times, sir knight. Many of the old castles built after the Conquest have fallen. Some had no more purpose, some never got the repairs they needed, and some just got abandoned."

"How did Pierce know about Willesden? He can't have had much warning when he had to leave Malvern."

"Pierce has always had people who kept eyes on Malvern and all the country around. He paid well for any useful knowledge." Estmar didn't use the word, but it sounded as though Pierce had many spies.

They spent an hour or so riding through the area, scouting for places to hide in much the same way as an enemy would do. There were a few, but overall, the tower dominated the landscape and refortifying it would go a long way toward making the whole area safer.

Finally, Octavian looked up at the tower itself. "Well, we've come all this way. I'm going to go in."

The interior of the tower was dark, clammy, and cold. Steps ascended to the left, so he took them all the way up to the top. Estmar followed along, his breathing more labored as they went.

Tav passed one room on the upper level, which was probably just a place for men to get out of the weather between shifts. He peered in, then climbed on to the top of the tower.

From this point, Tav had a magnificent view of the countryside. The sun was now dropping to the west, where a line of hills rose up, colored purple in the light.

Estmar climbed up and joined him, panting as he leaned against the chest-high wall. "Dee Valley is beyond," he said, pointing toward the hills. "See the gap on the southern side over there? That's said to be where some of the Welsh lead their armies through to reach England. And that's where raiders come through as well."

"If so, this tower is in exactly the right location," Tav said. The more Octavian looked around, the more he thought that this whole excursion to examine the tower was a deliberate attempt to get Tav out of the way for a little while.

Estmar might have suggested the journey, but Pierce approved of it because he wanted to separate him from Robin. Was he interrogating her? Would he discover that Robin was connected to the de Vere family, who he undoubtedly hated?

"What's on your mind?" Estmar asked.

"Nothing. I hope Lady Robin is well."

"She'll be looked after," the guard said. "The lord seems to have taken a liking to Lady Robin—unusual women intrigue him."

That didn't soothe Tav's mind. Robin was still very innocent when it came to men, despite her outward brashness. She could fend off a man who simply thought she could be forced. But she could be susceptible to charm. The idea of Pierce charming her made Tav feel slightly sick.

Robin is smarter than that, he told himself.

"Tell me, Sir Octavian, why are you here?"

"You asked me to look at your tower."

Estmar shook his head. "England. What does England have that interests a man like you? You grew up in the very places pilgrims dream of seeing just once. You look different, your manner of speech is different. What brought you here?"

"The lord I serve has interests in England. So I'm here

to carry those interests out."

"And your lord swore allegiance to Stephen," said Estmar.

"He did. I fight on Stephen's side when fighting must occur."

"But it is not from personal conviction on your part," Estmar pressed. "If your lord served Maud, you'd have fought on her side during the same battles."

"Yes, I suppose I would have." If fate had gone that way, Tav never would have met Alric and the other knights he now called friends. He might have attacked them on the battlefield instead. He recoiled at the idea.

"Any army would be pleased to have a knight such as yourself," Estmar went on. "If you wished, you could leave your lord's service and make yourself wealthy fighting for another."

Tav dismissed that notion out of hand. "I've known free lances. They're lured in by the prospect of a fat payment, and most of time they get a fraction of what they were promised."

"There are ways to make up the difference," Estmar said with a slight smile.

He meant looting. Tav hadn't liked Estmar in the first place, and he was liking him less by the hour. But he also didn't want to make his distaste obvious.

"I'm happy enough as I am," he told Estmar. "My lord has always treated me well, and I'm not even sure how long I'll be in England after this. I plan to rest up, then leave Willesden with Lady Robin, just as soon as Lord Pierce realizes there's no point in detaining us further."

Estmar studied him for several moments. "You've no interest in Pierce or the battles up here?"

Tav shrugged. "As you say, I'm only here because I am on my own lord's business."

"But Lady Robin is not your lord's business," Estmar said.

"No. But I told her I'd see her safely home, and I will." Tav now faced Estmar. "That's the core of chivalry. And any man who gets in the way of that promise will regret it."

The other man held his gaze, then said, "I believe you."

"Good." He looked back toward the east, where the moon was just rising. It was bright yellow and nearly full.

"Let's go," he said abruptly. "We're riding back to Willesden tonight."

"But the plan was to camp and examine the structure of the tower and the surrounding country tomorrow," Estmar objected. "There is much still to examine before we know the extent of repairs needed..."

"I've seen everything I need to see," Tav said, starting down the stone steps.

At the bottom of the tower, Estmar once again objected, saying that they had the necessary supplies and that the way back would be too dangerous in the dark.

"The moon will provide plenty of light," Octavian said. "You can stay here all night if you like, Estmar, but I'd rather push through and get back late tonight. I think we could be behind the castle walls by matins."

"They're not expecting you!"

"I'm used to that."

Chapter 17

ROBIN WAS CONCERNED ABOUT OCTAVIAN leaving, but as the hours passed uneventfully, she began to relax. She went to supper after being again dressed in the fur-lined, vivid red gown that still made her nervous to wear.

The mealtime was much the same as the nights before, though Robin excused herself a bit earlier. She went to the chapel again, just to maintain "Lady Robin's" habits. While there however, she prayed fervently for Tav's safe return and then for their quick departure from this place, with or without Lord Pierce. After leaving the drafty chapel and stepping back into the keep, she was halted by a footman.

"Oh, my lady, Lord Pierce wishes you to come to his chambers."

"Is there bad news?" she asked, thinking that some rider must have come with a message about the war.

"I heard nothing of that." The servant paused. "It's not wise to keep the lord waiting, you know."

She climbed the stairs to the upper floor. It wasn't strange for Pierce to ask her to join him in his room, since many nobles' bedchambers also functioned as receiving rooms, places to entertain or take counsel. However, it was rather odd to ask her there so late in the evening. Once the serving boy poured wine and brought out a tray of little sweet dried fruits, Pierce dismissed him, saying that no one was to enter unless Pierce called.

Now alone with him, Robin felt a little queasy.

"You asked me here, my lord," she began. "For what purpose?"

Pierce handed her a glass of wine. "Simply to enjoy the company of a most intriguing guest. I've been rather isolated here since I arrived." The last words came out with a bitterness that took her aback.

"I thought you chose to come here."

"Hardly a choice." He spread his arms out wide. "Does this ruin look like a place any man wants to be?"

She said, "Many people would be grateful to avoid the turmoil wracking the country. If you wanted to, you could make Willesden into a haven for those fleeing the anarchy and violence of the war." That was what the de Vere family tried to do at Cleobury. That was what Alric's comrades Sir Luc and Sir Rafe attempted to do as well at each of the castles they were charged with defending. They took their positions very seriously, and she felt a surge of pride at knowing them.

But Pierce curled his lip in distaste at the suggestion. "I don't want to wait out this war as if it were a summer storm. What you call turmoil I see as opportunity. And to take advantage, I must be in the thick of it."

"Then why not go to London?" she asked.

"If I could, I would already be there, my lady." Pierce took a long drink of his wine, and strolled toward the fireplace, leaning on the mantel as he looked into the flames. "But as I told you before, I'm stuck here."

Robin watched him, seeing the frustration on his face.

"You're a lord. Can you not leave Willesden in the hands of your seneschal for a while? Or do you feel the need to oversee the fortification personally?"

"That does sound more noble, doesn't it?" He gazed moodily into the fire. "Lady Robin, are you a witch? I find myself saying things out loud that I never meant to reveal."

"If you wish to tell me something, you can. I know how to keep a secret." In fact, Robin felt a stirring of compassion for the man standing in front of her.

"I have so many secrets to keep," he said quietly.

"That's your gift, is it not?" Robin asked. "That's what you're doing at this moment. You say you'll give the king information, but only if he helps you out of the trouble you created for yourself."

Pierce looked back over his shoulder, a little smile on his face. "So he told you."

She realized too late she wasn't supposed to know that. She tried to mend her words. "Octavian did tell me a little, after you gave me that cryptic message while riding. Is it true?" she asked. "About you knowing a secret?"

"Very true, my lady Robin. I do not claim to be a good man. But I *do* have information that the king would like to know. And all I require is safe passage away from here. Then I'll hand over what I know."

Robin said, "You have horses in your stable. Take one and ride to the king yourself."

"If it were that simple, my dear, do you think I would not have done it by now?" Pierce walked over to her and touched her cheek with one finger. He surveyed her, his eyes warm with approval. Then he leaned down.

Robin stiffened, prepared to push him away.

But Pierce just grazed her cheek with his mouth, then whispered in her ear, "Everything I do is observed by my enemies. Every conversation in my hall, every letter I write. That's why I had to outrun the grooms to give you my message earlier. They're everywhere...watching and listening."

"What about now?" she asked quietly, thinking of this interaction being watched by unfriendly, judging eyes.

"Here in my chamber, I have a scrap of privacy...so long as no one thinks I'm doing anything useful. The walls are thick and I know of all the hiding spots. Hence my invitation to you. All they know is that I've asked a beautiful lady to my chamber. They *think* they know why."

"To seduce me?" Robin asked.

"Precisely."

"I'm armed," she warned. She wore a dagger concealed under her skirts, never one to let her guard down entirely. "I'll stab you in the gut if you try."

Improbably, Pierce just laughed. "I expect you might, for you're less a lady than you seem." He stepped back to survey her. "Pity. Are you sure you wouldn't like to be seduced? We do have the whole evening to ourselves, after all."

"Don't you dare." All her previous compassion for him vanished. He was just as bad as the stories she'd heard. Maybe worse.

"What's the matter, dear heart? Afraid that you'll not be able to resist?"

Robin frowned at him. "Do I look that naive? I assure you, you're not the first man who's offered to take me to bed. I have plenty of practice resisting."

"I can guess how many men you've been forced to fend off," Pierce said. "But those men weren't like me, were they?"

"How do you mean? Arrogant and entitled?"

"Handsome and skilled," he corrected, with an undeniably arrogant smile.

"I've been importuned by handsome men as well as ugly men. As for skilled, I never cared enough to learn if they were or not."

"Is that it?" he asked. "Or are you saving yourself for your knight? Hoping he'll offer to seduce you?"

"Take that back," she snapped, offended and defensive on his behalf. "Octavian has always treated me with respect."

"His loss," Pierce murmured.

"You're disgusting."

"Not so loud, darling," he cautioned, unmoved by her judgment. "We are still pretending to be enjoying each other's company."

She rolled her eyes. "How long must I continue to enjoy your company, then?"

"A little while, at least." Pierce's expression grew serious. "And when you leave here, at least try to look as if you want to return, because I'll likely need to call for you again. You'll be the trusted confidante between me and Octavian. Tell him to make a plan to get me far from this place, somewhere safe. We don't have much time, I fear. No more than a sennight."

"What happens in a sennight?"

"The Welsh are coming here to Willesden, and when they arrive it will be too late. I got word earlier today. There's nothing I can do to stop them."

"You should just tell Octavian whatever secret you're keeping," Robin said, alarmed by this new development.

"I know too much to commit to another's memory," he replied. "And besides, that would run counter to my plan to save my own skin. Speaking of skin..." He ran a fingertip along the edge of Robin's bodice. The trail of his touch sparked heat and then a chill in its wake. Robin shivered, though the feeling was not exactly repulsive.

"Stop touching me," she warned, her hand dropping to her skirt where a hidden slit would let her find her dagger.

"This hardly counts as touching." Pierce's smile widened. "Kiss me."

"Absolutely not. Why would I?"

"If someone happens to barge in, we should look appropriately inappropriate." He reached out and touched the hair she'd insisted on having braided earlier. "And you'll need to look more disheveled. The devil knows I've never left one of my lovers with such tidy hair."

"If this is just to preserve a subterfuge, I can undo it," she said.

"No, let me. Turn around."

He turned her and ran his fingers through her hair, separating the strands. The sensation was really rather pleasant. Almost soothing, if it hadn't been Pierce doing it.

"You have gorgeous hair," he murmured, his lips close to her right ear. "I'd like to feel it across my chest."

"You may dream," she snapped, recovering herself.

He gathered her hair up in one hand and pulled her a little closer to him. "Hmmm, that'll be a fine dream tonight. Or do you want to bless me with the reality?" He laid his free hand on her neck. "I can feel your pulse, darling. No woman's heart beats like that unless she's excited about something. So I have to wonder if you're excited to be here in my room."

"I'm more excited by the prospect of leaving it," she said, slapping his hand away. "And I think the time to do so is now."

"If you insist," he said with a sigh. "But first…"

He spun her around to face him again and kissed her.

Pierce's mouth was hot on hers, his kiss aggressive and demanding. Robin started to lean away, but she was held fast by Pierce's hands on her shoulders, keeping her rooted to the floor.

"Get—" *off me*, she meant to say. But the moment she opened her lips, his tongue invaded her mouth. Robin gasped in surprise and indignation. But that didn't stop the kiss, which was reaching an uncomfortable intensity.

When she actually felt a flash of pain at her lower lip, she raised her hands to his chest to push him away, shoving him with such force he had to move back a few steps.

"What are you *doing*?" she demanded. "If you try that again, you'll never leave this castle in one piece." Robin drew the dagger from its hidden sheath, no longer willing to indulge the lord.

Pierce's eyes widened slightly, and he kept well away from her. Still, he wore a pleased, self-satisfied smile. "No need for alarm. I was just adding the finishing touches. Now you look like a woman who is ready to leave my room."

Robin gaped at him, feeling the tang of iron on her tongue. "Am I bleeding?"

"Only a little. I just wanted to make sure your appearance was appropriately ravished. No, no, keep the sleeves of the shift down, dear. It's perfect as is."

Robin stopped pulling at the top of her shift's sleeves, having discovered that Pierce had managed to expose both her shoulders during the kiss.

"I'm going now," she announced. "And you disgust me."

"Your knight should be back tomorrow, if Estmar hasn't done something stupid," he said, almost as an afterthought. "Talk to him when you have a moment, will you?"

"Go to hell," she spat.

"That is assured." Pierce bowed to her, mockingly.

Robin wrenched open the door and darted out into the hall. What a churl. The horrible man actually *bit* her.

She couldn't return to her own bedchamber like this. The other women would see her and think the worst, and Robin's pride wouldn't allow that.

Tav is gone, she thought. He had a small chamber to himself. She'd hide there until she could restore her appearance to normal. Ugh. She never should have left Cleobury.

Chapter 18

OCTAVIAN KEPT UP A BRUTAL pace on the return to Willesden, much faster than their morning travel. Estmar followed him, sometimes falling behind to the point that Octavian could barely see him if he turned back. But Tav's focus was ahead. He couldn't say precisely why he felt so uneasy, other than because Robin was on her own, a bird in a nest of snakes. Knowing she was far more skilled at fighting than anyone would expect didn't help him feel better. She was still one person against a garrison's worth of soldiers.

When he arrived at the gates, it took a few shouts to get the attention of the guard, who was undoubtedly trying to stay warm in the gatehouse.

The man slid back the small grate on the door to let him see who was asking admittance. He blinked at Octavian in confusion. "You're back?"

"Obviously. Open the gate."

"I'm not supposed to do so without approval."

"Estmar is going to ride up in a moment. Get the approval from him, *after* you open the gate. He won't like being kept waiting."

The guard looked at Octavian, mumbled something, and then closed the grate. The large door creaked as it was slowly opened. As soon as the opening was wide enough to admit a horse, he rode through.

The courtyard was deserted, and only a few torches burned. Tav dismounted and walked his horse to the stable. A sleepy-looking boy poked his head out of the loft, saying he'd be down in a moment.

Leaving the horse in the care of the boy, Tav strode over to the keep itself. Inside, he stomped his feet on the cold stone. Only a footman was present there.

"Where's Lady Robin?" Tav asked him.

"She was with Lord Pierce earlier this evening, sir. I assume she must be abed now." The footman had a sly smile. "Do you want someone to rouse her?"

"No. I just wanted to be sure that she's still within the keep."

He made his way to his chamber, meeting no one else along the way. The hallways were dark, all the candles extinguished. The moonlight filtered in through the few narrow windows, providing barely enough illumination to walk safely.

The chamber given to him was cold as well, but a fire had been laid. He pulled off his cloak and outer garments, draping them over a stool. Then he crossed the room and knelt to light the fire. Within a few moments, the kindling caught and a hint of warmth reached him.

Without warning, the door swung open and Robin flew in. As soon as she crossed the threshold, she turned and pushed the door shut again, leaning with her forehead against the wooden frame, a long sigh escaping her lips.

Tav stood up from where he'd been crouched by the fire. "Robin?"

She whirled around. "I didn't know you were here!"

she said. "I'll go!"

Tav barely managed to reach her before she left the room. He caught her arm and pulled her to a stop. "Wait. What's the matter?"

He opened the door, glancing into the hallway. All was silent.

"No one's chasing me," she said, waving a hand to indicate that the matter wasn't very important. "I wasn't running away from anything."

Tav closed the door and turned to look at her more carefully in the increasing firelight. Her hair was loose and wild around her face, her gown half-unlaced, the undershift pulled askew. And her lips were unusually deep with color. "Then why were you running?"

"I just needed a place to...to think for a moment. I didn't know you'd be back already. I'm sorry."

"Did someone hurt you?"

She looked rather offended at the notion. "Hurt me? As if I'd let it get so far!"

"So far as what? Robin, what *happened*?" From the state of her hair and clothes, the only possibility he could think of was that she had just come from a bed...and not from sleep.

She took a big breath, as if just realizing he wasn't privy to her thoughts. "Oh. Yes. Well, I just left Lord Pierce's chamber. He summoned me there long after supper."

"He asked for you to come to his room, and you went," Octavian said, trying to keep his voice calm as his worst suspicion was confirmed.

"I had my dagger," she said quickly. "I could have won any fight he gave me."

Octavian muttered a curse. "Tell me what happened."

"He wanted to talk."

"Talk," he repeated incredulously. Robin didn't look like a woman who'd just been *talked* to.

"Yes. He wanted to talk to me so I could pass another message to you." Robin looked back at the door, then leaned closer to him. She said in a low, urgent voice, "He says there's less than a week until escape from this place will be impossible—for all of us. He says an army of Welsh are marching here soon. Pierce claims he's being watched by agents of the empress and the Welsh, and he fears that one of them will kill him for what he knows."

"And why did Pierce have to unlace your gown to tell you that?" Octavian asked, indicating the state of her dress.

"It was his stupid *trick*." Robin glared at him, and then looked down, fussing with the lacing on the left side of her gown. She tugged angrily at the thin cord, only succeeding at tangling it. "He said it ought to look as though I'd only gone to his room for…you know…"

"Well done, then. That's exactly what it looks like."

"You think I enjoyed being alone in a room with him?" she snapped.

"Did you?"

Her eyes rounded with shock, and he knew he'd hurt her. "No! He's a miserable, infuriating man and I wanted to slap him the whole time he was kissing me."

"How long was that?" Octavian despised himself for asking the question, but he needed to hear the answer.

"Only a moment, really," Robin replied, rolling her eyes. "But it felt like years."

He put a hand out to her shoulder. "Robin. Look at me. Did he hurt you?"

She raised her chin unwillingly, her whole manner righteously offended. "He couldn't if he tried. After he got too attentive, I pushed him away and showed him I meant it." Robin flicked her hand, and there was the slim blade, flashing the firelight. She smiled, then returned it to its hidden sheath, somewhere in the folds of her dress.

"So he didn't push you into anything."

"Never." Robin set her jaw. "But he did…well, he laughed at me the whole time. He enjoyed using me as cover for his own purposes. He wasn't violent, though. Aside from the bite." One finger edged up to touch the corner of her mouth, where he saw a spot of blood. The sight of it made Tav want to find Pierce and throw him out a window.

"The *bite*?"

Robin misread his fury, because she said, "And now you're angry with me for going there in the first place."

"No, I'm not angry with you," he said quickly. "I'm angry at Pierce for using you like that. And at all the other men before who you had to keep at knifepoint because they didn't listen to a simple no. Why do all your encounters with men end up badly?"

"Not my encounters with you," she said with a faint smile. "Those I thought ended quite well…if a little too quickly."

The smile caused another bead of blood to well up at the corner of her mouth. He raised his hand to wipe it away. His thumb lingered on her bottom lip. She looked up at him with those deep blue eyes, and her lips parted. "Tav."

She raised her own hand up to take his, and tipped her head upward.

Knowing he shouldn't, Tav leaned down to kiss her.

She let out a tiny sigh.

"Now that's a proper kiss," she said.

He wanted to hear that. He wanted to hear it a little too much.

Robin's hands dropped to her sides as he pulled away. "I'm sorry. I know we said we wouldn't do this. Should I go?" she asked, her eyes locked on his, trusting him to give her the answer.

"Yes. You should." He stroked her jaw with one finger, loving how she inhaled in reaction, opening her mouth, inviting him to taste her a little deeper. "But I don't want you to go."

He bent to kiss her again. When his tongue touched hers, Robin's fingers dug into his skin.

"Oh," she breathed. "Oh." Her voice was throaty, almost entirely unlike the Robin he knew. But he liked the Robin who was revealing herself now—more mature, but still innocent. More vulnerable, but still trusting. She licked her lower lip without knowing she did it.

That was what broke him. The expression of desire from her.

"Stay," he said. "Until you want to leave."

"You'd let me?" she asked hesitantly.

It was madness to let her stay in his room with him in the middle of the night, but it was what he wanted. What he needed. He reached for her again, twining her hair in his hands while he sought another kiss.

She moaned softly when his mouth touched hers, and the sound vibrated through him. Then her tongue flicked against his just for a moment. Tav tightened his grip instinctively and his own body reacted to her presence.

Robin took a ragged breath, and whispered, "I want to stay, but…"

She said something else, but the words were too soft to hear. "What?"

Robin raised her head slightly, her expression half anxious and half defiant. "I don't want you to hate me." Then she ducked her head down, tucking herself into him.

"Why would I hate you?" he asked.

"I saw your face when I first came to the door, when you thought I'd gone to his room for…well," she mumbled. "I disappoint you. Just as I disappointed Rainald and Cecily and Alric. Everyone I love, I fail them. I try. I want to be the sort of woman you're all trying to make me into. Truly. But I can't seem to ever forget the girl I used to be. Rude and thoughtless and uncivilized. Always ready to make a mistake. And whoever sees me gets this look in their eye. Just as you did at the door. A look that says I'm not what anyone wanted."

"You are wanted," he told her. "Stay with me and I'll show you."

Chapter 19

ROBIN HEARD OCTAVIAN'S INVITATION, BUT her heart didn't quite believe his words. "You want me to stay?" she asked.

"Yes," he said, looking at her intently. "But only if you want to."

"I do," she confessed, her breath rushing out of her. She was certain she'd made a fool of herself when he kissed her before, but why pretend at this point? He already knew she desired him in the most desperate way possible.

"I'm not sure I'm ready...for..." She trailed off.

"You are definitely not ready," he said flatly. "Whatever else happens tonight, you're still going to be a virgin in the morning."

"It's all right?" she asked with a frown. Her experience with men was limited to fending them off because as far as she could tell, they always wanted more than what she was willing to grant. Never less.

"If you think that's the only thing I can enjoy doing with you in a bed, Robin, you do need a bit of an education."

She exhaled in relief. "Then educate me. Please. Because I spend too much time thinking about you, and just wondering…"

"Is that true?" He kissed her again, and Robin closed her eyes, enjoying the sensation of his mouth on hers, and the promise of more at last. But not too much more.

She edged closer, eager to remind herself just how good it felt to be in his arms. Except for the constant irritation of the fur lining against her skin.

She squirmed. "Wait," she said. "This dress is horrible. The stupid fur keeps tickling me in the worst way. I have to get out of it."

His eyes slid downward to the lacing, which was growing more tangled by the moment as her nervous fingers knotted the cord.

"Stop that." Octavian put his hand on hers. He knelt down, his attention on the lacing at her right side. His hands had a golden cast from the firelight, and she inhaled at the thought of those beautiful hands on her skin.

"These laces really are in a tangle," he said, as if it were perfectly normal for him to be undressing her. "Just be patient."

Patient? She was practically shaking with eagerness and embarrassment, but Tav didn't seem to notice. He loosened the lacing on both sides, and then lifted the gown carefully over her head, leaving her clad only in her shift, which went down to her ankles.

He put the gown aside and turned back and surveyed her. "The firelight behind you makes for a pretty picture."

She glanced over her shoulder, realizing that the light silhouetted her body against the fabric. "Do you want the shift off?" she asked.

"You can keep it on if you prefer," he said. "Your choice."

Robin took a breath, and then gathered the fabric up and pulled the shift off. She swallowed nervously. If she was going to spend a night with him, she wanted him to see all of her.

Tav's eyes widened, and he took a long moment to consider her from her feet up to her head.

"Well?" she demanded, putting more defiance in her voice than she felt. "Am I acceptable?"

"You're lovely."

She melted instantly. *Lovely.* She wanted to be lovely to him.

He reached out and drew her hair over one shoulder, partially covering her breasts. "Go to the bed before you get cold," he said, his eyes locked on her.

She obeyed, though cold was the last sensation she was feeling at the moment.

Tav undressed himself, a lengthier operation since he was still wearing boots and had multiple layers on.

But at last he stood naked at the side of the bed, and she could take in the sight of him—the bulk of his shoulders, which she already loved, to the expanse of his chest and the tightly curled hair dusted across his front and down to…well. She bit her lip, wondering if she'd been a bit too impulsive when she agreed to stay.

Tav slid onto the bed and slipped an arm under her and pressed his hand against the small of her back, bringing her closer to him.

Robin slid her leg over his before she realized what she was doing. All she knew was that she instinctively wanted to mold her body to match his as closely as she could.

"Educate yourself," he challenged her. "Touch me."

Under the covers, she let her hands slide over his upper body, his arms, his shoulders. She reveled in the feel of him, the smoothness of his skin over most of his body, and even the dozens of faint scars and scratches where he'd suffered injuries over the years. She traced the lines made by the hidden muscles, smiling as she went.

"I don't know what to do next," she said.

"It's not a test," he told her. "You can do whatever you like."

"And you won't tell me it's a sin?" she asked.

"It is," he said simply. "But it's a sin I seem destined for, so how can I pretend that I don't want to sin with you?"

Robin felt the thrill of victory run through her. "Then tell me exactly how you want to sin."

"It would take too long. I'd waste the whole night talking and never get to any of the sinning." He smiled and pushed her hair away from her face. "Lie back, and I'll show you one sin I've been dreaming of."

She rolled so she was on her back, and he shifted to his side. Then he lowered his head to begin a trail of kisses along her chest until his tongue met her nipple.

Robin let out a whimper of pleasure because whatever he was doing stirred a heat inside her belly. He licked her nipple over and over, the tip of his tongue swirling around it, keeping the bud hard and responsive. Robin felt warm and weak and utterly adored.

"Now the other one," she ordered softly.

He laughed low in his throat and kissed his way to her other breast, treating that nipple to the same gentle pleasure.

"That feels wonderful," she whispered, her hand resting on his shoulder. She decided she adored his shoulders.

"I've been wanting to taste you," he said, his breath hot against her skin. "I never should have kissed you that one night, Robin, because since then I've only wanted more."

Their bodies were pressed together, his muscled frame holding her close. She felt how hard he was, and curiosity overcame her. "Can I touch you?" she whispered.

"You're already touching me," he whispered back, teasing.

Robin slid her hand from his shoulder to lower on his body, down to his stomach, where she paused. "I meant…" Was he going to keep teasing her? He was going to make her say something crude, something that Robin never said to a man except as an insult hurled in the heat of a fight.

But he didn't make her say another word. He lay back on the bed, then put a hand over her own and drew it downward, leading her to his erection.

He let out a shaky breath as soon as she curled her fingers around the hard shaft. Curious, she began to touch him, noticing how every little move seemed to drive him to distraction.

She said, "Is this how it's typically done?"

"Who cares," he responded. "All I know is that I love the way you touch me, and I don't care if it's typical or not."

"Oh," she said with a little sigh. "Good. I just didn't want to make a mistake and turn you away."

He laughed, his voice warming her. "No chance. Keep doing what you're doing, and I'll never turn away."

She smiled and continued to stroke him. When she ran her hand up to the tip of him, though, he grabbed her hands and sat up in the bed. From that angle, she had a perfect view of his whole upper body, outlined in firelight.

"Did I do something wrong?" she asked.

"Not at all. If you'd been using your mouth, you'd

have finished me just then."

"Oh." Robin knew exactly what he meant—she'd lived among numerous people in close quarters, and she'd glimpsed women pleasuring men in that way. She'd just never done it herself. "Would you want me to? Use my mouth?"

He pulled her over to him, laid a soft kiss on her neck, just below her ear, before answering. "Yes, but that falls under the rubric of acts you're not ready for yet."

"Shouldn't I decide that?" she objected.

He shook his head. "You have a record of deciding to do things you've got no business doing. For now, you listen to me." Once more, he captured her mouth.

Robin ached with desire as he deepened the kiss. Her wrists were still caught in his grip, a reminder that she was utterly under his power. Yet she had no wish to be anywhere else. The need she felt for him was actually rather frightening. Robin shuddered when she realized that she would do anything he asked...and whatever might happen tonight was entirely up to him.

"What's wrong?" he asked then. He studied her face, his eyes glinting in the firelight.

She'd frozen up, consumed in the swirl of thoughts that made her so weak around Tav.

"I think I'm scared," she whispered.

He immediately stopped kissing her and released her hands. He leaned back against the pillow, waiting for her to decide what to do next.

She knelt beside him, using her hair as a curtain. "I'm not scared of you," she said. "I'm scared of...not being able to refuse you. If that makes sense."

"I told you that I'd never make you do something you didn't want to."

"But you could."

"But I wouldn't," he said, his gaze steady on her.

"I believe you," she mumbled, trying to explain the conflict, the different voices clamoring within her. "But…"

Tav reached out to sweep her hair away from her face. "Turn around, Robin. Trust me."

She turned, and he shifted, pulling her back against him until her hips rested against the insides of his thighs, and her back lay against his chest. He was a much bigger person than she was, so it felt like being enfolded. He pulled the blanket up over them both, covering her breasts, leaving just her shoulders and head exposed.

"I didn't mean to ruin everything," she whispered.

He encouraged her to lay her head back on his chest. "You've had terrible luck regarding men, Robin. I'm actually astonished you're trusting me as much as you are now."

"I've always trusted you, Tav," she said. "Since the first time I saw you."

His arms tightened around her. "You didn't know anything about me then."

"No, but I saw how other people trusted you. And you always treated me like I had a mind of my own."

"You definitely have a mind of your own," he said.

She smiled. "You know what I mean. Everyone else wanted to make me into something new. You just let me be who I am."

His lips brushed her cheek. "You're perfect as you are."

Under the comforting weight of the blanket, he touched her lightly, his hands roaming her body without lingering on any particular part. Robin sighed, relaxing against him.

"Are you still scared?" he asked softly.

She shook her head. The worry that plagued her before had fled again, now that she realized Tav had more patience than she did.

"Can I kiss you?" he asked quietly.

"Please."

He began to kiss her neck and the top of her right shoulder, slowly teasing her with his mouth and tongue until Robin was no longer relaxed but growing needy once more.

"Can I show you how I want you?" he asked. "Just to touch. Nothing more than that."

"Yes," she gasped.

He slid his right hand over her breast, and her stomach, then slowly reached between her legs. Robin's breath left her body the moment she felt his fingers there, bringing an instant heat to her core. "Oh," she gasped.

His voice was low as he ordered, "Open up for me, Robin."

She let her knees fall apart, inviting him to touch her as much as he wanted.

He teased her gently, circling the sensitive bud without touching it directly. Robin's hands tightened on his legs, and she began to push her hips back toward him in a steady rhythm. "More," she whispered. "Please."

Tav kissed her neck, and then she felt the pressure of his finger entering her body.

"You still want this?" he asked.

"Yes!"

"Good." He continued that steady in and out, using her body's slick heat to make her squirm with need.

"More," Robin begged, even though she loved the way he took his time.

"More," he promised. The pressure grew. She craved his attention, and her hips rose to meet his hand. When his thumb rubbed slowly against the nub above her center, in a counterpoint to the thrusting of his fingers, she knew she was going to lose herself. She needed his touch to feel complete.

"Tav," she murmured, feeling a little desperate. "That feels so good. It feels…"

She arched her back just as the orgasm broke over her. He slid his free hand over her mouth, and she bit down, stifling her moan, which otherwise would have woken half the castle. Her whole body shook in the aftermath of the sensation.

Then he held her tightly with one arm around her shoulders, even as his fingers kept tormenting her gently, drawing out the exquisite shock that left her so weak. He murmured, "So that's one way I can enjoy you in a bed without actually coupling."

He withdrew his hand and laid it on her stomach.

"No, *I* enjoyed it," she corrected. "You just…made me enjoy it."

"Mmm, no. I enjoyed it as well. Hearing you, seeing you react to my touch…it's like nothing else."

"You want more though," she guessed, feeling the hard length of him under her body.

"I *want* more," he said, "but the point was to show you that it's not about what I want. Or what any man wants."

"So we've enjoyed each other and there's nothing more to it?"

He sighed. "Of course there's more to it. But I don't want to think about that now. Just enjoy the night. Please."

He shifted to lie beside her, one hand roaming over her skin, from her shoulder to her thigh and over her back. His touch made her happy and drowsy at once.

She curled up on him and closed her eyes, drifting in and out of sleep. The fire flickered against the walls and she sighed as she felt Tav's touch on her back and on her arms, and his fingers in her hair.

A while later, he nudged her. "Robin. Wake up."

She blinked, and saw the fire had died to embers. "I need to get to my room before morning!"

"Sadly, yes. I'll take you back."

"No!" she said, alarmed. "If I'm going to be sneaking around at night, let them think Pierce is the reason for it, not you. I'll go alone."

"You're sure?" he asked, obviously concerned.

"I'm sure." Robin knew he'd take her the whole way, but she didn't want to sully his reputation along with her own.

He slid out of the bed and helped her dress, his hands skimming her body as he pulled the gown over her head.

"No lacing this time," he said quietly. "You'll just have to endure it until you get back to your room."

"I hate the lacing," she said. "It's far too tight."

"It's meant to please the viewer, not the wearer," he said. "And for what it's worth, the sight of you in the gown pleases me."

She ducked her head and smiled. Perhaps it was not such an ordeal after all.

One more lingering kiss, then she slipped out of Tav's room and made her way through the utterly silent keep.

The large bed in the women's quarters where Robin slept was occupied, of course, and there was no chance of Robin slipping in unnoticed, since she had to rouse at least one person to make room.

The servant named Irene was on the end, and she woke up when Robin prodded her in the shoulder.

"Where have you been all night?" Irene asked in a

grumpy tone as she shifted to the left, allowing Robin room.

"Pierce asked me to visit him in his chamber," Robin mumbled, looking at the floor.

"Hmmm," Irene responded, still only half awake. "Better you than me. I only go when he insists, or when Estmar needs me to. Just don't get it into your head that it's love."

"I'm not in love."

"Good. Love is for fools. You'll have a few late nights, till he tires of you. And he will. He cares for no one but himself."

Robin only shrugged. "It matters not to me."

"Aye, that's the spirit. Take what you want from men, because they just take what they want from us." Irene yawned and rolled to the other side, burrowing down amid the blankets.

Robin crawled into the bed. It was warm on the side where Irene lay, but cold on the outer edge. When she'd lain with Tav, she'd been deliciously warm all over. She wished she hadn't had to leave him. But she also refused to let him suffer for her impetuousness. She would go to hell on her own.

Chapter 20

AFTER ROBIN LEFT, TAV COULDN'T get to sleep. What had he been thinking? Nothing, other than that he wanted Robin.

He reached for the pitcher by his bed, and managed to pour some water into the cup without spilling. His arm was shaking, a consequence of the agitation in his mind. He'd experienced that feeling many times before, usually when a life-changing choice loomed before him. Tav preferred decisions that had to be made in the moment. How to parry an attack. Whether to stand or run. Respond to a challenge in the same language, or to pretend not to comprehend it.

It was the choices that he saw coming that pained him. The choice of whether to remain in the Levant, or follow a new lord to France. He'd agonized over that for days, weighing the options, praying for guidance, doubting his own impulses till the very morning Denis would depart.

Take wing when you can, the brothers once told him. Granted, they'd meant it in warning to avoid the bullies and rough men in the streets of the city. They'd beat or rob children, or steal them to sell as slaves in the markets. But Tav applied the advice more generally in later life, almost always choosing to go somewhere new, to keep journeying, whenever he had the chance. That was what led him through Europe and to the distant isle of Britain. That was what let him meet the other knights who served the same king. That was what made him meet Robin, a woman born so far away from him, in such different conditions, that their paths never should have crossed.

And now they had shared a bed. Even if he hadn't done the one thing his body was screaming at him to do, he'd absolutely taken advantage of Robin's innocence and inexperience. All because he wanted her.

Tav had always prided himself on keeping his lust in check. Unwarranted pride, apparently, because he had many chances to end what he was doing with Robin that night, and every time, he chose to go on. Was he just that desperate for a woman?

No. He had other opportunities. Plenty of them. Prostitutes would have happily taken payment for the night, but he'd also been made offers by women who thought him an interesting challenge. The farther north and west he traveled, the more often it happened. Some women saw the shape of his body, and in particular the shade of his skin, and wanted to know if he was different from the other men they'd had in bed. Women like that were easy to turn away because nothing was less alluring than pure disgust, which was all he felt when he heard such offers.

Robin was different. When Robin looked at him, when she shyly confessed that she looked forward to seeing him more than she looked forward to spring, he felt like he was the only man in the world. She didn't regard him as a curiosity. She regarded him as himself.

But Tav couldn't think about the ramifications of his

night with Robin now, because he was *not* the only man interested her. Pierce's attempted seduction drove Robin to his room, and Tav hated the fact that the other man laid a finger on her.

He sat up. If he wasn't sleeping, he saw no reason why Pierce should slumber away peacefully. It was time to talk.

The moon had set and dawn was still an hour away. Tav dressed and made his way through the icy, dark hallways to Pierce's doorway. It was unguarded, and when he tried the handle, the door swung open easily.

Only embers lit the room now. The bed was curtained off, hiding the sleeping figure of Pierce. Tav took a candle from its sconce and lit it with the glowing embers. Light flared. He walked over to the bed and yanked the curtain aside, in no mood to be gentle with his wake-up call.

He grabbed Pierce's shoulder. "Get up. You've slept long enough." The white cat sleeping on the pillow yawned.

Pierce's eyes flew open, and he took in the sight of Tav with near panic. "What are you doing here? You've come to assassinate me!"

"Shut up. If I were here to assassinate you, I wouldn't have woken you up first." Tav lit the rest of the candles on the great iron fixture near the bed. He pulled the rest of the curtains aside, to Pierce's ineffectual protests, and then sat on the most comfortable-looking chair.

"You weren't supposed to get back until tomorrow," Pierce said. "Or later tonight, if it is tomorrow."

"Change of plans. Estmar's tower wasn't actually that interesting. Why do you think Estmar wanted me to go there?"

"I don't know. Perhaps just he wanted you out of Willesden because he figured out you arrived in response to 'Govannon's' message. I tried to be discreet, but I know I'm being watched carefully."

"Speaking of that, let's discuss Govannon's message to the king."

"It's the middle of the night!" the other man protested. The cat seemed to be in agreement.

"It's the end of the night, and coincidently, also the end of my patience. We talk now and you tell me what is truly going on, or I'll leave you here to stew on your own."

"It's not safe. We'll be overheard."

"So you told Robin," Tav noted. "But at this hour, everyone is asleep. Now is the time."

"Lady Robin was quick with her message," Pierce said, looking more alert. "When did you speak to her?"

"What does it matter? She told me, and I'm here. Tell me about why you need to get to the king personally."

"Other factions do not value me highly at the moment," said Pierce. "The empress has grown sluggish in her fight for the crown, and the Welsh...damn the Welsh."

"Even Myfanwy?" Octavian remembered the black-haired Welsh woman who had been Pierce's lover.

Pierce's eyes narrowed and his mouth thinned. Though subtle, it was the first sign of real anger that Tav had seen from him. "Myfanwy left me, and Govannon here is my only ally. The one exchange in which I can definitely say I profited." He rubbed the cat's ear affectionately. "Govannon has never betrayed me. Not yet, at least."

Tav wholeheartedly agreed that the cat was the better companion. Though he'd had only a few exchanges with her, Myfanwy had struck him as a petty, vicious person. "I thought you were well suited to each other," Tav said coolly.

Pierce chuckled. "A little too much alike, perhaps. If you can imagine it, the beautiful Myfanwy was not to be trusted. She worked with her damned family in secret to overthrow me and hand Malvern over to a warlord they liked better, all because he promised them more spoils from his constant raids."

"Raids?"

"In the name of the empress and her vassals, he claims," Pierce said with disgust. "But the truth is that he's no better than a cattle thief. The raids aren't against enemy strongholds. He sends his soldiers to raid farm-steads that have nothing to do with strategic safety, taking everything from herds of swine to farmers' daughters. He'll inspire a peasant uprising, the idiot."

"I heard about some raids in the area, but I assumed they were your doing."

Pierce's eyes narrowed. "I'd never condone that. We've gathered what we found near here, that's true. But all the livestock you see, all the servants, I paid for them. I'm not a thief."

"So you wish to regain Malvern for the good of the people?" Octavian asked, not bothering to hide the skepti-cism from his voice.

"Regardless of what you think of my politics, sir, I never allowed the people in the very shadow of Malvern to starve. And this winter, with their food stores raided by the new overlord, they will starve."

Tav had been wondering something else as well. "You knew who I was when you sent that message under the name of Govannon. You asked for me specifically. Why?"

Pierce sighed. "I needed to know that it was really a king's man who came, not some imposter or a traitor. Even with the code name of Govannon, the message could have been intercepted. You're a difficult man to impersonate, for obvious reasons. I knew you'd be you."

That was what Tav had suspected. "All right. Explain, in detail, what information you've got for the king."

Pierce said, "Earl Ranulf is planning another rebellion in the north, and he's going to start with an attack on an important city early in the new year, while it's still winter."

"So Stephen won't have time to send reinforcements," Tav guessed.

"Exactly. Ranulf will win, and that will cause more cities and towns in the north to fall, one by one. The result will be dissolution. The northern barons don't want to help the empress Maud rule. They want to rule themselves. Think of a hundred little duchies, all squabbling and fighting and killing for the next generation. They say it's anarchy now, but what will come next is far worse. Is that what you want?"

"It doesn't matter what I want," Octavian said. "You're the one who claims to be able to stop this."

"I am." Pierce leaned in. "I know what city Ranulf will attack, and how, and when. I know which allies he is relying on for aid. And I'll tell Stephen everything I know in exchange for his support so I can take back Malvern Castle, and once again be the lord, as I should be."

"You don't need me for that," Tav said, frowning. "You can just go."

"As I tried to make clear to your little companion, I'm a prisoner here as much as you two are. The moment I do anything to reveal a change of heart—"

Tav gave a snort at the idea of Pierce having a heart at all.

"—agents of my enemies will kill me."

"So what do you suggest?" Tav asked. "You think that

the three of us can succeed at an escape?"

"Three?" Pierce asked blankly. "I only need you, Sir Octavian. As a soldier to protect me on the way to London or wherever Stephen is at the moment, and then to get me an audience with the king."

"I'm not going anywhere without Robin," Tav said flatly. "So if it's an escape you're hoping for, it will be three."

Pierce said, "Very well, but don't think I'll tolerate a woman's whining on the road. Nor slow to her pace."

Tav almost laughed out loud. He didn't bother to explain that Robin's presence was likely the only thing that would keep the men alive once they were in the depths of the Ardenwood.

"I'll make a plan to get out," Tav muttered. "I'll need to know where the guards are posted and when the guard changes. And which men are actually agents of your enemies, as you claim."

Pierce ground out, "All I know is that Myfanwy turned many of my men with promises and payment in coin. But I was so desperate after the attack on Malvern that I couldn't afford to cut men loose without knowing for certain. I'd be living here alone, with no force at all."

"You'd probably be better off."

"Too late now," Pierce admitted. "I made my move, and I am paying for it. But my opponents underestimate me if they think it's my last move. You and I will escape here and then I'll show them."

"We'll escape with Robin," Tav reminded him.

"Lady Robin…" Pierce said suddenly. "Who is she, really?"

Tav wasn't going to fall into that trap. "You mean is that her true name? I'm sure it is, but I've no idea who her parents are, or exactly where she was born." Which was true enough.

"So the woman was a stranger to you when you met her? And you believe her story?"

Tav shrugged. "Believe me, I was certainly not expecting to see her in the middle of the forest. As for her story, I've heard less believable ones. A man doesn't travel from the Holy Land to here without hearing some incredible tales."

Chapter 21

LATER THAT DAY, OCTAVIAN FOUND Robin in the great hall and suggested a walk along the battlements, the one place they could be reasonably assured that no one would be able to listen in to their discussion.

The weather wasn't conducive. The sky was a low, solid grey, and the wind whipped up from the west every few moments. Still, Robin wrapped a borrowed cloak around her body and followed Tav up the stone stairs to the top of the walls.

"Did you sleep well?" she asked.

"No."

"Neither did I."

"I'm sorry," he said automatically.

A fleeting smile crossed her face. "I'm not."

The simple phrase was enough to make him feel better. At least Robin didn't regret what happened between them. Not yet.

He turned to the more immediate problem. "I spoke with him, and he's agreed to do as I say to get him out. But *how* do we do that?"

Robin looked over the castle courtyard, busy with activity as men worked on the walls and servants carried out daily tasks.

She chewed on her lower lip, obviously working out possible choices. "We need to leave Willesden, and we're not permitted to ride out like ordinary travelers. So what options are left to us?"

"Pierce had no suggestions," Tav noted sourly.

"You're a knight in the service of the king," she said. "Can't you just…"

Tav shook his head. "We can't fight our way out. Even if all three of us were armed, there's a garrison's worth of soldiers to fend off."

"So we'll be facing a few dozen swords. Or we'll be shot dead by the archers," she added miserably.

"No direct confrontation will work," Tav went on. "That leaves stealth. We can sneak out of one of the smaller gates during the night."

"We may be able to get through the door ourselves," Robin said, "but we need horses and supplies. How will we manage that?"

Tav sighed. "I don't know."

She folded her arms on the high stone wall, looking out. "I can't think of anything he wouldn't have already tried. Bribe a guard?"

"He's not sure who's bribable," Tav explained. "He could give a guard money, only to be recaptured an instant later when the man reports when happened. He trusts no one."

"Except us, apparently." She frowned. "Even if we slipped out ourselves, bearing our weapons and supplies, how would we get our horses out? It's just too…noticeable."

"We could do it in phases."

"How? There's no way to get horses outside the walls without causing far too much suspicion. And we can't leave separately. They might let *us* go, but the instant Pierce disappears, there will be a massive search party mobilized to find him."

"We need a distraction," Tav said, watching the activity happening outside the walls of Willesden. A small group of men herded a few sheep toward the castle gates. "Looks like mutton tonight."

"They bring in animals," Robin mused. "Always from the eastern track. The direction we came from. But there are no farms there. Where do the animals come from?"

"Farther afield," Tav guessed. "Perhaps they sent these men yesterday and they're just returning now."

"I saw them at breakfast," she disagreed. "The fat one in the red cap likes to look at me."

"So it's not far to get the sheep."

"Nor the goats, nor the horses. It's all sorts of livestock." Her eyes widened. "The raids! Our suppers must all be stolen meat."

Tav told her, "He says the raids are not his doing, but the new overlord of Malvern."

Robin gave an unladylike snort. "We heard about the raiding while we were in the village of Sutton. That's at least five days hard riding from Malvern. No lord is raiding out that far. These raids are happening closer to home."

"Pierce is lying, then." Tav should have known. The man was a liar by nature.

But Robin put her chin on her folded arms, saying, "I agree, but it's not like him to lie about this sort of thing."

"Liars lie."

"Pierce does have a sort of code," she argued. "When it comes to his loyalties, he's all over the map, and he treats women and anyone beneath his station like a bug. But he takes the idea of being a lord seriously. I don't think he would order a secret raid from his own home. It would reflect badly on his honor, and he cares about that."

Tav considered her words. "If it's not the old lord of Malvern and not the new lord of Malvern, where does that leave us?"

"The raids are happening, but they're directed by someone else."

"Someone who has a lot of sway over the men to get them all to go along."

"I remember something Irene mentioned to me. She said she only went to Pierce's bed when he insisted, or when Estmar needed her to. Why would Estmar ever want Irene to go to Pierce, let alone need her to?"

The conclusion she was leading to was simple.

"Irene kept Pierce occupied while Estmar took a group of men out to raid in the middle of the night." Tav frowned, thinking it over. "Estmar is conducting raids, acting on his own initiative. He doesn't want Pierce to know about it, so Irene is the distraction. And Estmar and his men have the whole night to ride out, raid whatever target they've chosen, and return with the spoils."

She nodded. "And because Pierce would be suspicious when the castle gets fresh livestock, or whatever else it is they're stealing, Estmar is instead keeping the livestock close by and under guard. Then, when Pierce gives the servants money to purchase livestock needed for food, Estmar pockets it, and they return with a stolen animal from his store. It's an excellent scheme...rather more clever than Estmar seems capable of."

"Perhaps he got the idea from someone else, as a sort of favor for his loyalty." The idea was unproven, but it felt right. "He acts with far more authority than he should. He did ask me in a roundabout way if I'd like to switch sides. And when we were at the old tower, he mentioned the possibility of keeping livestock there, if guards were manning the tower anyway."

"Another spot to keep his spoils that his own lord won't see," Robin said, her eyes bright. "I'll bet anything it is Estmar leading the raids. And if they go on another raid soon…"

"…the castle will have far fewer guards that night." Letting them escape with a much better chance for survival.

"Those must be the nights Irene goes to Pierce unasked! We can get everything ready and put the final part of our plan into place when we're certain a raid will occur."

"We could let her show up in Pierce's room, and then restrain her…somehow." Tav didn't like the idea of hurting the woman, even if she was part of Estmar's raids.

"Or I could say that Pierce asked for my company instead. Folk around the castle already know he's asked me to his room once. They'll believe it."

"You can't risk your reputation—" Tav started to say.

"There's not much risk," Robin said bluntly, "since no one knows who to tell. Nor will the common folk particularly care about spreading rumors surrounding a lady they can't name."

"I can't let you do that, Robin. And anyway, you'll probably be needed elsewhere. We're going to need all three of us to carry the supplies."

Robin looked to the keep, her gaze on the exact spot where Pierce's personal chamber was. "I have an idea."

Tav knew he wasn't going to like it.

After hammering out the details of Robin's plan—which Octavian objected to but couldn't counter with anything better—both of them spent the next few days subtly watching Estmar and the men around him, waiting for a sign that another raid was imminent. Meanwhile, Pierce played up his role as the moody lord. He only spoke to Tav in very public areas, to allay any suspicions. However, Pierce frequently found reasons to spend time with Robin, flirting with her shamelessly, using the situation to his advantage.

Worse, Robin not just tolerated Pierce, she actually seemed to enjoy being with the man. Tav told himself that she was playing a part, but it didn't help. He was jealous. He'd never been jealous of any man, and now he had to sit back and watch as Pierce toyed with a woman Tav couldn't get out of his mind.

He couldn't get out of this place fast enough.

On the fourth day, Robin found him in the castle courtyard in the early morning. She was bundled against the cold, wearing a thick velvet cloak, though her head was uncovered.

"It's happening tonight," she murmured, skipping all pleasantries.

"How do you know?"

"Irene told me that I was to refuse any invitation from Pierce this evening. She was adamant that she was going to entertain him all night, no matter what. And that must mean a raid is planned."

"What will Pierce do, now that his preferred companion won't be available?"

Robin shook her head. "Who cares? If I have to lose another game of chess, I'm going to toss the board into the fire."

"That's what you do with him? Play chess?"

"He adores it. And he adores winning at it even more. And I'm terrible. But I told him if he tried anything else, or even laid a finger on me, I'd slice the smirk off his face."

Tav repressed a laugh. "There's the Robin I know."

"I'm always the Robin you know."

Her words weren't meant to be suggestive, but the way they fell between them led Tav to remember exactly how well he'd got to know Robin the other night, how he'd touched her until she unraveled in the most innocent and sensuous way possible, and he couldn't think of anything else.

Robin must have been thinking the same thing, because her gaze was locked on him, and the desire in her eyes was unmistakable.

"Tav…" she began to say.

We can leave, he thought. Right now. Forget everything we're supposed to be doing here, and just leave together. We can go anywhere we decide to go.

That was what he wanted. He was certain she wanted it too, in the moment. And it was the most enticing idea he'd had in years.

But he made promises, and he had to deal with the matter at hand.

"How will you deal with Irene?" he asked, dragging his mind away from the memory of Robin turning to silk in his arms.

"Who?" she asked, sounding a little dazed. "Oh. Irene. The plan will still work. She'll help me get ready for bed before she goes to him. I'll take care of her then."

"You're certain this will work?"

"I'm not certain of anything!" Robin said. "But if we spend another day here, I'll hand him over to the Welsh myself."

Octavian took a breath. "Then tonight it is. By tomorrow morning, we'll be gone from Willesden."

She smiled at him, once again the trusting smile he associated with her before this maddening journey. "I can't wait."

Late that evening, Tav made his way through the manor house. The guards were easy enough to evade since only a few were around, the other men having gone off on the raid conducted by Estmar. The servants were more likely to appear in odd places, though Pierce promised when possible, he'd order tasks that would leave the path of escape clear. Still, Tav had to duck into a doorway when a kitchen boy hurried through the corridor with a covered dish in his hands. Tav waited until the smell of mutton stew drifted away after the boy, and then continued on.

He reached the place where he and Pierce were supposed to meet—a storeroom at the back of the keep, now empty. In better days it would have been filled with sacks of grain or other supplies, when Willesden supported three times the number of people who were there now.

Tav was early, so he leaned against the side wall and took a few long breaths, steadying himself for the possible confrontation to come. If everything went perfectly, then there would be no violence and no need to draw his sword. But Tav had been in enough situations to know things rarely went perfectly. It was entirely possible that he'd either kill or be killed by the time the sun rose.

The idea of death didn't frighten him. Death was inevitable, and there were far worse fates than dying with a sword in hand. What made him anxious was the idea that by dying, he would fail those who put their faith in him. His lord, Denis, who trusted Tav to such an extent that he could roam the whole island of Britain on his own. King Stephen, who needed Tav to succeed so he could stop a rebellion. The other knights, Luc and Rafe and especially Alric, who offered friendship to a stranger with no expectation of reward for it. And Robin, who might have got herself into this web, but who certainly needed Tav to get safely out of it.

To keep his promises to all of those people, Tav needed to live long enough to finish this. He'd get Pierce to a safe location and get the vital information to Stephen's forces in time. If he could do that, the other promises could be kept…somehow.

But for all that to happen, Pierce needed to actually arrive. Tav shifted from one foot to the other. Where was the man? Not for the first time, Tav wondered if Pierce was intending to betray Tav and Robin as part of some obscure plot of his own. This escape plan could be a trap so Pierce could have both of them ransomed, or executed, or worse.

Except that Pierce already had that power. He could have had both of them under lock and key if he wanted. Tav took another long breath. Pierce himself brought up the need for escape. He wouldn't betray Tav and Robin, because he needed them.

He thought of an old story he heard from Brother Petrus when he was at the monastery's school in Aleppo. Petrus loved little parables, whether from the Bible or elsewhere. One day, he told the story of the frog and the snake. A frog was hopping along in a forest when he smelled the terrible scent of smoke. The forest was on fire! He hopped as fast as he could to the river, intending to jump into the water and swim to the other side where the fire could not reach him. Other animals had the same thought, and those who could swim jumped into the water and swam frantically for the safety of the far shore. Others, those creatures who could not swim, moved about frantically, some going upstream in hopes of escaping the flames, some going downstream with the same idea. But the smoke was getting thicker and the heat was growing.

PEREGRINE'S CALL 178

Then the frog heard a hissing. It was a snake—a terrible, poisonous snake. But the snake very politely asked the frog if it could ride on its back across the river. A few other animals warned the frog not to listen. The snake would bite him and kill him. It was in the snake's nature and no one could trust such a creature. But the snake pleaded for its life and promised that it would never harm the frog, who would be its savior.

The frog allowed the snake upon its back, and began to swim across the river...and just in time. The fire raged toward the bank, and destruction was imminent. The snake raised its head and encouraged the frog to swim faster. When a log caught in the current rushed toward them, the snake warned the frog so they would not get hit. Later, he encouraged the tired frog to keep going, saying the other bank was very close.

Just as the exhausted frog climbed onto the bank, grateful to have escaped the fire, he felt a painful bite at his neck. The frog cried out, asking the snake why he'd done such a thing after promising not to, and after the frog saved the snake's life.

The snake looked sadly at the frog, saying, "You did save my life, and I am grateful. But the others warned you that I was not to be trusted. To bite and kill is in my nature."

Then the snake slithered away into the forest. The frog's vision clouded and it died upon the riverbank.

The moral of the story was obvious. Evil preyed upon good by exploiting good souls' natures to trust and forgive. Lord Pierce was definitely a snake. Betrayal was in his nature. He should have been here by now, and he wasn't.

Just as Tav was about to rise and leave with the intention of finding Robin on his own, he heard a new sound.

Footsteps. He gripped the hilt of his sword, ready to fight.

Then Pierce stepped into the dim room. A small pack was slung over his shoulder, and he carried a woven, covered hamper with leather straps on both sides. "Sir Octavian?" he asked softly. "Are you still here?"

"Here." Tav moved forward half a pace.

"Oh, thank God." Pierce heaved a breath. "I thought you might have left without me. I felt like I had to wait so long to move unseen."

"Did Irene come to your room?"

"No, I never saw her. Why?"

"No reason." Tav was relieved because it meant Robin did her part.

They moved to the back door of the keep, then Tav stopped. "Hold still, my lord. There's a guard about to cross the western courtyard on his way to the barracks. Then we'll have a few moments to move undetected."

"Why are there still so many people in this damned place?"

"Because you're a lord," Tav responded drily. "You wanted all those people here, and moving about unseen isn't your strength."

They both waited in silence, Pierce shifting on his feet with barely suppressed impatience until Tav signaled him to move.

Tav led the way, pointing to the direction where the curtain wall was damaged very badly years ago. Though men had been working to repair the massive breach, a large gap still remained. Even better, heavy scaffolding concealed the hole itself, and a few stacks of rocks and building materials provided even more cover.

They had less than a quarter hour before another guard was expected to pass by. Tav moved as quickly as he could from shadow to shadow. Pierce followed along, his own footsteps surprisingly silent for a man who was used to making himself known.

When they reached the first large rock pile, Pierce paused, looking furtively behind him. "Where's Robin?"

"Don't worry about her. She knows what to do."

"I thought you weren't leaving without her."

Tav signaled silence, having just seen a man's shape across the courtyard. Pierce nodded and took a step back...and bumped right into an armed guard.

"Sorry, Brower, I forgot my flask..." The young guard stared at Pierce. "You're not Brower...my lord! Halt."

At least he didn't shout, Tav thought as he continued to moved forward.

"I said halt!" the guard repeated, putting a hand on his sword hilt.

"Stand down," Pierce said, his voice calm and full of his usual authority. "What's your name?"

"Kevan, my lord," The guard saw Lord Pierce's grim face in the nighttime and abruptly took his hand away from the weapon. Respect for nobility was so ingrained that the guard would find it difficult to harm Pierce directly.

But even if the guard respected Pierce's nobility, he didn't look like he was about to let them leave.

"You can't be here, my lord. We've got orders! I can't let you leave. Either of you." He gripped his short sword tightly, but the glance he shot at Octavian betrayed how nervous the young man was. Octavian was better armed and better trained. Kevan took a breath and blustered, "Come along quietly, all right?"

"Shut up," Pierce growled. He turned to Octavian, saying, "He'll report everything. Kill him."

"Climb through the gap, my lord," Tav ordered. "I'll deal with the guard."

Tav moved, his frame effectively shielding Pierce while he scrambled over the rocks.

"I tell you, kill him!" said Pierce.

"Wait on the other side," Tav returned, not taking his eyes from the guard.

Kevan watched in consternation as Pierce began to vanish into the darkness, and then he suddenly rushed toward Tav.

Tav countered the attack easily and reached to grab the hilt of Kevan's sword.

Kevan gave a short cry of dismay as the weapon was unexpectedly wrenched from his hands. Then he stared at Octavian, who now held both swords.

"How'd you do that?"

"You overextended on your thrust," Tav explained. "Now, on your knees. Can't have you running away."

"I won't get a chance to learn not to do that, will I?" Kevan asked, swallowing nervously as he slowly sank to his knees. "You're going to kill me."

"I'd prefer not to," Tav said with absolute honesty.

Hope flickered in the young guard's eyes. "I won't say anything!"

"I'd like to believe that, but I can't take the risk."

"So you're going to kill me after all?"

Tav said, "I suggest that you close your eyes and pray for mercy."

Kevan bowed his head, muttering quickly and fervently to a whole pantheon of saints.

Octavian quickly swung the hilt of his sword toward Kevan's left temple. The guard went silent and sagged forward.

Tav caught him by the shoulders just before his head hit the ground. He laid the short sword nearby and then turned to the curtain wall. He clambered through the gap, praying that no one heard the brief clash of swords, or if they did, they'd assume it was just a clumsy man dropping a weapon, rather than a fight.

"That was quick," Pierce said once Tav reached the other side. "I didn't even hear a cry."

"I didn't kill him," Tav said. "I just knocked him out."

"What? Why did you let him live when you could have silenced him forever? That will come back to haunt us sooner rather than later. Fool!"

Tav shrugged. "It's in my nature."

Chapter 22

FROM HER VANTAGE POINT IN the shadow of the trees, Robin saw Pierce emerge from the broken part of the curtain wall. He pushed a large sort of basket through, then sidled several feet over, but didn't move farther. She could hear nothing from where she hid, and she waited in an agony until she saw Octavian appear a little while later. When no yells or flares from torches followed him, she allowed herself a small sigh of relief.

The men made their way to where Robin waited. She was once again dressed in the brown monk's robe, and it fluttered around her as she stood up.

Pierce stumbled backward, startled by her movement. "God's wounds!" he muttered. "What's there?"

"Me, my lord," she said in a low voice. "I've got our supplies." She had dropped the wrapped bundles over the walls earlier, using the darkness as cover. She slipped through the gap after waiting for the guard on duty to pass by, long before the men followed.

The most nerve-wracking part had been getting Irene safely out of the way. The maid came up to help Robin prepare for bed, bringing the mulled wine Robin specially requested. Robin had to slip a dose of poppy syrup into the glass without Irene noticing, and then trick Irene into drinking it herself. Luckily, the maid's desire for a warm, rich drink outweighed the expectations that a servant should not indulge in the luxuries meant for her betters.

Robin waited until Irene succumbed to the medicine, got her to bed, and then pulled the blankets over the sleeping woman. Drawing the curtains helped even more. With luck, Irene would slumber till sunrise, blissfully unaware of the escape until it was far too late.

"Any issues with your side of the plan?" she asked Tav.

Pierce answered before Tav could. "He didn't kill the guard who saw us."

"Knocked him out," Tav explained.

"Will we regret that?" she asked him.

"Possibly. But I'm not dwelling on it." Tav gave Robin a quick smile, and bent to gather some of the bundled supplies. He heaved them over his back, and ordered Pierce to do the same with the others.

The lord grumbled at the need for labor, but mimicked Tav's actions. Finally, he hefted the woven hamper he'd brought himself, holding it as though the contents might break. "Where are the horses?"

"Hidden," Robin said, slinging her own pack and quiver across her shoulders and picking up her bow. "Follow me."

She led the men on a more or less direct route to where she'd seen that barn on the day she and Tav first came upon the Willesden woodgatherers. As she picked her way through the nighttime forest, she prayed that the barn held the animals they needed to escape. She'd ride a mule if she had to, but the men would require suitable horses.

Pierce cursed every time branches whipped past their faces or a tree root rose up too high. Behind him, Octavian warned him to be silent.

"Where are the horses?" Pierce asked instead. "How'd you get them out of the castle unnoticed?"

"We didn't," Robin explained in a low voice. "We're going to retrieve some horses that Estmar stole in one of his raids."

Then Robin told him of their suspicions, and how the raid happening at the moment was actually the key to their escape. Pierce sounded livid about Estmar's actions, swearing to discipline the man if he ever got his hands on him.

"Best to hope we don't encounter Estmar and his company anytime soon, my lord," Tav said. "We want to be gone by the time the raiders return."

They reached the hidden barn. Robin eased open the door, hoping no one was within. She heard only the quiet sounds of farmyard animals at rest, and inhaled the smells of hay, feed, and manure. She lit the lantern kept inside and saw their prize—a half dozen horses stabled at one side.

She moved over to them, surveying their quality. Most were farm nags, but one was lovely looking creature of good quality stock, with a coat that glowed a reddish-gold in the lantern light. She pointed to it. "Octavian, saddle that one for yourself. Pierce should ride this grey one, and I'll take the roan." The roan looked attentively at her, and Robin suspected the horse would run well if given leave to.

"I should have the finest," Pierce said flatly.

"Octavian needs the strongest, biggest mount in case of a fight," she countered. "Now work quickly."

A short while later, they led the saddled horses out of the barn. They'd just mounted up when a shout echoed through the woods.

"You there! Stop! Thieves!" A contingent of men was approaching on horses. They didn't yet recognize Robin, Octavian, and Pierce, but they would.

Slowing them down was imperative.

Mounted on her horse and with a good view of the advancing group, Robin had an arrow ready almost instantly. She aimed and let the arrow fly. A moment later, one of the attacking men cried out in surprise and pain. He fell off the horse, the arrow protruding from his thigh.

By then, Robin already had the next arrow nocked.

"I thought he was the soldier!" Pierce hissed, looking at her with newfound horror.

She loosed the next arrow, which whistled past the leading horse's ears, spooking it and forcing the rider to wheel about to regain control, fouling up the progress of the others.

She smiled in satisfaction, but then heard more hoofbeats in the distance.

Octavian looked to Robin, yelling, "We can't fight them all off. Ride!"

She wheeled about, plunging forward along the eastern track.

The three horses pounded along the narrow path. Robin was in the lead, her gaze locked on the ground, a pale strip illuminated only by moonlight. Pierce followed. She could hear him muttering under his breath, urging the horses to go faster. Tav rode last, since he was the most capable of defending the group should anyone catch up. He was also the only one of them wearing armor.

Still, Robin feared an archer might sent an arrow flying toward them long before any riders caught up. Tav's chain mail would do little to deflect an arrow. Whether shot from a sturdy longbow or with the terrifying power of a crossbow, a metal arrowhead could easily bite through the chain links to strike the flesh underneath.

She took a ragged breath, trying to shake the image of Tav being injured. Ahead of her, the track split.

She turned in the saddle and shouted, "To the left!" The left path was likely to turn toward the north, and she hoped that their pursuers would assume they went the other way—south to lead them most quickly to a road eventually reaching London.

She guided her horse down the left-hand path and heard hoofbeats behind her, signaling that both Pierce and Tav followed.

"Faster!" Pierce called, his voice just loud enough to be heard.

Robin grimaced. Any faster and they'd all stumble on the path, leading to injury or worse. She chanced a look behind, but could see nothing beyond Tav. The original path was hidden.

A splashing sound brought her attention back to the front. Her horse trod through a shallow stream, one of hundreds in the Ardenwood. She tugged the reins to guide the horse into the water, walking upstream until she could find a good crossing point. Any method to fool dogs or trackers would be a boon.

Icy water droplets splashed up at her, but she continued onward to the pebbly bank on the other side, beckoning the others to follow suit. Octavian kept looking over his shoulder.

Picking up a new track, Robin felt confident for the first time since they bolted out of Willesden. The land around her, the way the streams flowed, even the smell in the air...all of it was deeply familiar. She kept up the pace for another half hour or so, and then Octavian called out just loud enough to be heard.

"Robin. Halt for a little while. They're not following us any longer."

She pulled the roan to a stop, glad of the break. She looked to Tav and smiled, then noticed Pierce's expression twisted into a scowl.

"What's the matter, my lord?" she asked. "You asked to be taken safely away from your castle, and we've done so. You should be pleased." *Or at least grateful.*

"Why should I be pleased, here in the cold and the dark with no sleep and no hope of finding a haven before we all freeze to death?"

"You're exaggerating," she said.

"Am I? We're in the middle of a dangerous forest at night, with few supplies, no help, and very likely about to be pursued by an even greater force of armed men. As soon as Estmar hears of what happened, he'll chase us with dogs. He'll send word to Ranulf too, and Ranulf will do everything he can to kill me. Meanwhile, we'll just wander around the woods, completely lost."

"You're lost," she said. "But I'm not. If we keep up a good pace, we'll reach shelter by dawn."

"Dawn?" The lord looked aghast.

"Sorry your rescue is inconvenient." Tav sent one glance at the other man, then nodded to Robin. "Lead on."

She straightened up, the weariness fading a bit with Tav's encouragement.

"Why is *she* leading us?" Pierce asked.

Exhilaration flooded through Robin's veins. She was free, after days of confinement. "Because the Ardenwood is my home!"

Chapter 23

ROBIN KNEW THE WAY TO Rainald's old camp in her
bones. She couldn't explain why she turned right when
she saw a certain hill, or why she laughed when she
passed by an ancient tree with wide, twisted, moss-covered branches.

It was an hour past dawn when she saw the outer walls
of the old camp. She drew an arrow from her quiver and
readied it, just in case unfriendly types had moved into
the camp since she'd left it. Behind her, she heard the men
drawing steel, responding to her own movements.

But the camp was deserted. The quietude filling the
place was broken only by the soft sounds of the forest—
birds in the high trees, and the wind playing with the few
leaves left on the branches.

"It's safe," she announced as she rode in through the
open gate.

Octavian looked around skeptically, his eyes darting
from one place to another as he assessed possible threats.
Pierce just exhaled, his spine bent with weariness.

They all dismounted and walked around the old camp.

It had been five years since she left this place, but time
and the forest were already devouring the evidence that
people had lived here. The wooden stockade fence sur-

rounding the camp was green with moss. Many of the posts were rotting from the top, causing the fence to lean inward at some points and outward at others. Some holes at the base were large enough to allow wildlife through.

The structures inside fared better, probably because they'd been built out of sturdier materials. Cottages that had been barracks for the outlaws still stood, the roofs mostly intact. The house that had been Rainald's own—tucked under a spreading oak—also stood, but Robin felt uneasy about entering it. Even when she lived here, Rainald's home was something special. She was called there by the lord himself, and never entered without permission.

"This is your so-called haven, Lady Robin?" Pierce asked at last. "It looks like an outlaw's den."

She smiled. "You're not entirely wrong."

The lord turned to Octavian. "So she's dragged us to a deserted lair for raiders and masterless men. Is this where she learned her archery?"

"I stand before you, my lord," Robin said. "You could ask me. And yes, I learned it in the Ardenwood. I hunted game like all the others who called—" She broke off abruptly, just before she was about to announce Rainald's name. Pierce must never realize she was connected to Lord de Vere.

Pierce noticed her odd silence, but he said only, "Why did you not flinch when you had to shoot at men instead of game?"

"I defended the camp when I had to, and I defended myself whenever the need arose. You think women can't fight?"

"*Ladies* are not meant to fight."

"Lady Robin seems to be unusual," Tav said from where he stood nearby.

"Oh, don't keep up this charade," Pierce sneered. "I've heard you both. I've seen you both. I accepted your flimsy story about a meek Lady Robin being stranded in the woods until the brave Sir Octavian happened by to rescue her. But you both talk and act as if you've known each other for your whole lives. I won't ask what the truth is. Just don't think you're fooling me."

Robin looked to Tav, who gave a shrug and said, "Let him think what he likes."

The words were noncommittal, but Robin sensed the warning in them. Pierce was pretending not to care, but he was man who thrived on secrets. If he found out who Robin was, he'd use it to hurt her somehow. Tav wouldn't tell him, and neither would Robin.

"Yes," she said calmly, with a slight nod to Tav. "Let him think what he likes."

The sun was rising higher, a pale yellow disk in the hazy sky. They'd have to rest—both themselves and the horses.

"We'll use this cottage," she said, pointing to the best preserved one. "There's plenty of dry wood around to make a fire. Pierce can gather it and stack it by the door."

"I will not," he retorted. "I don't take orders from those beneath me. Not a knight from some desert waste. And especially not a common-born girl playing at being a lady."

The words stung. Robin opened her mouth to reply, but her words failed her.

Octavian, however, had no trouble responding. Tav didn't even draw his sword. He just stood at his full height and looked down at Pierce. "You'll do as she says. From this moment, until you're no longer my responsibility, you have one duty, which is to obey every little instruction given to you."

"Or what? You'll kill me? You're charged with my safe passage to the king."

"I won't kill you," Tav said. "But I can shut the cottage door and leave you outside to sleep in the cold."

Pierce only laughed.

Tav went on, "And you'll have to learn to sleep with your wrists and ankles bound. Can't have you stealing a horse and riding off."

The laugh died in Pierce's throat. Robin saw the flash of anger in his eyes, either from the insult of being tied up...or the fact that Tav guessed Pierce was planning on slipping away if he could.

She said, "The horses need a full day's rest, and feeding, before anyone can ride again. Let's unload everything, and tether them away from the gate." The horses could crop the grass that had grown all throughout the clear areas of the camp. As for their own food, she could easily set some rabbit traps nearby, but first she wanted to sleep. She was bone tired.

Octavian had begun to unburden the horses. He reached for the woven, boxy basket on Pierce's horse.

"Don't jostle the basket!" the lord warned suddenly.

"What's in it?"

The basket emitted a meow just as Pierce said, "Never mind."

"You packed Govannon?" Robin asked. "We're fleeing from your enemies, we each could only take the essentials, and you took a *cat*?"

"He's an essential ally," said Pierce. "And what does it matter to you?"

Tav just shook his head. "If the cat runs off, we're not going to chase after it."

Pierce dropped the single chunk of firewood he'd picked up and stormed over to take charge of the basket.

He undid the leather strap, and the head of the white cat popped up, its eyes surveying its new surroundings with much the same expression as Pierce himself first had. Robin stifled a hysterical giggle. Was she so exhausted that the mere sight of a cat could wreck her?

Soon enough, a fire was burning, warming the cottage they'd chosen to use. They all rolled out the bedding Robin had packed as part of the bundles she'd tossed over the walls. Octavian said someone should stay awake, but the next thing Robin knew, it was late afternoon. All three of them had slept the entire day.

She sat up, yawning and fiercely hungry. She'd packed some food, and now she retrieved it from the supplies.

Octavian woke next, looking much more alert than he had in the morning. Then Pierce, who'd fallen asleep with Govannon perched on his chest, yawned and carefully removed the cat.

"We're still alive," Pierce said, sounding surprised.

Tav nodded. "Despite being completely unconscious and defenseless all day. The Lord has been kind to us."

"But the men who are chasing us will not be," said Robin. "Can we assume they want us all dead? Can they be bargained with?"

Pierce looked despondently around the water-stained walls of the cottage. "Some of the men who took bribes from the Welsh might be. But Estmar is in the pay of Lord Ranulf, and he won't stop following me until I'm either captured or dead."

"If you knew Estmar was Ranulf's man, why didn't you get rid of him?"

"Because part of the terms I struck with Ranulf included taking Estmar in my retinue," he admitted. "Ranulf does that with all his alliances. Estmar kept an eye on me, to see that I didn't betray Ranulf."

"How does he send messages to Ranulf to let him know what's happening?"

"He had a whole cage of pigeons that knew where to fly. You can be sure he'll have sent one to Ranulf already."

Tav was frowning. "Why do you want to switch sides at all? You could simply have gone to Ranulf himself and asked for help to get Malvern back."

"Ranulf lacks both the strength and the time to aid me. He's wholly focused on his own ends." Pierce, a man also wholly focused on his own ends, sneered, apparently despising the trait in other people. "I knew that my only hope for regaining Malvern Castle on my own terms was to act myself. So I'll exchange the information I have about Ranulf's plans for the support I need to retake Malvern."

Octavian looked to Robin. She sensed he wanted to talk to her in private. She finished her food and stood up, stretching. "Well, nothing to be done about that now. I'm going to set a few traps for tonight. With luck, we'll have a better meal tomorrow than we do now."

Tav also stood. "I need to check on the horses and the equipment. My lord, you can remain here."

"This is where the fire is," Pierce said, as if it were only natural that he should be idle while they worked.

Robin used the last of the afternoon light to set a few rabbit snares just outside the camp's wall. Rabbits were not the brightest creatures, and she anticipated catching a brace at least. That task done, she set out to find Tav.

She found him sitting near Rainald's old dwelling, out of sight of the cottage but with a view of the camp's gate. He was cleaning his sword, examining the edge of the blade with critical eyes.

"I thought you didn't have to use that during the escape," she said, wondering if he'd blooded it and then told her otherwise to spare her feelings.

But Tav said, "No, but I still drew it several times, so I want to be sure there's no moisture to corrode it."

She nodded, knowing how meticulous he was about his equipment. All the knights were.

Tav put the sword aside and stood up, facing her. "How are you?"

Robin rolled her shoulders. "I'm well. Why?"

"Because we're here, in Rainald's old camp. One of the few places you called home, and now it's empty and decaying."

His insight made her pause as she considered both his words and the fact that he was astute enough to guess her feelings. "It's a little sad," she confessed. "But only a little. Rainald is back in his true home now, with the power and authority he always should have had."

"That's well for Rainald. But what about you?" He stepped close and reached out to cup Robin's face in his hands. "You've been peering into every corner of this old camp."

Robin had to tilt her head up to meet his eyes. "Just... remembering."

"Good or bad?"

"Mostly good. You needn't worry about me. And anyway, we won't be here long. We need to keep moving."

"You're certain you're all right?" he asked, his eyes still on her face.

Without consciously deciding she would do it, Robin stood on her tiptoes and opened her mouth for a kiss.

He responded with a fierceness that lit a fire in her, starting in her belly and spreading outward to her limbs.

She wrapped her arms around him, needing the kiss more than she'd ever anticipated. She wanted to have his hands on her again, feel his mouth all over her, and she wanted to taste him in all the same ways. She clung to him, her breathing rough as he sucked on her lower lip until she was whimpering against his mouth.

Finally, he broke it off. "Enough, lovely," he told her, even though his expression suggested he hadn't got nearly enough of what she was offering to him.

"You don't want more?" Robin asked. *She* wanted more. She wanted days and days of this strangely wonderful torture, the anticipation and then the fulfillment. Possibly months. Or years. A lifetime would be best.

"What I want and what's going to happen are two different things," he said. His fingers grazed her neck, and the shivery pleasure shot straight into her core. "Though the idea is extremely tempting." He leaned toward her and kissed her again, this time with a tenderness that left her breathless. "It's not the time or the place to indulge in something like this."

"It's never going to be the right time or place for us, is it?" she asked, her chest aching.

"I don't know, Robin." He shook his head and stepped away. "We're still far away from where we need to be. And we're not safe in any sense of the word."

For a moment, she *had* completely forgotten they were likely being pursued by people who wanted them dead. She was much happier before she remembered it.

"How long do you think we can stay here?" he asked, sounding much more collected.

She thought about it. "A few nights. The camp was designed to be difficult to reach unless you know where it is. But we can't just hole up here. The information Pierce carries grows less useful with every passing day."

"The main road will be far too risky. We've got Estmar's men chasing us from one angle, and now perhaps a force from Ranulf himself coming soon."

She nodded. "Not to mention the usual dangers in the Ardenwood—outlaws and the Welsh."

"And the weather itself is turning against us," Tav said. "Every day shorter and every night colder."

"I'll get us through the forest," Robin said. "And I don't need the main road to do it."

"You've already proven that." He gave her a smile. "I just hope—"

Then he broke off, looking at something to his right, in the clearing of the camp.

"What is it?" she whispered.

"Not sure." His eyes narrowed. Then he exhaled. "Never mind. It's only the cat."

"I can't believe he brought the cat." She sighed. "It's so sad."

"It's idiotic."

"Well, it was poorly planned, yes. But it's mostly sad."

"Why?" Tav watched her now.

"Because it just shows that he has no one. He's with two strangers and a cat. His enemies are chasing him. And his best chance for salvation lies with a king he never supported."

"Don't be tricked into pitying him."

"It's not a trick," she said. "It's a simple observation. Anyway, Pierce doesn't want to be pitied—he wants to be feared. But no one fears him now, which is why he's being such an ass."

Tav gave a short laugh. "That part is true enough. If I have to live with his complaints for much longer, I may have to gag him."

"I'd be quite comfortable with that," she said.

Chapter 24

DESPITE A FULL DAY OF sleep, the trio was tired and quiet that evening. Two fresh rabbits provided the meal. They had two wineskins left, one of which Robin concealed in the supplies.

Tonight, Pierce didn't complain about the quality of his meal and accommodations. In fact, he was uncharacteristically sedate. Robin was melancholy, and kept watching the flames leap in the small hearth.

After eating, Octavian stood and said he was going to check on the horses again, and then walk around the camp to ensure all was well. Robin nodded, grateful he was so alert.

After Tav left, Pierce looked over to her. "Who are you, truly, that you know this forest so well?"

"I already told you." She looked up from the fire, giving him a smirk. "And as for who I am, you may call me Lady Robin of Ardenwood."

"That's no real title."

"Titles are only as real as the power behind them," she said. "Right now, I know where we are, how to stay alive, and how to get where we want to go. Whereas you have no money, no allies, and no sense of direction. Perhaps you'd better stop whining about titles and such."

Pierce's expression twisted into something dark for a

moment, but then he sighed. "You make a sound argument...my lady."

He looked into the fire, then said, "Where are we, specifically? How far are we from Willesden, or Malvern? How far from Hereford? Or Lincoln?"

"We're well south and west of Malvern, as you can guess. Willesden is many leagues from here, though I think that by crossing all those rivers and streams as we did, it might as well be over the sea and in Ireland. Your pursuers won't pick up our trail."

"So we're safe. We can ride out to a main road and ride to London tomorrow."

"Not so fast, my lord. I said your pursuers won't pick up our trail. But they will certainly guess our ultimate destination. If I were them, having lost my quarry, I'd reach the main road as fast as I could and then lie in wait, hoping to catch my quarry again."

"We can't hide here," he protested in dismay.

"Of course not. We'll continue toward London, but not by the expected path."

"That will take too long," he said.

"The other option is that you could tell *us* what you know. What precious message do you have for the king? Tell Octavian and he could pass the message on within a few days."

Pierce shook his head sharply. "No. I'm not a fool. If I give up what I know without a promise in return, I'll have no leverage at all."

"Telling what you know without expectation of reward would be a show of faith. You'd be rewarded for that."

He grimaced. "You're a naive little girl, aren't you? Didn't you hear how King Stephen rewards men who offer him aid? Do you not know of what happened to Ranulf himself?"

In truth, Robin had no idea. There were so many earls and barons involved in the war, it was hard to keep track. "What happened?"

"Last year, Earl Ranulf changed his allegiance from the empress to King Stephen. He went to Stephen and offered to share what he knew about Maud and her Welsh allies. In return, all he asked was for Stephen to allow him to retain Lincoln Castle."

"It sounds as if you've a similar plan," Robin noted.

"Yes, but I know that I must be more careful than Ranulf. You see, Stephen heard what Ranulf had to say. He used it to win against his enemies at Lincoln. But how did Stephen repay his new and loyal supporter? He imprisoned Ranulf, despite swearing an oath he would not. For months, Ranulf was at the mercy of the king, who accused him of treason."

"But he was released," Robin said.

"Only after his friends begged the king to do so. Stephen gave in after wringing the harshest terms from Ranulf. He was to surrender all his lands and castles—even Lincoln. He was to give hostages. And for the final touch, he had to take an oath not to resist the king in future."

"Did Ranulf give such an oath?" asked Robin.

"He said the words, but his oath lasted less than a day after he was freed. He gathered his forces and attacked Lincoln, hoping to recover it for himself. He failed. But he is not finished. Stephen will regret crossing Ranulf."

Robin frowned. She didn't say what she was thinking, which was that both Ranulf and Pierce seemed to hold contradictory views on loyalty. They switched sides on a whim, yet frothed with rage when King Stephen himself showed any breach of trust. She sighed. "This war is so confusing. Is there any alliance that will last until the end?"

"All I know is that neither Maud nor Stephen think of others beneath them." Pierce shrugged. "So I must think of myself and protect my life and my legacy as best I can." He caught her skeptical look, and added, "It's easy for you to sit in judgment, Lady Robin of Ardenwood. But tell me, have you ever been called into the presence of royalty and asked to give your lands or your funds or your men to the cause? Despite not knowing if that same royal figure would truly help you in return?"

Robin shook her head slowly. "I'm not important enough for any king or queen to care about. But I do know that it's men like you, who change sides every season, who make kings and queens demand such oaths in the first place."

"How important are you, Lady Robin?" Pierce asked curiously. "You've been very coy about your birth and your associations."

"And I will continue to be so," she snapped back. "All you need to know, my lord, is that you won't want to marry me, and you won't want to ransom me. Both of those things would end in great disappointment for you." Robin had no political or monetary worth.

Pierce nodded, but didn't look quite convinced. "You say that, yet you're worth something to Sir Octavian, are you not?"

The memory of their kiss that afternoon flared up in her mind. But she responded cautiously. "Only in the sense that he is too honorable to leave me somewhere alone. But when he takes me back home, he'll leave afterward. He must return to his own lord. That is how it is for knights, especially in a time of war."

Pierce nodded. "We're living in anarchy, and anarchy is kind to no one, unless you're strong enough to make your own way. But you're far stronger than you let on, Lady Robin."

She glanced at him. "Was that a compliment?"

He smiled, a real smile, his eyes crinkling at the corners. In that moment, she understood how he got so many people to listen to him over the years. "A compliment, yes. But also the truth. And don't think I'm not grateful for what you've done for me, getting me away from Willesden when I thought I'd be trapped there forever. I'll remember that."

She didn't know what to say in response, and then Octavian entered, and she felt flustered.

"You both should sleep," the knight said, his expression unreadable. "We'll ride out tomorrow at dawn."

In fact, Robin awoke well before dawn, eager to be on the road. The men woke and ate quickly. They saddled the horses and confined Govannon to his basket once again. To Robin's surprise, the cat hadn't run away in the night.

Octavian rode last in line, and he took the time to push the great wooden door of the outer stockade wall closed before he mounted up. The whole wall blended into the forest, nearly invisible. Tav's action was likely a tactical decision to discourage anyone noticing the place and going in. But Robin felt her heart lurch a bit when the door shut, as if she'd never be able to get into the camp again.

Why would I want to? she asked herself. The camp was abandoned and slowly decaying, and there was no reason for her to return.

She shook off the feeling and directed the party through the deepest part of the Ardenwood. This was the area of the forest that people told stories about. Stories of lawless men who attacked travelers, monsters who dwelled in caves, fairies who snatched children away, and even stranger tales of spirits and ancient beings. The only common thread in the stories was the warning that the Ardenwood was dangerous.

Robin respected the message behind the stories, even though she didn't believe most of them. She still rode carefully, keeping her eyes out for danger, and never letting herself fall into daydreaming, lest she lose the path.

They made good time for the first part of the day. They crossed countless little brooks and ridged hills, threading through the quiet woods. They startled a herd of deer, and were in turn startled by a fox dashing past the horses.

Cloud-covered skies meant that it was difficult to see exactly which direction they were going. Robin, using her knowledge of the area, kept turning to the south whenever she had the chance, but the twisting paths and the hills made it almost impossible for the others to know she was doing so.

Pierce called a halt at one point. "I need to piss, and I don't need a guard along the way."

"All right," Tav said evenly.

"No objections? No warnings?"

"No objections…as long as you dismount and leave the horse with us."

Once Pierce walked off into the trees, Tav rode up closer to Robin. "Which direction are we going at the moment?"

"Almost due south," she replied. "I haven't seen a good route leading back eastward yet."

"That's not my concern," he said, shooting a glance toward the way Pierce had gone.

"Don't we want to go to London?"

"Pierce suggested that rather strongly, but I'm not inclined to bow to his whim on every matter."

"You don't trust him."

"Not even a little bit. Pierce is being too sanguine about this whole escape. He's definitely not told us everything, and he won't share what he knows unless he has no other choice."

"So what do we do? If you fear he could run away, you could restrain him."

"I don't want to alert him to my suspicions, and restraining a man for two weeks of travel is far more trouble than it's worth. We need him to cooperate."

"We could go somewhere besides London. Or stop our journey somewhere, send a message, and wait for aid." She didn't say it, but the obvious answer was Cleobury.

"We can't go to Cleobury," Tav said, just as if she had spoken out loud. "Pierce would fight us the moment he realized the destination."

"Then how about Martenkeep?" she suggested. Martenkeep was a newly refortified castle lying very close to the Welsh border. Robin had been there several times, since the castellan was a close friend of the de Vere family. Sir Rafe had worked endlessly to make his castle a stronghold that even the fiercest enemy would think twice about attacking.

Tav shook his head. "Rafe was also involved in the fiasco. Pierce will remember him."

"But that happened before Rafe learned his true name and title. At most, all Pierce would know is that Martenkeep has a castellan named Raphael Corviser. What are the chances that he'd connect that name to a soldier he once encountered five years ago in a different place entirely?"

Octavian stared into the distance, his expression considering. "Very well. We'll head for Martenkeep. But keep our destination to yourself. The less Pierce knows, the better for all of us."

At that moment, a rustling in the trees signaled Pierce's return. He remounted, and they continued on.

The weather grew colder throughout the afternoon. Robin doubted they'd find any sort of shelter as good as the camp, and she was correct. The best she could discover was a shallow cave, barely more than an overhang in the rock. On the journey north, she and Octavian had slept in a similar place with no difficulty. But it was weeks later, and the shift toward winter was dramatic. The horses remained close together all evening, as did the people. The fire burned fitfully, and sleep proved elusive when a cold rain began to fall in the middle of the night.

The next day, the group continued, their moods all much worse. Robin wore the monk's robe over her boy's clothing and wrapped her cloak over that. She still shivered. Pierce grumbled to himself, and snapped out answers to even the most benign questions. Octavian said very little, remaining stoic about the weather. But whenever Robin glanced back at him and he didn't realize she was doing so, his expression was miserable.

The rain stopped shortly before noon, but then a sharp wind swept through, chilling them further. Robin sensed snow in the air and worried about the horses if the path should turn icy.

An hour later, Robin called for a halt by the edge of the creek. The horses all came to a standstill, nickering in the frigid air. She turned her own horse in a small circle, looking around carefully.

"What is it?" Pierce asked nervously. "Are we being followed?"

"No. I mean, yes, I'm sure your onetime friends are somewhere to the north, hoping to find us and kill us, but that's not why I'm stopping."

"We should keep moving," he said. "I *insist* we keep

moving."

"Shut up," Octavian said. "Let Robin think."

"Why?"

"Have you learned nothing?" Tav sounded irritated as he replied. "Because she's our guide and our only chance to get through the Ardenwood in one piece."

Robin nodded. "See that stand of pine trees by the creek? There's another path that begins very close to here. The creek is a marker. I just need to remember if it's upstream or downstream from this point."

"Guess one and let's move," Pierce said.

"No. If I'm wrong, we'll lose precious hours and perhaps walk right into our enemies. Now hush."

Robin took a deep breath and closed her eyes, listening to the sounds around her. She remembered a time many years ago when she stood in this very place, a lone girl in the woods, hoping to track down game or find a homestead or farm where she might beg for some food.

More memories came flooding back to her. She had found a farm nearby. An old couple gave her bread before she could even ask, and then told her how to get to the nearest village.

"We go upstream," she announced, nudging her horse forward.

Pierce looked worried. "You're sure?"

"She said we go upstream," Tav nearly growled, his usual patience evaporating in the cold. "After you, my lord."

Robin grew more confident as she went on. When the light began to fail, the sky sliding into ever deeper shades of grey, Octavian called out, "Shouldn't we look for a place to sleep tonight?"

She turned in her saddle. "There's a village up ahead. And it has an inn."

Pierce smiled, but Tav shook his head. "Inns mean people, and people mean gossip. Is there somewhere else, somewhere protected from the weather?"

Robin bit her lip. "Maybe."

"I have money to pay for an inn," Pierce said. "And I for one think that another night in the cold will hurt us." Hearing a meow, he loosened the buckle on the basket tied to the horse. The lid was pushed up from within, and Govannon's face appeared. The cat looked at them with pure sadness in its eyes.

Robin's heart lurched. She didn't mind seeing Pierce shiver, but to abuse the cat or the horses any further would be cruel.

"We must risk it," she said to Tav. "We'll arrive after dark, and if we leave early in the morning... Anyway, Estmar and the others don't know what route we're traveling since we never even stepped onto the main road through the wood."

Octavian looked unsure, but then nodded. "The horses will recover far better in a stable than outside. We might actually make better time tomorrow."

Pierce muttered praise to God on hearing he'd sleep indoors. But if Robin thought that meant he'd be more pleasant to deal with, she was mistaken.

Chapter 25

NOT FOR THE FIRST TIME, nor for the last time, Robin wanted to slap Pierce across the face. From the moment he entered the inn, Pierce seemed determined to display the worst traits of the upper class. He talked down to the innkeeper, who was a perfectly pleasant woman of middle age. He looked around the ground floor as if it were no better than a sty, when in fact the front room and the tavern beyond were scrubbed, with clean rushes spread upon the floors, and had several lit sconces to chase away the darkness.

The innkeeper said that the upper sleeping loft was empty, but Pierce waved the suggestion off.

"I require a private chamber. It's absurd to think that I would be content with anything less."

"We do have a separate bedchamber," the innkeeper said, her eyes taking in Pierce's travel-stained but expensive clothing. "Though there is no need since we have no other guests now. You and your companions would have the entire floor to yourselves." She spoke slowly, as if debating whether she ought to have mentioned it. Many innkeepers would have jumped at the chance to earn a few more coins by renting as many beds as possible.

"You don't need a private chamber," Tav said, his eyes narrow. "And I'll feel better if I know what you're up to."

Pierce sneered. "You can't stay awake all night."

"Care to wager?"

The innkeeper held up her hands. "Oh, no. That's enough! I don't know what you're about, sirs, but I don't want to host trouble. You can eat in the tavern, but no rooms tonight."

"Wait, wait, wait." Pierce pulled out several coins, the shine of copper and silver gleaming in the candlelight. "You don't want to make a living?"

The innkeeper gnawed her lip, eyes locked on the money. "Well…a private chamber for you and your wife, and the soldier will sleep in the common room himself?"

"I am no man's wife," Robin said before she thought better of it. Then she remembered Geoffrey Ballard for the first time in weeks and wondered if he'd even heard or cared that Robin was missing from Cleobury.

The innkeeper was clearly puzzled at how such an odd collection of travelers ended up at her door. "Oh. I have only one private bedchamber, but you may sleep with my barmaids if that is preferable?" Perhaps she was offering Robin escape from the two men.

Robin just shook her head. "I thank you, but a pallet in the common room is fine. My assistance may be needed at any time." Such as if Pierce decided to run away in the middle of the night.

Tav said, "You can stay with the women if you like. The choice is yours."

"So she can sleep where she likes, but you tell *me* what to do?" Pierce complained.

"I trust Robin. I don't trust you." Tav's words were as blunt as they were honest.

Pierce muttered something under his breath.

Robin suspected he hoped that the lure of a hot meal and a soft bed would make Tav sleep while Pierce escaped. Pierce underestimated Octavian, though. The knight would never let down his guard. He'd watch until dawn if he had to, no matter if it deprived him of his own rest.

But he'd already suffered several days and nights of short sleep and hard travel. No matter how highly trained and dedicated he was, Tav was mortal. If only Robin could talk sense into Pierce, or exact a promise that he'd stay put. But how could she trust the ever-changeable lord?

A short while later, Robin wondered if Pierce would even survive long enough to make an escape attempt. The inn's servants would surely want to murder him, given the chance. He wanted more firewood stacked up in his private chamber, just in case. He wanted fresh rushes strewn near the bed. He wanted chopped meat brought up expressly for Govannon. He wanted a pillow expressly for Govannon. The servants were a maid of about fourteen years old and younger boy. Their coloring and expressions were so similar that Robin didn't even ask if they were siblings. The girl nodded mutely at every request, though her expression grew pinched by her third trek up the stairs. The boy groused at the many trips to the woodpile, but looked astonished when Octavian offered to help.

"No, sir! Mum would strike me flat if she saw a guest doing my job!"

So the two weren't just siblings, they were the children of the innkeeper herself, Robin thought. They lived and worked together every day of their lives. She watched the girl pause in her duties to whisper a joke to her brother and felt a pang at the closeness they shared.

Then Pierce demanded hot water for a bath, which the servants brought. Then he claimed the water wasn't hot enough. So they brought hotter water, enough to scald a person. Just as Pierce was about to tell the girl to assist him in bathing, Robin dismissed her. The girl gave her a relieved glance and fled the room.

"Now who will help me?" he asked.

Robin said, "You seem old enough to bathe yourself."

"It's less satisfying that way."

She sighed in annoyance at his innuendo, but she still felt a flush creep into her cheeks. However, Pierce ceased his taunting and took his bath without further discussion. Robin kept her attention on the fire, tending it more than necessary. Behind her, she heard only some splashing and one warning for Govannon to stay away from the folded towel.

A moment later, Pierce said, "Robin, the cat is sleeping on my towel! Grab it!"

"The cat or the towel?" she asked as she stood up. She turned around, and only then realized that Pierce had stood up in the bath, his naked, dripping-wet body fully on display from the back.

Robin squeezed her eyes shut. "Some warning would be appreciated!"

"Apologies," he said, not sounding sorry at all.

She edged past him to reach for the towel, which was indeed beset by a feline conqueror. She picked Govannon up, earning a hiss as he tried to wriggle free. Then she snatched the towel and held it out to Pierce, trying not to look at him more than necessary.

Pierce was handsome, she had to admit, and not for the first time. He was much more slender than Octavian, but well muscled and well proportioned.

"Like what you see, my lady?" he teased.

"I wasn't looking!" she denied.

"You were."

"You may dream," she retorted, unconsciously echoing a phrase she used before, on the night he kissed her without asking leave.

"Perhaps I do, little Robin," he said in a lower voice. Something in it made her shiver. Robin wasn't used to the idea of being dreamt about—and part of her felt a thrill to be told she was. Even if it was by the liar Lord Pierce.

"Get dressed if you want to eat supper," she said, avoiding the uncomfortable topic of whether Pierce dreamed about her. "I'll wait outside."

She was leaning against the corridor wall when Octavian came up the stairs. He looked curiously at her. "What's happening?"

"His lordship is taking a bath," she muttered. "I'm here making sure he really finishes the bath and doesn't sneak out of the inn. What were you up to?" She was so glad she stepped out when she did. She would have died of embarrassment if Tav knew she'd overseen any part of Pierce's bathing.

"I saw to the horses, and I also needed to re-oil my armor and weapons. I'd neglected them too long."

By which he meant a day, Robin knew.

All three of them went down for supper. Robin's stomach was nearly folding in on itself, she was so hungry.

In the tavern room, the other guests were locals who came to enjoy a meal and a drink in a friendlier, livelier atmosphere than their own homes. They didn't bother the newcomers, but Robin noticed how they kept looking over and talking to each other about the three strangers. Confusion and curiosity showed in their eyes. And why not? The trio was unique. First there was Pierce, a man who spent money and acted like a lord, but looked like a beggar. Then Octavian, a man with skin darker than anyone here had ever seen, but attired and armed as a knight.

Some people were no doubt wondering where Tav was from, and others were trying to sort out whether he was Pierce's vassal or his jailer.

And Robin herself defied all logic. She was dressed in a simple, modest green wool gown she'd taken from Willesden, so at least she looked like a woman instead of a boy. She wasn't a wife to either of them. By her actions, she wasn't a servant to either of them. So what was she? Society tended to frown on women without an obvious role.

A barmaid brought them food and ale. Predictably, Pierce complained about it with every breath.

"This is appalling," he said, poking at the meat in front of him. "I'm sitting in a tavern, drinking some half-brewed swill, and dining off tables so filthy they might as well place the food on the floor. If I'd known, I'd have chosen the woods."

"I doubt that," Tav muttered.

Robin saw how irritated Tav was and knew it wouldn't take much for the knight to do something physically painful to the lord. How on earth could she shut Pierce up?

As if delivered by an angel whispering in her ear, the answer came to her. Robin almost smiled at the simplicity of it. Rooting around in the small satchel she carried, she found what she needed.

"If I go plead for the innkeeper's finest ale, will you drink it instead of complaining?" Robin begged Pierce.

"I make no promises. I have grave doubts about any ale from this sort of place."

Robin stood up and made her way to where the other barmaid was tidying up. In a low voice, she asked as nicely as she could for a quality beverage, offering to pay more than what even the finest ale would be worth. The maid raised an eyebrow at the coin, and then nodded. "Just because it's you asking, mistress, and not that pig."

A few moments later, Robin bore a full tankard back to the table. "Here. A special batch of dark ale. Suitable for a lord."

Pierce took a sip, and his sour expression melted into pleasure. "Now *this* is worth drinking."

"I'm so glad," she murmured. Tav looked on silently, obviously annoyed at Pierce's high-handedness and Robin's eagerness to appease him.

Pierce drank more. "I'd buy this from a brewer to ship to Malvern," he said, licking his lips as he stared into the tankard. "A trifle sweet, but good. Very good."

"I hope so, considering the cost."

"This is why money is important," he said, taking another quaff.

"So that means you'll reimburse me?" Robin asked. "I paid with my own coin."

"Oh, don't fret, my little Robin," he said with a wink. "I'll pay you back in one way or another."

Robin sighed. Why did Pierce persist in his flirting, long after they'd left Willesden? She'd made it clear she wasn't interested. Hadn't she?

A seed of doubt sprouted in her heart. Though she certainly didn't want to ever go to Pierce's bed, she hadn't been as forceful in refusing his frequent hints as she normally would be. With all the men who'd propositioned her before—from the time when she was barely more than a child—Robin turned them down fast and flat. If they didn't get the message at first, she had no compunction about following up with a threat of violence.

But it was different with Pierce. They needed his cooperation, and in any case, Robin had been trying to act more like a lady, and ladies were not supposed to threaten men with death when they got too attentive. Perhaps she'd mistakenly led him on by remaining in the room when he took his bath. All she wanted was to ensure he didn't harass the poor maid, but he probably assumed Robin couldn't resist him.

"What's your problem?" Pierce asked her.

Robin had been lost in thought, and both men were watching her.

"Nothing," she said hastily. "I'm just tired."

"It's been a long day," Tav said with just a hint of dryness as he glanced at Pierce, who'd made the day feel much longer for everybody.

Pierce yawned. "Indeed. Didn't feel tired until you mentioned it, but…"

Suddenly, Pierce slumped forward onto the table. The now-empty tankard was knocked to the floor and rolled slowly from side to side. The others in the main room all looked over at the collapsed man, their eyes widening.

Robin leaned over and held her fingers at his throat. "He's not dead," she informed the room at large.

A murmur of disappointment rippled through the crowd. The barmaid in particular looked as if she hoped for a different outcome.

Tav frowned at the prone figure. "Are you sure? He was talking a moment ago."

"He's just unconscious. He'll stay that way till morning."

"How do you know?"

She held up the little glass vial she'd secreted in the palm of her hand. "I still had some of Cecily's poppy syrup in my bag, even after I used part of it during our escape at Willesden. I dumped it into Pierce's ale. Believe me, he's not going anywhere."

Tav coughed, covering a laugh. "That's devious. Why,

though?"

"Because you need some rest. You can't stay up all night to make sure he doesn't run away."

A warm smile lit his face. "Much appreciated. I suppose I should carry him upstairs."

"Finish your meal," Robin suggested. "He won't mind." She picked up the empty tankard from the floor and placed it carefully on Pierce's back, where it stayed upright and rose and fell slightly with the sleeping man's breathing.

They took their time eating. The barmaid brought over more stew when they asked, and every time Tav looked at Pierce's face mashed on the surface of the table, he laughed a little. When he finished his plate, he placed it on Pierce's back as well. Robin followed suit, until his back was covered with the dirty remains of supper. The other guests enjoyed the game, cheering every time an object was added.

Robin's sense of amusement turned to giddiness by the end of the meal. It was just too funny to watch the once haughty lord become a fixture of tavern furniture.

Finally, Tav stood up. "I'll get him upstairs, if you'll remove the dishes from him."

"Very well," she said with a false pout.

He hoisted Pierce over his shoulder and carried him up the stairs, cheered on by the patrons.

"When you get to the top, toss him out the window!" one called out.

"There's an idea," Robin murmured. "If only we didn't need him alive."

Upstairs, Tav heaved the sleeping Pierce onto the bed of the private chamber he insisted on. Govannon had been sleeping on the bed already, and only gave a short, annoyed meow at the disruption.

He closed the door, but lingered there in the hallway. "You're certain he'll sleep through the night?"

"I've seen Cecily use this syrup many times. I know how potent a dose is, and this was a full dose. Trust me, we'll have to drag him out of bed in the morning."

"Still…" Tav opened the door, walked in, and gathered up Pierce's few supplies, most notably his weapons and his money. "There. Now no one can sneak in and steal anything while he's dead to the world. And he can't slip off without us since he can't pay his way on his own."

They crossed the hallway to the common sleeping room. There were several beds with thin curtains to cordon off each area for a modicum of privacy. However, as the innkeeper said, they were the only guests using the sleeping accommodations. Late fall was simply not a time to travel if one could help it.

Tav knelt down to push Pierce's supplies under his bed. Then as he stood up, he started laughing.

"What is it?" Robin giggled too, partly because she was already giddy, and partly because Tav's laugh was so nice to hear.

"From now on, every time I look at Lord Pierce, I'll picture him wearing a kitchen's worth of dishes. That's a gift that will never get old."

Chapter 26

THE TENSION OF THE DAY drained out of Robin when Tav smiled.

But then the smile vanished, replaced with something else, something that sparked a new tension, beginning low in her belly.

"What is it?" she asked.

"Where will you sleep tonight?" he asked with so much heat in his voice that she felt warmth spreading through her body.

"With you, if you want me to." She'd walk through fire if he asked her to.

"Yes," Tav said, pulling her to him. "Yes, I want you to."

Then his mouth was on hers, and she gave herself over to the desire his kiss always seemed to create. She moaned when she felt his tongue flick against hers.

Tav said something in a low tone, another phrase in a language she didn't speak.

"Tav, say it again so I can know," she begged.

"Forgive me," he said, his lips against her throat. "I keep forgetting how to behave around you. You're too difficult to ignore."

"Good," she murmured, her head spinning with being so wanted.

She wasn't shy about showing herself before, and she wasn't shy now. Their clothing was off and forgotten within a few breaths. Robin ran her hands over Tav's chest, then his shoulders and back. He in turn used his tongue to taste her neck and shoulders, creating waves of shivery, delicious sensation that spread lower, through her belly and between her legs.

Robin sighed when she felt him press against her, fully aroused. She slipped one hand between their bodies, her fingers circling the hard length of him.

His breath caught for a second, but he didn't say anything. Instead, he just tipped her head up a little, so she had to look him in the eyes.

That was how she had to learn what he wanted. She kept her eyes locked with his as she began to slowly stroke him. His reaction was instantaneous—his jaw clenched, his eyes widened, and his lips parted as if he were about to speak. But he said nothing.

Robin continued to touch him, fascinated by how he felt in her hand. She knew he enjoyed it from the way that his breathing grew heavier and more eager. There was immense pleasure in giving someone else pleasure, she realized. She loved knowing that Tav wanted her touch so badly. That he *craved* her.

Wetness beaded on the tip, and Robin ran her palm over it. That was when Tav pulled her hand away and swept her up in his arms, striding over to the nearby bed. He yanked the covers aside with one hand, and then set her down.

"I could have walked, you know."

"I do know, I just don't care."

She leaned forward. She needed to feel his mouth against her skin. She pressed herself up to him, shamelessly seeking the heat of his body against her own. Her breasts betrayed her desire, the nipples grown hard. Robin sighed when he pulled her closer, kissing her cheeks, her neck, her chest.

After a little while, he shifted in the bed, moving to a kneeling position where he could survey her below him. He pulled the covers aside, baring her breasts to the cool air. Robin whimpered when he grazed his palms across her nipples, teasing her. "You're playing with me."

"You like it?"

"Yes," she whispered.

He lowered himself so he could take one nipple in his mouth, sucking her and licking her until Robin was clinging to him. Heat flushed through her body, stirring most between her legs.

He switched his attention to her other breast. "Tav," she moaned. "More."

He slid one arm under her back, lifting her body to his. He kissed the valley between her breasts, then said, "If you want more, you have to trust me."

"I trust you," she breathed as he shifted again, moving to kneel between her legs.

With his hands on her thighs, he urged her to spread her legs wider. She did, expecting him to touch her as he'd done before, his fingers slipping into her body and stirring her desire.

But then he lowered his head.

Robin inhaled when he ran his tongue against her body, right where she ached most, his touch gentle but soul-searingly intimate. Robin put both hands on his head, rubbing her fingers over the close-cropped hair, unknowingly guiding him.

Her hips rocked as he circled the bud with his tongue. Then again. And again. She was breathless by the time his finger slid into the damp heat of her body, creating ripples of tantalizing pleasure, wonderful but somehow not enough.

"Oh," she gasped. "Oh."

He kept touching her, driving her mad as he teased her body, drawing out the slick moisture she made, making her as wet on the outside as she was on the inside. She said his name in time to his strokes. The sensations in her core intensified until she reached her peak, a sudden flush of pure *yes*.

A moment later, he lay next to her on the bed, cradling her against him. Robin spread her fingers over his chest, feeling the heavy beat of his heart.

"Tell me how you feel," he said, his voice hot.

"I feel divine," she whispered, still half-shocked by what he'd just done to her. "I didn't know that was something that could feel so luscious."

"Luscious," he echoed, pulling her a little closer to him. "That's how you tasted."

She blushed. "Tav, did you just do that to please me, or…"

"I did it because I wanted to," he said bluntly. "And I'll do it again." The words were spoken with a calm confidence. There would be a next time, and she would want his mouth, and she'd do anything to experience this intimacy again. With him and only him.

He caught her hand in his and drew it downward. Robin again circled his erection with her fingers and began stroking him slowly, enjoying the way his breathing grew faster.

"Would you like to know how my mouth feels on you?" she asked.

"This wasn't meant to be a way to—"

"I know. I asked because I wanted an honest answer."

"Then yes."

She was already curled against him, so she wriggled her body downward, the side of her head resting on his stomach. She carefully tasted the tip of him with her tongue.

His reaction was gold—a strangled moan and a ripple of the muscles in his torso.

Salt. Musk. Heat. She opened her lips wider to try to take all of him in her mouth. He was hard, but still smooth, and sensitive. He reacted to her every lick and touch with raw satisfaction, encouraging her in at least two languages to keep going.

He put one hand on her head, his fingers slipping into her thick hair. Very gently, he let her know exactly what he wanted by the way he guided her, and Robin realized again how much she liked pleasing him.

Tav's breathing quickened, but then he restrained her from continuing. "Stop, love. I'm too close."

Rebelliously, she flicked her tongue along the tip of him, a move she already knew he loved. But he pulled her back with one quick move of his hand.

"Enough," he said with far more command than before. "You listen to me, or we're done."

She nodded, her breath quickening at the change in his voice.

He let go of her hair and slid his hand to her shoulder, pulling her upward. "Come here. I need to see you."

Instinctively knowing what he wanted, she straddled him. He grabbed her hips and held her tightly to him, groaning as she moved. His eyes roamed over her, and he looked more aroused with every passing second.

Robin took a deep breath, feeling how firmly he held

her hips. It would be so easy for him lift her up and bring her back down, penetrating her and destroying the last fragile scraps of her virginity.

From the covetous expression on his face, he was thinking the same thing.

He kept one hand on her hip, holding her tight, but the other slid to her shoulder, drawing her upper body down so their faces met. "I want you so badly," he said.

"You can have me," she told him, meaning it. "There's no other man I'd rather give myself to."

He closed his eyes, obviously torn. "Robin," he said at last. "I can't. Don't ask me again."

Disappointment rippled through her, but then he pressed against her once more, spreading her wetness over himself. "Do this, though," he said, his voice raw. "Just as you are, all along me." He sounded dazed, needy.

He directed her with his hands on her hips, drawing her forward and back along the ridge of his erection. She squeezed her legs around him and rode him until he growled, "Faster." Then he stiffened, throwing his head back against the pillow. She watched as he gave himself up to the same feeling that exploded in her before.

"Robin," he ground out, his muscles contracting as he came. "I wish I was inside you."

"You chose not to," she said, her tone more hurt than she intended.

Suddenly, his eyes flew open. A moment later, he had her flipped onto her back beneath him.

"You know why," he said, every word clear. "You know exactly why I can't do this one act with you. You know why."

She nodded. She did know why. Because of who she was, and how much Tav cared for the people who took Robin in. Betraying them was a far greater sin in his mind than anything he'd done in a bed with Robin. "I know," she said. "I didn't mean to..."

He sighed and lay down on his back again, pulling her into his arms. "I just don't want to hurt you," he said. He brushed a kiss against her forehead. "Not in any way. Did I hurt you before? Your hair?" Tav ran one hand over the back of her head.

"No. And I did get carried away." She had, driven to prove herself to him.

"*You* got carried away?" he said. "I lose my mind around you, especially like this, only you and me. If things were different..." He stopped. "But they aren't."

She rested her head on his shoulder.

He laid another kiss on her hair. "You deserve so much more."

Tears welled up in her eyes. No matter what she did in her life, however cultured or brave or learned she might become, she'd be bound by her humble birth. She depended on the charity of the de Vere family. Her virgin status was her only path to a worthy marriage, and thus the chance to rise out of her origins.

Tav was being kind by denying her the one thing she wanted—him. Perhaps one day she'd be grateful, but now she was miserable.

Thank God he didn't know anything of what she was thinking. He'd risen off the bed and poured some water onto a cloth. He washed her clean, and then himself, all without any fuss. Then he lay back down and pulled her into his arms.

Robin took his hand and raised it to her lips. She kissed his palm gently and heard him inhale.

"Did I ever tell you how much I like your hands?" she asked.

Tav actually laughed, the sound low, partly muffled by

the bedclothes. "My hands are a wreck. Blistered, cold-cracked, and ugly."

"No." She kissed the pads of his fingers, one by one. "Your hands are so beautiful. All the times you stayed at Cleobury, I would always notice them, no matter what you were doing. Training with a sword, riding, even at prayer. I love your hands. Strong." She laid her own hand up against his palm to palm. Her fingers barely reached halfway up his.

He laced his fingers through hers, her pale skin sharp against the dark brown back of his hand. "You expect me to believe that you were attracted to my hands," he said, his voice warm.

"It's true. Perhaps because it's all I could see of you, aside from your face—also beautiful, I should add." She especially loved his cheekbones.

"You need to see more faces," he suggested. "My face is plain."

"No," said Robin. "I'm the plain one. Please remember how I once passed for a boy."

"Remember that no matter how you dressed, you never fooled me," he reminded her. "That very first time you came to Cleobury, I knew exactly what you were. A most unusual young woman, who was more comfortable with archery than weaving. Wear what you like. Crop your hair as short as you can. I'll still see Lady Robin of Ardenwood."

"Don't say that name," she whispered.

"It suits you. You are a lady in all the ways that matter, and who knows the Ardenwood better?"

"But the Ardenwood is wild. There's no honor in it, no title attached to it."

"So? All the more reason to claim the mantle for yourself, then."

"And do what with it?" she asked. "Embroider offerings for the deer? Forests have no need of ladies."

"What's wrong?" Tav looked over at her, his brow wrinkling in concern.

She shook her head. "Nothing. I just don't want to discuss this topic."

"I didn't mean to upset you." Tav reached out to pull her close to him. "Forgive me?"

"I'm not angry with you," she said. Indeed, it was difficult to be angry when she was in his warm embrace, in a soft bed, on a peaceful night.

"Good," he said quietly. "I aim to keep it that way."

Before she could ask what he meant, Robin drifted to sleep, truly content for the first time in years.

Chapter 27

OCTAVIAN KNEW THE EXACT MOMENT that Robin fell asleep, her body easing into slumber as she rolled onto her side, her head resting on his chest, her arm draped over his torso. He couldn't understand how she could be so comfortable with him no matter what situation they were in. Robin seemed to be equally content to trek through a forest with him, or sleep naked next to him. She drew no distinctions, and instead told him silly, sweet things like how much she loved his hands.

Just lying with her, with a blanket and the low fire to keep away the chill, felt like an indulgence, and he wasn't quite ready to give that up. He brought up one arm to curl her in a half embrace. He closed his eyes. An uninterrupted night was a gift in itself. To spend it with Robin was bliss.

He kissed her forehead before he realized he might wake her, but she only gave a sleepy sigh, her eyes remaining closed.

Looking at her, he knew he had to decide what to do next.

Octavian had made a mistake with Robin. Many mistakes. He'd either gone much too far with her, or not nearly far enough…and even though he knew it was a mistake, the remorse just wasn't there. He couldn't ignore that it happened, or pretend it was an incident he could forget about. He was also certain that if another opportunity arose to make love to her, he'd do it without a second thought. He just wasn't strong enough to resist her again.

He lifted his hands and examined them in the dim glow of the embers, wondering if he'd overlooked something all these years. The skin on the backs of his hands was rough and crisscrossed with thin scars over his knuckles and fingers, remnants of strikes from blades that he'd defended too slowly. Thank God he'd improved as a fighter. His palms were just as work-worn. The cold chapped the flesh, and all his traveling required him to wear gloves, or grip reins or baggage, or scrabble to build a fire or dig a pit. There was nothing pretty about his hands or his fingers…though she did seem to enjoy how he touched her.

Tav sighed, the feeling of her next to him casting out all other thoughts. She was so lovely. He wanted desperately to know just how it would feel to have her completely, to know how her body would take him, to make her explode with pleasure and know *he* was the one responsible for it.

But she was as good as promised to someone else, and he wasn't going ruin the rest of her life for a few nights of lust. He loved her too much for that.

Then he realized what he'd just thought. He loved her. It wasn't just a physical need. He cared about all of her. Her odd mix of idealism and cynicism, her headstrong nature, her little jokes, and her fierce defense of anyone she felt was in danger. He couldn't think of a more perfect woman for him.

But he was not the perfect man for her. He had nothing to offer, not even a parcel of land or a home to take her to. He had no wealth and no way to earn wealth other than by his sword. And what sort of life would that be, him leaving her for months on end to campaign for someone else's war? He had no illusions about the likely fate of any man who made a living by killing. He was lucky to have survived as many battles as he had already. Who'd be cruel enough to marry a woman, knowing that he'd leave her a widow sooner rather than later?

Tav couldn't do that. That was one of the reasons he'd held himself apart. Not a reason he even admitted to himself until now, when he finally knew there was a woman he wanted to stay with for the rest of his life.

She just happened to be the one woman he should never have considered.

In the morning, Tav woke Robin up and was hit by her smile, which very nearly seduced him all over again. Only the urgency of their errand kept him from staying in bed with her all day.

Robin teased him about his dedication, and though she meant nothing by it, Tav took the jibe harder than he should have. He'd just been thinking about how his vaunted dedication to serving his lord was starting to feel more and more hollow. Especially when it meant he had to deny himself something as slight as an hour longer in bed with Robin next to him. But no, he had to avoid even that tiny comfort for the sake of hauling an irritating, occasionally traitorous lord to the king.

Fortunately, he was able to hide his mood from Robin. She kissed him sweetly after she dressed, saying she'd see the horses were ready and all the baggage packed. That left him to wake up Pierce, who decidedly did not want to wake. Octavian practically had to threaten him at sword-point to get him on his feet.

Govannon, by contrast, hopped into his basket with only the lightest coaxing. Tav gave the cat a rub behind the ears as a reward, then fastened the leather straps. He looked up to see Pierce frowning.

"That's my cat. Don't think you'll trick him away from me."

Tav stood up, enabling him to look down a few inches at Pierce, who wasn't as tall. "Animals can sense who's trustworthy—it's how they survive."

"Tell that to the lambs who go peacefully to the slaughter," Pierce retorted. "Most animals are stupid...so are most people, trusting until the last."

"Get your things together," Tav ordered shortly. It was too early in the day to deal with Pierce. "Don't make us wait."

Not long after, they rode out. Robin rode ahead several lengths while Tav remained near Pierce, who'd said almost nothing since they left the inn.

Pierce glared him, his mood not improved one bit from the morning. "Why is my head still so groggy?"

"Perhaps the ale last night was stronger than your usual fare, my lord," Tav suggested, just as he wondered if Robin had any more of the poppy syrup in her bag. Nothing would please him more than Pierce out of the way every night.

"I can hold my drink," Pierce said. "All I know is that I was eating my meal, and then I woke up in the morning with no recollection of how I even got to my bed."

"You were no doubt exhausted from the effort of traveling as we've had to do. I know you're used to better. You used to have a carriage, yes? Before you lost Malvern?" Tav couldn't resist needling Pierce. His faith taught him that he shouldn't *hate* anyone, but he was fairly certain the text of the Bible said nothing about *detesting* someone.

"I didn't lose Malvern," Pierce hissed. "It was stolen from me."

"Fortunes of war," Tav said with a shrug. "No doubt the current occupant feels he earned Malvern as a result of all his hard work to take it."

"Then he can die of a pox," said Pierce. "And as for you—"

Suddenly, Robin wheeled her horse around on the road ahead and galloped back toward them, causing Pierce to shut his mouth. *Small miracles are still miracles*, Tav thought.

He shifted in his saddle, watching Robin's approach. "Problem?" he asked when she was in earshot.

Her forehead was wrinkled in concern. "There are men ahead of us on the road. Dressed like soldiers. Armed like soldiers."

Pierce said nervously, "Perhaps they're just marching somewhere, and we can wait them out."

"Or, if they're men loyal to Stephen," Tav said hopefully, "we can travel with them and not have to fear Estmar's or Ranulf's men catching up to us."

Robin looked over her shoulder. "But none of us can exactly ride up and ask. We're all liable to be captured if they're unfriendly."

Tav said, "Then we should avoid meeting them altogether. Can you find a path around the group?"

Robin nodded. "It will take longer, but there's always another path."

She turned sharply to the right, leading her horse off the road and into the woods. Tav gestured for Pierce to go next and then he followed.

The land rose sharply on either side of the road, and

they had to switch back twice to reach the high ground. Despite the better views once they were over the ridge, Robin went slowly, pausing several times before committing to a route. She must have been more concerned than she let on about the soldiers she'd seen.

After a while, the route began to lead downward again, toward a flatter stretch of land that was less heavily forested—a valley between their ridge and the next. Robin's horse quickened pace, and the others followed. Tav breathed a little easier, not realizing until then how tense he'd grown thinking about an unknown force on the road.

Just as her horse reached the flat ground, Robin signaled a halt as she pulled hard on the reins, muttering a curse. Pierce imitated her, though his curse was louder.

"Hush," she mouthed at them, her expression serious. She pointed to the little valley ahead, to the left.

Tav squinted, seeing the shapes of men on the other side of the sparse cover of trees. Some were mounted, some were not, but they were all armed. He counted eight. Perhaps a scouting party split off from the main group that they wanted to avoid? Or another group all together. Either way, Tav didn't particularly want to fight eight men if he didn't have to.

One of the men looked their way and smacked a neighbor in the arm to get his attention.

Then two men were looking in their direction, alert and wary.

Robin gripped the reins of her horse, her body held frozen. Pierce's hand inched toward the sword he wore.

Tav put his hand to his own sword, even as he murmured a quick prayer for the men to ignore their presence.

"Do they see us?" he asked softly. Mounted, he felt like an entirely too obvious target, especially with the woods mostly bare of leaves. Thank God none of them were colorfully dressed. But the metal of their gear would glint in the light, and human shapes always jumped out of a scene when someone was looking for them.

After a moment of edgy silence, Robin said, "I don't think so. See? They're going now."

The two men who'd been looking their way had been talking, but now the whole group was moving back toward the road, and the two men joined them.

Tav exhaled in relief, but kept an eye on the place where the group had been, half expecting someone to charge back out of the woods.

"We must have been farther away than it seemed," Pierce said after a moment.

"I was certain they'd seen me!" said Robin. She looked worried rather than relieved.

"Let's keep going," Tav said. "The more distance we put between them and us, the better." He didn't know why, but he had a bad feeling about the men they'd just seen.

Robin nodded and led them onward, going farther to the right, putting even more distance between the main road and their new route.

They spent the next two hours picking their way through the forest. The going was slow, only getting easier when Robin ran across a deer trail that was fairly free of undergrowth.

Then, about an hour before sundown, the path intersected a little river, with a low hill rising nearby.

"We can stop here to rest." Tav turned his horse in a circle to survey the whole clearing. "We won't get much farther today anyway, and I don't want to risk the horses. It's too easy to stumble and get hurt."

Robin looked around. "This is a good place to camp.

Let's stay as close as possible to that hill, though. If there's weather from the west, it will provide a little shelter."

"So no inn tonight," Pierce said sadly.

Tav's eyes met Robin's, and he saw a secret flash of desire in her expression.

"We're all sad about that," she said, her gaze still on Tav. "But there will be other nights."

Chapter 28

ROBIN BIT BACK A SMILE when she saw Tav's reaction to her words. She was just being honest. She'd much rather be in a bed with him than sleeping cold in the forest. She couldn't wait to be done with this adventure.

"Misadventure," she corrected, speaking to herself as she began to unpack the items needed to set up their modest camp.

But when she began to walk away to harvest the firewood they'd need for the night, Tav intercepted her. "Stay here and mind the horses…and Pierce."

"I'm not going to try anything," Pierce protested from where he stood, spreading his hands wide in a gesture of innocence.

Tav just raised an eyebrow. "Nevertheless, Robin can send an arrow to stop you. I'll be back soon." He said to Robin, in a lower tone, "I'll stay within shouting distance."

"There's no need," she said. "Anything Pierce may try, I can counter it perfectly well on my own."

"So you can," he said, "but why should you have to? Call for me and I'll take care of it. Meanwhile, rest.

You're tired from all this travel—I can tell."

She was tired, but she didn't want to make a fuss about it. While Tav was off getting fuel, she sat against the rock face and instructed Pierce on how to build a fire, despite his initial protests.

"You should thank me," she said. "A grown man who can't keep himself warm is pathetic."

"I keep myself warm in other ways," he said, looking at her with a frankly comic leer.

She rolled her eyes. "You need a woman or a cat to make it through the night indoors, and you act like you know anything? What if you had to flee Willesden alone? You'd have died the first night."

"I'd have gone to a town immediately," he countered.

"And been captured because your weaknesses are so predictable. Put that big stick down. You need to lay the tinder and kindling first."

"This is servants' work."

"You have no servants here, my lord. That's too much tinder. You'll kill the fire before you light it. It needs air to breathe. Pack the tinder too tight and it will never catch. It will smolder, and smoke chokes the flame."

Pierce made a face, but did as she directed. Perhaps he wasn't completely foolish.

A short while later, the first flames were licking greedily at the tinder, and Pierce was grinning as if he'd accomplished a much greater task.

Tav returned with a supply of wood more than sufficient to get them through the night.

"Aha," Pierce said. "See, sir knight, a fire worthy of all your hard work gathering fuel. *I* made it."

Tav looked amused. "About time."

Aside from eating the food they'd bought from the innkeeper, there was little to do that evening. Leaning against the rocky hill, her feet poking out from under her monk's robe, Robin relaxed as the heat of the fire warmed her. In fact, she could barely keep her eyes open, even though the sun only set a while ago, the sky not yet full dark.

The snap of a twig was the only warning of the attack.

At the sound, Robin whipped her head around to see men rushing out of the forest toward them, their blades gleaming.

Tav lunged to his feet, his sword somehow already in his hand. He moved to block the attackers' path to Robin, and yelled for Pierce to draw.

Robin scrambled for her bow while trying to keep her eyes on the chaos breaking out all around her.

The three of them were badly outnumbered. She thought she counted eight or ten men, but everyone moved fast, and the leaping flames made it hard to see clearly.

"Kill the soldier! And get that monk before he can run off with the horses!" one of the attackers ordered.

"I'm not running," she said, knowing no one could hear her.

The force split into two groups, each trying to surround Tav and Pierce.

One man broke off and advanced toward Robin with a grin on his bearded, almost jolly face. "Forgive us, brother! We know not what we do!"

Robin raised the bow and shot before he could get any closer. He looked surprised at the arrow shaft protruding from his chest, and then slid slowly to the ground.

Her heart pounding, Robin focused next on the group going after Pierce.

Pierce countered the attacks against him with an agility that surprised her. He always seemed so idle, but now he stepped nimbly, parrying thrusts with both his sword and his dagger.

She drew another arrow and aimed once more, this time at the man who'd yelled out the orders. She shot and caught the man's upper arm. He howled in pain, and Pierce seized the opportunity to strike, a deadly hit to the throat.

Meanwhile, the men engaged with Octavian were quickly realizing that he was not just a common soldier, but rather a highly trained knight. Even fighting on foot, he outmaneuvered them and struck out whenever he saw an opening. One man fell, then another.

"Retreat!" a man fighting Pierce shrieked out. But since everyone was engaged, a coordinated retreat wasn't possible, and each man was scared of giving an opening to his opponent.

Just then, Robin saw one of Tav's attackers shift, getting behind him. She didn't even think. She simply stepped forward and loosed the arrow. The short distance was a hindrance for her longbow, but this time the arrow flew true, and the man took the hit in his eye.

The gruesome image made Robin lose her breath, but Tav just dispatched his last opponent with a heavy blow from the flat of his blade. The shorter man staggered backward, moaning.

Tav announced, "Half of you are dead. The rest of you can run or die."

His booming voice actually halted the fight for a moment. The attackers froze, and Robin saw frightened, furious eyes in the light of the fire.

Most of them took a half step back. Pierce slid into position next to Tav, ready to fight again as a unit.

That did it. The remaining men wanted nothing to do with two better equipped warriors. One said, "Please let us go! It was his idea!" He gestured to a fallen body. "Just let us leave."

"Go." Octavian's voice was deadly calm. "Drop the weapons. Walk away. One step toward any of us and that's the end."

They let the weapons fall and began to back up, but Robin caught one man whose gaze was fixed on Tav. As if he couldn't stop himself, when he drew level with Tav, he lunged, his hands curled like claws.

"No!" she shouted, her unexpectedly feminine voice startling everyone else. The man going to Tav was already in motion though, his face a mask of rage and fear.

She shot one last time. The man stumbled, the arrow jutting out from his shoulder.

"Devil take him," someone said in the darkness, pronouncing the man's fate as if he were dead already.

"You take him," Tav said. "Grab him and get out of here."

"Don't touch the swords," Pierce added, seeing another man reaching down to the ground. "Take your comrade and go."

Robin said nothing more as the group of would-be brigands took their wounded friends and vanished into the darkness. The sounds of a few horses echoed through the woods, and then the hoofbeats faded into nothing.

She still clutched the bow, an arrow tight against the string.

"Robin. Robin." It was Tav's voice. He must have said her name several times.

"What?"

"You can put that down now." He pointed to the bow. "You did your part."

"Where the hell did they come from?" Pierce asked, crouching near the fire, only to spring up again, clearly still feeling the tension of the fight in his veins.

"They were the men from before," she said dully. "The ones in that clearing. We thought they didn't see us, but they did."

"I should have guessed," Tav said. "Probably a scouting party. They thought they could follow us and take down a few travelers without the larger group knowing or caring. Then they'd take our horses and split the loot equally."

Pierce nodded slowly, thinking it over. "Ten to three… the odds sounded good."

"Not against Octavian," Robin said.

"Or you," Pierce said with an expression unlike his usual assurance. She looked away.

"Let's move these away," Tav said to Pierce, gesturing to the bodies. "Robin, pile up the dropped weapons."

She did, her limbs heavy with the rush of blood that surged through her before, and now lingered even after it was all over.

The men took the bodies away into the darkness, returning some time later. Robin wasn't sure if it was minutes or an hour.

"I can't believe you prayed for them." Pierce's voice came out of the shadowed woods. "They were enemies."

"They were," Tav responded in a lower, calmer tone. "And now they're dead. The least we can do is say a prayer."

They came into the circle of firelight. Tav said, "Pierce, I need to speak to Robin. Go and watch."

"Watch for what?" Pierce asked nervously.

"I have no idea. That's why we set watches." Tav's voice was stretched tight. "Now go. If you see something suspicious, yell. If someone attacks you, kill them."

Pierce took a last look at Robin, then moved off away

from the fire.

Tav moved closer to her. "How are you? Did you get struck in the fight?"

"No. I was just startled. No one hurt me."

He kept watching her, his gaze intent. "You're certain?" He laid his hands on her shoulders, then ran them along her arms, checking for injuries.

"I'm fine."

"You killed people tonight."

Robin raised her chin defiantly. "Not for the first time."

"But never more than one, and never so close. I was there when you had to do that before. And I remember how you pretended you didn't care then."

He was right. She'd been in more than one fight that Octavian also been involved in. Alric and his fellow knights always seemed to get tangled up in each other's troubles.

Robin always acted as if she didn't much mind the blood, but that was pure reflex, a need to appear strong when all she wanted to do was collapse. Some part of Robin was adamant that she could never show any weakness, particularly after striking an enemy down, a feat that made most men—men on her side—look at her as if *she* were the enemy. At least Tav was speaking to her.

She said, "I got a clear shot, and I took it." She was talking about every time she'd been forced to kill during a skirmish, but he took it to mean only today.

Without hesitation, Tav replied, "They would have killed you. Every one of them."

"I don't regret what I did. And I'd do it again. But..." She couldn't stop her body from shaking. The attack was over, she told herself. Why was she so out of control? The face of the last man she killed—pallid and sweaty with fear—jumped into her mind.

"You can say it, Robin."

"I'll always remember the faces," she whispered, hating herself for feeling so weak. Hot tears slid down her cheeks. "That man...I don't have a name for him, but he'll always follow me. Just like the other people I killed. Every time it happened, it was because I had to defend myself and the people fighting with me. But I wish I didn't wonder if he had a family."

Tav took her hands in his. "It doesn't get easier," he said.

Robin gripped his fingers, needing something to hold. "Do you *see* the people you've killed?"

He paused for a long moment, then said, "Some of them. It's different on a battlefield because you can't always see what's coming. But I always remember. I can close my eyes and relive every battle. I can smell and hear everything. Including the dead."

"I hate it," she whispered.

"You're supposed to hate it. If you felt nothing, I'd be far more concerned about you. But you've got a good soul, Robin. That's why it hurts you to hurt other people. Even when it's your life or theirs."

She buried her head in his chest, needing the shelter of hiding in his embrace. Her tears slowed as she took in Tav's words. No censure, just acknowledgment of the horror. He understood, and he listened to her when she spoke about something that she'd never spoken of before. Not telling her she shouldn't have taken part in the first place...as if she could ever stand by when she could do something instead.

Tav held her for what seemed like a very long time. Robin breathed in, growing calm. How odd that sometimes being close to him woke every nerve inside her, and other times, like now, he could soothe her without a word.

Her shivering subsided, and he told her she should try to sleep.

"I don't think I can sleep at all tonight," she objected even as she moved to her rolled-out bedding.

"Lie down." Tav put the cloak over her. "You need to stay warm. Trust me. Even if you don't feel it, the cold is affecting you more than you realize."

"You need your cloak."

"I'll be near the fire," he said, forestalling her attempt to give the cloak back. "Someone needs to keep watch."

"Tell Govannon to do it."

Tav's smile flashed in the glow of the fire. "If he returns from his hunt, he can relieve me."

The addition of Tav's cloak helped. The thick wool stopped the wind's assault, and the heavy weight of it kept her from shivering. More than that, it carried the faint but unmistakable scent of Tav himself in the fibers, and Robin felt almost as if he were holding her, a thought that warmed her to a remarkable degree.

"It's better with the cloak," she whispered out loud.

"Good." He put two fingers to his mouth, then laid them on her cheek. A subtle kiss.

"Tav?" she asked in a small voice.

"Yes?" His eyes caught hers.

"Thank you for…everything. I know I've been difficult to deal with." From the moment he'd found out that she'd chosen to follow him.

"We've had a difficult night," he said gently, as if she only meant that night. "It's no surprise you're suffering the effects of hard travel. Anyone would."

"You don't."

"I do. I'm just better at hiding them because I've had more practice. Now go to sleep, Robin. I'll stay awake."

Then he stood up and walked out to the fire, his form silhouetted against the light from the flames. All she could see was the outline of him—a warrior in every regard.

And he said he'd stay awake.

That, more than anything, allowed Robin's eyes to slide shut. She cuddled into the wrapped cloak and blanket like a little animal burrowing in for the winter. She could sleep if Octavian was awake, keeping danger from her. It was a comfort to know that she did not have to fear anything or anyone sneaking up on her. Tav would never let it happen.

The early bird call woke her, and Robin blinked, realizing that not only had she slept, she'd actually slept well. She looked around in the dawn light, seeing Tav sitting before a low fire. Pierce was a little ways away from her, close to the rock wall, his prone form mostly hidden by blankets. What she first took for a fur collar turned out to be Govannon, draped across his neck.

She got to her feet, keeping the blankets wrapped around her as she walked toward the fire.

Tav turned at her approach, but didn't get up.

"Did you sleep at all?" she whispered when she reached him.

"I dozed from time to time. It was a quiet night."

"Thank God."

"Yes," he agreed, meaning it.

Robin extended one arm and wrapped Tav in her blanket, bringing her body next to his. "You had to be cold."

He inhaled, turning his head to hers. "We shouldn't do this," he murmured, even as his lips brushed her cheek.

"I'm just getting you warm," she said with a smile. "What's wrong with that?"

His smile grew in response to hers, and Robin suddenly felt very warm. His hands skimmed her body under the layers of fabric, and he made a sound that a starving man might make when given a single bite of food.

"Robin," he breathed, "you don't know how much I wish we were alone right now."

"I know exactly how much," she assured him.

He kissed her once, and then extracted himself from her blankets. "Do me a favor and find some food in our supplies. I'll get fresh water." He stood up and moved away from the fire.

Robin shucked off the blankets and started to gather what she'd need to break their fast. Then she noticed Pierce awake and watching her.

"Good morning," he said, standing up and stamping his feet to get the blood flowing. "I suppose we're getting an early start."

"Unless you like the surroundings so much you want to linger?" she asked.

"Certainly not. The sooner we get to civilization, the better."

She nodded, in complete agreement.

Pierce looked to where Tav had gone, then said, "What you did last night was remarkable. I knew you were a good shot, but not that good, under such difficult circumstances."

"I was always skilled with a bow," she said.

"That's obvious." He paused, then said, "Speaking of obvious…"

"What?"

He leaned forward, his voice more confidential, even though they were alone. "If you're truly a lady, as you occasionally claim to be, you'll have to get better at hiding your attraction to unsuitable men."

"I don't know what—"

Pierce held up one hand, waving her objections away.

"Don't pretend, Robin. I'm not blind or stupid, and you and Octavian aren't exactly masters of deception."

"What we are or aren't is no business of yours."

"True, and I don't care one way or the other. Ladies have lovers, just like women of any other class. But ladies do need to be more discreet."

"We're not lovers," she insisted.

Pierce laughed a little. "No? Then that's the first time I've been mistaken about a man's interest, especially when the woman is as eager as you are for him."

She didn't need insults in addition to whatever else Pierce was saying. "Stop it."

"Robin, I'm not jealous," he told her, and indeed, he looked sincere. "Yes, I teased you before, that one evening at Willesden. I was bored, and you were a breath of fresh air. I'm not sorry I kissed you. And I would have bedded you if you hadn't been so icy about it. Now I know that you've only got eyes for another."

"If you're not jealous, why say he's unsuitable?" Robin asked. "For pity's sake, Octavian saved your life."

Pierce nodded quickly. "And I'm grateful for it. He's a model knight. All I'm saying is that he's unsuitable for a lady…in terms of a formal match, that is. Knights are just soldiers. Unless Octavian is more than a knight, of course. If he's a castellan, or if he also holds some land or a title…"

Robin didn't even have to answer that. Pierce guessed the truth. "So he's merely a knight. Which means he can't ever be more than a lover, and one who must be kept secret. You've neglected to tell me your family name or connections—and that's your prerogative, dear—but if you're a lady, you must marry for position, as your family dictates. That's how the world is, yes?"

Robin bit her lip, knowing Pierce's words were true.

Then she said, in a voice that lacked conviction, "I thank you for the advice. Even though it's not needed, as we're not lovers."

"But you wish you were," Pierce said with that unsettling confidence. "And since you're a little naive, I'll give you one last piece of advice."

"What is that?"

"Knights, lords, commoners...men are men. Men take what they want, and the moment they get it, nothing they promised before means anything."

"You'd know," Robin said tartly.

"I do know," he replied, his voice gentle. "Better than anyone, I know how men use women. Octavian may say all sorts of sweet words and treat you like a goddess when you're alone. But he's a man with all the same drives and flaws as other men. Be careful, Lady Robin."

She frowned, trying to understand Pierce's motives. "Why are you telling me this?"

"Because you saved my life too, and regardless of what you think of me, I *am* grateful. Let this be a way to repay you...a truth you need to hear."

"You don't know him," she blurted out. "Even if you think you're offering good advice, you don't know Octavian at all."

He sighed. "The question isn't how well I know Octavian. It's how well *you* truly know him."

Then he turned away, leaving Robin to ponder his words.

After leaving the scene of the attack, they kept traveling, roughly south and east, as best as Robin could devise, considering the untrammeled nature of the Ardenwood. The weather warmed again, with a watery sun offering at least a little warmth at midday. The trio did its best to remain unobtrusive, and they avoided all inns and villages. A few times, Robin risked going to a farmstead, dressed in her monkish clothing, to buy a little food. She was usually given bread, but she offered a small coin for cheese and meat.

Nights remained cold, but weren't disturbed by any more attacks. They took turns watching for danger, even Pierce sitting up for hours. Over the past several days, he'd turned almost docile, still out of his element, but no longer the abrasive, arrogant lord he'd been at first. He confessed one night that he found it difficult to admit he'd lost so much of the power he was accustomed to holding. His bad temper was the result.

He was actually becoming a fairly competent traveler, though. In addition to learning how to build and tend a fire properly, he also knew much more about the care of horses than before, and how to set up a camp to avoid waking up in a rain puddle. Robin even pointed out some star signs one night, explaining the few she used most when she had to travel in darkness. Tav knew even more of the constellations than she did, all their names and the stories behind them.

"Brother Petrus taught us," he said when she asked how he'd learned so much. "The monks felt all of creation needed to be named and categorized and understood if we ever want to truly know the mind of the Creator."

Robin wanted to curl up next to him and listen to all the stories of the stars, but the presence of Pierce made that impossible. And perhaps it was for the best, considering what Pierce had told her. It was hard to tell what Octavian thought, and they had no opportunity to discuss anything so private. He often found reasons to touch her hand, or smile at her when Pierce's attention was elsewhere, but now she wondered exactly what it all meant... if it meant anything. She couldn't wait to get to the castle of Martenkeep, where they hoped to find the first real shelter since beginning this mission. Then she could speak to Tav and discover what he truly wanted.

If she dared. What if the answer broke her heart?

The next day, Robin was certain they'd crossed out of the Ardenwood, and were now heading toward the safer, more populated environs of the Long Forest and the lands to the south. The area was not free of danger—the nearby Welsh were always a threat, and many of the local lords were weak, only protecting their own estates—but it was far better than the wild, unpredictable Ardenwood.

She told the others and got two sighs of relief.

"That's good news," Pierce said. "Does this mean we can find the main road now and head to London directly?"

She glanced toward Tav, who said, "Remember that we're still likely being pursued by either Estmar's force or Ranulf's men, or both. We have to be alert and let Robin continue to choose the path."

"You know this area?" Pierce asked Robin.

"I've been here before," she replied noncommittally. "I'll get us to a safe location, and then we'll find out where the king is. We've been too long without news."

Robin knew that from the north, there was only one good way to Martenkeep. A river ran through a deep gorge somewhat north of it, a natural barrier that helped protect the lands around the castle in that direction. A bridge crossed the gorge at one point, very near the main road through the Long Forest, and that was where they had to cross. Otherwise, they'd have to spend days traveling around and through the ravine.

Later, she told Octavian about the bridge and said, "We're getting close. By tomorrow evening, we should be within the walls."

He nodded, his expression betraying weariness, especially around his eyes. The days and weeks of travel had been grueling, and Tav stayed up on watch more than she or Pierce did. Once they reached Martenkeep, he'd want to sleep for days.

Robin herself was dreaming of a warm bed, and clean clothes, and food cooked by anyone but her. The lure of sitting down while someone else poured mulled wine and offered it to her made Robin sigh audibly.

Tav glanced at her, and she blushed. "Just thinking of being inside a proper home again."

He smiled. "Soon." The way he said it hinted at something less proper in his thoughts, and she looked away, hiding under the hood of her cloak. If only Tav's mere presence didn't summon moths in her stomach. She could barely think straight around him.

They had to swing to the east for a short while before picking up the route to the bridge. Robin watched carefully for any sign of travelers, but saw no one. She rode out to the path itself and took a cautious breath.

They rode for about a quarter hour when a sudden shout echoed around the hills. "I see Pierce!"

Robin cursed under her breath and looked around. The sound of horses—too many horses—started to grow louder.

"They caught us!" Pierce said, fury on his face.

"Not yet." Robin grabbed the reins. "We can outrun them and then cross the bridge. Follow me!"

Robin saw Tav's face for only a bare second, and she didn't like the expression there. It was the soldier's expression, one she'd seen too often on Alric's face, and Luc's and Rafe's as well. When they got it, they focused only on battle, blind to anything else.

It meant Tav didn't think they'd get out of this without violence.

251 × Elizabeth Cole

Robin had to try. She knew the way to the bridge and rode at a breakneck speed through the woods, dodging trees and yelling warnings almost too late for the others to react.

When Robin saw the bridge in the distance, she thought they'd make it. Glancing behind her, she saw only the two men, but she knew the other force would be there in a matter of moments.

At the north end, she slowed her horse to safely cross the narrow wooden bridge. The others met her, but Tav inexplicably dismounted.

"What are you doing?" Robin asked, a pit forming in her stomach. She jumped down as well, rushing over to him. "What's going on?"

He didn't look at her. "Get back on the horse, Robin. If you get a head start, you can be safe. You know the forest well enough to avoid getting caught."

"But what about you?"

"Someone has to slow them down."

"Alone?" she asked incredulously.

"The bridge is a choke point," he said, sounding far too calm.

"I'm not leaving you to fight them off alone! I can cover you, even from the other side." Her longbow had sufficient range.

Tav actually pushed her back toward the horse. "No. You need to get out of here and take Pierce with you to Martenkeep. He's got the information the king needs to hear. I'll follow you when I can."

"Tav—"

He took her hand and kissed it, the gesture melting her even as it scared her.

Pierce looked back. "They're coming!"

Tav lifted her up onto the saddle as if she weighed

nothing. "Pierce, follow Robin. Don't let her circle back. Go!"

Pierce used his own horse to bully hers toward the bridge. Robin cursed him, but had no other choice. She cast a last look at Octavian, who was already hefting his shield upward. He didn't look back at her.

"Move!" Pierce snapped. "We need to get out of arrow range, or what he's doing won't matter."

She dug her heels into the horse's flanks and leapt forward. They crossed the bridge in a blink, and the horses lengthened stride into a gallop and then a canter, as if they were aware of the urgency.

Robin's vision was blurry with tears.

She'd abandoned Tav.

There was no other word for it. He stood there alone, against who knew how many men.

He's not expecting to get out alive.

And she left him. An ugly sob broke through, and she hunched over the horse's neck.

She had no recollection of how she reached Martenkeep. Time ceased to run sensibly. Perhaps it stopped altogether. All she knew was that the moss-covered stones of a castle's curtain wall suddenly rushed up to meet her.

"Halt!"

"Halt!"

The command came from ahead of her and behind her, as if more than one person called. Her horse skidded to a stop only out of a sense of self-preservation, lest it be smashed against the iron-studded gate.

"Let us in!" she yelled, her voice cracking with fury. "I need to speak with Sir Rafael Corviser! Let us in!"

Pierce rode up next to her. "It's Lady Robin," he called up to the astonished guards. "And I'm Lord Pierce of Malvern. Open the gate, quickly. We may have compa-

253 × *Elizabeth Cole*

ny."

Whether it was the names, or their obvious panic, or just the fact that two people weren't a threat, the gate opened.

Robin stormed through it the instant she could edge her horse into the space. "Where's Sir Rafe? It's urgent!"

She couldn't focus on anything. Hands reached for the reins, and then pulled her down to the courtyard stones. She caught only the vague impression of uniformed men and concerned faces.

Then a voice boomed out, "What the hell is going on?"

A nearby guard said, "Sir! These…people. They just rode up like the devil was chasing them. Demanded to speak to you."

"Let me through!"

All of a sudden, Robin was looking into the handsome face of a knight with long, dark hair.

"Robin?" he asked in disbelief.

Relief rushed through her, and she grabbed his arms. "Rafe! Tav was with us, but he stayed at the bridge to hold them off. You have to go help him! Please, there's no time."

"When did this happen?" he asked. "Who's chasing you? How many?"

"It doesn't matter!" she said, shaking. "Just go, for God's sake. Just take as many men as you can and get to him!" She gulped huge breaths of air, her limbs sagging with exhaustion.

Rafe straightened up. "Someone get her into the keep and call for my wife. And get this man in there as well. Simon! We're going to the bridge. Twenty riders, armed for a raid. Let's *move!*"

The last word spurred a flurry of action, but Robin

was on her knees and saw nothing more than a dozen pairs of boots running in all directions. Then Pierce was kneeling next to her, pulling her to her feet. "Come on, Robin. Up. You need to get inside. There's nothing more you can do."

"I hate you," she whispered. "He's going to die so you can live, and there's no secret message to the king worth that. I *hate* you."

Chapter 29

"WHO'S THAT?" PIERCE ASKED.

Robin looked up as a woman emerged from the keep. Lady Angelet's hair was the lightest shade of blonde, and everything about her, from the way she moved to her leaf-green eyes, hinted at something otherworldly.

When she saw Robin, those eyes widened in surprise. "Dear child, what are you doing here?"

"We were outrunning a force of men after *him*." Robin pointed to Pierce. "Octavian made us go ahead so he could hold them off, and…"

"Be calm, Robin," Angelet said, reaching to take Robin's hands in her own. "Everything that can be done will be done. You are safe here, just as he wanted—wants —you to be."

Robin swallowed, her throat gone dry. She swayed on her feet, and Angelet signaled two maids to assist Robin inside.

Pierce stepped forward. "I regret we couldn't give your household any warning before our arrival. I am Lord Pierce of Malvern."

Angelet curtseyed politely to Pierce. "And I am An-gelet. Malvern, you said? The name is slightly familiar to me. It's well north of here, is it not?"

"True, my lady," Pierce said, his eyes taking in the appearance of Angelet with some of his old calculation. "Please forgive our intrusion. You can't get many visitors here."

"The Marches can be lonely," said Angelet, her tone mild and agreeable—which reflected her personality. "But Martenkeep is lively enough, especially with all the young lads here for training. Several families have sent sons here to be fostered, knowing my husband's reputation as a swordsman."

"And what is his name again? I missed it in the chaos."

"Sir Raphael Corviser," she replied proudly.

Robin kept her eyes on Pierce, but saw no hint of recognition. He'd realize who Rafe was once he saw him for more than an instant—the man left an impression on nearly everyone—but by then the gates would be closed and Pierce would have no choice but to accept he was confined until he revealed the information he claimed to have.

"We are grateful for the hospitality, my lady," Pierce said. "We've been forced to travel for quite a while under less than desirable conditions."

Angelet said, "From the looks of you both, and the speed of your arrival, that seems an understatement. But the story can wait till you both have rested." She turned to Robin. "Come with me, dear. I will see to you personally. My lord, you will be quite comfortable in the care of my seneschal."

Pierce nodded, once again in his element as a guest in a well-run castle.

Angelet took Robin by the hand and led her toward the upper part of the keep, where the master bedchamber occupied a whole floor. Once there, Robin sighed in relief. Walls. A bed. Water in a pitcher. Fire in the fireplace. No enemies chasing her.

She sagged down onto the edge of the bed.

"Robin, I must ask exactly what is going on." Angelet's gaze was intense, and her eyes seemed to miss nothing. "What brought you here, of all places, and why were you traveling with Sir Octavian and this lord? What are you wearing? Do Alric and Cecily know where you are?"

"It will take some time to explain," Robin said hesitantly.

"Excellent, for it will also take time to scrub the dirt off you and wash your hair... Is that blood?" Angelet fingered a stain on Robin's cloak with horror.

"Possibly. Not mine," she added.

"Thank heaven! I will call for hot water."

Not long after, Robin was tucked into a wooden tub, luxuriating in a steaming bath scented with rosemary and lavender. The heat of the water seeped into her muscles, and she gave a long sigh.

Angelet sent her maid away and attended Robin herself, cooing over her like a motherly dove. As she removed the grime from her skin and the tangles from her hair, Angelet got nearly the whole story from Robin. She told her everything from sneaking out of Cleobury to join Octavian out of a misplaced sense of duty, to meeting the frustrating Lord Pierce, and to evading their tenacious pursuers on the road. When Robin got to the part of the story where Tav stayed behind at the bridge, she blinked back tears.

"No, don't cry," Angelet said. "Not till we know if tears are needed. You rode here so fast and sent Rafe back even faster. He and his men are probably to the bridge at this moment!"

"But what will they find there?" Robin whispered.

Angelet frowned and touched Robin's cheek, brushing away tears that fell despite her words. "When Rafe returns, we'll know. Until then, you're safe." Then she smiled. "You're weary of rough clothes and rough living. I have a gown that will suit you well."

The gown Angelet lent her was so unlike the one Pierce had her wear. Angelet favored soft colors and delicate fabrics, and because she was such a skilled hand at embroidery, all her clothing featured some astonishing details. The white shift Robin borrowed was the softest linen, with little flowers worked in cream and ivory all along the long, loose sleeves. The overdress she had Robin put on next was silk dyed in a pale lavender, and the feel of it under Robin's fingers nearly brought tears to her eyes. "This is beautiful," she whispered.

"It will be more so when I finish the lacing and find the right girdle," Angelet promised.

The lacing was made of a silken rope shot with silver thread, and the narrow belt Angelet girdled around Robin's hips was also embroidered with silver thread to resemble feathers lying end to end—both items made by Angelet herself.

"There," Angelet said with satisfaction. "A true lady is what you are, and everyone can see it now. Let me just brush your hair out and add in a little braid."

"Thank you," Robin said, sitting on a carved wooden stool. "Not just for the dress, but for everything."

"My dear, it's little enough to house you and clothe you when you come to our door. I'm happy to do it, just as Cecily is."

"I'm not sure she'll be happy to do it anymore, after how I snuck away."

"When you have a chance to explain, she'll understand." Angelet squeezed Robin's shoulder. "What you did was so brave. And it sounds as though Octavian might never have found his quarry if you hadn't been there to guide him. He'll speak for you and see that Cecily and Alric understand what happened."

Yes, Octavian would put the best possible face on Robin's actions. He'd never embarrass her, but he would also be overjoyed to get rid of her at last, putting her safely back behind walls in Cleobury.

Assuming he came back at all.

If he didn't, it was all Pierce's fault. She wondered if the hospitality of Martenkeep was up to Pierce's standards, and then wondered if Pierce was using this opportunity for some plan of his own.

She grabbed Angelet's hand, saying, "The man I came with, Lord Pierce, must not be permitted to leave here alone. Will you pass that on to the guards?"

"Is he a prisoner?" Angelet asked, puzzled.

"Not exactly. But neither is he quite a willing guest."

"I'll send the message." Angelet rose and went to the door, speaking briefly to someone on the other side.

"All taken care of," Angelet told her then. "And soon Rafe and Octavian will both ride up, and all will be well."

Robin desperately wanted to believe that, but the image of Tav standing alone at the narrow bridge, fending off a far superior force of armed men, was too terrible. She had faith in his abilities as a knight. But she couldn't stop her heart from turning to lead at the thought of him so outnumbered.

"It isn't fair," she said.

The other woman looked at her with sympathy. "Nothing ever is. Try to rest. And pray, though I am confident that Octavian always has a few saints watching over him." Angelet left her, closing the door quietly.

But Robin couldn't bear to be alone, so she went down to the great hall not long after. Servants moved about in the hall and in the courtyard outside. On the surface, everything was just as usual. But the disturbance of the afternoon, and now the absence of the castellan himself, gave everyone a troubled air. Robin walked up to the battlements, needing to see the men's return with her own eyes. But the woods remained still and silent.

When dark fell, Robin was called down by Angelet, who told her that she needed food.

"Why aren't they back?" she demanded, knowing the other woman couldn't answer. "Why isn't someone here with news? A runner, or one of the men. Something."

"For all we know, they're riding back now. Remember that you rode the distance far faster than anyone ought to, and now that the light's gone, it will take longer to go safely. Now come into the hall. Supper is ready, and order must be maintained."

The ladies sat at the high table, and the dining hall soon filled with people. Pierce joined them, looking as clean and well rested as ever. He didn't ask for news—the lack of news filled the hall like a cloud, dampening all efforts to remain cheerful.

Then the mood broke. Several very young men all came in together, laughing and joking as they walked through the center of the room. Robin guessed them to be the boys sent here for fostering and military training. Most nobles sent their boys to other houses during their childhood. It allowed them to learn from experts they'd never get to in their own homes, and also served to build alliances and friendships between families.

"Gentlemen," Angelet called. When they all looked up to her expectantly, she went on. "Please approach and make your greetings to our guests. I wish to demonstrate that your education does not happen solely on the practice fields. You have manners, do you not?" Her smile belied her words.

Robin found herself greeted with a chorus of polite *how do you do*'s and *my lady*'s. The tallest of the boys barely managed not to trip himself as he bowed, his limbs not quite under his full control yet.

"Careful, Torin, or you'll fall right at the lady's feet," his smaller neighbor teased.

"Shut up, Guy."

The one named Guy turned back to Robin. "Fear not, my lady. Torin's much more coordinated when he's attacking one of us with a sword than when he has to confront any creature wearing skirts."

"I'm relieved to hear it, since swords are rather more dangerous," Robin said. The boy Torin was scarlet with embarrassment, and she wanted to make him feel better. "Perhaps I'll see for myself tomorrow. You wouldn't mind if I watched a training session?"

The boys' expressions ranged from excited to alarmed. Guy nodded, and said, "Certainly, my lady. But tomorrow we practice archery."

Angelet said, "Then you gentlemen can show Lady Robin your skills, and even allow her to shoot."

"That would be most kind." Despite her stomach being knotted like a tangled rope, Robin couldn't suppress a smile, and she caught Angelet's tiny answering smirk. She'd teach these boys a thing or two about archery, and she couldn't wait to see their faces when she finished the lesson.

As if tomorrow will just be another day. Her mood sank. If Rafe didn't come back with Tav alive and well, tomorrow would be the bleakest day Robin ever faced.

One of the other boys spoke up, addressing Angelet.

"When is Sir Rafe expected back, my lady? We were training and only saw that a force left in a rush."

"The guards said enemies were close by," the fourth boy added, his eyes big with concern. "Is that true, Mother?"

"Nothing to worry about, Henry. A group of men were near the north bridge," Angelet said. Her tone was calm but Robin heard the tightness in it. "Now, take your seats for the meal."

The food came out of the kitchens, and Robin tried to eat. But nothing appealed to her. She nibbled on bread only when Angelet nudged her with a foot.

She kept looking to the doors of the hall, which remained stubbornly closed. All of supper passed, and still there was no word.

Pierce and Angelet exchanged pleasant, meaningless conversation after the meal while Robin sat in turmoil. Still there was no word.

She went to the chapel, accompanied by Angelet, and prayed with her hands clasped so tightly that her fingers grew cold and numb. Still there was no word.

She went up to the master bedchamber with Angelet, who asked her to share the bed during the night. "That way, if the men return and I'm woken up, you'll know the very same instant." So Robin prepared for bed along with Angelet and her maid. She tried to sleep, telling herself that the instant she did so, the men would ride through the gates, because wasn't that how things happened?

Eventually, her tired, dry eyes slid closed. But when she woke in the morning, after fitful sleep and tortured dreams, still there was no word.

Chapter 30

WHEN ROBIN WOKE UP, ANGELET and her maids were already gone, leaving her alone in the massive bedchamber. She stared up at the canopy, which was supported by four posts of oakwood carved to resemble tree trunks covered in ivy. The heavy fabric of the canopy and curtains hid much of the light, turning the bed into a warm, dark cave. And because this was Angelet's home, the fabric was embroidered with flowers and birds and magical beasts, all rendered with such skill that they seemed ready to emerge from the cloth into the chamber itself. Robin reached out to touch a lion worked in gold thread, and then a unicorn standing fearlessly beside it. The lion certainly looked fierce, but what could frighten a unicorn? She wondered if Octavian had ever seen a lion in the flesh. He might have, traveling as much as he had from the Holy Land to here.

"Octavian!" she gasped. The events of the previous day flooded back into her mind. She sat up, flinging the covers aside. She yanked her gown on over the clean white shift. Shoving her feet into the soft slippers near the bed—also from Angelet—she hurried to the door and then down the stone steps to the ground floor.

Angelet was speaking to a maid when Robin rushed in.

"Any news?" she asked, skipping any good mornings.

The answer was clear in Angelet's face.

"You have to send someone out to check!" Robin had no business telling Angelet what to do, and yet she couldn't stop herself.

"So I have done," Angelet replied, unruffled. "I sent a rider toward the bridge this morning, and God willing, we'll hear something soon."

Her calm air made Robin feel even more brittle. "Aren't you worried?" she asked.

"Of course I'm worried, but I can only do what I can do. In the meantime, I have my duties to attend to." She gave Robin a little crooked smile. "And you will need a distraction to make it through the day. Why not break your fast and then go to the south meadow? The boys are training there, and it's always lively enough to occupy a person for a while."

Robin recognized the implicit command and bent her head. "I will do so, my lady."

"I will send word to you the moment anything is known." Angelet squeezed her arm. "Have faith."

Robin nodded. After eating a simple meal of bread and butter, with small ale to drink, she put on her cloak and gloves and took her bow to the south meadow.

Along the way, she passed through the courtyard and out of the main gates. Guards watched from the top of the gate tower, and another guard nodded politely as she passed by.

Outside the castle walls, Robin followed the faint sound of clashing metal until the din grew louder and she saw several pairs of fighters sparring in a large field. Instructions and warnings floated out over the air. When someone stumbled, the other helped him up and began the fight anew. A couple of grizzled instructors—men who'd survived more war than these boys could imagine— walked through the field, surveying each miniature battle with practiced eyes. They stopped to offer a critique in one spot or to demonstrate a sequence of moves in another.

One of the instructors reached the end of the field where Robin stood. She recognized him as Adam, who'd come to Martenkeep shortly after Sir Rafe was placed in charge.

"Good day, Lady Robin," Adam said with a bow made stiff due to an old riding injury. "I suspect the boys are in for a drubbing when we haul out the archery targets."

She smiled, trying to keep her mind on the topic. "It seems that they are fully committed to swordplay this morning."

He waved a hand, as if sweeping the notion away. "These whelps aren't strong enough to keep up such practice for more than a few hours. They've got to grow into it, and that'll take years. 'Cept for Torin, that is," he amended, looking at the tall blond boy sweating on the field. "He'll be ready by spring. And with Sir Rafe to oversee his training, I suspect that Torin might be a legend in his time."

"How's he at shooting?" Robin asked, hefting her bow slightly.

Adam snorted. "Not a legend. For archery, it's Acer you'll want to watch out for. Little scourge."

Robin watched the boy called Acer. He seemed as quick and obedient as the others practicing, but she caught a hint of displeasure in Adam's tone. "You don't like him."

"Ah, I like him well enough. He's a bright boy. But he's the son of one of the rebel barons to the north, and sons take after their fathers. Acer's always got a look in his eye, the sort of look a wolf gives to a lamb. He might not *do* anything evil, for he's still young. But mark my words, he's from bad stock."

"Perhaps he just needs time," Robin murmured. "Rafe was thought to be from bad stock for most of his life, and now he's one of the king's trusted castellans."

"Well, the saints do work miracles," Adam said. Then he whistled, drawing everyone's attention. "Put the swords away! Let's get those targets out. Time to show the lady how archery is done at Martenkeep."

Considering her inner turmoil, Robin had more fun than she expected to. There was something pleasantly distracting about having multiple people constantly piping up around her, vying for attention and always asking something.

Torin was blond, big, and brash, clearly the one destined for a life as a fighter, and most likely a knight. Guy was Torin's opposite—slim and thoughtful, with a mop of dark hair and skin almost olive in complexion. Acer was polite and clever and had an answer for everything. Robin liked him in spite of Adam's dire predictions about his fate. And finally, the youngest boy, Henry, who happened to be Angelet's son from her first marriage, rounded out the group. He seemed constantly wide-eyed, and clearly idolized the older boys around him.

Robin challenged all of them to ever more difficult feats of archery. Torin and Acer ran to push the targets back each time, and the boys were impressed by her shooting. Robin had just let an arrow fly when she caught sight of something odd. She turned her head and saw none other than Pierce walking toward an outbuilding near the trees.

"Now where's he going?" Robin muttered.

Acer followed her gaze, but Pierce had disappeared behind a building wall. "Who, my lady?"

"Lord Pierce, over there by the storehouse. He's got no business poking around Martenkeep. I wonder what he's up to."

"Want some reconnaissance, my lady?" Guy asked, his eyes bright.

She smiled. "What a good suggestion, Guy. Let's have a lesson in scouting, shall we? Acer, Guy, find out what he's up to. Follow him, but stay back and *don't* interfere unless he tries to leave the area of Martenkeep altogether. Then report back to me. I'll stay here with Torin and Henry and keep practicing."

The two boys ran off. Henry looked relieved at not being expected to go, but Torin frowned.

"I could have spied, you know," Torin said.

"I'm sure you could have," Robin replied, nocking another arrow. "But Lord Pierce might notice a whole practice field gone silent. You and Henry are helping preserve the illusion that we didn't notice him. That part is just as important as what the actual scout does."

Torin's eyebrows rose. "Yes, my lady!"

So Robin continued to practice, offering Torin and Henry practical advice on their own shooting. She actually enjoyed teaching them, since it kept her mind focused and away from baleful thoughts of Octavian's whereabouts.

Then a guard came running toward them. "My lady! Come quickly to the gate! They're back!"

All the breath left her lungs, and Robin swayed once on her feet.

Torin grabbed her elbow. "Are you well?"

"I don't know. We need to run. I need to see him." She didn't say a name, and didn't have to. Torin kept near her even though his long legs meant he could have outpaced her.

Robin's mind raced with possibilities. The guard's expression gave no clue as to what she'd find once she got there. Was Octavian dead? Wounded? Was Rafe with him? What had happened?

She passed through the open gate of the castle and saw a cluster of riders on horseback, all looking worn out.

And there he was, right in the middle of the group. He looked battered and worse for wear, and one arm was wrapped in a bloody bandage, but he was riding under his own power, upright and alert.

"Oh, praise God," she breathed. "Thank you for sparing him."

Torin pulled her forward. Everyone was drawn to the new presence of Octavian.

Then Octavian saw her and smiled. "Told you I'd catch up."

Chapter 31

OCTAVIAN EXPECTED ROBIN TO HAVE a tart comment ready, or at least to laugh. Instead, she just stared at him, looking as if she might fall over at any moment. The very young man who stood next to Robin put a hand to her elbow, steadying her.

Before Tav could ask her anything more, his attention was taken by Rafe, who'd remained close by him as they rode into the castle gates. Rafe dismounted, already calling for the gates to be closed after all the riders were accounted for. He gestured for someone to help Tav down, which was good because Tav's left arm pained him so much that he had difficulty using it or putting any pressure on it.

When his feet hit the ground, he looked for Robin again, but there were too many people and horses crossing the courtyard and crowding his vision. "Robin?" he called.

A woman emerged from the crowd, but it wasn't Robin. It was Lady Angelet, wearing a relieved smile. "Sir Octavian! You are always welcome here, but you are very welcome today. We feared for you."

"As you see, I'm alive and well...thanks to the timely arrival of Sir Rafe and his men."

Rafe reached for his wife. "How are you?" he asked, surveying her carefully.

"I am quite well," she replied softly. "No need to be concerned for my health."

He squeezed her hand, tension clearing from his face.

Throughout her life, Angelet experienced visions and suffered from seizures that followed. It left her weak and helpless for hours at a time. Rafe did all he could for her, sending for healers and doctors, and even writing to the great universities in Paris for answers. But nothing seemed to prevent them, so Rafe watched over her to catch the earliest signs of an attack. In the aftermath of one, he babied her extravagantly, keeping her abed and not letting her so much as pick up an embroidery needle.

"Rafe worried that his leaving so abruptly might cause you distress," Tav said.

"He worries over me far too much," Angelet insisted.

"I love you," Rafe told her. "The worry comes with that."

She smiled at her husband. "I know."

Tav watched them, still amazed at how much Rafe had changed after finding Angelet. Rafe had once been a cynical rogue who viewed women as diversions—to be enjoyed but never kept for long. Then he met Angelet, who took down his defenses simply by being herself. And now Rafe was married, the castellan of a strategic keep in the Marches, and a respected instructor for families to send their boys to so they could learn how knights fought. More proof that anything was possible.

Angelet now looked around the courtyard. "Where's Robin? She should be here."

"I saw her a moment ago," Tav said. "Is she all right?"

"Robin's fine," a new voice spoke up. Pierce appeared from the shifting group of folk all milling around. "Prancing about the castle as if she lives here, and already surrounded by a retinue of boys who follow after her like puppies. Did you think she'd be pining?"

Tav would never picture Robin pining, and he wasn't sure why Pierce was looking at him with such hostility. Then he realized that the man was actually glaring at Rafe.

"I knew there was something familiar about you," Pierce said to Rafe. "But I only saw you for an instant before. I know you."

Rafe nodded, having been told about what happened as he and Tav rode back. "Indeed, my lord. Five years ago. We met at Malvern when you were still Lord Pierce of Malvern. I hear your fortunes have declined since then."

"And yours have improved. Landless, bastard knight to trusted castellan!" Pierce glanced at Tav with anger flashing in his eyes. "Why did you send me here?"

"I sent you here because it's the closest place of shelter I trust," Tav said. "And don't forget, my lord, you *insisted* that I was the one who come to meet you. You wanted a specific man so you knew you weren't getting an imposter. Well, that means that you get all the specific connections that come with me. Such as Sir Rafe, your gracious host."

"I am not sure this is the best place for me, after all," Pierce said, looking as if he expected to be escorted directly out.

"The gates are closed, my lord," Rafe said. "Apart from the group that chased you, the Welsh are a constant threat, not to mention ordinary raiders and cutthroats who use the marches to hide from the law. You may not like it here, but at least within my walls you'll keep breathing."

Pierce recoiled at the knight's blunt words, but nodded. Then he noticed something else, and he smiled. "Ah, it's none other than Lady Robin."

Tav turned, eager to see her up close. She looked back at him, her deep blue eyes clouded with some sadness, though he couldn't think why.

"Octavian," she said, her voice barely loud enough to be heard.

"Robin." This was not how a reunion between them was supposed to happen. He remembered the awkwardness of seeing her at Cleobury when she shocked him into idiocy by being a full-grown, lovely woman. This was worse, because now all he wanted to do was reach for her and kiss her and tell her how very happy he was that they were both alive. But he couldn't do that in the middle of a crowd that would ask questions, and certainly not when she wasn't even smiling to see him.

Her gaze dropped to his arm, and she frowned. "You were hurt."

Tav's arm was held stiffly against his side, and the bandage he wore had soaked through enough to reveal a few bright red spots of blood. "Yes, but it will heal."

"We must tend to it immediately," Angelet declared. "Your wound and any others the men suffered. Come with me, Octavian."

Tav allowed Angelet to lead him toward the steps of the keep. He saw Robin following, much more slowly. She was still accompanied by the boy Pierce called one of her puppies—though he was big for a puppy, almost as tall as Tav himself, despite being probably a decade younger and still growing.

"Who's the boy?" he asked Angelet in a low voice.

"Torin? One of our fosterlings. He'll be a fine fighter

one day. And he seems quite struck by Robin." Angelet gave a little laugh. "Fear not for her safety while he's defending her."

"I'm glad she's protected," Tav said. In truth, the fact that Robin was on the other side was all that allowed him to fight for as long as he did. The bridge was the only thing between the attacking force and the woman he loved, so he would hold it until he faced capture or death.

He expected death.

Coming out alive was a miracle. Tav had no other explanation.

Because of Angelet's unusual ailment, Martenkeep actually had a doctor within the walls. The man was small in stature, less than five feet tall. His hair and beard were both iron grey, and he spoke French incessantly, peppered with Latin phrases, while he worked.

Octavian had seen his share of doctors and surgeons during his life. Some were lifesavers and others were quacks. Brother Andre at the monastery of Saint Thomas had been the former. He knew all the phases of the moon and which stars were ascending, and how to balance the humors of the body, as well as how to stop a wound from bleeding and stitch the flesh back up without killing a patient. Tav had seen women set bones at the sides of a battlefield without blinking an eye at the carnage around them. And he'd seen learned doctors in the cities across Europe who couldn't save a fish from drowning.

This doctor acted pompous but wasn't afraid of blood. He muttered in French about the need to wait for the moon to start waning before the wound would truly knit, but he also cleaned the cuts well and bound them all tightly with the bandages Angelet and her maids supplied.

"There now," the doctor proclaimed at last, his mumbled words coming out quickly. "The cuts are bound, the bruises treated. You must drink a tisane which I've ordered prepared. And you must rest, praying every time you wake up and every time you are about to fall asleep."

"Octavian does that anyway," Rafe said from the chair by the bed where he'd been sitting.

"Many people were praying for you," Angelet added, smiling softly.

"Many people pray for kings," Rafe noted, "and kings still die."

"Kings are rarely good Christians," the doctor grunted. He looked back at Tav. "I will tell my assistant to change the dressing every day. If the wounds fester or if you take a fever, death may come for you anyway, despite all I've done. But you are lucky. Very lucky. God may have plans for you yet upon this earth."

Tav had plans himself, but he nodded in thanks.

The doctor left, and Rafe said, "The man's a bit odd, but he's saved lives here. He doesn't fuss, whether it's tending to Angelet after a seizure or tending to soldiers after a battle. The other doctors in Paris didn't like him. He was happy enough to come here."

"You should sleep now," Angelet said. "Call if you need anything. But please sleep—that's the best medicine."

"Tell Robin I want to talk with her," he said quickly.

At the doorway, Angelet cast a sympathetic look over her shoulder. "When you wake up again, I'll send her."

Tav was given a private bedchamber specifically so he could rest uninterrupted for as long as he needed to. As soon as his head touched the pillow, he succumbed to sleep. He'd been deprived of it for too long.

Even in sleep, his arm still ached from the wound he'd received at the bridge. And even though it had been nearly a full day since the fight ended, he still felt the vibrations of every sword striking his shield, and how his shoulders felt permanently bunched up from the effort of parrying and lunging with his longsword for such a long time.

He had sent Robin ahead and told Pierce to enforce the order because Robin had a fire in her eyes. She wanted to fight, and left to her own, she would.

But he couldn't think clearly when she was in danger, so he forced her away. Then he turned to cover their escape, remaining on foot. The horse he'd got from Willesden was sturdy, but not trained for battle. The last thing he wanted was a horse that spooked during combat, so he sent it off into the woods.

He didn't want to die, and he didn't intend to give up, but the odds were not in his favor. One man against many required a miracle for the one man to win.

The first wave of attackers rode up a few seconds later—about eight men on horseback. They saw only Octavian there and immediately split up, riding on either side of the gorge as if they'd find another way across. Only two came up to within twenty paces of Octavian at the end of the bridge. They stopped and waited with grins on their faces, confident that he could go nowhere unless they allowed it.

He just stood there, waiting for the inevitable clash.

Not long after, the other riders returned, reporting that the gorge was impassable. "To get Lord Pierce, we need to cross and chase him down," one proclaimed.

"Easy enough," another said, looking at Octavian. "You two. Go take care of him."

Two riders charged up, swords drawn, expecting little trouble.

Octavian crouched low and struck—not at the men, but at the horses. He hated to do it, but it was necessary. The horses reacted the way all sensible animals did to pain. They reared up and instinctively retreated, ignoring all commands from their riders. Two more attackers tried to stop the retreat, and the result was confusion and chaos.

Octavian defended himself and took opportunities to wound his opponents only when he could. His aim wasn't to win, just to keep them from crossing the narrow bridge.

And he did, though it got more difficult with every passing moment. Battles were usually short for a reason—not even the strongest man could fight with a sword and heavy shield endlessly.

Then he felt a searing pain in his left arm, just above the top of the shield. An attacker howled in triumph as the blood welled up.

Tav shook off the pain and struck back, though he knew he wouldn't last long if he got struck like that again.

A fresh fighter edged up at one point, darting between two others. He got close to Tav and said in low voice, "They don't want you! You can jump over the side and escape into the gorge. They won't follow."

He then whipped his sword toward Tav, but in a way that Tav could parry. He recognized Kevan, the young guard back at Willesden.

"I can't," he grunted back.

Kevan struck again, and again, he deliberately aimed poorly. "Pierce. Isn't. Worth. Defending," he got out.

It wasn't Pierce who Tav was thinking of. He just shook his head. "Back away," he cautioned the other fighter.

"More are coming," Kevan warned, even as he retreated.

Other men replaced him, men who aimed better and more intently. Tav blocked their attacks, feeling more and more tired. He heard distant hoofbeats. Another wave of fighters would be here any moment.

Just when his shoulder dropped, when he knew that he couldn't stop these men much longer, he heard a few cries of dismay.

He glanced back for an instant and saw a storm of riders. A single figure with night-black hair, wearing mail and a black surcoat, riding a black horse, rode ahead of the others.

Tav redoubled his efforts, despite the weariness taking over. Then he heard a shout behind him as a horse clattered along the bridge span.

"Get the hell out of the way, Tav!"

It was Rafe who yelled, and Tav slid to the right just as a glossy black horse rushed past him directly into the fray. Rafe was followed by more men who fanned out around Tav. Six of them blocked the bridge, and the rest flowed into the skirmish, shifting the balance of the fight.

Tav sank back against the stone wall, dropping his sword beside him. His whole body ached, and his left arm was throbbing. He clapped a hand over the wound in his arm, feeling the sticky warmth of blood.

He didn't see the rest of the fight clearly, but he heard Rafe shouting orders and then the well-trained horsemen chasing down the already tired opponents. The second wave of attackers that Kevan warned him about had appeared, but lingered only long enough to cover the escape of their comrades.

Rafe, enraged that any hostile force got so close to Martenkeep, began to pursue them, his own men riding in a way that scattered the attackers into the woods.

Tav closed his eyes, concentrated on breathing, and only roused himself when he heard Rafe calling his name.

At least an hour had passed. Twilight was taking over the sky. Rafe ordered Tav's wounds bound, and then announced that they'd all stay at the bridge to keep anyone from circling back and crossing during the night.

"Let them wander through the trees or find a way through the ravine, and may they stumble and die in the night. This bridge is *ours*."

Blazing fires were lit, both to keep the men warm and to make it clear the bridge was defended. The horses got herded into a spot where they could crop the grasses and rest after the breakneck ride to reach the bridge. They wouldn't want to ride them back tonight anyway—they were exhausted.

In the morning, the men took their time gathering up the makeshift camp, the sun well up when Rafe finally ordered the whole company to ride back to Martenkeep at a careful pace. Along the way, Tav recounted to Rafe nearly all that happened, up to Rafe's seemingly miraculous appearance at the bridge.

Rafe just laughed. He wasn't usually in league with saints and angels.

Now safe at Martenkeep, Tav woke again to the soft light of a grey afternoon. Or he thought it was afternoon. He didn't know if he'd slept a few hours or many days. He'd believe either.

He called out, his voice emerging dry and hoarse.

An older maid opened the door. "You're awake! Do you need anything?"

"How long have I been sleeping? Where are Rafe and Angelet?"

"Oh, it's been near a day since you got here. I'll fetch Sir Rafe."

Not long after, Rafe appeared with the doctor at his side. Tav had to argue his case for getting out of bed and being allowed to eat his supper in the great hall. "I'm not an invalid, but I will be if I don't eat at least half a roast by myself. I'm hungry."

The doctor insisted on redressing the wound on his arm and frowned in concentration as he sniffed at the cut. "Looks and smells well enough. It seems to not be festering," he said cautiously. He held one hand to Tav's forehead. "No fever. That's good."

"So you're saying there's no reason why I can't stand up and walk about and act as I normally would?"

"I suppose not," the doctor said, "but don't overexert yourself. Avoid all food that is green in color. Drink wine instead of ale. And don't consort with any women. It overheats the blood and taxes the body. Even looking at women can stir up the humors and destroy a man's inner balance. Women are in general a detriment to a calm mind and healthy body."

Rafe's laughter boomed in the small chamber and echoed through the hall. "That's why we keep them around!"

The doctor wrinkled his nose and declared his advice too good to waste on bloodthirsty, brainless knights.

Rafe hustled the doctor out, and Tav dressed in new, clean clothing that had been folded neatly on a chest at the foot of the bed. The long sleeves of the tunic covered all the bandages completely. He felt at his bruises, his fingers gingerly testing how sensitive they still were. Thankfully, the ointment the doctor used worked well, and he was much improved.

Downstairs in the great hall, fires burned in each of the fireplaces at the ends of the large room, and candles flickered in sconces set all along the walls, as well as in the great iron chandelier hanging from the massive central beam. Tav made his way to the high table, speaking to several people along the way, thanking the soldiers he recognized and greeting others he didn't know before. Then he took his seat, more weary than he'd ever admit out loud.

Angelet and Robin entered together, their figures briefly framed in the doorway. The sound in the hall dropped to almost nothing for a brief moment.

What had the doctor said about women destroying a man's inner balance? Robin, looking like a vision, was destroying Tav's inner balance. And his calm mind. And the sight of her was certainly stirring up something in his body.

Supper seemed to go on without end. Despite being seated next to each other, Robin barely spoke to him or indeed even looked at him for longer than the space of a glance. At one point, a boy of about thirteen years—not the same boy as earlier—dashed up to her, leaned over the table, and whispered something.

Robin's eyes lit up and she whispered something back.

"Acer," Angelet said sharply, having seen the boy approach. "What are you doing? You shouldn't be out of your seat and you certainly shouldn't be whispering. It looks like gossip."

"The fault is mine," Robin responded, her words shielding the boy from Angelet's censure. "I asked Acer to do a favor for me earlier and he's merely keeping me informed."

Acer winked and scampered away.

"What was that about?" Tav asked.

The smile she gave the boy evaporated the moment she looked over at him. She gave a brief shake of her head and mumbled, "Probably nothing."

"What does that mean?"

"It's not important," she said. "A diversion for the boy…something to occupy him. That's all."

It clearly was not, but Tav couldn't interrogate her in the middle of the dining hall. So he'd just have to wait till he could speak to her alone.

That might be difficult, considering how she seemed to be avoiding him ever since he got to Martenkeep. She hadn't gone to his room once, despite Angelet and Rafe stopping by several times. She could have joined them for any visit. And then there was this strange aloofness, which was so unlike Robin, who normally wore her heart on her sleeve. Was he imagining it? Because she was dressed so finely, with her glossy hair falling down her back rather than in her practical braid, was he assuming her behavior was also different?

No. His Robin was an honest, even blunt, person who never kept silent when she had something to say. This Robin was mysteriously circumspect. Entirely too…lady-like.

When Robin excused herself after the meal, Tav waited only long enough for her to leave the room, then he also stood.

"What's wrong, Octavian? Are you not well?" Angelet asked, her eyes wide with concern.

"I just need some air," he said, wondering how many steps Robin was from him right now. "And then I'll rest."

"We'll send the doctor up," she promised, but Rafe put a hand on her arm.

"Tav is on his feet and he's a man who can ask for help if he needs it. Haven't you got enough boys around to mother?" He grinned at Tav. "Go and get some air. I'll tell the doctor to check on you…on the morrow."

Tav nodded gratefully, and then left the loud, busy hall in search of Robin. He found her only after climbing a flight of curving stairs and then checking down two dark hallways.

A flash of pale silk the color of her dress caught his eye, and he quickened his steps. "Robin?"

She looked back and stepped aside as if to let him pass. "What are you doing here?" she asked when he stopped in front of her. She made a motion as if to dart back downstairs. "I should go."

"Wait." He reached out and put one hand against the wall to prevent her from sliding away.

Robin raised one eyebrow. "If you think you're trapping me…"

"I don't want to trap you, I want to talk to you."

"We spoke all through supper."

"Not true. In fact, you've hardly spoken to me since I got here."

"You've been asleep for most of that time," she countered, quite correctly.

Still, he wasn't about to let her evade the question. "Not during the meal. I could have reached out and touched you, but you behaved as if I wasn't even there."

"I wish you would," she said. Or he thought that was what she said.

"What?"

"Reach out and touch me."

That was easy. He lifted his other hand and touched her face, right along her jawline, which was one of his favorite features of hers, since it was so often set to reveal her mood. Her skin was warm under his fingers, and he stroked up and tucked a strand of hair behind her ear. And then he had her hair in his hand, playing with the silky locks before he knew that's what he wanted to do.

At his touch, her breath rushed out of her like a storm pent up for too long. "I was so scared," she whispered. "I still don't believe it. That you're alive. And here."

"I am," he assured her. "I got through it and I'm in one piece."

"I left you." The words came out in a hiss. Angry

words, but her anger wasn't directed at him. She looked up at him, and he was surprised to see her eyes were glassed over with tears that hadn't fallen. The anger was for herself, and he started to understand her reserve from earlier.

"Did you think I was upset with *you*?" he asked. "I told you to go."

"But I wanted to stay, so I could do something to help. Not just run away to where I couldn't even see what was happening. I might have run to the other end of the world."

Tav shook his head. "You didn't run away. You retreated, which was just what you should have done."

"Then why did it feel so horrible? I left you alone." At *alone*, her voice broke off.

"I'm not alone now." He held her, and once he held her, he couldn't stand the idea of not holding her. He needed her. Because she was right about one thing. When she'd left, he felt the distance between them stretching into something far greater than a few leagues.

"Come with me," he said, pulling back enough to see her face. "Right now. Come with me and stay all night."

Her mouth fell open, but before she could raise any objection, he said, "Please. I spent last night alone, dreaming of things I'd rather forget. Now that I'm here with you, I don't want to be alone another night."

Robin's chest rose as she inhaled, her thoughts racing behind her eyes, most of all an uncertainty that he wanted to erase. "You just don't want to be alone?"

"I want to be with you," he said.

Her smile was the answer he needed—a slow smile that started on her lips but then suffused her whole face and lit her eyes. "Then yes."

He took her to his own room on the next floor, moving

fast, as if that would ensure she wouldn't change her mind. But when they got inside and closed the door, she didn't seem inclined to change her mind. Her arms slipped around him, and her mouth was on his before he managed to say a word.

Robin's kiss fed him in a way no food or drink or medicine could. How long had it been since he got to feel this, to feel her touch? Too long. He thought he'd be dead the day before yesterday, but he was alive now, and all he wanted was to prove how alive he felt.

They were tangled together and yet clothing still came off. Robin lost her gown and then her shift, lying gloriously naked on his bed, which was exactly where she was supposed to be. He got rid of his offending clothing as well, but only earned a furrowed brow from Robin as she rose to her knees on the bed, scanning the various wounds he'd got.

She cautiously touched the bandage on his left arm. She said, "The cut could have severed the limb if you'd been standing a little differently! Does it still hurt?"

"No." Yes, it hurt. And he didn't care. Not when she was with him.

"How else were you injured?" she asked, her hands moving across his body, delicately, afraid to bring any further pain.

"A few scratches and bumps," Tav promised. "It's nothing a little time won't cure."

"Are you lying to make me not worry?"

"If you're worried, you should think about something else." He leaned forward and kissed her, running his hands through her loose hair. He might never get enough of her hair.

"Tav," she whispered. "I'm so, so grateful you're here."

So was he. He was grateful that he could kiss her all over, grateful that he could taste her breasts and slide his hands over her stomach and her legs and grab her feet in a way that made her wriggle against him and accuse him of tickling her on purpose.

"Of course it's on purpose," he told her, loving the way her body pressed against his erection. Everything he did now was with the express purpose of showing her how happy he was to be alive with her and making her as delightfully satisfied as it was possible for a woman to be.

"Hand or mouth," he said when he'd kissed his way back up to her ear.

"What?"

"You know what I'm asking," he told her. "I'm going to make you come for me, and you choose whether you want it from my hand or my mouth. This time, that is."

"Oh." Robin's rapid breaths told him how excited she already was, how much she had missed him. "I...I've always loved your hands."

He smiled, adoring the sudden shyness in her voice. "Then that's what you'll have." He liked that because then he could watch her respond to him.

And she responded instantly when he touched her center, already wet with arousal. She spread her legs and let him do whatever he liked, which was to make her weak with need, drawing out little gasps of pleasure as he teased her and played with her.

He'd been lying on his side, but when she began to roll her hips in response to his touch, he shifted to put his body above hers, loving how she looked beneath him on the bed.

"Come for me," he told her at last, his tone harsher than he expected. "I need to feel you come against my hand, Robin. It's been too long since I felt you do that for me."

"Is that what you need?" she asked a little breathlessly. "Or is it something else?"

He was already painfully hard, and when she reached out and curled her fingers around him, he somehow grew harder still.

She stroked him, her eyes locked on his face. "I think you want me."

Tav couldn't stop a laugh, even though it wasn't funny. God, yes, he wanted her. "You have no idea," he managed to say.

"I want you," she told him, her voice soft but unwavering. "I want to feel you inside me."

"Robin—"

But she went on, "When I wasn't sure if you were alive or dead, I couldn't stop thinking that I might never know how it would be to truly be with you. A very worldly, sinful regret, I know."

"I had the same regret," he confessed. There was nothing like getting sharp blades pointed at one's belly to make a person reflect on what he truly desired in life. Namely, to live, and to prove just how alive he was by coming inside the woman he loved.

"Then it's what we both want," she breathed. "Please, Tav. Don't deny me."

She meant it. He knew that by how she guided him right to her center, and how ready she felt when she teased the tip of him with her body.

He was done with denial. He braced himself on his good arm, slid one hand to her hip, and thrust once.

This was it. This was home. She was home. He had never felt so complete before.

When he entered her, Robin let out a huge breath and then lay perfectly still for a moment. He worried he'd hurt her. But then she slipped her arms around him, her hands spread out on his back.

She brought her mouth to his ear, and he heard a whispered command to keep going.

Tav never needed an instruction less.

He shifted slightly and pushed farther into her. She arched her back and raised her hips in a way that made him want to howl.

He grasped her left hip hard, keeping her still. "Robin. If you move like that again, you'll finish me."

"How should I move, then?" she asked, her eyes both innocent and mischievous.

"Don't move at all," he ordered. "Just feeling you like this is all I can take. Feeling how…tight you are." He closed his eyes. "Don't move."

She obeyed, stilling beneath him, her body hot and wonderfully soft inside and out.

"How do you feel?" he asked. "Any pain?"

"None. Just…" She couldn't stop from shifting her hips. "Just need."

He groaned when she moved. "Need for me." He withdrew a little, then returned.

Robin gasped, her eyes widening. *"Yes."*

He repeated the move, drawing another yes from her. And another.

"Tav," she said desperately. "I think you're driving me mad."

He liked that. Slipping one hand to her backside, he lifted her hips up, pulling her to him as he thrust. He didn't go fast, but he let her feel every inch of him as he slid in and out of her, filling her with an increasing frenzy of need. Far from easing her tension, he stoked it, keeping his eyes on hers the whole time.

Robin's breath came in half gasps, and then she

whimpered his name. Tav cupped the back of her head with one hand, bringing her mouth to his shoulder. She bit down on his body to keep from making any more noise as she came undone.

He felt her whole body shudder and knew he couldn't hold back any longer. He needed to join her wherever she was.

Tav was so close to coming, he wanted to scream, but Robin raised her hand to his mouth, knowing what he needed. He caught the heel of her hand between his teeth, stifling the shout. Then he moaned, his eyes closing as he lost himself in her.

"You're what I want," he swore, and then pushed into her as he came. He spent himself and reveled in how blissful she looked. "Robin," he said, breathing hard, his body stunned from the intensity of being inside her at last.

He recovered slowly, not entirely sure what had just happened was real. Robin lay beneath him, her eyes closed but with a smile on her lips as she slowly rocked her hips against his. *Oh.* That's why he felt like he was still coming. She was using her body to draw out the pleasure, a slow pulse that he'd happily enjoy for hours, if only he could stay awake that long. Then again, if they slept for a little while, he could recover and then take her again, showing her just how much he wanted her.

He withdrew, and she let out a discontented little mewling sound that was arousing all on its own. He would never get tired of hearing her and seeing her like this, completely exposed and yet still at ease with him.

After cleaning her up with water and a cloth, then doing the same for himself, he slid next to her and stretched his body out along hers. He reached for her, drawing her against him, her back against his chest, her hair spilling out everywhere, teasing his skin and making him eager for their next coupling.

Oh, Christ.

He'd done it. Coldness spread through his chest. He'd done the one thing he swore he would never do. As if he could somehow take it all back, he pushed himself away from her.

She turned toward him, her eyes opening, her lips curving into a sleepy smile. "I liked that," she whispered. "No, I loved it."

"Good." He should have *something* more to say, but his mind was utterly blank.

No, not blank. It was running rampant with all the consequences of what he'd just done. He'd ruined her best prospects for a marriage, he'd shredded the last of her innocence, and he'd possibly destroyed her life. All for a few moments of pleasure. Intense, perfect pleasure that he wanted to repeat as soon as she'd let him.

This was why people kept sinning. Because it felt so astonishingly perfect in the moment.

She could bear my child. The thought took his breath away. Was Robin going to suffer that much because he couldn't control himself one time? Then the even more selfish thought followed—*I want her children to be mine.*

Not now, he protested in his mind. But someday. He absolutely could envision Robin cradling a child to her breast, a child with richly colored skin like his own, contrasted against Robin's own light complexion.

If he made Robin a mother before she wanted to be a mother, she'd loathe him for trapping her into a life she despised—the life of a matron, safe behind walls and with a child tied to her apron strings. He could picture the fury in her eyes when he rode off to fight and she had to remain behind where it was safe.

He had to prevent that future, and that meant he could

never repeat what he'd just done. If it wasn't already too late.

Octavian held Robin in a vain attempt to pretend that everything was as it should be, and that he hadn't just ruined her life. She was blissfully unaware of his thoughts, or of how complicated everything had just become. Nestled against his body, she was asleep within moments, her breathing soft and even.

Tav's mind was humming, and he couldn't even close his eyes. He watched the rise and fall of Robin's chest and trailed his fingers along her skin, unable to resist her allure.

Unable to resist summed up his soul at the moment. How was he going to face Robin when she inevitably realized the consequences? She'd hate him, and there was nothing he could do to reverse what had happened.

And what if she did become pregnant after just one night? He'd marry her in a heartbeat, but the only benefit that would provide was legitimacy for the child. It didn't change the fact that Octavian wasn't suited to marry anyone because he had no lands or income of his own, in England or anywhere else. That had been the problem from the very beginning, and nothing had changed, except that he knew he loved her and that he'd also just destroyed her.

After hours of him turning the same thoughts over in his mind with no different solution appearing, the fire had burned to nothing and the room grew cold. He held Robin closer, and she stirred, turning to face him, her hands curling against his chest.

"Robin," he murmured.

"Hmmm?" She tipped her face up and kissed him without fully waking, a gesture so sweet it made his heart ache.

"Robin," he said again. "You have to wake up."

"What time is it?" she asked, alarm invading her voice.

"The middle of the night," he assured her. "But it would not be wise for you to be found here in the morning."

"I don't want to leave you."

And he didn't want her to have to leave, but what could he do? "It's safest if you go," he said. "Any questions at all wouldn't be good."

"Kiss me goodbye, then," she said with her usual impudence.

He kissed her, because he wasn't made of stone. She melted into him, and he wanted to keep her there forever.

But he couldn't. When her kisses grew more demanding, he pushed her away as gently as he could. "Enough, Robin. Get dressed."

She bit her lip, frowning for an instant, but then flashed a smile. "As you command."

Robin slid from the bed, threw more logs onto the fire, and then found her clothing in the dim light, pulling her shift on and then the gown over the top.

He sat up in bed, but she stopped him from getting out of it by leaning over to kiss him again. "Stay there, Tav," she said, her expression suddenly serious. "Don't forget you're wounded."

"Not that wounded."

"Yes, you are. So wounded you slept all night. That's what you'll tell everyone, won't you?"

He paused, weighing her words. "If that's what you want me to say."

"We can talk tomorrow?" Robin asked more hesitantly. "I think...we need to talk."

"Tomorrow," he promised. "Now go." He reached for

her and put two fingers on her mouth. If he kissed her again, she'd never leave the room.

Robin smiled and left without another word.

Tav slept fitfully after that, his waking thoughts tangling up with dreams. He walked through the streets of Aleppo he remembered as a child, only to go into a house and see Robin with two children with skin like his, asking him if he'd remembered to buy her more arrows in the market. He walked out, finding that Aleppo was gone and he stood in a church decorated with stained glass depicting English saints. Brother Petrus stood up from where he'd been sitting in the front of the church and advanced toward Tav, reciting the fable of the snake and the frog.

"Who is the frog, Octavian? And will the snake escape justice?"

Tav shook his head. "It's just a story."

"Everything is a story, Octavian," the monk declared. "One single story written by the hand of God. Every chapter in order, every page with a purpose. Will you let the snake kill the bird?"

"The frog," he corrected. "The fable is about a snake and a frog."

Brother Petrus turned around walked away. Tav started to chase after him, but tripped on the uneven stones.

He looked up and saw the church had melted away. He now stood in the courtyard of a very familiar manor. Alric was standing in front of him.

"Tav, I thought I'd never see you again." He pulled Tav to his feet. "We're glad you're home. Robin is lost."

"Lost?"

"Someone stole her." Alric now held a sword, the blade pointing down so that it looked like a cross in his hand. "I swear I'll kill him when I find him."

On either side of Alric, the figures of Sir Rafe and Sir

Luc appeared, also holding swords. Rafe spoke, promising Alric every aid a knight could provide a brother knight. Luc echoed the sentiment, his eyes burning.

Tav woke in a sweat.

He got up and struggled into his clothing. His arm seemed to have stiffened up, the wound aching more this morning. He put his head out the door and called for someone to send up the doctor.

Tav turned around and walked to the narrow windows, opening the shutter, letting in the light and cold of the morning. He looked around the newly bright room. Something glinted under the bed frame, and he knelt down to pick it up off the floor. It was a long, thin cord in a silvery color—the lacing from the side of Robin's gown. Tav swallowed and wound it into a tight coil. If anyone had found it, there was no innocent explanation for its presence in his room.

He had to hide it until he could return it to Robin, but he had nowhere it would be safe. He heard footsteps in the corridor and began to panic. The doctor was coming. His eye fell on his boots and he dropped the balled-up cord into one just as someone opened the door.

He turned, but it wasn't the doctor who stood in the doorway. It was Lord Pierce.

"Made it through the night? Excellent."

"Kind of you to check on me," Tav said.

"Well, we are not finished with our business. I need to speak with the king himself, and the king is not here. I think we should continue on today. You and I. Leave the lady behind."

"I'll never leave her," Tav snapped before he thought better of it. "And you don't tell me what to do. Try it and I'll show you what I mean."

"You can't harm me," Pierce said in a smug tone.

Tav grabbed him and shoved him against the stone wall. Astonished by the mere fact of being handled like that, Pierce gave an undignified yelp.

"How dare you try—"

"I'm not trying," Tav said. "I'm doing. You say I can't hurt you. But I can."

"Wait! The king won't permit it—"

"The king isn't here."

"The whole country will suffer if a rebellion succeeds…"

"Look at me." Tav grabbed Pierce's jaw and forced him to face Tav directly. "Do I look like your countrymen? Do I look like I care what the king of this island wants? It doesn't matter to me if you live or die. I could kill you, leave your body for crows, and then leave Britain forever."

"You swore service to a lord."

"I'll find another. Or serve no lord. It matters not to me. There's always someone willing to pay for a fighter."

"A knight has lands."

"Not me. I have none. Nothing holds me here."

"What of your companions that you claim to hold dear?"

"I lived without them before and I could do so again." Besides, they had each other, not to mention support from countless others.

"Even the little Robin who follows you so faithfully?"

Tav shoved Pierce against the wall, harder than before. He hated the man for mentioning her name. "Forget about her. Robin can take care of herself."

Pierce struggled against Tav's grip, but he had no leverage and couldn't free himself.

Tav released him, disgusted at how craven the other man was. "And don't talk to me of a greater good. You

295 x Elizabeth Cole

claim to have information that will prevent a rebellion that will kill innocent people. Yet you keep it to yourself."

Tav turned away, leaving Pierce to gather himself. He was sick of the whole mission, of responding to every call, of riding on other people's business instead of his own.

When Robin came to see him this morning, he'd tell her that. He'd confide how empty his duty had started to feel, and how he could strike out on his own. He'd ask her to come with him, no matter the consequences. He just hoped she'd arrive soon, before his usual resolve asserted itself and kept him from explaining his true feelings, the way it had too often done before.

Robin would understand.

Chapter 32

FORGET ABOUT HER. ROBIN CAN take care of herself.

Robin heard those words and abruptly stopped just before she reached Octavian's door. She'd come to visit Tav in his room during the respectable hours of daylight, when the door would remain open and they could talk without fear of someone thinking it was clandestine.

But then she heard Tav and Pierce. The words cut through her chest and into her heart. She'd only caught the last part of whatever discussion the men had been having, but she wished she had stayed away a moment longer, so she didn't know what Octavian actually thought of her. It wasn't just the words that hurt so much. It was the way he said them. He would discard her along with everyone else he knew whenever he decided to leave England.

Leave. She blinked back tears that sprang from nowhere. Weeks ago, Tav admitted to reconsidering his search for his family, but he hadn't mentioned he was actually leaving. She realized how little she knew of what he thought of anything, and how much she'd just assumed he held the same feelings for her as she did for him.

Obviously, she'd been wrong. Robin wheeled about

and fled silently down the corridor, down the stairs, and outside.

The courtyard was busy this morning. Several women were sorting through baskets of late harvest vegetables, deciding which would be eaten first and which could be stored through the winter. Boys hauled off the baskets to various places, struggling with the weight. It was all so everyday, so normal.

Robin closed her eyes, her mind spinning. She felt faintly sick to her stomach, thinking of how she'd thrown herself at Tav at every opportunity. What had Pierce told her before? To be careful, because men took what they could and then left as soon as they could. She should have listened.

"My lady?"

Her eyes flew open at the voice. The young man Acer was approaching, his smile sunny and open, though his eyes were more crafty. He'd told her last evening that he was continuing to spy on Pierce, following him discreetly. Robin was a little ashamed at instigating the game, but the boy clearly enjoyed it, and what harm could it do?

"Good day," she said. "When did you wake? You look as if you're the early bird with the worm."

He nodded, his hair catching the sun as he did. "It's been interesting. Lord Pierce went to the storehouse again. The one by the practice fields. I watched, and when he left for the castle, I peeked in. There's not much in there now, but I found a whole bundle of clothing and several full wineskins. They were hidden under a pile of hay. I left everything there, but it's an odd thing for a lord to do, isn't it?"

"Very odd." Why would Pierce hide such items when he already was in a safe place like Martenkeep? "What did he do after?"

"Just went to the hall to break his fast. Torin was there too, and by the time I joined them, they'd been talking for a while. Pierce was asking Torin all about Coventry—that's where Torin's from, you know."

"What does Pierce care about Coventry?"

"I think he was just making conversation. Asking about the land around, and if Torin ever went hunting in the woods nearby—where the best places were for game and such, which rivers were wide and which were narrow enough to ford, and which had the best fishing. He loves to talk. Lord Pierce, that is. Torin's rather quiet, but he got him chattering like nothing."

Robin nodded. Pierce was always good at charming others, even boys he had no need to manipulate into alliances. It was just in his nature to draw people out and get them talking.

"Then Pierce said he had to go speak to Sir Octavian," Acer added.

Yes, and Robin knew how that had gone.

"Would you keep an eye on him throughout the day, if you can?" she asked Acer.

"We've got to practice," he said. "But after that, I'll watch."

"If you see anything else strange, let me know. Should we meet here again after supper?"

Acer gave a bow—he was a budding charmer himself. "As you wish, my lady."

The boy strolled off, leaving Robin in no better state than before. First she overheard Octavian revealing his true thoughts and crushing her soul, and now Pierce was up to something. Could any man in the world be trusted?

A headache began to pulse at her temples. She decided to return to her room and hide until she could think clearly again.

But even in her room, she wasn't permitted to sulk alone. First Angelet came by, all concern and commiseration for Robin's mostly imaginary illness. Then, not long after, Octavian himself walked in while Robin was sitting by the window, inhaling the brisk air blowing in from the west.

"Robin?" he asked, with every suggestion of concern. "I heard you weren't well."

"I'd be better if I wasn't bothered every quarter hour." Her voice came out bitter, and she hated how fragile she felt.

Tav regarded her in silence for a terribly long moment, then just said, "I won't stay long, though you did want to talk."

She had said that. Last night when she was still caught up in a dream. "Later," she managed.

"Good." Tav nodded as if everything were settled. "But perhaps not too much later? Pierce says he wants to continue to London as early as tomorrow."

"Well, you were charged with doing so, weren't you?" she asked listlessly.

"Robin? What's wrong?" Tav looked at her, frowning. Before, she would have confidently shared her every thought. Now, she doubted if he cared about her in the slightest, and was just being polite.

"I slept poorly. That's all."

"I thought you slept well enough," he countered in a low voice. Then he came forward and touched her chin, raising her face to peer at it. "Robin, if you need to truly rest, you can stay here at Martenkeep," he said. He gave her a smile. "I can find the way from here. No more hidden paths in the Ardenwood that only you know how to navigate."

So that was her sole usefulness after all...just as a

guide through the Ardenwood. "I imagine you'll want to get to London as soon as possible. And from there, who knows?" Probably back to the Continent, or the Levant, as far from Robin as he could get.

Tav gave her an odd look. "It's true that the earlier we get Pierce to London, the better. But I don't like the thought of leaving you, especially if you're not well."

She said, "I'm not sick. I told you, it was just that I slept poorly."

"Robin," he said, reaching for her.

Robin wanted so badly to step into his embrace. She wished he would just hold her and let her shelter with him, trusting that he'd be a bulwark against whatever the world plagued her with.

"Robin, you're not just tired. What's—" Before he could go on, the sound of someone in the hallway made him drop his arms and step away from her.

A maid came in with more firewood, and Tav walked toward the door, saying he hoped to see Robin at supper that evening. She didn't even answer.

She spent the afternoon brooding, but did join the others in the hall for the evening meal, more to keep Angelet from worry than any desire to be among people.

Robin picked at her food, uninterested in eating. Acer caught her eye at one point and tipped his head toward the door, wordlessly asking if she still planned to meet him. He looked excited, and she guessed he had news. She nodded once and got a quick smile from him.

After supper, people began to leave the great hall to prepare for bed. The shorter days meant the long twilight evenings of the warmer months were over, and most folk wanted to remain warm near the fires or huddled in beds, like animals ready for winter.

Robin announced she was also going to bed, but once

in the cold, dark foyer, she instead walked to the doors of the keep. She peeked out at the courtyard, dazzled by the glimmering of the frost on the stones. Looking up, she saw a crescent moon hanging high, with wisps of clouds catching the light and threading the whole sky with a silvery-white glow. Awed at the sheer beauty of it, she stepped out into the courtyard and then walked to the stairs leading to the parapet along the walls.

At the top, she stared out over bare trees with branches dipped in silver. The frosted ground sparkled as if someone had spilled diamonds over it. Winter was all but knocking on the door. Soon this land would be covered in snow and buffeted by wind, made into a deadly fairyland for anyone who was unprepared.

Robin was entranced by the scene and didn't notice when she first began to shiver from the cold. She wrapped her arms around herself, wondering just where Acer was. He seemed so eager to meet.

Then something moved in the courtyard, and Robin squinted at the shadows. Finally, she saw him. It was Pierce, quietly leading a horse out of the stable and over to the gate. Why didn't the guards stop him? She waited, sure that someone would shout or run up to keep Pierce from passing under the gatehouse. But the silence persisted.

She dashed down the stairs and into the stables, then nearly tripped over a body lying in the darkness. She gasped, seeing Acer's still form. Had Pierce murdered the boy to keep him from sounding the alarm? She knelt down, put her hand to the boy's neck. She was rewarded with the feeling of warm flesh and a steady heartbeat. Acer had only been knocked out. He'd seen Pierce up to no good, but never got the chance to pass it on to Robin or anyone else.

Her fists balled up, her nails biting into her palms. Pierce *had* planned something, and now he was going to get away, unless she could catch him first. Robin rushed back into the keep. In her room, she discarded Angelet's lovely gown and pulled on the boy's clothing she felt most comfortable in. Robin looked around the room, hoping she had what she needed. She grabbed her satchel, the quiver, and the bow. No food or supplies, but she'd catch Pierce before he got too far.

In the stables again, Robin tried to wake Acer, who only moaned and told her to let him sleep because it was Sunday. Which it was decidedly not.

Leaving the boy to be helped by others, she saddled a horse as fast as she could, and then led it from the stables. The gatehouse was quiet, so she went to the massive doors of the gate itself. They were closed, but unbolted. No, they weren't even properly closed. She pulled on the righthand door and it groaned open slowly.

She walked the horse through and pulled the door closed, a task that took most of her strength. How had Pierce managed to unbolt the doors and get out undetected? Robin had no time to find out. She had to track Pierce's path before all signs of his progress vanished. She mounted up and began to follow the tracks in the direction she'd seen him go.

The cold night and the frost aided her. The clear imprint of iron horseshoes showed in the icy white rime covering the ground. She kept her eyes on the trail until it led into the thicker woods surrounding Martenkeep. With the castle well behind her, Robin was truly on her own. She couldn't call for help or hope that someone saw her.

Octavian would not be coming to save her.

Well, Robin knew how to survive on her own. She always had. Tossing her head, she pressed her mount forward. She'd catch Pierce before he got to wherever he was going.

As she tracked her quarry, Robin tried to understand Pierce's motives. Why try to run away when he was going to be escorted safely to the king by none other than Sir Octavian? It made no sense.

"He's not told us everything," she muttered to herself.

Of course. Pierce gathered secrets for himself and only told the minimum of what he knew in order to get others to do his bidding. He'd lied to Tav and Robin more than once. He must have lied about even more than that, and now he was escaping so he could meet someone or reach some destination of his own.

She knew this area of the country far better than Pierce did, almost as well as she knew the Ardenwood. In fact, if the trail kept going southeast, they'd be heading directly toward Cleobury itself by tomorrow. She rode at a steady pace, not wishing to catch up to Pierce *too* quickly. A man on the run always looked over his shoulder, and she wanted to stop him on her terms.

In fact, she'd do that best by overtaking him. She left the established path Pierce was using and rode through the woods, following deer trails and streams to avoid getting her horse caught in the thick overgrowth. She increased her pace, thinking of a particular spot a few miles ahead where all travelers had to cross a river at the shallow point. She increased her pace to reach it in time, and then tethered her horse and got ready to hunt her quarry.

Not long after, Robin was perched in an oak rather like a bird herself. She sat on one of the sturdy lower branches in sight of the narrow road. The sound of hooves echoed through the woods. Robin wrapped her hand around a slender branch to brace herself, and then swung her upper body downward to get a better view.

The clear ring of iron meant a well-shod horse, and the particular volume and frequency of the ringing suggested a heavy animal, moving at slow pace. Pierce. She began to track him from above.

At first, the dense tree cover allowed her to keep to the higher branches, but when the trees thinned out, she slipped down to the forest floor and moved among the trunks, using the smaller shrubs and brush to hide her passing. Robin stepped quietly, with only the occasional crack of a twig or a rustle of leaves as she moved forward. She wasn't worried, though. Even if Pierce heard it, he'd mark it up to a squirrel or some other creature prowling the woods for food.

She kept him in view, which wasn't difficult, since he had slowed down since she first saw him. Why slow down when he was trying to escape?

Pierce seemed to be in no hurry, though. He bent down to say something to his horse. She wondered if the horse had gone lame, and when Pierce dismounted, she guessed that was exactly what happened.

He walked the horse onward. Robin actually matched him step for step, despite having to pick through the undergrowth. Still, he didn't even glance her way. She gripped her bow tighter. The natural tension she felt before any fight began to flow through her blood, making her muscles tense.

A little while later, the path turned sharply to ford the river, and Robin saw the horse standing by the water, happy to take a drink. Pierce was nearby, frowning at the horse and frustrated at the delay in his escape.

Nocking an arrow, she took one step closer to the horse, keeping herself in cover. Its ears flicked backward, and it nickered in response to her approach.

She let the arrow fly, aiming just past Pierce's head.

When it hit the trunk of a tree behind him, Pierce went still.

"Next one hits you if you try to get away," she called, even as she readied the next arrow. "Step away from the horse and unfasten your swordbelt."

He looked back. "Robin?"

"Who else around would want you alive instead of dead, my lord? Get rid of the sword, and don't delay."

He unbuckled the leather belt that held his scabbard, dropping it to his feet. "Now what?" he asked, sounding very confident for a man in his position.

"Dagger."

"You'd leave me defenseless?"

Robin laughed. "I'm naive, but not that naive. Drop the dagger and step ten paces away from the weapons."

He dropped the dagger and dutifully walked back. Robin sprang forward, seized the weapons, and then said, "All right, let's move so we're not out in the open."

"Where are we going? My horse can't carry me."

"Then you'll walk him. There's a forester's hut very near here. It will do until morning."

She directed Pierce to the hut, keeping her horse behind his and her bow ready in case he tried to bolt.

The hut was a tiny building, existing only as an emergency shelter for the people who worked in the woods throughout the year, whether it was herding hogs through the woods to fatten them up, or to cut wood, or to hunt the small game that lived here. The hut provided shelter for anyone who couldn't reach home.

It was empty tonight, but well stocked with wood for a fire and feed for any animals that needed shelter. Robin directed Pierce to tether both horses and then go inside the hut.

He insisted on getting his basket first, and Robin realized that he'd spirited Govannon out of a castle once again.

After he got the basket and went inside, she hid his weapons in the deepest part of the hay pile and leaned her bow against the wall. It would be useless inside.

The interior of the hut was almost stygian until Pierce located the lantern and lit it, illuminating the rough walls and the modest wooden platform that served as a bed.

"Good," Robin said, her hand on her dagger. "Now start a fire. I know you can, because I taught you."

When the fire was burning, Govannon curled up in front of it as if he were lord of this little hut.

Pierce petted him, and then stood up, his gaze intent on her. "You can't take me back to Martenkeep. You know Ranulf's men are still crawling through the woods between here and there. We're lucky they haven't found us yet."

"Then I'll drag you to Cleobury and Sir Alric will lock you up there," she snapped.

Pierce's eyes widened. "Cleobury?"

Instantly, Robin knew she'd made a terrible mistake. She never should have revealed her idea, and she definitely shouldn't have mentioned Alric's name.

"You know Cleobury," he said, his eyes gleaming. "You know the knight Sir Alric. Damn me. It was obvious you knew Octavian long before you pretended to meet, and you both know Rafe very well. And here's Alric in both your circles. Tell me who you are!"

Something in his voice made her answer before she could stop herself. "My name is Robin. Just Robin. I'm not a lady and I have no family."

"But you know this part of the country, and the Ardenwood as well. How?" He shifted back, inviting her to share more, and she was surprised to find that she wanted to. Keeping her ordinary identity to herself had never been comfortable.

"I was born in the Ardenwood, to common folk. When they died, I lived alone until I encountered Rainald de Vere there in the woods, while he was living in exile. He took me in. He fed me and let me live in the camp. I scouted for him and his men."

"But then he returned to Cleobury."

"Yes, and he took me with him. I owed him everything. His daughter Cecily and her husband Alric became my guardians. Cecily taught me to be a proper lady…or she tried."

Pierce snorted. "Had her work cut out for her, poor darling. How *is* Lady Cecily?"

"As if you care."

"I quite liked her, you know," he said mildly. "I would have treated her very well as my wife."

"God did not care for that fate, apparently," Robin said with a little bite to her tone. "For Cecily is now wedded to her love, with children, and she is happy."

"Children?" Pierce said in that same distant, musing tone. "She did say she wanted children. And Hawksmere was quite the protector, after all."

"So you remember Sir Alric."

"The man who undermined a carefully crafted alliance among three different factions simply by stealing my bride? Of course I remember him. And I am glad for her, to have got what she wanted."

He sounded sincere, and Robin frowned. "I thought you'd hate her. She was the one who discovered your treachery and reported it to the king."

Pierce shrugged. "She may have been the first to report that news, but she would not have been the only person who sought to undermine me. The Devil knows there's no shortage of people who want me dead."

"Perhaps you should stop betraying every person you encounter."

"Not every person, little Robin. Just the important ones."

Not her, his tone implied. She was utterly unimportant.

But she said, "Like Ranulf, and Estmar, and who knows how many more men who are looking to kill you even now. What do you know that's so essential? Surely the king has spies among the northern barons. They've been restless for years."

"He does have spies, and most of them are known to Ranulf. He uses his knowledge to feed those spies the wrong information. He'll get Stephen to head to the wrong place, or keep him from moving at all."

"But you have the right information?" she asked skeptically.

"Yes, and I can prove it. The hints of attacks at other towns across the country are a diversion to mass Stephen's forces elsewhere. Meanwhile, Ranulf is gathering everything he needs to build a counter-castle at his chosen site."

"You can't build a castle without someone noticing!" she objected.

"Oh, you can if you've got enough hands. I've seen the preparations and the supply routes, all planned out with the northern rebels and the Welsh mercenaries they've hired to help. Then he'll be able to lay siege to the city from a position of strength. The city will fall before Stephen can get any reinforcements there. And once it is under Ranulf's control, the other northern towns will follow. The independent barons retake power in the north, and Cadwallader seizes control of the Marches, free of

309 × Elizabeth Cole

any fear of the English attacking from the northern strongholds near the border."

"So you'll tell the king of Ranulf's true plans, and you expect Malvern back in return."

"Simple, isn't it?" Pierce sighed. "Except that Ranulf is a clever bastard and made spies out of some of my own men. So I had to devise a new way to get an ally."

She pointed to the sleeping cat. "By sending the message to get Octavian to help you escape your own castle."

"Yes, and thanks to him—and you—I'm out of Willesden, out of the Ardenwood, and nearly to a main road to London. Why not come with me?" He smiled at her suddenly. "There's nothing for you at Cleobury. Just a life of hanging around your betters, like a dog hoping for scraps."

"That's not how it is," she protested.

"Oh, I'm sure they treat you well. Cecily has a soft heart—I could tell that the moment I met her. But it doesn't change the fact that you're a pet. A forest urchin they're dressing up so they can feel they've saved you from yourself."

"It's not like that," she said with less conviction.

"Isn't it? Is it not all womanly pursuits and sewing and mending and minding your tongue because you're not important enough to speak up? You're not meant for that life."

She frowned, suspecting his real motive in asking her to join him in London was simply to avoid the reckoning he'd face if the king's true allies got hold of him. And wasn't Robin an ally of the king herself? She'd never taken an oath, but everyone she knew and loved swore allegiance to Stephen.

"We're going to Cleobury," she said flatly.

He shook his head sadly. "So that's how it will be? It's

too bad you're not better at chess."

"Why?" she asked.

"Just because you'd know the most satisfying move isn't a checkmate. It's the move that happens before checkmate, when you place the piece that your opponent doesn't notice. The move that gives you multiple paths to victory, before your opponent even knows the game is over, Lady Robin." He looked not the least bit perturbed to be bound up in rope by a girl half his age.

The way he said *lady* made her shiver.

The next morning, Robin woke Pierce up by nudging his stomach with her foot. She'd bound his wrists and ankles before he slept—she was done playing.

"Time to ride on," she said as she untied the rope at his ankles.

"How can I ride if my hands are bound?" he complained as he struggled awkwardly to a standing position.

"You'll manage. Follow me, my lord."

She readied the two horses, strapping Govannon's basket to one. Pierce's hadn't gone lame, it just had got a stone wedged into a hoof, which she managed to get out.

She then had to help Pierce mount up, practically shoving him into the saddle, him cursing all the while. They rode eastward along the paths that Robin knew well. She kept her bow handy, just in case Ranulf or Estmar or anyone with them happened to cross their path. But Robin thought it unlikely since they were getting closer and closer to a more populated and well patrolled part of the country.

It was an uneventful journey, until late in the day. The sound of hoofbeats behind her made Robin turn in her saddle. It was difficult to see in the fading light, but two figures were emerging from the trees to the west. Robin already knew one of them was Octavian. The other figure, dressed in black and riding a black horse, had to be Rafe.

She waited until the men caught up to her and Pierce.

Rafe said with his usual sardonic laugh, "We came to save you, Robin."

"Oh? Well, thank you. I don't know what I would have done without your assistance." She glanced at Pierce. "His hands are bound and I've got his weapons, so you can see I've managed fairly well so far."

Tav just looked between her and Pierce as if they were hiding something. "We found you both missing this morning, after learning that the gatehouse guards had mysteriously fallen asleep on watch." Tav looked at her as he said it.

But Robin turned to examine Pierce. "You got into Martenkeep's medicine chest, didn't you?"

The lord smirked at her. "A little poppy syrup dropped into the ale served with their evening meal...all I needed for a quiet escape."

"How's Acer?" Robin asked, remembering the boy being barely conscious on the floor of the stable.

"Acer?" Rafe echoed. "Why?"

"Because Pierce knocked him out when he tried to stop him from leaving, I suspect."

"As far as I know, Acer is perfectly well, and he didn't say a word about either Pierce or you leaving." Rafe gave her a searching look. "It was a little unclear whether you left together or if one followed the other."

Pierce chuckled. "Yes, Sir Rafe. Robin finally succumbed to my charms and agreed to run away with me."

"Shut up," Robin hissed. "Pierce left Martenkeep in secret, and I chased him down."

"You could have told someone," Tav noted quietly.

"It was late and there wasn't time," Robin said, knowing it wasn't entirely true. She wanted to catch Pierce on her own, to show that she needed no one's help to accomplish what she needed to do. "And anyway, he's bound and he's going where I'm taking him."

"Where are you taking him?"

"Cleobury."

When she said the name, Tav glanced at Pierce to get his reaction, but before he could say anything, Robin went on, "He knows who I am. And in truth, it no longer matters."

Tav looked unsure of that, but didn't protest. "If you say he ought to go to Cleobury, then we'll get him there."

"Looking forward to wandering through Lady Cecily's gardens," Pierce said, his tone smug. "Perhaps I'll pick a few late-blooming roses."

Robin shook her head. The man was half-mad. There would be nothing in the gardens for him now.

The rest of the journey went more easily for Robin, now that she had two other people who could help keep an eye on Pierce. Thankfully, both Rafe and Tav were better supplied than she was, so food wasn't a concern. Tav even brought out some cheese, which made her mouth water.

She wished he didn't pay so much attention to her. Robin didn't want to talk to Tav, even though she couldn't seem to look away from him. Every time she thought she was getting him out of her mind, she'd realize she was contemplating the curve of his shoulder, or the proud way he rode, or the depth of his eyes…which was the most mortifying, because it meant he'd caught her staring.

Robin couldn't wait to see the gates of Cleobury, despite the agony of not knowing what awaited her inside. She caught sight of them just as the last light glimmered in the west. Torches on either side of the gates blazed brightly, signaling to any travelers or locals in need that warmth and protection lay within.

Everyone quickened their pace, and even the horses perked up, sensing the end of the journey.

Despite the quiet all around, Cleobury was well guarded. As soon as they approached, someone yelled, "Who goes there?"

"Octavian," the knight called out. "Along with Lady Robin and others."

The guard's reaction was swift. Within moments the huge gate swung open. "I've already sent for de Vere," the guard announced, his attention fixed on Robin. "We've been awaiting any news, but we didn't expect to see you."

She gave him a weak smile. "Too bad. I've come back after all."

Then Cecily was running from the manor house, her skirts flying behind her. "Robin!" she called.

A moment later, Robin was in the arms of the other woman, being held like she'd been gone for a year. In some ways it felt as if she had been gone half a lifetime. She'd been a child when she left, and now she was no longer.

"I'm sorry, Cecily," she said.

"No, no," Cecily responded instantly. "No apologies, my heart. We're just so happy to see you back safe."

Robin wiped her eyes. Would she never stop crying? And was it possible that Cecily wasn't furious with her?

"You're not angry? I ran away."

"We can discuss everything later. I'm just grateful you're back home. And it must be thanks to Octavian?" She now looked to the knights. "And here's Rafe as well. There's a story here. And this is…" Suddenly Cecily put her hand to her mouth.

"Lord Pierce of Malvern at your service," he said, bowing as well as he could, considering he was partially bound. "It's been too long, Lady Cecily."

"Not long enough," she returned. "Are you Octavian's prisoner?"

"To be accurate," Rafe said, "we must say he's Robin's prisoner, for when he escaped Martenkeep, she was the one to track him down and catch him. Very tidily done too. She hardly needed us to rescue her."

Just then Alric strode up to the group, his eyes taking the scene in at once. "Pierce," he said in the same tone that a person said *vermin*. "What are you doing here?"

Pierce gave him a lofty nod. "I'm on my way to London to negotiate with the king."

"Is that what you think?" Alric gestured to the guards who surrounded the whole group. "Take this man to the south tower room. Untie him and then lock him in."

"You can't do that!" Pierce objected, his calm shaken at last. "I am a lord! I have certain privileges, and you can not impede me."

"Watch me."

The guards obeyed Alric instantly, taking Pierce by each arm and leading him away. Robin watched him go and felt only numbness. It was over. She was back where she started, and everything she'd set out to do was accomplished. Cecily kissed her and welcomed her home. Her life could resume exactly where she'd left it.

The thought should have been reassuring, but instead it rang hollow.

She looked to Tav again, unable to do otherwise. He was watching her with an unreadable expression, but then took a small step toward her, his hand rising as if to reach for her.

"Please take me inside," she said to Cecily. "I can't bear anything right now."

"Of course." Cecily wrapped an arm around her,

blocking out the world. "Come with me. You don't have to worry about anything."

Robin walked with Cecily and didn't look back, because she was a coward and she was terrified of what she'd see on Tav's face now.

Chapter 33

OCTAVIAN SHOULD HAVE BEEN RELIEVED the mission was almost over. But he wasn't. As promised, Pierce was confined in a room that featured narrow windows, no other exits, and a sturdy bolt on the door. Two men were posted outside as an extra precaution, but Pierce wouldn't be leaving the room until Alric decided he would.

After that, everyone gathered to discuss what must be done. Everyone, that is, but Robin. Cecily had spirited her away to the women's bedchamber, where Robin would be doted on like a lost lamb. She had looked incredibly tired and drawn, but Tav could never get her to say what was the matter, so he'd been unable to help on the way.

In fact, he couldn't get her to say much of anything since…well, since the night he'd ruined her. Which was understandable. But despite the fact that he couldn't change anything about what he'd done, he still desperately wanted to talk to her. However, Robin didn't want to talk to him.

"Tav?"

He looked up, realizing that he'd drifted off. Alric had been talking to him. "What?"

"I was saying that since we can't be sure if the men after Pierce are still pursuing him and might find him on the road again, a better solution might be to keep Pierce here and send word to London."

"You think the king would come here?" Tav asked, surprised.

"Not the king," Rafe broke in. Clearly Tav had missed a large part of the discussion. "Remember Lord Drugo? He'd be well placed to know how valuable Pierce's information is, and how best to get that information to the king."

"Ah. Yes. Good idea." Drugo was King Stephen's spymaster. The knights in this room had dealings with him before, and although he was one of the coldest, most calculating men Tav had ever encountered, he was fair-minded.

Rafe nodded. "All right, then do we send word to Drugo and hope he hurries?"

"Better to ask directly." That was from the elder Lord de Vere, who'd been mostly quiet, allowing Alric to lead the discussion. "A letter can't convey the urgency, and in any case, a letter may go astray. Someone should ride to London and bring Drugo back."

Alric looked to Tav immediately, and before he could ask, Tav said, "I'll go."

He should go because it was his duty, and because he couldn't stand being this close to Robin when things were so awful between them.

"You've spent the past several weeks riding up and down the country," Rafe pointed out. "We could easily send a different person. One of the men-at-arms…"

"No," Tav said more firmly. "It should be me. I'll leave at first light. And now, if you'll excuse me, I'm going to the chapel before I sleep."

Tav wanted peace, but he was mistaken in thinking he'd find it in the chapel. He sat on one of the benches, staring at the altar without seeing it. No matter where he was, he thought of Robin and the mess he'd made of her life. And his own. He needed to speak to her, to touch her, and to see her laugh. He needed to ask her how he could repair the damage he'd done, what she wanted him to do.

Perhaps the few days of separation would give her some time to forgive him a little, and then they could talk.

"Am I interrupting?"

Tav turned to see Alric standing next to the bench. He sighed. "Interrupting what? I'm just sitting here."

"I thought you might be at prayer."

He shook his head. Prayer required thought, and at the moment Tav could barely keep hold of a single idea within his head.

Alric sat down near him, his gaze also on the altar's flickering candles. "You must be glad to have completed the task set for you," Alric said. "And the information the king will gain is probably more valuable than he dreamed it could be. You should be proud."

Tav shook his head. "I'm not proud of anything I did. In truth, Robin deserves more credit than I do. Without her, I'd have got lost in the Ardenwood or simply never even learned where Pierce was at all. The king should reward her."

"Perhaps he will, but we just want her to be safe. That's what any family wants."

"She's safe now."

"Thanks to you. I don't know what she was thinking, running off like that. God grant no one speaks ill of her... *we* all know she's an honorable girl, but it would be all too easy for someone to get the wrong idea with her leaving Cleobury for weeks with no explanation."

Tav said, meaning it, "She doesn't owe the world an explanation. She wanted to help find someone we thought would contribute to the king's cause. And she did. I never would have succeeded without her." And look how he'd repaid that help.

"Thank you," Alric said suddenly. "You watched over her and saved her from God knows what fate. The whole time Robin was gone, I worried about her, but Cecily said that if she was with you, she'd be in good hands."

Tav bent his head. How many more people would he need to ask forgiveness from?

Alric went on, "Robin isn't family by blood, but both Cecily and I will do whatever we have to in order to protect her."

Thus ends any hope of talking to Alric about my mistake, Tav thought grimly. *And Robin will hardly even say two words to me. So where does that leave us?*

"After all this is done, what's next for you?" Alric asked, echoing Tav's own line of thought. "Do you need to return to your lord?"

"Not immediately, but soon," Tav said slowly. "The last time we spoke, he hinted at some more business in France. Family matters with his estates, not the war."

"You don't sound very happy about that. Don't you want a little peace?"

"I might need more than a little peace."

Alric shifted his gaze from the altar to Octavian. "What do you mean?"

"I've been thinking. The pope has made a call for another crusade, and Bernard is preaching it all over Europe, and at last a few kings are answering and gathering forces of their own."

"Yes," said Alric. "And already they're bickering about the best routes to take and who owes allegiance to whom."

"I don't think these new fighters know what they're getting into."

"Are you feeling the call to go? You have no need to wash away your sins. You're the most pious man I know, and that includes some priests."

Tav felt the sting of Alric's unwitting words. "I'm no saint. But to answer your question, no, I wasn't thinking about joining the fighting. I am concerned, however, for those I knew in the Holy Land. I've been gone longer than I expected, and it may be time to go back. Have you heard some of the stories? After what happened to Edessa, I'm worried about Aleppo."

"Your city."

"Yes. I've been thinking about it more and more this past year. I have friends I've not seen in a long time and I worry about them, and if the city is being fought over, I should be there to try to keep some measure of peace for the residents."

"As you think best," Alric said slowly. "You owe no term of service to your lord, or to the king. You are free to leave Denis's retinue at any time and do as you wish."

"I've decided nothing yet," Tav said. "It was just a thought."

"Have the English winters got to you at last? Or has something else changed your mind?" Alric sounded more tense than before.

Tav paused, then said, "No." He couldn't tell Alric the real reason for his worry. If Alric ever found out that Tav had slept with Robin, that would be the end of any friendship between them. Alric would take it as a violation of trust, which is what it was. Indulging in his desire for Robin was the stupidest thing Tav had ever done, because there was no honorable conclusion to it. "I need to think it over."

"You're in a church," Alric said. "Best place for thinking there is, especially for you. I'll leave you to it."

Tav found no peace that night, and when he woke in the morning, he felt as if he hadn't slept at all. He rode out at first light, long before Robin would wake up, so he had no chance to even tell her he was going.

He felt a sense of relief when he passed through the gates of Cleobury, and then instantly hated himself for it because he knew he was running away.

Chapter 34

"He left?" Robin's heart constricted. She'd wondered why she hadn't seen Octavian all morning, and then Cecily broke the news.

"Just to bring Lord Drugo back from London," Cecily clarified. "He'll return within days. Are you missing his company already?" she added with a little laugh.

"No," Robin said, too quickly. She missed the man she thought she knew, before he revealed the truth in his conversation with Pierce. But even so, she wasn't ready for him to leave. "I just wanted a word with him," she said to cover her flustered reaction.

"Hmmm," Cecily murmured. "Well, you'll be happy to hear that your Geoffrey will arrive soon. He's been quite concerned about you in your absence."

Robin had almost forgotten the existence of Lord Geoffrey Ballard, and the reminder was not a pleasant one. "He has?" she asked.

"Shouldn't a man be concerned for the woman he expects to marry?" Cecily's eyebrow rose. "You don't sound very excited, Robin."

Robin was not excited. The thought of Geoffrey merely brought a new wave of confusion. How was she supposed to look on a man such as Geoffrey and smile and be sweet and unassuming when she'd just endured weeks of hardship and had her heart swept up and then dropped to the ground? And how could she lift her face for a kiss from Ballard when she had the memory of Tav's kisses all over her body, and the feel of his hands on her skin, and the completely heart-scorching moment when she took him inside her own body…

"Robin, are you quite well, dear? You're so flushed." Cecily, healer and herbalist, put a hand to Robin's forehead, testing for fever.

I should ask her if she knows how to heal a broken heart.

"No fever, but perhaps you should rest." Cecily regarded her thoughtfully, as if she were about to prescribe some concoction for Robin to drink.

"What will you tell Geoffrey?" Robin asked.

"What will *you* tell Geoffrey?" Cecily replied. "You're the one who went away. It's your story to tell."

"But it was to be kept secret," Robin said. "At least, at the beginning, until the king knows what to do with Pierce's information. And I don't think he'd like to know the details, truly. Geoffrey, I mean. I didn't behave as he thinks I ought to. I slept outside and disguised myself and got into fights and spent far too much time with men who…weren't Geoffrey."

"You think he'd be jealous?"

"I don't know. He never seemed the jealous type." Then again, Robin had never been swarmed with suitors before Geoffrey Ballard expressed interest in her. He probably never considered the idea of her being pursued by others, let alone losing her heart in a matter of weeks. *No, I lost my heart to Octavian years ago. I was a foolish child then, and I'm a foolish woman now.*

"A good man will understand your reasons and trust

your word," Cecily said. "Geoffrey must know how lucky he is to gain you for a wife."

Robin tried to smile. She knew how much Cecily wanted this for her, to be well married and well cared for. Geoffrey Ballard was a man who could provide for Robin's future. What was a little broken heart compared to a lifetime of comfort? It was a trade that many women faced, and Robin couldn't afford to indulge her whims. Not when the de Veres had all done so much for her. *I have a duty*, she reminded herself.

The next day, Geoffrey arrived at Cleobury. Robin watched him emerge from his carriage, his attire perfectly arrayed and his face the picture of concern. She studied him from her vantage point on the upper floor and tried to fall in love with the man she saw. She never could before, and she certainly couldn't now. To say she loved him would be a lie.

She'd be expected to lie her whole life—as bride, as wife, as mother. "Mary, Mother of God, save me," Robin whispered. She'd have to submit to Ballard in bed. She knew that, of course, but the notion had never seemed quite so…real before.

Now that she had shared a bed with a man—not just any man, but Tav, who had kissed and stroked and worshipped every inch of her—she couldn't imagine performing such an act with someone like Geoffrey. Would he do what Tav had done? Would he expect Robin to do the same things for him? Would he tell her to choose his hand or his mouth, knowing that she wanted both and would take either because absolutely no one in the world had ever made her feel so exquisite and lovely before?

Would Geoffrey call her lovely, as Tav had once done?

Would Geoffrey then tell another man to forget about Robin, and that she could take care of herself?

Robin closed her eyes, the pain of Tav's words springing up again to wound her. How was it possible that he could be so sweet and kind to her one night, and then so callous about her the next morning? And how was it possible that she still couldn't put him out of her mind?

"My lady," a maid said, interrupting her brooding. "Please come downstairs. You're wanted."

If only that were true, she thought, trodding down the cold stone steps.

The whole day, Lord Geoffrey was polite and attentive to Robin, expressing great relief that she was home safe and asking what had driven her to leave Cleobury without so much as a message. Robin told the truth…mostly. And she was right that he didn't care for it. Fortunately, both Cecily and Alric spoke warmly of Robin's commitment to helping the king's cause, so Geoffrey could only nod. When he heard Lord Pierce was confined at the manor, though, he leaned forward and asked Alric, "May I speak to him?"

"Lord Pierce? Why, do you know him?"

"Not at all. But this whole situation is so far beyond anything I've heard. I'd like to hear what the man has to say."

"I suppose it is unique," Alric said. "I'll tell the guards to let you in to speak with him tomorrow."

Robin thought nothing more about it, happy enough to not need to entertain Geoffrey all the time. But after the midday meal the next day, she found herself summoned to the solar where Alric, Cecily, and Geoffrey greeted her.

Robin looked around at them. "Yes? Has something happened?"

Alric gestured for her to take a seat. "Lord Geoffrey just informed us that he has a most vital topic to discuss."

"But he hasn't said what it is," Cecily added, looking

a little annoyed. "Come sit by me, Robin, and we'll all find out together."

Geoffrey waited until everyone was seated, then said, "I spoke with Lord Pierce this morning and learned some very disturbing things."

Alric nodded. "Well, Pierce is a rather disturbing man, who's served all sides during this war."

Geoffrey shook his head impatiently. "Not about him. About Robin."

"Robin?" Alric frowned. "Explain."

"He told me that she spent the night with him, quite willingly. That she chased after him, in fact." Geoffrey looked around the table coldly, but he refused to meet Robin's eyes, as if she weren't worth addressing directly.

She rose to her feet. "Hold a moment. On the way here, I was *forced* to spend a night in the company of Pierce, during which time I tied his hands and feet so he couldn't escape again. I did nothing shameful that night. If he said otherwise, his words were merely spiteful and mean, revenge against a woman who got the better of him."

Geoffrey was unmoved. His mouth was a mere line as he told her, "Words are all you have as well. I for one will not take the word of a woman who might be no better than a whore."

"Watch yourself," Alric said in a low voice. He didn't move, but his fury was obvious.

"Apologies for the crudity of the term," Geoffrey said to Alric. "But consider my position. A man takes a wife for specific reasons. I am already compromising in this matter."

"How?" Robin spat out. "How are you going to suffer in a marriage to me?"

"It's one thing to marry below one's class, and the

generous dowry Lord de Vere offered does make up for your birth. But to have a wife of a lower station and impure as well? Intolerable."

So this was what Pierce had been so smug about before, when she captured him following his final escape attempt. He took revenge on Robin by suggesting that he slept with her, thus destroying any chance she had for an advantageous marriage.

"Pierce is a liar. He lies as much as he breathes." Her voice trembled as she spoke, partly from anger, but also from the knowledge that she could no longer prove her virginity if it came to a test. She *was* impure in the eyes of nearly everyone who cared about such things. And to say she lost her virginity to Octavian instead of Pierce would not improve her position in the least.

Geoffrey looked her over with disdain. "A lady's reputation is her most important asset."

"More than a dowry?" Cecily asked drily.

"More than a dowry, more than an alliance. I will not suffer the indignity of gossip. I will not be called a cuckold or a fool."

"I'll call you worse than that," Robin said. "Or did you forget how you kept trying to get me alone during those hunts earlier this autumn, how you wanted a kiss and then more?"

Cecily's eyes narrowed. "What is this?"

"It happened on more than one occasion, my lady," Robin explained. "Geoffrey would ride after me and when no one else could see us, he tried to kiss me. I let him because I thought it was just his clumsy way of courting me. But when he wanted more than a kiss, when he tried to grope me, when he tried to lift my skirts, I left him. I rode off to find the others."

"You never told me that," Cecily said, her face ashen.

"I was supposed to marry him," Robin said, feeling ashamed, and then angry that *she* should feel shame for it. "I didn't think anyone would care if he took liberties."

"It was very...restrained of you to not hurt him when he tried," Alric said. "I'm surprised you didn't draw blood."

"I was supposed to marry him," Robin repeated. In fact, that was the only reason she'd avoided drawing her knife on Geoffrey Ballard the last time he had tried to take advantage of her. A proper lady did not threaten her betrothed's life.

Cecily sighed, looking at Geoffrey in disappointment. She said to Robin, "Well, I wish you'd told me, but I'm proud of you for refusing him."

"I refused him," Robin said, "precisely because I do not give in to men who think of women as playthings." *I just gave in to the one man whose every word I believed, until it was too late.*

Geoffrey sneered. "Yet you travel for weeks on end in the company of strange men and still expect to be thought a clean and wholesome lady? I'm not stupid. I know a slut when I see one."

Alric pushed himself up from the chair, clearly ready to challenge Geoffrey to combat based on his insult.

"Don't!" Robin shouted at Alric. "Please don't challenge him. I wouldn't marry this man if he begged me to, but I don't want to have any role in his death. And if you fought him, he'd die before he got in a single parry."

"As you wish," Alric said, still looking enraged. He turned to Ballard, his expression barely controlled. He bit off every word as he spoke. "We thank you for your visit, my lord. But it is clear that our interests do not align. Naturally, everyone at Cleobury will do their upmost to see that you can depart without delay. You must wish for the comfort of your own home. And we will speak no more of a marriage."

"Lord de Vere will…" Ballard began.

"Lord de Vere will agree with me," Alric declared. "Because we both want what is best for Robin. Now go. I won't ask again."

Geoffrey bowed stiffly to Alric, ignored Cecily and Robin completely, and then stormed out of the hall.

After a long moment, when Robin thought he might chase Geoffrey down out of principle, Alric slowly sank back down in the chair. "Well. That seems to be the end of that."

"My dear," Cecily said, squeezing Robin's hand. "I am so sorry."

Robin let out a huge breath, the tension draining out of her with Geoffrey's departure. "For what? I didn't want to marry him anyway, and now we know what a stubborn, small-minded man he is."

"He seemed so attentive at first when he took you hawking and riding…." She trailed off.

"The attention to Robin happened because he was currying favor with de Vere," Alric said shortly. "Robin was an afterthought to him, if that. We won't make that mistake again."

"There won't be an *again*," Robin said. "You heard him, and you know what he'll do. He'll spread his version of the story throughout the whole shire, and he's a man, so he'll be listened to. Thanks to Pierce's words, my reputation is destroyed, and I am to blame for it."

Cecily frowned, clearly trying to set the situation to rights. "This whole business has been unpleasant, and Robin must want to rest. I'll walk her to her chamber."

Upstairs, Robin wanted nothing more than to curl up and shut out the world, but Cecily still wanted to discuss the matter. She sat with Robin on the edge of the bed.

"We could call for a doctor," Cecily suggested. "An examination to verify your virgin—"

Robin cut her off. "Absolutely not! If you try, I'll... run away again."

"Oh, my dear. Please don't. It nearly killed me to let you go the last time."

Let me go?

"What do you mean?" Robin asked, all thoughts of her reputation suddenly upended. "What do you mean you *let me go*?"

Cecily gave her a gentle, rueful smile. "I must confess that I...steered your actions a bit. I knew it wouldn't take much. A little information on the task Octavian was assigned, an afternoon free of chores so you could prepare..."

"You actually *wanted* me to run away?" Robin asked, aghast.

"I wanted you to have the chance to go, if you wished to do so. It was right to help Octavian, and you were the only person who could help him. And I have faith in your skills to survive in less than ideal conditions, since you've done it before."

"But to join Octavian..."

"Who better? He would protect you from all dangers that you might not be able to deal with on your own." Cecily smiled wider. "And so he did."

Robin took a ragged breath, hoping to stall the tears she knew she was about to shed. "Not all dangers," she confessed.

"What?" Cecily asked, her brow wrinkling. "What happened?"

"I... We..." Robin wiped away a tear with her sleeve, the wool rough against her cheek. "That's why I can't endure that exam. But it was my fault! I...pursued him."

Cecily raised one eyebrow. "Pursued?"

"Yes!" The words were pouring out before Robin knew she wanted to say them. "Because I never wanted to be with someone as much as I wanted to be with Tav. And I knew it was wrong, but I couldn't stop myself, and I did everything in my power to make him give in to me."

"Robin. Octavian is more than twice your size, not to mention a trained warrior. I do not believe you forced him into anything he did not already want to do."

She twisted her fingers in her lap, her cheeks going hot. No, she didn't force him to lie in a bed with her, but... "But I led him into sin because I couldn't control my own desire."

"If you're so sinful and wicked, why did Octavian remain with you after this occurred? Why did he see you safely back to Cleobury?"

"That was just because he had to get Pierce here. He doesn't care for me at all."

"What makes you say that?"

"He said as much in a conversation I overheard."

"Are you certain that's what he meant?"

Robin opened her mouth, but then doubts rushed in.

She *had* been certain. The way the words stabbed at her and took her breath away made her certain that she never wanted to face that pain again, and confronting Octavian would force her to do just that.

But now, with Cecily's cool, calm enquiry in her ears, she was no longer quite as certain.

"I...I don't know," Robin whispered.

"Darling, I don't pretend to know your mind or his, or what happened between you. And people can be deceitful, whether it's witting or not. But for the years I've known Octavian, he's shown again and again that he's worthy of trust. That's why I trusted that you would be safe with him."

"He did keep me safe," Robin admitted. "There were so many times that I'd have stumbled into something or exposed myself to danger, but he never let anyone harm me. And at the bridge by Martenkeep, he sent me ahead and stayed there, and he knew it might be his death. But that was before we..." She trailed off, newly mortified at her behavior. "I think after we...were together, he changed his mind about me."

"He's going to be back in a week or so at most. Would you like me to send him away?"

"No!" Robin took a breath, then added in a low rush, "I don't want him to leave me behind. I think I'll die without him."

Cecily embraced Robin, who was horrified to realize that her face was wet with tears. "My sweet little Robin," she murmured, her cheek pressing against Robin's own tear-stained one. "I remember when we first met, and you laughed at the idea of falling in love. You thought it was a lie troubadours told."

"Then I am paying for it," Robin said. "I am in love, and I'm miserable. You can laugh at me now."

"I would never do such a thing. I never want to see you in pain."

Robin sniffled. "I don't know what to do."

Cecily pulled back and looked Robin over carefully. "You say you love him. Does he know it?"

"I never said it." Robin couldn't bear to tell him that and risk being turned away. "It's too humiliating for me to say. Besides, he would be better off not knowing how I feel."

"Why is that?"

"Because eventually he'll go away, whether on his

lord's business or his own. He shouldn't have to think of…"

"…a little robin who misses him?" Cecily finished. "My darling, you must talk with him as soon as he returns. You owe him the truth. And he owes you his own truth," she added.

"He won't want to speak to me. He regrets what happened between us."

"You don't know that, not until you speak to him." Cecily put her hand over Robin's. "And no matter what you decide, you will always, always have a place here."

Robin closed her eyes, unwilling to look at the woman who worked so hard to make Robin into a lady, only to learn how thoroughly Robin failed. And then still offered her a home.

"Speak to Tav," Cecily said softly. "You won't have much time before he leaves again. And then it *will* be too late."

Robin spent the next several days in quiet misery, increasingly aware that she'd behaved like a petulant child and had leapt to the worst conclusion she could have, all without benefit of a scrap of evidence. Every day Tav didn't return felt like another punishment, and she worried he might never return at all. Perhaps he'd just pass the message to Lord Drugo and then…keep going, to wherever he chose. Somewhere far away from Robin, because why would he want to return to her? They had no understanding, no agreement, and in the end, no future.

Cecily offered the same quiet, calm support every day. She kept Robin's secret, and only once did she bring up the issue of Robin's transgression.

"My dear," she said one morning. "I must ask you to tell me when your monthly courses return. Or if they do not. So that…we may plan, if necessary." She patted her own gently swelling middle to make her point.

Robin swallowed hard and nodded. "I'll do that, my lady. Do you think it's…likely?" *Oh, Mary, Mother of God, I am* not *ready to be a mother myself.*

"You said you only engaged in the act once, and once is enough. But it is a slim chance."

"I was so stupid." She closed her eyes. How could something that felt so right end up being so terribly wrong?

"No. You were thinking with your heart. That's all. And there's no help in worrying until you know there's something to worry about."

Nevertheless, Robin worried. She wandered about the orderly environs of Cleobury as if she were lost in a forest, seeing multiple paths and not knowing which one would take her home.

And then one morning, she discovered she had no need to worry after all, and paradoxically burst into tears. The relief of not being pregnant warred with a strange sense of loss, and she wasn't even sure why. All she knew was that her heart was wracked and she couldn't take another blow.

How would she ever speak to Tav and confide her true feelings for him when he might not return her affection in the same way? Perhaps it was better to stay silent, to stay safe at Cleobury for the rest of her life. She had a place here, and she could make a life for herself. A helper to Cecily, a part of the daily routine of the manor, a woman alone. She'd so often leapt into fire. Her whole life, she'd acted on impulse and never thought of the consequences. Perhaps she'd finally learned her lesson.

The next day, Octavian returned. Robin saw him ride in, and half of her wanted to run to him and beg him to speak to her, while the other half ordered her feet to stay still, to not disrupt the fragile balance she'd found here over the past week.

He wasn't alone when he arrived. Lord Drugo rode with him on one side, and on the other, Robin was surprised to see another man she knew. It was Luc of Braecon, one of Alric's brother knights. He was the son of an important baron, and his family was close to King Stephen. If he was here as well, it must mean they were very serious about dealing with a potential rebellion.

Not long after, Robin was called down to the solar. Knowing the status of the guests, and how much store Cecily set on proper behavior, she had dressed carefully, in the same green gown she'd been wearing when she first saw Octavian all those weeks ago. She brushed her long hair and let it fall down her back. Braiding was too much effort when her hands were shaking at the thought of being in the same room with Tav again.

When she stepped into the solar, *everyone* was already there. And everyone turned to look at her. Pierce, looking more like a host than a prisoner, stood by the fire and smiled widely, not bothering to hide his appraisal of her.

Lord Drugo examined her with a cold eye. He was about fifty years old, bald with a pointed beard, and possessed an air of quiet power. Stephen's spymaster was not a man to be trifled with. "You are Robin," he said. It wasn't a question. "Sir Octavian told me you accompanied him on his assignment of your own volition."

"Yes, my lord," she said in a voice that nearly came out as a whisper. Would she be punished for such presumption?

"He said you were essential to both locating our informant, and later in preventing his escape."

"Yes, my lord." Octavian told Drugo about her? She dared to look over at Tav. He was in the opposite corner of the room, but she swore she almost felt the heat of his gaze from that distance. Lord, he was so handsome. She could stay with him forever. If he'd let her.

"Let's not waste more time," Drugo said shortly. "Rumors of a rebellion increase every day, and yet all we have are rumors. You have promised facts, Lord Pierce. You have promised more than that. I trust you will not disappoint me."

"What I know is more than enough to guarantee the king will be able to counter Ranulf's plans. But I require a guarantee of my own before I share all I know." Pierce was polite, but his eyes were gleaming. He was in his element, playing his favorite game—politics. And now he was making his final moves, using all the pieces he'd gathered and held close for just this moment.

With his typical flare for the dramatic, Pierce laid out what was already known about the impending rebellion. Ranulf's rage, the northern barons' discontent, the Welsh alliance for their own ends. Then he added precious gems of knowledge at Drugo's feet—the name of a key ally, the existence of a supply route, the revelation of a spy in the king's own castle.

By the end, Drugo was nodding, and Robin understood in a flash how Pierce built up his whole story in a sort of intellectual seduction. Lord, *everything* was a game to him. A game where he had to control everything to feel that he'd won.

"This is valuable intelligence, my lord," Drugo said. "But you have not yet shared the name of the city Ranulf plans to attack. And without that, we cannot confidently plan a counterattack."

Pierce smiled. "I will reveal that when I hold Malvern again."

Drugo's eyes narrowed. "Absolutely not. We don't

have time to besiege a castle, particularly not a castle such as Malvern!"

"My lord, would I dare propose an impossible task? No, there is another way." Pierce gave a slight bow. "If I might make a suggestion?"

At Drugo's nod, he went on. "We can march to Malvern and retake the castle, using it as a staging point for the next phase in marching to the city Ranulf has set his sights on. I know a secret way to get inside the walls. I can raise the gate, and then even a small but prepared force will take it with a minimum of casualties."

"A bold proposition, Lord Pierce." Drugo gave him a cold, doubting smile.

"I have confidence we will triumph. At which point, I shall be reinstalled as the true lord of Malvern. The king must understand I will not compromise on that."

"The king will understand what I tell him," Drugo returned. "But I am intrigued by your proposal."

Robin listened to the negotiations, furious at the way Pierce once again seemed to get all he wanted. Must he manipulate everyone, from kings down to peasants?

She wasn't the only one annoyed by the situation. Luc, who'd been silent until now, said, "Once Lord Pierce is back in Malvern, he has no incentive to reveal the rest of Ranulf's plans."

"A risk you'll need to take," Pierce responded, his tone lazy as he looked at the people in the room. His eyes lingered on Robin for a moment.

"It's Coventry," she said suddenly.

Robin spoke before she fully realized what she knew.

All eyes turned to her.

"How do you know?" Drugo asked. "Pierce might have told you that as a diversion."

Robin kept her attention on Pierce, who'd gone quite

still, his face pinched and white. "He didn't tell me anything. He doesn't think I'm important enough to play politics with, and he's right. But there's a young man in training at Martenkeep who is from Coventry, and Pierce spoke to him, asking him about the city and land around it. River crossings. Hills. Hunting. He was seeking strategic information that someone would need to know if he expected to lay siege to a city. And he thought because Torin was little more than a boy, no one would ever think to monitor such a conversion. But Acer overheard it and mentioned it to me."

"A wild guess based on a child's word," Pierce said.

But Robin wouldn't let Pierce steer her mind any more. "It's Coventry. Send your spies there, Lord Drugo. Verify it, but I think you'll find someone already preparing to build a counter-castle, just as Lord Pierce says."

Pierce's chest rose and fell as he tried to restrain his emotions. "Lady Robin," he said, very quietly, "what I wouldn't give for a moment alone with you."

At his words, four knights all took a step toward Pierce. He saw it and froze, aware at last that he'd lost his game.

"That will do," Drugo said, once again taking command.

Robin saw Tav slowly relax his hand on the hilt of his blade, and a wild hope took wing inside her. The other knights looked to Alric.

"What now?" Luc asked him.

"Pierce has told us what we need to know," Alric said, signaling two men-at-arms who'd been standing on either side of the door. "Take him back to his room."

Rafe rose to his feet. "I think I'll go along, just in case." The black-haired knight gave Robin a wink as he passed her. "Well done," he mouthed.

Pierce wouldn't be foolish enough to try anything as crude as trying to outrun guards and a well-trained knight. No, he'd go to his confinement and begin plotting his next move.

"What will you do, my lord?" Robin asked Drugo. "You don't need Pierce anymore."

"Not at the moment. But who knows when a snake like that will be useful? He'll be kept under lock and key somewhere very remote until he's either proven he can be trusted, or the war ends. Or do you think he ought to be put to death, Lady Robin?"

She blinked, not expecting the question. But Drugo was obviously expecting an answer. Forced isolation was the greatest punishment Pierce could suffer, and as horrible a person as he had been over the years, Robin didn't want him to be killed. "Let him live. It will annoy him more."

Drugo gave her the tiniest nod of approval.

Then he addressed Alric. "I assume Lord Pierce will not be a welcome guest here. I suggest an armed transport to London until I find a suitable place for him."

"Indeed, my lord," Alric said. "I will provide vehicles, horses, and as many men-at-arms as you deem necessary."

"Good." Drugo looked at Tav. "I'd like more than just men-at-arms, though. Sir Octavian, you must need to come to London anyway, for Lord Denis will leave word for you there. We leave tomorrow."

Tav glanced at Robin, his eyes flashing with an emotion she couldn't decipher. But an order was an order. "Yes, my lord," he said, his tone neutral.

Tomorrow? Robin's heart collapsed again. Tomorrow was too soon. If Tav left tomorrow, before she could even speak with him, he'd never come back at all.

Drugo bowed to Cecily. "My lady, if you'll take Robin

and leave us to discuss some other matters of a military nature?"

Cecily nodded. "Of course, my lord." She took Robin's hand and led her out. Robin turned back and caught Tav's gaze, wishing he didn't seem so far away.

Chapter 35

OCTAVIAN DID NOT CARE ABOUT wintering armies or preparations for a spring campaign.

He did not care about another threat from the empress's forces.

He did not care about anything unless it was named Robin.

Drugo's discussion seemed to drag on interminably, and all Tav could think of was that he was expected to ride out from Cleobury again in the morning. In a matter of hours. He was sick to death of riding mile after mile on the business of other men. He'd done it for years because it allowed him to see the world he wanted to see. But he could no longer do it for anyone but himself.

Once I get to London, I'll send word to Denis that I'm done. I'll tell Drugo that I'm done. I'll send a message to Alric and tell him too. Saying it in person was too difficult, especially with the matter of Robin unresolved.

What was he thinking? He couldn't leave Cleobury until he could actually talk to her. He needed to ask her forgiveness for what he'd done, for hurting her when that was the last thing he wanted to do. He had to let her know he loved her because if he didn't, he'd be a coward.

"Tav?"

He jumped, not even noticing Alric beside him. "What?"

"Can I have a word with you? The others can discuss how many horses we need to get to Lincoln by January—they won't miss us."

Alric led him to a corner of the room, and then asked in a low voice, "What's wrong? You look like you want to kill Drugo."

"No. I just don't want to go to London tomorrow."

"Then we'll send someone else. I'll go."

"He ordered me to go. Besides, you'll be needed here anyway. Isn't a wedding happening soon?"

"Whose wedding?" Alric asked blankly.

Was Tav losing his mind? "Robin's. I thought she was to marry some lord."

"Oh." Alric blinked and shook his head. "No. Did you not hear what happened?" He related it all to Tav, who was glad he wasn't in the room himself at the time, because he probably would have thrashed the man.

"Why didn't you challenge that idiot?" Tav asked. "He slandered Robin."

"Robin ordered me not to. She said she didn't want Geoffrey's death on her conscience."

Considering that a combat between Alric and a petty lordling could end only one way, Robin had a point. And Tav didn't want her to suffer anymore, either.

"How is she?"

Alric rolled one shoulder. "I've never been able to read Robin very well. She's defiant one moment, and then sweet the next. As it turns out, she didn't actually care for Geoffrey Ballard at all, so that's a relief. But she hasn't been the same since she got back. Perhaps you could spend some time with her. She's always loved seeing you."

"I would do that in an instant, believe me. But..." He gestured to the table where Drugo, Luc, Rainald, and Rafe were all arguing hotly about some minutia of military planning.

"Go," Alric said. "If we absolutely need your opinion on how much feed seven hundred horses require, I'll send word."

Tav asked every person he saw where Robin was, and eventually learned from one maid that she'd last seen Robin heading outside the manor house. He found his cloak and went after her, a part of him convinced she was running away again.

He looked for her in the dwindling light of the day. The gardens of Cleobury were prepared for winter, with straw laid out over the soil as mulch to keep the frost from killing the bulbs and seeds below. But she wasn't there.

He walked into the church where candles burned on the altar and everything else was wrapped in velvet shadows of twilight. But she wasn't there.

Then he looked up and saw a familiar outline on the battlements near the gatehouse. Robin. He took the stairs through the gatehouse to get to the top.

"Robin," he said, as breathless as if he'd climbed thirty flights of stairs instead of three.

She turned at Octavian's voice. "Yes?"

"Can we talk?"

After a second's hesitation, she nodded.

Unfortunately, all words flew out of Tav's brain then. He struggled to think how to begin. "I heard about...the marriage. I'm sorry you had to go through that. Pierce hurt you just because he could. I thought I was the frog. But you were."

Robin was perplexed, and rightly so. "The frog? *What?*"

"Never mind. I'll explain later." He knew that wasn't the right thing to say. Of course it wasn't. It was inane.

"Anyway. I'm well rid of him," she responded at last. "Ballard, that is. He wasn't what I wanted at all."

"What do you want?"

She caught her lower lip in her teeth for a moment, which caused his body to react in a completely inappropriate way. Then she said, "It seems like such a simple question, doesn't it? And yet I can't quite answer it." She stared out over the trees, unwilling to look at him. A breeze swept up from the stone wall, and she shivered.

Tav moved next to her and wrapped half of his own cloak around her shoulders, drawing her into his warmth. He touched her chin with one finger, trying to turn her face to his. He needed to ask her forgiveness and he couldn't do that if she wouldn't look at him.

She resisted, but then suddenly turned toward him and wrapped her arms around his middle, pressing her head to his chest. He inhaled the scent of her hair, which was clean and sharp and green with herbs, and thought he'd never get enough of that smell.

"Tav, I'm so, so sorry." Her voice was muffled, but he heard the ache in it. "I've been so awful. Right from the beginning, I put you in a terrible position, and then when everything became more complicated between us, I kept hounding you for more because I was selfish and curious and I didn't think what it would mean to you. And then I just fled from the whole thing as if it were something I could outrun, which is madness because how can I outrun myself? And I'm sorry—"

He put a finger on her mouth to hush her. "Robin. I came to apologize to you. Why are you apologizing to me?"

Her eyes widened at his touch. He couldn't resist running his finger along the softness of her lip, and her lids dropped in a way that made him want to take her somewhere private, preferably that instant.

Robin leaned away a fraction. He dropped his hand, angry that he couldn't resist touching her even when he was apologizing for touching her.

"May I ask you something?" Robin began.

"Anything."

"At Martenkeep," she said, inhaling nervously, "I overheard you speaking to Pierce, and you told him…you told him I could take care of myself. What did you mean by that?"

"Did I say that?" he asked, not remembering the conversation.

"You said to Pierce, 'Forget about Robin. She can take care of herself.' It was the morning after we…"

Then he remembered, because that was the moment when he'd honestly wanted to throw Pierce off the side of the curtain wall for being such a hideous person. "He knew how much I cared about you, and he taunted me with it. But yes, I did say that. I told him to forget about you because he wasn't worthy of being stepped on by you. And I said you can take care of yourself because it's true. You're the most independent and resourceful person I've ever met. I can't think of anyone else I'd rather have had with me during that journey."

"Oh."

That was all she said, but it was clear she was turning something much more significant over in her mind. He waited, and then realized that he'd never actually got around to asking her forgiveness. "Robin," he said slowly. "I hurt you."

"When?" she asked, startled.

"When we spent the night together," he said, exasper-

ated. "Or don't you remember the little matter of you being a virgin? I ruined that, and ruined you, and your future. That matter."

"It didn't feel like ruin to me," she said.

"Well, it was."

"You don't get to decide that," she said. "And I won't
forgive you for it."

"You won't?" This was going worse than he thought
possible.

She shook her head. "You see, I remember that whole
night perfectly well. I pleaded for you to take my virginity. I didn't want it. I wanted you."

His breath caught, but then he registered her use of
wanted. Not *want*.

"There's another matter," he said then. "You could be
pregnant."

"I'm not," she said bluntly. "I learned that a few days
ago. So you're under no obligation."

"It's not about obligation."

"It's not?" She arched one eyebrow.

"No! I want you to be happy."

"And what do you think will make me happy?" She
stepped away from him, her expression now challenging.

Tav wasn't sure where this was leading, but he knew
that he had to answer honestly. "I think…that of all the
times I've seen you, you've been your happiest, and your
truest self when you were in the Ardenwood."

Her mouth opened a little in surprise, and her eyes
softened. "Go on."

He resisted the urge to tell her that she also looked
extremely content in his bed, and the urge to tell her that
she'd be happy with him. He could never ask her to leave
her homeland. Asking her to leave would be like taking a
bird from its nest.

"There's something wild in you, Robin," he said. "You can hide it from some people, for some time, but it can't be contained. It bursts out of you like spring."

She took a breath, her palms coming up to rest on his chest. "That's true. Cecily could live in a garden until the end of days and she'd be happy...so long as she has her husband and child with her. Angelet would say the same, though she grows her gardens from thread and needle. I can't do that. The moment I feel walls around me, I want to climb out and over. I want to see things, new things that won't come to me."

"You come alive in the Ardenwood. It's your home."

Robin frowned. "Octavian, how can you be so intelligent and still miss what's right in front of your face?"

"What do you mean?" What had he missed?

"I wasn't happy because I was in the Ardenwood. I was happy because I was with *you*. I come alive when I am free to roam. When I have a good horse, and a road to travel...and the one I love beside me." She leaned closer, her voice dropping to a whisper. "Does it mean nothing to you that I love you?"

He couldn't believe her. Not yet. "You don't love me more than your home, or the people who care for you," he objected, even as his heart wanted to take her and hold her and never let her go.

"I care for myself, and my home is where I make it." Robin raised her chin. "I love you," she repeated, like a challenge. "I think I've always loved you, Tav. First as admiration because you were a knight and strong and wonderful. But then as *love*, as I got to know you and your thoughts and how you treated me and everything in the world around you with the sort of care that so few people do."

"Robin." He touched her face, hoping the right words

would come to him, somehow.

"Tav, you have to say you don't love me."

"What?"

"I need to hear you say that you *don't* love me. It's the only way I can have a future, so that I can start from nothing, knowing that my love for you never had a chance and there's no hope for us."

"I can't do that," he said.

She froze, uncertainty vibrating in her whole body. He felt it, and felt it seep into his own being. He was at a point when a dozen possible futures awaited him, and everything hinged on what he did next.

Tav reached out, his arms circling her waist, drawing her against his body. He ran one hand up her back and to her head, cradling her close. "I can't tell you I don't love you, Robin, because I do. I never meant to fall in love with you, and it probably doesn't matter when I did. But I love you now, and I will keep loving you, whether I'm with you or not."

He told her he loved her in every language he knew, including the language that had no words, just the touch of his hands to hers, promising that he'd always be there for her, no matter where they went in the world. Robin raised her head and he captured her mouth, a deep but tender kiss that promised even more.

* * * *

Hearing Octavian tell her he loved her was like summer returning. Robin sighed, resting her head on his shoulder. "I love you so much," she whispered. "Only you."

He kissed her hair and held her even closer.

"Since I first saw you," she went on, dreamily, "I realized how much of the world I had yet to see. I want to see it with you."

"The world is a very large place," he said at last.

"I want to see the whole of creation, but I'm content to begin where you lead me."

"You think we ought to travel together?" he asked, a new look in his eyes.

"Dear Lord, Tav. That's what I've been saying!"

"If you want to travel with me, and stay with me, and sleep and eat with me, then you'd have to marry me. That's the only condition I'd accept."

"Of course I want to marry you!" she said. Only days ago, she'd been cursing the very notion of marriage. But a marriage to Tav was an entirely different matter. "Do you think we could get married tomorrow?"

His hands closed around her shoulders to keep her grounded. "Wait. It's not quite so simple, Robin. We're not marrying without permission from your family. And there are several reasons why they might refuse to give it."

"Name one! You're a knight. You're one of Alric's closest friends. You've saved his life. You've saved my life! Cecily adores you. Rainald thinks you're wonderful. I think you're wonderful." Robin was aware that her list of reasons in favor of a marriage wasn't quite typical, but what did it matter? She loved Tav and Tav loved her.

"I'm a knight, and I serve at the pleasure of my lord, and I have no lands or income of my own. Lord de Vere sought to marry you to a man of a much higher rank than I'll ever have. He may like me well enough as a man, but not as a match for his chosen daughter."

She bit her lip. Would Rainald really oppose Tav's request to marry her? "We have to try," she whispered. "Let's go now and find him. I'll go mad if we have to wait until tomorrow to even know what he says."

Tav nodded, then pulled her close and claimed her mouth in a rough kiss. She responded in kind, her need for him suddenly turning her wild.

"If he says no, I'm stealing you," Tav said, his voice low in her ear, thrilling her. She believed him and loved him even more.

The sky turned to night by then, and it was barely possible no one noticed their behavior at the top of the walls. Certainly, the Octavian who descended the steps was the man people expected to see—calm, collected, unfailingly attentive to Robin, who walked beside him.

"Where is Lord Rainald?" Robin asked of the maid who greeted her when they entered the manor house.

"In his chamber, I believe."

Robin nodded, and they went up to find him. Robin began to shake a little, and Tav cupped her elbow to steady her.

"Ah! My sweet Robin," Rainald said when she knocked on the door. "And Octavian. Come in, come in. A busy day, was it not? But soon the odious Lord Pierce will be gone from Cleobury, and we'll have peace again." He turned to Tav. "You must come back as soon as you're able. I did not care for Lord Drugo snatching you away so quickly."

"About that," Robin said. "We wanted to speak to you, my lord."

"Then sit with me and speak. My goodness, such serious expressions on your faces."

They sat by the fireplace, the heat blazing forth from the hot stones.

Tav looked as calm as ever, but Robin could sense how nervous he was. "My lord," he began, "you are Robin's guardian. So it's you that I come to...for your blessing, in fact. I want—"

"He wants your permission to marry me," Robin broke in, "though if you don't give it, we'll marry anyway because I love him."

Rainald smiled slightly, not looking nearly as surprised as Robin expected. "You love him? That is good, but not enough."

"What more do you need to give your blessing?" she asked.

"Octavian," Rainald said, "why do you want to marry my little Robin?"

"Because I adore her," Tav replied. Robin's heart soared at the words—he'd told her he loved her, but now he was saying it aloud to another person, and she recognized the difference.

"Can you provide for a wife?"

"I can try," said Tav. "I have nothing to offer her in material goods. I have no land and no legacy. But I can earn a living by my sword, and I promise that I won't eat unless she's fed. I'll do whatever I need to do."

"A worthy sentiment, but not a practical one," Rainald said. "What if you become injured? Or are killed? Who cares for Robin then? She needs more than promises."

Robin looked at Tav anxiously, seeing that he had no counterargument. She knew Rainald was advocating for her, but if the result was that he'd refuse to let Tav and Robin marry, what good was it?

"I know the risks," she said, leaning forward and reaching for Rainald's hand. "And I don't care. I'll have Tav whether you like it or not! Why don't you want me to be happy?"

He took her small hand in his larger ones, squeezing gently. "My dear, your happiness is all I want. That's why I ask about your future as well as your present. I know

Octavian's heart is good, and there's no one else I'd rather trust you to. But powerful as love is, it will not feed you or clothe you."

"Then what can we do?" she asked, her voice breaking. Tav slipped an arm around her shoulders.

"You can accept a gift," Rainald said.

Robin looked at him, confused. "A gift?"

"I decided years ago that you deserved more than providence offered you in your childhood. Therefore, I have set aside some land for you, to be yours legally upon my death. But I will make it a gift to you now. The land will provide the income necessary to support a knight and his family."

Robin felt light-headed. "Land? For me?"

"Yes. I thought to give you my old estate of Aldgate, in the Long Forest. Not quite the Ardenwood, but I think you will feel a certain kinship with it."

The generosity Rainald was showing rendered Robin speechless.

"That would…seem to solve the problem," Tav said, also sounding stunned.

"Excellent. I shall see that a contract is drawn up to make the gift official, to have everything in place before the wedding, which will be here at Cleobury—I insist. And after you return from your journey, you will have a home ready for you."

"Our journey? You know we intend to travel?" Robin asked, still overwhelmed.

"My darling, you are both inveterate wanderers. Anyone can see that. My Cecily needs a garden, my Robin needs a road. And there is no better man to travel that road with you than Octavian."

Rainald stood up, and Tav did as well, waiting for the man's next words. Rainald put one hand on the knight's shoulder. "I give you my blessing, Octavian de Levant. You may have my sweet Robin's hand in marriage, and though neither of you are of my blood, you have both found your way into my heart. I wish you great joy together."

Tav bowed his head. "Thank you."

"Thank you!" Robin did not bow her head, but instead threw her arms around Rainald. "Thank you!"

Epilogue

THE NEWS COULD NOT BE contained, of course. Robin
herself could not be contained. She rushed to Cecily to
tell her first. Then they told Alric, and Luc, and Rafe.
Rainald announced it at supper, as calmly as if it had all
been planned for months.

Lord Drugo accepted the news that Octavian would
not be joining him in taking Pierce to London, largely
because Luc said he'd go instead.

"And you must take Govannon along too," Robin ordered.

"Why such effort to keep the pet with his owner?"
Alric asked. "You owe that man nothing after all he tried
to do to you."

"I'm not doing this out of obligation. Pierce did terrible things, and I don't mean to excuse what he did. But I
know that much of what he did was out of loneliness.
Perhaps if he learns to care for another creature, he'll
have a chance for redemption."

"A small chance."

"In any case, it's up to him. Sending him Govannon is
how I forgive him. And henceforth, I'll never think of him
again." She smiled at Tav. "I have far too many joyous
things to occupy my mind."

"Very well. Pierce and his cat shall go to London. But

I'll be back for the wedding, and I'll send word for Domina to travel here as well," Luc promised. "Weddings are best when everyone can be there."

"Learned from experience, did you?" Rafe needled him. Luc's own marriage had been a little hasty.

"Oh, shut up," Luc returned. "This is important. Who knows when we'll all be together again?"

Luc's comment, airy as it was, hinted at the melancholy truth. These friends who had fought together and lived for each other and watched over each other through good times and ill times were going to be separated. By distance. By time. Nothing lasted forever.

"All the more reason to have a wedding," Cecily said. "We celebrate when we're together, so we may remember those times when we're apart."

A date was set a month hence. The banns needed to be read out, and a few distant friends needed to travel to Cleobury to be there in time. And the preparations for Robin and Tav's journey afterward needed to be made as well.

Rafe went back to Martenkeep to fetch Angelet and the boys in training, saying it would be a holiday for them. Robin was glad she'd get to see Torin, Acer, Guy, and Henry once more. They'd be full-grown men the next time she saw them…if she ever laid eyes on them again.

Robin and Octavian were married in the chapel of Cleobury, amid their friends and the many good folk who lived on the manor grounds and the lands around it. A feast in the coldest days of winter was always welcome, and Robin had never felt so much joy around her.

The wedding night was full of joy as well, though of a much more intimate nature. Robin lay in Tav's arms at one point, lazily tracing patterns on his chest.

"I've been thinking," she said.

"Yes?" He laid a trailed of open-mouthed kisses along her neck. "Tell me."

"All the talk about forbidden fruit tasting sweeter is a lot of nonsense."

He laughed. "You're sweet no matter how I taste you."

She smiled and then licked his shoulder, making him moan. "Whereas you're more salty, not that I'm complaining."

"No complaint from me, either," Tav promised. Then he caught her in his arms and rolled her onto her back, intent on denying her any sleep at all.

She loved him for it.

The next several days were a whirl of activity as Robin and Tav got ready to leave Cleobury. Robin regarded the stone walls of the manor and the gentle hills around it with deep affection, and a sort of longing, even though she hadn't even left yet. People asked over and over about their plans to travel all the way to the Holy Land. They asked if she was excited, or nervous, or scared. She was all of those things, but she looked at Tav every time and knew that whatever they faced, they'd face it together.

She walked to the open gate of Cleobury and studied the landscape, committing it to memory, for it would perhaps be years before she saw it again.

"Almost time." Tav walked up to where she was standing and slipped one arm around her. He smiled the slow smile that always melted her heart.

"Almost," she agreed.

They both turned their eyes to the road. It stretched out before them, familiar now, but promising a wide world beyond.

ABOUT THE AUTHOR

Elizabeth Cole is a romance writer with a penchant for history. Her stories draw upon her deep affection for the British Isles, action movies, medieval fantasies, and even science fiction. She now lives in a small house in a big city with a cat, a snake, and a rather charming gentleman. When not writing, she is usually curled in a corner reading...or watching costume dramas or things that explode. And yes, she believes in love at first sight.

CPSIA information can be obtained
at www.ICGtesting.com
Printed in the USA
LVHW010455020920
664776LV00001B/227